THE GATES

OF

SHEOL

THE GATES
OF
SHEOL

A Civil War Novel
THE SHILOH TRILOGY BOOK 3

KARL A. BACON

Historical Chronicles Press

The Gates of Sheol

Historical Chronicles Press
www.kbacon.com

ISBN: 978-1976382338
ISBN 10: 1976382335

All Scripture quotations, unless otherwise indicated, are taken from *The Holy Bible, King James Version, KJV*.

Editor: Julie Gwinn
Cover design: Tatiana Willener
Maps: Karl A. Bacon

Printed by CreateSpace, an Amazon.com Company
Please report errata directly to the author.

Publisher's Note: This is a work of fiction. Names, characters, places, and incidents are a product of the author's imagination. Any resemblance to actual people, living or dead, or to businesses, companies, events, institutions, or locales is completely coincidental. Historic places and persons that do appear within these pages are presented as accurately as possible.

And he said unto me,
Son of man, can these bones live?

And I answered,
O Lord GOD, thou knowest.

Ezekiel 37:3

A Civil War Novel

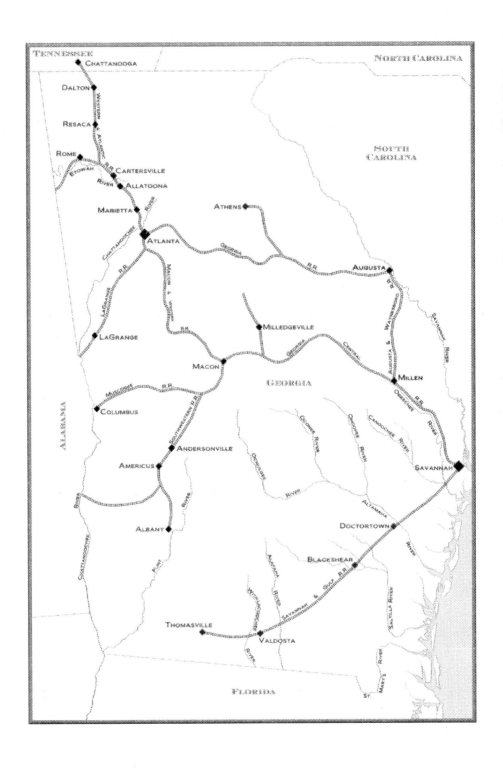

CHAPTER 1

Thursday, June 23rd, 1864

*T*HE HEAT INSIDE THE CATTLE CAR WAS FOUL, UNBREATHABLE. When the cars had been moving, at least the air inside had stirred, but now the sweat and stink of sixty-five men sitting elbow to elbow hung like a heavy pall over a coffin. Indeed, the car had become a coffin for one of their number— Stanley had heard someone weeping and calling the man's name over and over, "No, Thatch. Oh, Thatch, no."

How long had the train been stopped? Stanley reached for the watch he always carried in the left hip pocket of his frock coat, but that habit had cost him, the pocket was empty. A guard had noticed the bright silver watch and had liberated it the day after Stanley was taken prisoner, laughing and sneering as he did so, "No use fer it where yer going, Yank."

How long? Half an hour? An hour? More?

The sky had been overcast when they had been herded aboard at Macon early that morning, but for now the rains that had bogged down Sherman's advance north of Atlanta had stopped. True, the clouds were a mercy, shielding the cars from the heat of the midday sun, but still, the moment the heavy door had slammed shut, the corruption of the car's air had begun.

When the train finally had departed, the slow speed at which the car rumbled along admitted small puffs of fresh air. It would be enough, Stanley told himself again and again, it had to be enough. Men whimpered pleas for relief, knowing the only ones who heard were as helpless as they.

1

Stanley bowed his head and echoed their pleas silently, a pitiable offering to the Almighty. *Lord, please give me one deep breath of fresh air.*

Stanley listened closely to the sounds outside the cattle car—tramping feet, barked orders, groaned complaints of prisoners too long immobile suddenly forced into activity. He was in the last car of the train. As the guards worked their way from the front of the train to the rear, the sounds grew louder by degree. At last, he could make out the words. The prisoners in the car just ahead were ordered out. *We will be next.*

First a rapping sound, then the rasping squeal of the heavy door sliding open. It was about midday and still cloudy, but Stanley squinted against the sudden light. Two dozen flint-eyed guards greeted them, rifles leveled and cocked. Stanley was sitting near the door. He moved aside to allow the other men to pass.

Shouted orders, cries of relief, groans and grunts as men jumped from the car to the ground, heavy thuds as some fell flat, followed by curses from prisoners and guards alike. One man remained slumped against the rear wall of the car. *Must be Thatch. He'll never get home.*

Stanley swung his legs over the edge. It would be a drop of about three feet and his walking stick would be of no use. He set it on the floor of the car, still somewhat amazed that he still possessed it, that no guard had taken a fancy to it and liberated it as well.

A sergeant with a long red beard glared up at him. "Today, Yank. All us-ins is waitin' on you-ah."

There would be no help from that direction. Stanley pushed himself off. His right foot landed first. He pitched himself forward and to the right, rolling to the soft, muddy earth at the sergeant's feet.

Stanley's leg muscles burned from sitting all day in the car. He clenched his teeth and forced himself to stand upright.

"He-ah," the sergeant said, holding out Stanley's cane, "Look like you-ah be needin' it."

Stanley nodded. "Thank you, Sergeant." Another small mercy.

"Squad up with the rest." Then to all the prisoners from the car Sergeant Red-beard shouted, "Fo-um column of fo-ah."

A clerk in Federal blues with corporal stripes counted the prisoners and recorded the number in the ledger he carried. "Sixty-four, Sergeant Peck, plus one deceased en route. All accounted for. Does anyone know the deceased?"

The squad remained silent.

"Raise a hand if that dead-un is known to you-ah," Sergeant Peck said.

One hand went up. "He's Percy Thatcher from Ithaca, New York."

The clerk noted the information in the ledger. "What is his rank and unit?"

"Corporal, Company H, Eighth New York Cavalry."

Don't much care for cavalry anymore.

"I'm a prisoner just like you," the clerk said after he finished writing. "I work in the prison office keeping the rolls of prisoners for the commandant. The prison population is organized in detachments of two hundred seventy men. Each detachment consists of three companies of ninety. Rations are issued to each ninety sufficient to feed the full complement of prisoners. I will assign each man in this squad to a detachment and company. To put it bluntly, you are replacing dead men so that each detachment is kept full. When you enter the stockade, you will search out your assigned detachment and join their ranks. How you do that is up to you."

Sixty-four new prisoners to take the place of sixty-four dead ones? That must be for several weeks. Men died of disease all the time in the army. This place should be little different.

The clerk started at the front of the squad. "You, private, will report to detachment thirty-five, third ninety." Then the clerk repeated the assignment as he wrote in the ledger, "Thirty-five, three." The clerk worked his way quickly through the ranks. The highest detachment number Stanley heard was ninety-one. His stomach tightened at the result of his figuring. He figured it again—ninety-one detachments of two hundred seventy. *That's over 24,000 prisoners.*

Finally, the clerk stood in front of Stanley. He glanced at the stripes on Stanley's sleeve. "Quartermaster Sergeant. Which regiment?"

"Quartermaster Department, Fifteenth Corps."

The clerk let out a low whistle. "Only one or two others like you inside that I know of. You must have really messed up to get yourself captured."

"You're right about that, Corporal," Stanley said. He looked down at his cane and then back at the clerk. "I can't run nearly as fast as you."

The clerk huffed and flipped through three pages in his ledger. "Fifty-five, one," he said. Then he slammed his ledger book shut and stalked away.

A dark-bearded Rebel officer astride a pale gray horse approached the new prisoners at a trot. Sergeant Peck turned and saluted the officer. A few words were exchanged. Then the officer turned his mount around and started off at a slow walk up a narrow lane that led away from the railroad toward the dark wall of the prison stockade several hundred yards away.

The sergeant's command rang out like a clarion. "Forward, march."

The column of new prisoners, surrounded left, right, and rear by almost fifty guards, moved forward. The lane was mired ankle deep with red, sticky mud from days of heavy rain. Stanley struggled to keep up. To the left of the lane stood dozens of tents, the camp of the prison guards. To the right a brook, swollen to about ten feet wide, babbled gaily as it flowed swiftly along.

"Sergeant," a voice near the head of the column called out, "let us stop to fill our canteens."

"Yes, yes," the men echoed up and down the column. Stanley's canteen had been dry for hours, as had those of the other men.

The officer, several yards ahead, wheeled his mount around and rode back toward the prisoners. It appeared that he would ride straight through their ranks, but he stopped short with his horse nose to nose with the men in the front rank.

The officer drew his pistol and waved it at the new prisoners. "Who say dat?"

No one moved.

"WHO SAY DAT?" The officer jumped down and brandished his pistol in the face of the first man he came to. "Any of you Yanks go for dat water, I shoot every one. Der plenty good water inside." The Rebel officer mounted his horse and glared down at the new prisoners, his eyes hard with contempt. "NO TALK. NOT. ONE. MORE. WORD."

The march toward the stockade resumed across a wooden bridge that arched over the stream. Stanley longed to wade in and revel in it's cool, soaking, cleansing flow, as surely every other man did, but it would have meant swift and certain death. They marched past corrals of mules and horses, and a small herd of beef cattle. The area reeked of animal excretions.

The lane led up an incline away from the brook. With the added elevation, the road became less muddy and the footing better for Stanley. To the right, a small house was built on higher ground. Surrounding the house was a large earthen fort. The barrels of at least six artillery pieces protruded through the parapet.

As the column passed in front of the fort, Stanley's breath caught in his throat. The ground upon which the fort had been built overlooked the stockade. Much of the interior of the prison lay open to his view and to the deadly fire from those guns.

Even in the light of midday it was impossible for Stanley to distinguish within the walls a single living form he could positively identify as human. In fact, all of the ground inside the walls of the stockade seemed to be a single rippling, flowing, living being with no common direction or purpose. A thick, putrid stench hung over the place unlike anything

Stanley had ever smelled before, a sure sign of disease, decay, and death.

A constant hum came from within the stockade, like the sound of swarming hornets when their paper nest has been poked with a stick, except the sound seemed to have a pulse like a living, breathing thing—like his own heart which seemed about to burst out of his chest—though much slower than a heartbeat, and somehow ominous and peaceful at the same time.

To the left of the lane, less than a hundred yards from the gate of the prison, a mule-drawn wagon stood off to the side in front of what appeared to be a large, ramshackle three-sided shelter. A pair of black workers were removing small, naked, stick-like man-figures from the shelter and stacking them in the wagon, loading the wagon to its fullest capacity, like the black firemen had done aboard the *Evangelina* whenever they stacked cordwood in her fuel bins.

The ground had been covered with hundreds of his dead Federal brethren when Stanley had passed between the lines at Vicksburg. Intent upon his purpose, he had lowered his gaze so he would see only the path in front of him rather than the bloated, rotting corpses.

But he couldn't look away now. The wagon jerked forward. The dead rattled noiselessly against each other. Stanley swallowed back vomit that swelled in his throat. *You saved me for this, Lord? Am I replacing one of them? How long before I'm carried away in that wagon? Death at Shiloh or Vicksburg would have been honorable. Even death at the hand of Anna's brother, Luke, would have been better.*

The officer at the front of the column stopped within ten yards of the gate and reined his horse around to face the new prisoners.

"Halt!" Sergeant Peck yelled.

"I am Captain Wirz." It sounded like *Veerts* to Stanley, high, strident, and forceful. "I am commandant of dis Andersonville prison. You Yanks will do what I say or you will be shot. Der will be no escape. Der will be no complaint. And if you t'ink to start trouble," he pointed up the lane toward

6

the fort, "I tell dem to fire and dey won't stop until all you Yanks is dead."

Then he laughed, low and cynical. "I hear some of dem inside say dis is hell. Maybe it is, maybe not, but I know dis. Won't be long and you Yanks be saying de same t'ing."

CHAPTER 2

THE GIANT DOORS OF THE GATE OPENED. SERGEANT PECK
ordered the four-abreast column of sixteen ranks
forward as Captain Wirz moved off to the side to watch the
prisoners pass. The gate permitted entrance into a nearly
square stockaded chamber with a second pair of doors,
which remained closed and bolted, in the opposite wall of
the chamber. Stanley was barely inside when the outer
doors slammed shut behind him.

The inner doors were thrown open. A narrow path, lined
with thousands of men, lay ahead. The pulsing buzzing of
hornets he had heard from outside the walls was actually
a chant, two simple words that welcomed the new
prisoners to the stockade. "Fresh fish. Fresh fish."

"Forward, march," Sergeant Peck cried out above the
chant.

They were a practiced swarm of prisoners. Their chant
was in perfect unison, the first word long, growing in
volume, the second nearly as long as the first, but dying
away in a diminishing "ssshhh," until the chant started
again. Here and there, small groups of men linked arms
and swayed slowly side to side as they chanted—to the
right on *fresh*, to the left on *fish*—making a game of it, their
entertainment for the day. The way the hundreds chanted
reminded Stanley of the peaceful sound the wake-waves of

a paddle steamer made when they broke upon the shore of the Mississippi. "Fresh fish. Fresh fish."

The new band of prisoners marched along a narrow path until they were about half way across the breadth of the prison. Men crowded on either side. Some appeared in perfect health, well-dressed and well-fed. Many others seemed at death's door, mere skeletons of real men, seared dark by the merciless sun, their scant, tattered clothing dyed yellow-brown by the ground, themselves just a breath away from being thrown into the dead wagon. And still the chant continued, "Fresh fish. Fresh fish."

But the faces of the men betrayed them. The hale and feeble alike, and every stripe in between, pressed close against the new prisoners as they walked slowly toward the center of the prison. Hands grabbed at Stanley's clothing, tried to rip away his canteen, reached for his black slouch hat. Fierce expressions and burning eyes spoke only one message—*what can I take from you today?*

Sergeant Peck never called a halt; he and the other guards simply slipped away, leaving the new prisoners to the mercy of the crowd. Several of the new men crouched low, fists raised, ready for a fight. A brawl seemed unavoidable, but the crowd suddenly backed off.

A band of rough-looking men appeared. Each was armed with a cudgel, a length of tree branch or sapling, or steel knuckles. Several carried long, thick-bladed Bowie knives that looked twice the size of Luke's hunting knife. These men moved among the new prisoners, beating several senseless, without any provocation that Stanley saw.

A large, burly man stepped out of the crowd. "Mosby, that's Mosby," said someone close behind Stanley.

Mosby wore a long sergeant's frock coat, a crimson sash, a large floppy crimson bow-tie, and a black slouch hat like Stanley's, but with cavalry insignia. He was also clean-shaven, except for a dark, bushy mustache that ran down the sides of his mouth to his chin. "You see that?" he said, pointing at the men writhing in pain at his feet. "You fight us, that's what you get. You fresh fish have just been netted. You belong to me now, and all you have is mine too."

Dozens of Mosby's cronies moved among the new men. Mostly they wanted money, but if they took a particular fancy to a man's shirt or hat, that was taken as well, along with whatever they pleased of the man's possessions.

Two of these ruffians approached Stanley. "My word, Wally, this one's a big one. Big as Mosby, I'd say."

Wally brandished his club in Stanley's face. "Ha! Big one's die fast, Jack, everybody knows it."

Jack's wry grin accentuated his thin mustache, reminding Stanley of some of the dandy gentlemen he had seen in river ports like Natchez. "Give you three to one he don't last a month," Jack said.

"Nah. That's a sucker bet. Yep, this one will shrivel up and die right quick—inside of three weeks, I'd say. And he's lame to boot." Jack snatched the walking stick from Stanley's hand.

"I need that to walk."

"You plan on leaving?" Jack asked, at the same moment rapping the side of Stanley's neck with the cane.

Stanley's knees buckled, but he didn't go down. He touched the place; his fingers came away red and sticky with blood.

"What else you got? Put your hands up."

Both men searched the pockets of Stanley's jacket—Wally on the right and Jack on the left—but the only thing either man found of interest was Stanley's Bible, which Wally found in the right hip pocket.

Jack grabbed the Bible from Wally and rifled through its pages. "Nothing here." He tossed the Bible to the muddy ground a few feet away and pointed at Stanley's trousers. "Turn your pockets out."

Stanley did as he was told and produced a most disappointing haul for the two thieves—a few coins amounting to less than a dollar and a soiled handkerchief.

"Nice hat," Wally said, swiping Stanley's black slouch hat from his head. But the hat was much too big for Wally. "Here, Jack. You try it. Wait. What's this?"

Losing the hat was bad enough. "Those are my personal letters," Stanley said. "There's no money there."

"Look at these, Jack. They're from a girl—his girl, I bet. Sure make good reading around our campfire tonight."

"Keep the hat, but please leave me those letters."

Wally ignored Stanley's plea. "What else you got?"

"Sergeant's stripes," Jack said. "I always wanted to be a sergeant." He motioned to Stanley to hand over his dark blue frock coat. "Looks good on me, don't you think, Wally?"

Wally hooted with laughter. "You swim in that coat, Jack, hangs almost to your knees. Take off them boots, big fella."

Stanley lifted his right leg. "You'll have to take it off yourself, since you stole my cane."

Wally pulled the boot off. He reached inside and found a few bills. "Thirteen dollars, Jack. Federal greenbacks."

"Fresh fish never learn," Jack said. "If it ain't in his pockets, it's in his Bible; if it ain't in his Bible, it's in his hat; and if it ain't in his hat, it's in his boots. Now the other one."

Stanley lifted his left leg toward Wally. "Pull it straight. Don't twist it." A look of disappointment passed between the two thieves at not finding another stash in Stanley's left boot.

"Muddy and worn," Wally said, "but Mosby might want them. He's always looking for bigger boots. And I'll take that nice green-checked shirt, too. Never had me a green shirt before."

Stanley slid his suspenders off his shoulders, unfastened the three buttons, and shucked the shirt off over his head. Then he raised the suspenders back over his shoulders and ran his thumps up, then down along the inner seams of the suspenders to make sure they were smooth.

Stanley looked at Jack. "You took all I had." It wasn't true, but a lie to such a scoundrel was certainly excusable. "May I please have my cane back?"

"Nah. I like the feel of it. The carving's nice too. We ain't heartless, you know, we let you keep your canteen—and your trousers."

Then Jack and Wally slipped away into the crowd.

CHAPTER 3

STANLEY BENT AND PICKED UP HIS BIBLE, BUT WHEN HE straightened, he reeled from the stench of the place. His head seemed to spin, first to the left, then abruptly back to the right, then end over end. He bent over again to stop the spinning, and tried to think of clever words to describe the smell. *Appalling* came to mind, but it seemed far from adequate. Light headed, feeling about to faint, he closed his eyes and hoped it would pass.

A firm hand gripped his elbow.

Stanley tried to stand to fend off yet another assault.

"Whoa there, big fella. Steady now. One man fell faint not two steps inside the gate. Don't you be another." The voice was nasal and reedy, like Mr. Poteete, the peevish clerk aboard the *Evangelina*, but it was also gentle and calming. "Know you don't want to, but breathe—breathe deep and slow. Always be there—the stink, I mean. Give it a couple of days, maybe a week or two, and you won't notice it so much. Been here four weeks tomorrow and it still makes me retch sometimes."

Stanley opened his eyes. A dark-bearded young man stood before him. He was short in stature and of slight build, and his left cheek appeared quite swollen.

The man eased the Bible from Stanley's grasp and wiped the mud from it. "You just met the Raiders and you got off easy."

13

"Easy? My neck doesn't agree."

"Sure. You're still alive." The small man grinned, revealing gums that were swollen and a little bloody. "Your neck will need some looking after, but you still have some clothing and your Bible." He handed the Bible back to Stanley. "That's what caught my eye. Any man that treasures the Word is kin to me."

Stanley stuffed the Bible into the pocket of his trousers. "But they took my walking stick, my jacket, my shirt, and my hat." His voice rose suddenly. "And they stole all of Anna's letters. What could they want with them?"

"Your wife?" The man's concern seemed genuine. His hazel eyes were wide and earnest, but dim and a little empty.

Stanley shook his head. "Not yet. Maybe not ever."

The man removed his cap and scratched at his scalp for a moment. Then he replaced the cap and looked up at Stanley. "Can't be talking like that if you ever hope to see your Anna again, Sergeant. I saw the stripes on your jacket before those rascals took it."

"Rascals? I've got a list of names for them in my head, but *rascals* isn't one of them."

The young man laughed and extended his hand. "Just being charitable." His hand was cold and bony, but his grip was firm.

"Mitchell, Stanley Mitchell, Quartermaster Department, Logan's Fifteenth Corps."

"Ah, rear echelon duty. Makes sense. Saw your cane too. Where were you taken?"

"Cartersville, about forty miles north of Atlanta."

"Austin Oglethorpe, Eighth Michigan Volunteers with Burnside's Ninth Corps. Passed the exam for Lieutenant just three days before I was captured at the Wilderness, but the papers didn't come through yet. Would have been a second lieutenant. Guess the army will just have to owe me my officer's pay. Which detachment did they put you in?"

"Fifty-fifth, first ninety," Stanley said.

"You're joshing. I am too, third ninety rather than first. And this *is* a first. Rank fillers—that's what I call replacements like you—they send some in nearly every day, and I always come over to find ours and bring them across to our little village. Been doing it the last ten days or so, but this is the first time the first fella I come across is for the fifty-fifth. First ninety, that's Stew's bunch. You'll like him. Always see him at the Christian meetings and we're getting to be good friends. I take it you were wounded. Recent?"

"No," Stanley said, finding it a challenge, because of the long toilsome day, to keep up with Austin's rapid manner of speaking. "I almost died at Shiloh."

Austin's head bobbed. "Whoa, that was over two years ago and they didn't discharge you on medical?"

Stanley shook his head. "And that's a long story."

"Can you walk without your cane?"

"Yes, but slow."

"Now your head's better, let's get away from this rabble." Austin pointed across the valley through which the stream meandered to the hill on the opposite side. "All three nineties are close to each other across the swamp near Broadway."

"I just met you, Austin," Stanley said. "How do I know you aren't going to deliver me to another band of thugs over there?"

"You don't, Mitch. You can trust me or not, your choice. This I do know. Loners die fast here. Cast your lot in with somebody—friends, if you can find them—if you ever hope to survive this place. Already offered you my hand. If you got any better offers, I'll be on my way."

Austin set off without waiting for an answer, and Stanley hastened to stay close behind him. Austin led

Stanley between a dozen or more shabby dwellings—some of them just a blanket supported at the corners with sticks covering a hole in the ground—to a narrow path that led back toward the gate through which Stanley had entered the prison. Voices cried out as they passed, some in recognizable, spoken words, others in only pitiful, plaintive wails.

Stanley tried to fix his attention on every step, so he wouldn't stumble or fall, but living, skeletal corpses of what used to be men lay out in the open. It was impossible to turn away. It was impossible not to see those wretched remnants of men who had hopes and dreams just like he did, and in the few moments Stanley had been among them, he had seen his own future. Hunger would weaken and wither his body. Disease would strike him down. Without shelter, his skin would redden and blister, then blacken in the summer sun. Finally, he would die alone in some miserable hole.

Austin paused and allowed Stanley to come abreast of him. "Looks like you saw a ghost."

Stanley swallowed hard. "I think I did—my own."

"Don't say that, and don't think it."

A loud cry came from a shanty a few yards ahead to the left of the path. A pale, sickly man lay unmoving on the ground. A second man stood over the sick man. He drew his bare foot back and kicked the motionless man in the ribs.

"Why won't you die, Peterman?" the kicking man screamed. Several more kicks thudded into the prostrate man's body. "Die and leave me in peace, you miserable wretch."

How can anyone survive this place, Anna? I'll never return to you and you'll never know what became of me.

Stanley took a step toward the shanty to intervene, but Austin's fingers gripped his arm.

"Just one of the horrors of this place," Austin said, "men living like wild animals, like there's no God. That man probably just wants the dying man's shirt."

Austin led Stanley away. "Very common to see only the misery, but good is here too. If you hope to survive, you must see the good. Even more, you have to do the good."

Austin walked on. Near the gate, he turned right onto a well-worn path that led down a slope into the valley of the stream, the same stream Stanley's squad had marched beside on the lane from the depot. A narrow, planked bridge allowed passage from the southern portion of the prison, where Stanley had entered, to the northern portion, which appeared larger, but was no less crowded.

Austin stopped in the middle of the bridge. "Welcome to Andersonville Springs, where the healing waters are known to put many a man in an early grave." He pointed at the water flowing below. "Local folk call it Sweetwater Branch, but it's far from sweet. Tell yourself again and again—you can't be reminded often enough—drink this water and you will die. Not *might*. You *will* die. Think you're parched now? Look at that water. See the shiny blue streaks? Grease from the cook-house. Doesn't look so bad. Maybe just a sip won't harm you. Don't do it. Garbage and filth from the cook-house are dumped into it, and the offal from the enemy camps and the corrals outside—you saw them on your way in here—all goes in the water before it comes in under the wall."

Stanley studied the path of the stream across the prison. Its black muddy banks seemed to pulsate, to ripple to and fro and up and down, without any apparent cause. "Austin, the surface of the soil on either side seems to be moving—like it's alive."

"It *is* alive," Austin said, "with millions and millions of flies and maggots, and all sorts of other vermin thriving on the same filth that kills us."

Austin led Stanley off the bridge. He pointed at a thin wooden slat railing that ran parallel to the stockade and about fifteen feet from it up the hill toward a second gate that allowed access to the northern portion of the prison. "That railing is the deadline. It goes all the way around the camp. Cross it or touch it and you will be shot. Again, not *might, will*. Look there, about fifty yards up the path."

A nearly naked man was weaving his way down toward the stream. His gait was uneven; he seemed about to fall at any moment.

"Look at that guard," Austin said, pointing at the sentry box atop the wall nearest the man. "He can't be more than fifteen, but he's drawing a bead on him just hoping he'll reach out his hand to steady himself on the deadline. Probably wants to tell the folks at home how he shot down one of them Yankee rascals."

Another man approached the unsteady man and guided him away from the deadline. The moment of danger passed.

Austin and Stanley walked up the hill on the north side of the stream toward what Austin called the North Gate. Then they turned right onto a narrow street like the one on the south side of the prison.

"This is Broadway," Austin said. "Dozens of shops sell food, cooking implements, clothing, shoe repair, knife sharpening, whatever the shopkeeper thinks might pry a few dollars from the prisoners' fingers. There's a Confederate sutler too. He sells fresh fruit, vegetables and baked goods, but his prices are very high."

"Austin, how long have you been suffering from the scurvy?" Stanley asked.

"You noticed. Started on the trip here. You some sort of doctor?"

"No. I was an orderly at a hospital in Vicksburg for a couple of months. Some of the soldiers had swollen faces and bleeding gums just like you."

"Vegetables would clear it up in a week or two, if they gave us any—only a few cow peas once in a while. Can't pay the sutler's prices."

Austin turned off Broadway and wove his way between scores of miserable hovels. He stopped in front of a small tent-like structure. A single blanket had been draped over a thin ridge pole supported at both ends by sticks. A small sign with the numerals "55" hung from the ridge pole.

"Sergeant Beckwith, Oglethorpe here."

A face appeared from the tent, a dark face, too dark, it seemed, to be only from prolonged exposure to the sun. "Who?"

"Ogre. I was at the meeting two nights ago."

"Ah, Ogre, right. Maybe my last meeting; thinking of quitting. Who's this?" Sergeant Beckwith crawled out of the tent and stood—a shriveled, shrunken man with darting eyes and an uneasy smile whose only clothing was a pair of severely tattered trousers.

"This is Sergeant Stanley Mitchell," Austin said. "He's with the Quartermaster Department, Fifteenth Corps."

Beckwith eyed Stanley. "Corps Quartermaster? Only one of *them* I met in here, getting caught back where it's safe and all. Another Bible thumper?"

Austin nodded. "Always trying to look out for the brethren after the Raiders finish with them."

"I need three, they send me one. Which ninety, Mitchell?"

"First, Sergeant Beckwith."

"That's Stew's group. He's a true believer too, and he's got a couple of others in that lot. Know the way?"

"I know the way," Austin said. He led Stanley off through more rows of low, flimsy hovels. "You'll find most here just go by one name. Most everyone calls me Ogre because of how I look. Personally, I think I'm too small to be a real ogre, but I don't mind. I figure another day or two, you'll be known only as Mitch."

"That suits me," Stanley said, "I'm used to it, but I think I'll still call you Austin. I'm sorry for doubting you."

"Apology accepted," Austin called back over his shoulder. Then he stopped and turned around. "A month ago, I was in your shoes. Know how hard this is at first. And it will only get harder."

"There was a wagon outside the gate," Stanley said. "Two slaves were loading dead men in it, more than a dozen, I think. Is that just for today?"

"Probably their third or fourth load of the day. We're losing between forty and fifty a day now."

The two men walked on among the dilapidated tents and hovels. The arithmetic was easy, at least twelve hundred dead in a month. "Those two thieves said I'll be dead in a few weeks. Is it true bigger fellows like me die fast?"

"Unfortunately, yes," Austin said. "The rations they give us aren't enough to keep a little guy like me going. Most larger men can't abide it and just give up. They're broken the moment they arrive and won't live a month. That's why I said what I did before. You can't give up and you can't do it alone."

"Right now," Stanley said, "I wouldn't know where to start."

"Depends more on a man's heart whether he lives or dies. What's inside you, Mitch? Terror, likely, but don't give it room to grow. Like I said, look for the good, do the good, and let good grow inside you instead of evil. And you got to have friends, good friends."

Austin grabbed Stanley's elbow, causing him to stop. "That's Sergeant Stewart just ahead. See the barber's shingle hanging on his tent pole? One thing you got to do before tomorrow. Decide who you'll be in this rotten place."

"I'll do my part and I won't make any trouble," Stanley said.

"Not what I mean, Mitch." The two men stood facing each other in the middle of the narrow path. "You'll fight every day to survive, if you want to live, that is. But how will you fight? If all you see is filth and misery, you'll be carried out to the deadhouse in a month. And if you aren't a man of the Word, you could throw in with the Raiders and live at the expense of others."

"No." Stanley shook his head vehemently. "I could never do that."

"Never? Good men do bad things all the time in here. Seen it already, haven't you? A man kicking another to death. And before they came here they were probably the best of friends."

CHAPTER 4

SERGEANT STEWART SMILED THROUGH HIS NEAT AND TIDY beard as he shook Stanley's hand. "Albert Stewart, Eleventh New Hampshire. Ogre's a good man. I can always count on him to bring in a wayward sheep."

The sergeant had the brightest blue eyes Stanley had ever seen. His hair was light in color, perhaps further lightened by the sun to the color of the sands along the bends of the Mississippi when the water was low. He had a narrow but pleasant looking face, not dour and pinched like Mr. Poteete of the *Evangelina*. Sergeant Stewart was of medium height and very lean, with dark, leathery skin, and the overall impression was that he looked exactly as every hardened survivor of many battles should look.

The sergeant's attire was almost identical to Stanley's, although his undershirt was stained a pale shade of the yellow-brown Georgia soil. His trousers, standard issue infantry light blue, were now tattered and faded and held up by canvas and leather suspenders. But there was one glaring difference from most of the other prisoners Stanley had seen thus far. Sergeant Stewart wore shoes, the cracked, split, and muddied remnants of army brogans.

"I guess you already met Sergeant Beckwith," Stewart said. "He's our detachment sergeant and an army First Sergeant, too. He's trustworthy, but he has little use for our small band of Christians. I'm sergeant of the first ninety. Each ninety is divided into three messes, and I'm assigning you to the third mess. Your mess sergeant is Hiram Pickens. He was a private outside these walls, but the men elected him their mess sergeant. Pickens has got the scurvy in a bad way. He mostly hides in his shebang with a couple of chums and comes out only to go to the latrine, or for roll call, or when the rations come in. In here, it's prison rank before army rank, so you'll answer directly to Pickens, and then to me and Beckwith. Will that be a problem for you, Sergeant Mitchell?"

"No, Sergeant Stewart, and Mitch is fine with me."

"And call me Stew. Everyone does. I'm twenty-three years old, married, two wee daughters, and I'm feeling particularly low about not being home for my wife's birthday. But everybody in here is low about something. I see you're somewhat lame."

"I was at Shiloh with the Fifty-third Ohio Infantry. I got wounded at the start of that fight. Now, I'm with the Quartermaster Department of General Logan's Fifteenth Corps. I'll be nineteen in September."

Stew whistled softly. "Sixteen when you joined the ranks. Glad to have you, Mitch, but I wish we had met under better circumstances."

Stanley swept his arm in an arc that encompassed dozens of nearby burrows. Three or four or more ragged, emaciated men occupied each one. "Are these huts all part of the Fifty-fifth?"

"Most, but not all, and to call them huts is to elevate them above their station." Stew laughed. "We call them shebangs, except for that big Raiders' tent across the way near the south wall. That's the Castle, and the area around it is the Citadel. If you like, I can assign you a bed-down place for now, but you may bunk with anyone you wish—maybe with Ogre, if he's got room." Stew pointed toward the valley of the swamp. "But don't look for a place down there. Stay up here where it's almost flat."

"Why is that?" Stanley asked.

"Some of the Indian tribes believe Earth-Mother is a loving, life-giving spirit, but the ground we're standing on proves she's a fickle hostess at best. The earth is somewhat soft and forgiving from all the rain, but soon it will be baked hard, nearly impossible to dig into."

Stew tried to dig the toe of his shoe into the ground. "The rain ended just before dawn, but even now, it's getting hard again. And when the rain pours down, little of it soaks in. Instead, it runs off in a torrent and all the mud and filth from this upper part of the camp sweeps through all those shebangs down there before it dumps into the swamp. Two men dug a hole into the slope for shelter from the sun. For a while they had cool shade by day, but one night last week, a sudden storm swept through, and the two men were buried alive and killed when their dugout collapsed."

"Stew, if I'm to survive, I must learn how. May I bunk with you?"

"Until now, I've always preferred to be by myself. Here's what I'll do. Fresh fish never sleep the first night, so I'll put you on watch. The three fellows down in that corner house always stay together and don't say much, but their shebang is a good spot to keep watch."

"What will I be watching for?"

"Raiders, Mitch, and any other person that doesn't belong in my ninety."

Stew knelt and reached into his shebang. It was a tent-like structure like that of Sergeant Beckwith, but instead of a single blanket, Sergeant Stewart had two, held together at the peak with a neat row of six buttons, just like a shelter tent.

Stew rose and handed a canteen to Stanley. "You're parched, Mitch. Drink. It's all right. It's from a well and it's been boiled."

The water was warm and tasted bitter, but Stanley thanked God as he drank. "A well, Sergeant?"

"Yes. There are several wells between here and the north wall. A man from my old regiment owns one of them. He still charges me for the water, but at a lower rate, sometimes for just a trim and a shave."

Stanley took another long drink and handed the canteen back to Stew.

Stew ducked into his tent again and took an extra moment or two to make sure the canteen was hidden from passersby.

When he reappeared, he looked troubled. "I shouldn't have put you off so fast about bunking with me. I'm sorry."

"It's all right, Stew. I understand."

"Truth is, I've been thinking about a change. A week ago, before he got sick, Frank spoke at our evening meeting on a very familiar verse from John. 'He that loveth his life shall lose it; and he that hateth his life in this world shall keep it unto life eternal.'"

"Is Frank a preacher?" Stanley asked.

Stew shook his head. "There aren't any real preachers here, but Frank knows the Scriptures. Most times he speaks for only five minutes, but that night he hit me square on the head, and I've been chewing on it ever since. And Ogre has very little, but he always finds a way to help somebody worse off." Stew looked back at his tent. "I've been living high on the hog here with two blankets and a rubber one besides. Always justified it thinking I have to get home to my family."

"That's only natural."

"Sure, but now I'm thinking I should either take on a mate or give one of those blankets to someone like you who has none. Tonight, while you're on watch, I'll think about it. Pray about it too."

"Whatever you decide is fine with me, Stew."

Stew started down the narrow path. "Let's go and see if we can find Sergeant Pickens, and introduce you to the members of your mess. For roll call in the morning and drawing of rations in the afternoon, you must stand with your mess in the same place every day. Pickens will show you when the time comes."

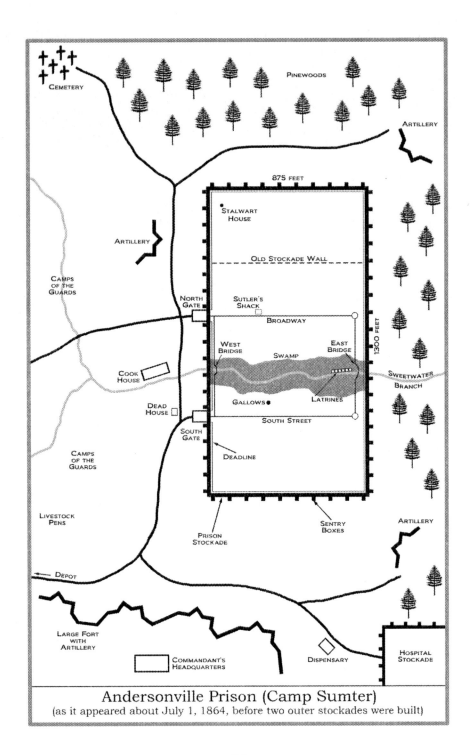

Andersonville Prison (Camp Sumter)
(as it appeared about July 1, 1864, before two outer stockades were built)

CHAPTER 5

STEW PULLED STANLEY ASIDE BEFORE THEY REACHED THE group of a dozen men sitting around a small fire pit. "Be careful what you say," Stew whispered. "Some of these men have been here for months and they think Sherman will be here any day to save them. It's their last hope, the only thing keeping some of them alive."

"I understand," Stanley said.

"Don't lie, but the truth might crush them."

Pickens was nowhere to be found, and had Stanley expected to be welcomed by his new messmates with smiles, handshakes, and pats on the back, he would have been greatly disappointed. The haggard, filthy men Stew introduced Stanley to sat shoulder to shoulder and stared up at him in silence for an uncomfortably long span of time. Then, as if a silent cue had been given, the men started to talk all at once.

"I'll be happy to answer your questions, if I can," Stanley said, "but please, one at a time." He pointed to the man closest to him on the left.

"Were you with Sherman?" the man asked.

"Who's asking?"

"Josh Bradford, Seventy-third Pennsylvania."

There was no place for Stanley to sit except on the damp earth, so he remained standing. "Yes, I was with Sherman. We started from Chattanooga the first week of May. Our troops were only twenty or so miles north of Atlanta when I was captured."

27

"Ken Daly, Seventh Michigan Cavalry. Does he know about us? Is he coming to get us?"

Cavalry again. Stanley stared at Daly for a moment and then glanced around at the others. "I don't know anything about General Sherman's plans. I was busy at the rear on the railroad, getting supplies to the front lines and evacuating our wounded back to Chattanooga."

"Walter Poole, Nineteenth New Jersey. The guards keep saying we're to be exchanged soon. Is it true?"

Pleading eyes stared up at Stanley. "I hope so," he said, "I haven't been inside two hours and already I want out."

A few thin smiles answered Stanley's attempt at humor, but most of the men just shrugged and looked away. No great news today.

What else could he say? That the exchange of prisoners of war probably wouldn't resume until this war was done?

"We should go," Stew said, taking Stanley gently by the elbow. "We need to go see Sergeant Cleary. He's in charge of Ogre's bunch, the third ninety of the fifty-fifth."

They started along a narrow path toward the east wall of the Stockade. "Mitch," Stew said, "I know the army policy against prisoner exchanges. Most of the newer prisoners do. But many of the older prisoners, like the ones you just met, don't know. You wanted to say more. What didn't you tell them?"

"General Grant himself stopped the exchanges, Stew. I was at Vicksburg when Grant paroled thirty thousand Rebel prisoners of war. Each man signed a paper stating he wouldn't take up arms against the Union again. But many thousands of those same men tore up their paroles and went right back to the Confederate army. Some of them were captured two months later at Chickamauga and General Grant was furious."

"Thanks, Mitch," Stew said. "I thought Grant cut us off on a whim. I guess he didn't, but I don't agree with his decision."

Stew stopped in the middle of the path, dropped to one knee, and peered into a low shebang. Stanley could just make out the dim motionless form of a shrunken man, bony legs drawn up—dead, Stanley thought, until the man gasped for air.

Stanley pulled the neckline of his undershirt over his nose and mouth and turned away from the stench.

"That's how it is here," Stew said as he stood. "To send a man to the hospital is death, so most times they lie where they are. I've seen it all too often. It's like they start to rot on the inside before the breath leaves them."

• • •

Sergeant Cleary's shebang was larger than most, and slightly more luxurious for he had two blankets for the roof of his tent and a rubber blanket to cover the earthen floor. Cleary was in a foul mood and made no secret of the fact that he was suffering an affliction that plagued nearly every prisoner sooner or later—chronic diarrhea.

Stew didn't bother shaking Cleary's hand. "This is my new man, Mitch. Came in just after noon. I just saw Rodgers. He's at death's door, and this morning I saw Father Whelan give that man the last rite. I was thinking it would be good if you would grant me Rodgers' ration for Mitch here."

Cleary eyed Stanley up and down. "Big fella needs to eat, but you know how it works, Stew. He wasn't here for roll call this morning, so he can't draw a ration this afternoon."

Stew's face reddened. "I know for a fact Rodgers hasn't eaten anything for several days—"

"And I can do as I please with his ration."

"Yes, I know. One of your pets will get it, or you'll take it for yourself while this man goes hungry."

"Whichever. The ration stays in this ninety."

Stew glared at Cleary. "Then may I ask you to please assign Mitch and your man Ogre to Rodgers' final muster?"

Cleary looked at Stanley again. "As you wish. Now, go."

Stew brushed past Stanley and started to walk away.

Stanley tried to catch up. "Stew. Wait. Stew, what was that? You should have asked me. How could you think I would take food from—"

"From a dead man?" Stew said, turning to face Stanley. "Yes, Rodgers is a dead man. Even if he could eat, which he can't, the food will do him no good. You wanted me to teach you to survive and this is lesson one. You will eat whatever food you can get, even if it's from a dead man, even if it's spoiled, even if it's full of bugs, and even if you know it will make you sick."

"But—"

"But nothing, Mitch. Every morsel, every crumb is life in this place."

"But what was the final muster talk about?"

Stew took a deep breath and calmed himself. "I'm sorry, Mitch. Cleary's pigheadedness always sets me off. I got you an extra ration though."

"How?"

"Rodgers' final muster, Mitch. You and Ogre have just been detailed to carry Rodgers' body across to the gate and identify him to the death roll clerk. You get an extra ration for that."

Stanley couldn't restrain the dark sarcasm. "So I'll get more food from a dead man."

"If that's the way you want to look at it."

"Excuse me, Stew." Neither Stanley nor Stew had noticed that another prisoner had taken a keen interest in their conversation.

Stew's eyes brightened. "Ah, Ogre. We were just talking about you."

"Heard you and Cleary going at it," Austin said, "and want to offer a solution, if I may."

"Of course," Stew said.

"Got some soup," Austin said, "not much, but Mitch can have it so he doesn't starve."

Stew looked at Stanley. "Is that all right?"

"Of course," Stanley said.

"Good," Austin said. "See you at meeting tonight, Stew."

"Will you be there, Mitch?" Stew asked.

"He'll be there," Austin said before Stanley could respond.

"Until then, gentlemen." Stew nodded and walked back toward his shebang.

"What meeting?" Stanley asked Austin.

"Christian meeting over at the circle. Have one every evening."

"And what was that between Stew and Cleary?"

Austin laughed a little. "Stew riles Cleary just to show how different they are. Thinks he's setting Cleary an example. Can't see it's doing much though."

"So, what if the shoe was on the other foot?" Stanley asked.

"That *is* the question, isn't it? I'm just over here next to Cleary. See the red strip of cloth tied to the ridge pole? Let's see about that soup. Good thing Stew got you that extra ration. Rodgers is my friend and I figured Cleary would put me on taking Rodgers' across, but I didn't know who would help me. I'm glad it's you, Mitch."

A medium-size cooking pot sat steaming over a small fire inside Austin's shebang. "You cook soup? In here? How?"

"I'll tell you after I fix you up. Sit here."

Stanley eased himself down onto a small crate, not sure it would bear his weight. "Do you have a mate?"

Austin poured some of the brown liquid into a small soot-blackened tin can with a wire bail for a handle. "Yes. His name's Dell, and he's a bit of a crazy man. Goes about wearing almost nothing, telling everybody he's the prophet Elijah. Doesn't believe it—he's not religious at all—just wants people to think he's insane. I got clothes for him, but he won't wear them. Think he'll die soon. Tragic, really." He handed the can to Stanley. "Careful, let it cool for a bit."

Stanley's stomach growled in protest, but he set the can aside.

"Got here a month ago," Austin said, "with a few dollars hidden away, so I bought this three-quart soup pot. But now I'm dead broke, and can only make soup from my rations, and Dell's, of course. Today, we have a special treat—beef broth. Traded yesterday's beef ration for a large beef bone." He held up a knife blade with several teeth cut along the back edge. "A bone saw, made it myself. Cut that bone in half and worried out all the marrow with the pointed end of my spoon. Turned out pretty well. With a little salt, it would have been perfect."

Stanley remembered what Stew had said. *"Ogre has very little, but he always finds a way to help somebody worse off."* I *guess that makes me one of the worse off.* Stanley hooked his thumbs inside his suspenders and watched the wisps of steam

31

curl upward from the can of soup. "I should pay for this, Austin."

Austin held up his hand. "No need. It's on the house." His eyes darted around at his humble surroundings and he smiled. "On the shebang, that is."

Stanley bowed his head and gave silent thanks for the simple meal. How good it was, both the broth and the company. Austin had said Stanley would need friends to survive, and Stanley had already shared a meal and a laugh with Austin.

When Stanley looked up again, Austin's smile had vanished. "I forgot about your stolen cane, Mitch. You going to be all right carrying Rodgers down to the South Gate? It'll be soon, two or three days, at most. Can't weigh more than eighty pounds, only forty apiece. I can do that, even feeling low as I do."

"Then I guess I can too," Stanley said.

"Stew was right, you know. You must be willing to take food from a dying man when there's no hope for him."

"Who's to say there's no hope, Austin?"

"Seems to go against basic Christian law, to love your neighbor as yourself, but you will soon know when a man has passed the point from which there's no return. You'll know without a doubt when life may be spared and when further effort is futile."

There was truth in Austin's words. Stanley had witnessed several such turning points at the Duff Green Hospital in Vicksburg. "How old are you, Austin?"

"Twenty. Too young to know things I wish I didn't know at all. But, well, there it is."

CHAPTER 6

*T*HERE WAS NO POINT IN RETURNING TO HIS MESS FOR ration call, since he wouldn't receive any food until tomorrow afternoon. Instead, Stanley stood guard over Austin's soup pot and watched the pompous Cleary go through the daily ritual of dividing up the mess's meager allotment into thirty equal portions.

Austin returned to the shebang shaking his head. "Corncob bread and hard peas today. I was hoping for rice. Cleary always gives me double, because I take care of Dell." Austin dumped the peas, about two cups in all, into the pot with the last of the beef broth. "Here," he said, handing one of the hunks of cornbread to Stanley. "What do you think?"

The bread was about one-third the size of a loaf but weighed more than any cornbread Stanley had ever eaten before. It was charred almost black on the outside and uncooked in the middle. Stanley turned up his nose.

"Break off a corner and try it," Austin said.

It tasted the way it looked, dark, dull and coarse, with no sweetness or saltiness to improve it. Stanley had only one word for it. "Ugh."

"We call it corncob bread because they grind up the corn and cob together. Very rough on the stomach. Eat only half that piece, and you'll be running for the latrine within ten minutes."

33

Austin took the bread from Stanley and crumbled it into the soup pot along with Dell's portion. "Always cook your rations. Even if they give us cooked meal mush, cook it again to kill any bugs or worms. Cooking it awhile seems to make it easier on the stomach and it doesn't go right through." He then added some water from his canteen to the pot.

"Where do you get your water, Austin?"

"Several places. It's been raining a lot since I got here, so I pitched my blanket toward the back corner and put my pot there to catch it. There are several wells and a few small springs. The owners charge for their water but are usually willing to trade for soup."

"But then you're giving away your food," Stanley said, "yours and Dell's."

"Only when I have to." Austin stirred the pot with his spoon. "Putting it back to what it was before it went in the oven—mush, peas and corn meal mush—but at least it's all cooked. Got water from the swamp too, but only a few times, and only when the flow was clean, like after a hard rain. Also, I like to check the deep footprints in the muck by the swamp. Found fresh water in them sometimes, mostly near the west bridge. Very strange, but it's better than what's in the stream. Wherever I get it, it goes in my soup pot with my rations and whatever else I can get. That's the only way I get my water, and it's keeping me healthier than most, I think."

A gaunt, balding man, thin as a rail, with a long graying beard hobbled up the path toward the shebang. Dressed only in a pair of sun-faded trousers that ran off to tatters about mid-thigh, the man steadied himself with a wooden staff. Had the man been clad instead with a long cloak of coarse material, he would have looked like Moses or one of the Old Testament prophets.

The man ducked under the blanket roof of the shebang and laid down on a rubber blanket in the rear of the shebang as if to go to sleep.

"Did you wash today, Dell?" Austin asked.

"Don't remember."

"Smells like you didn't. Have you picked at the bugs in your beard, Dell?"

"Don't remember."

"Dell, you know the rules. Wash and skirmish every day. Don't want your bugs, Dell. It's common courtesy."

Dell turned on his side, away from Austin.

Austin closed his eyes. "Father, we ask you to bless this simple food. We may not want it or like it, but may it be sufficient to our need, and may it do us more good than harm. Amen."

"Interesting blessing," Stanley said.

"What you pray for and what you don't changes quickly in here." Austin spooned some of the contents of the pot into a can. "We have mush tonight, Dell."

"Had mush every day this week."

"Yesterday, we had beef soup, but I can only cook what they give us. Got a visitor tonight just in from Sherman's army."

Dell grunted. "Sherman ain't coming."

"Come on, Dell. Sit up and have some mush, and let's chat with Mitch."

And he did, at least the first part of it. Dell sat up, ate a few spoonfuls from the can Austin gave him, and then laid down again without saying a word.

"His appetite's been failing the last several days," Austin said in a whisper. "It won't be long now." He held Dell's can of mush toward Stanley.

"Won't he want it later?"

Austin sighed and shook his head. "He was sick when we were taken and he's only gotten worse. We always looked out for each other. Now, he's all but slipped away."

35

Stanley would have much preferred the standard army ration of hardtack and salt pork to the mush Austin served him. It wasn't tasty, the texture was lousy, and no enticing aroma drove away the pervading stench of the prison. Also, it was hardly enough to feed a mid-size cat. Still, it was food, and Stanley remembered that, although he was entitled to no ration until the next day, he had been fed, not just once, but twice.

CHAPTER 7

AS EVENING OF STANLEY'S FIRST DAY IN THE PRISON
stockade approached, the overcast lowered and
thickened, casting a dark melancholy over the camp.
According to Austin Oglethorpe, it had rained nearly every
day since the beginning of June. Everyone was weary of
sleeping not only on the damp, muddy earth, but often
almost within it, as many of the prisoners had excavated
several inches to a foot of the sandy soil from the floor of
their shebangs to form dugouts. All seemed destined to
endure another wet, miserable night.

From somewhere out of sight, down in the valley,
perhaps near the swamp, a solitary voice began to sing, a
clear baritone that cut through the still, humid air.

"That's our call to meeting hymn," Austin said. "Let's
go." Austin took up the hymn and started toward
Broadway.

Come, ye disconsolate, where'er ye languish,
Come to the mercy seat, fervently kneel;
Here bring your wounded hearts, here tell your anguish,
Earth has no sorrows that heaven cannot heal.

From all around the camp, men walked toward a central
point, the wagon turnaround at the head of Broadway.

Men came singly, as Sergeant Stewart did, or in pairs, like Stanley and Austin.

> Joy of the comfortless, light of the straying,
> Hope of the penitent, fadeless and pure!
> Here speaks the Comforter, in mercy saying,
> Earth has no sorrows that heaven cannot cure.

A few men hobbled forward with crude walking sticks or crutches. Others, stooped and feeble, shuffled along, sometimes aided by a stronger brother.

> Here see the Bread of Life, see waters flowing
> Forth from the throne of God, pure from above:
> Come to the feast prepared, come, ever knowing
> Earth has no sorrows but heaven can remove.

Stanley and Austin were among the first to arrive at the meeting place. The men began the hymn again and the singing continued until all had gathered, a crowd of a hundred or more. One man carried a friend in his arms to the meeting all the way from the lower end of Broadway near the North Gate. A blanket was spread on the ground and the helpless man was laid upon it.

A slender, somewhat sickly looking young man holding a Bible, removed his cap and moved to the center of the group.

"That's Frank Griffin," Austin said. "He's been here just two weeks, but he's taken the lead in our little company. It's good to see him up again; he's been sick the last few days. It's him that started the singing to gather the people. You'll learn the hymn quick enough."

The assembly grew quiet, expectant. There was nothing exceptional about Frank. He was of average height with dark hair and beard, like thousands of other prisoners. His eyes were hazel in color like Anna's, but dull, with none of the brilliance of her eyes, perhaps due to his illness.

Frank called the group to order with a short prayer. His voice was pleasant and his words simple as he asked God to bless the meeting.

"I was reading my Bible this morning," he said, "trying to finish the Old Testament today, when I was brought up short by a verse written by the prophet Zephaniah. 'The LORD thy God in the midst of thee is mighty; he will save, he will rejoice over thee with joy; he will rest in his love, he will joy over thee with singing.'

"What stopped me was a question that came to me over and over as I lay sick. Do I really believe God is here with us amid all this suffering? Death has become a usual thing for us, even the wholesale slaughter Jeff Davis is inflicting upon us here at Andersonville. Zephaniah's time was little different; his nation of Judah was under the oppressive heel of Assyria. And yet God gave his people these promises: I am mighty, I will rejoice over you with joy, you will rest in my love. And then God repeats his promise to make it even more marvelous to our ears, I will joy over you *with singing.*

"In my twenty short years of life, I was never sick like I was this week. Was God singing for joy over my miserable condition? Or our brother Josiah Talbot lying here, is God singing for joy seeing him so low and wretched?

"No, God takes no pleasure in our afflictions. He knows we are dust and he knows our weakness. And yet he does rejoice, even to the point of singing over us, when we trust him to bring us through those afflictions. What are our sufferings compared to Job's? He was faithful and God commended him, and it certainly gave God great pleasure to poke a finger in Satan's eye.

"So, I plead with you to take comfort from the countless promises God has given us. Before you sleep tonight, think about how these promises are a blessing to us here and now. And if anyone would like to speak privately about God and his word, I will be happy to meet with you.

"Let me leave you with a few more words from Zephaniah. 'At that time will I bring you again, even in the time that I gather you: for I will make you a name and a praise among all people of the earth, when I turn back your captivity before your eyes, saith the LORD.'

"What sweet music to our ears. Let it be so."

Another hymn was sung; then Frank held up his hand. "Now, gentlemen, as we always do, let's have our season of prayer. Pray aloud, if you wish, or pray silently, but please, all of you, give up to our Almighty Father the desires of your hearts."

Several of the men did pray aloud, while most of the others, from their frequent deep moans and sighs seemed to be caught up to the very gates of heaven with their unspoken petitions. Stanley's prayer was simple: *Lord, please let me survive this place and return to Anna.* He voiced those words over and over within his mind, and with each repetition it sounded more superficial and selfish when, at that very moment, dozens of men like Talbot and Rodgers were at death's threshold.

It was something of a relief when Frank, after the gathering had grown quiet again, spoke three words that ended the prayer time and dismissed the meeting, "Go in peace."

Austin led Stanley forward and introduced him to Frank.

"You speak well," Stanley said. "Are you a pastor?"

"My father is back in Ohio."

"I grew up in Ironton on the Ohio River."

"I'm from Cleveland, First Sergeant of Company D, 124th Ohio Volunteers."

"I was in the Fifty-third."

Frank peered closely at Austin. "I see you've gotten worse. When I was sick, I saw some of that red root sticking

40

out of the side of my dugout." He reached into the pocket of his trousers and produced the root. "Take it, Austin. It should help with your scurvy. Are you an early riser, Mitch?"

"I guess so."

"If you're a friend of Oglethorpe," Frank said, "he's always up before the birds." He pointed down the slope toward the swamp. "A few of us meet at dawn each morning at the west bridge to bathe and wash our clothes and talk. Perhaps you'll join us."

"Thank you, Frank," Stanley said. "I will, but I think I'm in for a long, sleepless night."

CHAPTER 8

Matthews Hill Farm
McNairy County, Tenn.

MAMA CLOSED THE BIBLE AND SET IT ASIDE. "IT'S Thursday evening and before I dismiss you from the table, Anna has—"

"Another letter from Stanley," Ruthie said.

"How many is that now?" Mama asked.

"Twenty-eight," Anna said. "Remember his letter from Chattanooga? He wrote the date, 'President Lincoln's Day of Thanksgiving.'"

"Sure," Luke said. "He wrote it while he was on top of Lookout Mountain two days after the battle. He was looking west, wishing he could be here."

"That's right," Anna said. *So, Luke has been listening all along.* "That was the first letter. I got it on the 10th of December and I've gotten one every Thursday since. On Monday, it'll be two years he was taken, nine months since I, I mean we, saw him in Corinth. But every time I see Mr. Burns come up the lane, I know Stanley's safe. Every letter makes me more sure he'll be coming up that lane himself someday, and I'm starting to think sooner rather than later."

The growing lump in her throat belied Anna's confidence. *Am I really that sure? How many sleepless nights I've spent thinking of dozens of ways my Stanley—my betrothed—could die. He might fall under the wheels of*

42

one of those trains he's always writing about, or get some dreadful disease, or get kicked by a mule again, this time in the head.

"Go ahead, dear," Mama said. "We're all anxious to hear the latest."

Sgt. Stanley Mitchell
QM Dept., XV Corps
Chattanooga, TN
Saturday, June 11, 1864

My Dearest Anna,

As I wrote a week ago, I'm safe and in fine health, though wearying of humid, stormy weather. I long to soak in the cool water of Owl Creek, but I must make do with the muddy, tepid, and mosquito infested puddles that pass for creeks in these parts.

Twice, when my duties and my captain allowed me leave, I rode out the busy south road about a mile to the Etowah River. The water is much better there, and as I cooled and cleansed myself, I watched the engineers hard at work building a new railroad bridge high above the river next to the charred ruin of the old bridge that was torched by Rebel cavalry.

Most of the army has moved on, while my unit has remained here at Cartersville for two weeks, awaiting completion of the bridge. That good news arrived this afternoon, so there will be no going to church for me tomorrow. We'll be busy getting the trains running again, and by tomorrow evening, we expect to be up to our new forward depot at Allatoona.

You may wonder that I'm able to write details of our movements. The simple truth is that each side in this long, running fight knows where the other is. Every day our armies drive the Confederate forces back toward Atlanta, and every few days, up until our current sojourn at

Cartersville, the Quartermaster Department moved its main supply depot forward as soon as repairs to the railroad were complete. We are in constant communication with the front and yesterday I learned that Johnston has fallen back upon a formidable mountain called Kennesaw. I think it's about halfway between Cartersville and Atlanta.

Before leaving this place, I should tell you about an incident that occurred here two weeks ago on Sunday, just after we arrived in Cartersville. About a dozen men from the QM Department walked across town to the Presbyterian Church for the morning service. Ever since I attended First Presbyterian in Corinth—what a blessed day that was to see you and...

Although Anna had read the letter that afternoon, she envisioned Stanley's face as she had last seen it at Corinth, glowing warm in the October afternoon sun.

"And what?" Ruthie said. "Come on, Anna. What's he say?"

"Ruthie," Mama said, wagging her finger in her twelve-year-old daughter's face. "You do this near every time Anna shares one of her letters with us. Some of it's private, just between them two."

"It's all right, Mama," Anna said. "I don't mind. It's personal, but it's not stuff you all don't already know."

Anna felt the color in her face rise. She took a deep breath and began again. "'What a blessed day that was to see you and hold you and kiss you and tell you I love you.'"

"Wow! That's beautiful," Ruthie said, while Davy, four years younger, just laughed.

Luke remained still, neither smiling nor frowning.

"All right," Mama said. "Settle down. What was Stanley saying about the church?"

Ever since I attended First Presbyterian in Corinth, I have come to favor their plain style of worship. But when we

44

arrived at the church, it was obvious there would be no worship in that place, because—it shames me to write this—the church was heavily infested with a detachment of Federal cavalry.

"How is this possible?" I asked any trooper who would listen. "Jesus Christ was born in a stable, but to treat God's house as one is a crime."

Many of the troopers just laughed or ignored me altogether.

Others said things like, "Them Rebs wouldn't let us use their liveries," or "Serves them godless Johnnies right."

One cavalryman sounded slightly more reasonable. "It's the only place large enough to shelter our mounts from the rain."

My horse was corralled out in the open near the depot and he seemed to fare much better in the rain than I did, even when I was inside my tent wrapped in a rubber blanket.

I asked to speak to their commanding officer, which I did. He told me to return to my unit and file a complaint with my commanding officer, which I also did.

Because my complaint involved a breach of army policy prohibiting the mistreatment of otherwise law-abiding local citizens, it was sent about thirty miles south to the headquarters of General Logan near New Hope Church. Since he took command of the Fifteenth Corps, I have seen him several times during his regular inspections of the Quartermaster Department. Each time he passed in review of the men, he never failed to pause a few moments to chat with me, to inquire after my well-being, to offer a good-natured bit of advice about life, army life in particular, or to reminisce about the quiet days at Stonehaven after Vicksburg was won. A couple of times he asked if I'm still planning to marry "that pretty Tennessee gal," to which, I can assure you, I responded with a firm, "Yes, sir."

"He *will* come back, Anna," Willy said from across the table. "I pray he'll come back every day, sometimes a bunch of times."

"We're all praying the same," Anna said, "and because Stanley was so good to you when your eyes were going bad, I saw he was no common Yankee devil." This last she said with a wink at her Mama, and her heart seemed to flutter a bit when Luke nodded his agreement.

"All right," Anna said, turning her attention to the letter again. "So, Stanley's complaint against the cavalrymen was sent to General Logan's headquarters."

My name on the complaint must have caught his eye, for within three days, not only had the cavalry vacated the church, they had also swept it clean, mopped the floor, and replaced all the furnishings. That evening, the people gathered for their regular Wednesday evening prayer service.

Apparently, by last Sunday, the 5th, word had spread throughout the congregation that the tall Yankee sergeant with the cane had been instrumental in restoring them to their house of worship. I was rewarded with many smiles and warm handshakes, countless whispered words of thanks, and one beautiful blackberry pie.

As we close operations here at Cartersville tomorrow and move on to Allatoona, we will be protected by a screen of cavalry all along the way. The detachment detailed for this duty is the very same company that was banished from the church. I do hope they are at heart a merry band and are willing to let bygones be bygones.

Anna folded the letter and held it in her lap.

"That's it?" Ruthie asked.

"Yes, that's it. The rest is for me and only me. You'll just have to wait for Stanley's next letter."

46

"Aw, come on, that's a whole week. You read the I love you part."

Anna shrugged and grinned at her sister.

"You know, Sis, I think he sounds happy." It was the first comment Luke had made about one of Stanley's letters for several weeks.

Anna saw Mama's smile before she answered her brother. "He knows his work is important—getting all the wounded Yankees on trains for Chattanooga. The dead ones too. He only wrote about loading coffins the one time, good and useful work, he said it was. I wish somebody had sent Papa back here."

But no one had. Her father was buried in some unknown grave up near Fort Donelson. Her tears had been many then, but now he occupied a special place in her heart, a place filled with many fond memories.

"When Stanley was on that riverboat," Anna said, "he wrote me sometimes saying he was trying hard to be content, you know, with where he was and what he was doing and our being apart and all. I think maybe he's done that and he's at peace with the way things are for now."

CHAPTER 9

Sergeant Stewart guided Stanley through the twilight toward a black, almost rectangular shape in the earth. "This will be your place for the night. The Raiders love dark, cloudy nights like this. Raise a cry if you spot any, because you're on watch until I relieve you."

In every direction, the prisoners were already bedding down for the night, so Stanley figured he should do likewise. The black shape he had noticed turned out to be three small, thin men—*the three mice* Stew had called them. Huddled together for warmth on a warm, humid night, they lay front to back, spoon-like, in a shallow depression, under a single woolen army-issue blanket.

The three men took no notice of Stanley's grunts and groans as he lowered himself gently to the moist, almost muddy, earth beside them. The strong hickory walking stick Levi Jackson had made him was gone. Anna's warm, loving letters were gone. Nothing remained of his time at Matthews Hill Farm except a bucketful of memories which had grown suddenly dim and distant. And the image of his lovely, dearest Anna seemed to have faded most of all.

Stanley sat motionless. Every half hour during the night, each of the sentries atop the wall called out in a southern twang with a lyrical lilt, "Post number fo-ah-teen, half past ten o'clock, and all is we-ell." Stanley counted the number of posts—the words were indistinguishable from

48

the sentries farthest away—thirty-six posts in all. Minutes trudged past until the next half hour. "Post number fo-ah-teen, eleven o'clock, and all is we-ell."

Shortly after the sentries called two o'clock, a heavy rain shower came up. Stanley lay flat on his back, mouth open to the black sky, catching what drops he could. A short time later the rain ceased.

Stanley was soaked to the skin and started to shiver. The night was still warm; it shouldn't have bothered him. Weakness—that's what it was—from the scant rations forced upon him ever since his capture. *That's probably why the three mice huddle together.* Austin's broth and the half-can of mush had helped for a while, but hunger gnawed at his insides like a burrowing rodent trying to consume him from within, trying to make him into one of those emaciated forms lying beside him.

He dared not try to rise and stretch. The dull lethargy already taking a foothold within him might cause him to stumble and fall, or faint away altogether. There was no hope for more food and no hope for anything more to ease his thirst for at least twelve more hours.

So, there he sat, his left leg out straight before him, his right leg bent, knee raised, upon which he rested his right arm so he could bury his nose in the bend of his elbow, his only defense against the oppressive stench of the swamp which seemed to have grown heavier and thicker after darkness had closed over the prison. From time to time, when his left leg began to twitch and cramp, he used both hands to knead the muscles and ease the pain for a while.

Stanley knew the sounds men made during the night. He had shared barracks with a hundred at Huntsville, Bridgeport, and Chattanooga, and during the campaign, he had slept in tents with a dozen others.

But the sounds of Andersonville were different. Instead of the usual dissonance of a hearty chorus of snores, it seemed the entire camp struggled to take its next breath

49

in a gasping sigh that rolled from one hovel to the next like a constant, muted, rasping wave of moaned distress, pierced from time to time by wails of purest anguish.

Once, when the night was darkest, he heard a sudden cry from somewhere not far away, perhaps from the other side of Broadway. The cry had been followed by several thudding blows which sounded like a club striking human flesh. A few minutes later, he heard a shot from down in the valley near the bridge over the swamp. A shriek of agony pierced the night..

Look for the good, Austin had said. Stanley had known night terrors after Shiloh, but they were nothing compared to the real, living horror that was swallowing him up the way a snake does a mouse.

Death. It lay all around him. One man clubbed, perhaps beaten to death; another shot, perhaps the man he had seen that afternoon had tottered near the deadline again. Either way, a quick, violent death was better than the slow agony of wasting away. *But I must survive. I must see Anna again. Someday. Somehow.*

Stew was the only healthy person he had seen besides the Raiders. Everyone else appeared sick, weary, and filthy, their faces blackened, not from the sun, as Stanley had assumed, but from huddling over pitch-pine cooking fires, as Austin had told him.

"Darken your face, too," he had said, "so it won't be so obvious you're new."

What sort of man will I be in this place? Austin's question wouldn't leave him alone. Perhaps I'll be dead in a month, just like the two Raiders said. What will the cane and letters matter then? Anna will never know what has become of me.

Stanley fingered the inside seams of his suspenders. *Look for the good. What good remains in me? The Raiders took much, but they didn't take everything. What they missed will be my deliverance—it must be—and that secret will be mine alone.*

Sometime during the night Stanley became aware of both a prickling and itching of his skin. He couldn't say which came first, but he knew exactly what it was. He had felt the same thing during the encampment at Shiloh and a few times during this past winter when he had been stationed along the railroad between Huntsville and Bridgeport.

Gray-backs. Critters. Bugs. Cooties. Lice. Regardless of the playful names men gave them, he hated them. Had Stanley seen the three mice during daylight, he would have seen the severity of their inhabitation. He could have taken measures to avoid becoming heir to their bugs which, finding pickings on the trio increasingly slim, were abandoning their hosts for a stronger, healthier specimen.

War will begin at sunrise.

Finally, the sky above seemed a little less black. The minutes dragged on and it became evident that dawn was approaching. Stanley had no idea what the new day would bring, but one thing he did know. There would be no respite from the dreadful sights he had met with in passing yesterday afternoon. There would be no escape from the countless horrors that would be revealed afresh in the light of the new day.

A hand touched his arm. "Mitch. Stew here."

"Good morning, Stew. You were right. I didn't sleep at all. Didn't even nod off for a minute. But these boys are infested and I think I am too. I need to get out of here."

"Then we must go wash at the stream. Here, take my hand. I'll help you up."

CHAPTER 10

Friday, June 24, 1864

FOUR YOUNG MEN, ALL SERGEANTS IN THE UNITED STATES Army, stood knee-deep in the murky flow of the stream that flowed through the swamp in the middle of the prison. In the half-light of early dawn, the easy banter of Stew, Frank, and Austin eased Stanley's night terrors, but if he allowed his attention to drift even for a moment, the evil sights and smells and sounds of the place lay in wait to carry him away entirely.

It seemed a natural companionship. Each man's circumstances and service differed, but all were of similar age. Stew was the oldest at twenty-three, and Stanley, three months shy of his nineteenth birthday, was the youngest. And each man had been turned into the stockade within the last month.

The water was cleaner at that early hour, just as Austin had said. In lieu of his cane, Stanley leaned heavily on Stew's arm as he inched down the slippery bank into the shallow stream. Stanley's feet immediately became mired in the slimy bottom of the stream and he couldn't move either to the right or left, or backward or forward without great difficulty.

Bluish streaks tinged the surface of the water. Black blobs of who-knew-what meandered along with the current and Stanley doubted how clean he would feel after washing in such water.

"You're something of a curiosity, Mitch," Stew said. "I'm itching to hear your tale of woe."

"My tale of woe?"

"Yes," Stew said, "a rear area worker getting snatched up. We'd just like to know who you are, how you got your bum leg, how you got put in this place—the usual stuff that makes good conversation."

It had been months since he had told anyone the full story of his life, and it seemed these three young men should hear it, but now was not the time.

"It's about as long as *The Iliad*," Stanley said. "I'll tell you all of it soon, but not today. My strength is gone and it will take all three of you just to get me out of this muck. What time is roll call?"

"Ten o'clock," Frank said.

"I must sleep before then," Stanley said. "Being dead tired only makes the hunger and thirst worse."

"Go up to my tent," Stew said. "Drink some water and lie down. You won't have to endure the bugs of the three mice and I don't have any barbering until this afternoon. Besides, it's your tent now too."

"My-My tent? Really?"

Stew grinned. "Really. I thought it over, just like I said."

"Thank you, Stew. Is there any soap?" Stanley asked.

Stew roared with laughter. Frank and Austin laughed too, but it was obvious their merriment was tempered by their illnesses.

"They never give us soap," Frank said. "To the Rebels, cleanliness is more a frame of mind than a physical reality."

CHAPTER 11

STANLEY HAD SLEPT FOR AN HOUR OR TWO, BUT IT SEEMED only minutes. Already, weariness had worked its way deep within him. He felt weak and lightheaded from lack of food and water. And to make matters worse, the beating of the drums for roll call had awakened him with a splitting headache.

Mess Sergeant Hiram Pickens was about what Stanley expected, a thin, filthy, shoeless man, with a pasty-complexioned face that reminded Stanley of the prunes he had been introduced to at Stonehaven during the quiet days after the surrender of Vicksburg. But what Stanley had not expected was how affected Pickens was from scurvy.

Every soldier knew the threat of scurvy, and how proper food was key to preventing it. Stanley had seen boxcar after boxcar laden with fruits and vegetables—canned, desiccated, and fresh—roll into the depots from the north. But within the walls of the prison, not one green thing remained, except for two lone pine trees that, for some unknown reason, had been left untouched across the swamp in the southeast corner of the stockade.

Pickens moved slowly among the ten shebangs of the mess, calling out the men to stand in line, front to back, along a portion of Eighth Street, a narrow path that ran through the mess. He walked hunched over. His leg

54

muscles had stiffened, locking his knees at an awkward angle which forced him to walk on the balls of his feet. *That could be me in a month or two.*

The mess sergeant must have been in agony, but as each man fell in, Pickens reached up a trembling hand, patted the man on the back, and with bleary, pain-filled eyes, greeted the man by name. "Good morning, Lou." "Pleased to see you up again, Trotter." "Welcome to the Spa at Andersonville, Mitch."

Such youthful innocence and good humor from one so afflicted—a little good in this prison of death, just as Austin had said there would be. *Never again,* Stanley determined, as he watched Pickens continue down the line*, will I feel self-conscious about the awkward way I walk. It could be far, far worse.*

Roll call was a necessary part of every day. It was a prison, after all, and the Rebel guards took the process of taking the roll count most seriously. Pickens gave an accounting of the thirty men of his mess to Sergeant Stewart, who then passed the count of the three messes in his ninety up to Sergeant Beckwith. Then Beckwith reported the final tally of the three nineties of the Fifty-fifth Detachment to a sergeant of the guard, and each sergeant of the guard was responsible for counting ten detachments—twenty-seven hundred men.

That was when the lunacy began, as Stanley saw it. The guard, of course, never trusted any prisoner, and so, after receiving the roll count, the guard was obliged to view every man declared present to ensure there had been no escapes, but more importantly, it seemed to Stanley, to ensure that only the exact number of rations were allotted later in the day. After all, it just wouldn't be good policy to allow any more food to enter the prison than was necessary.

After a long wait the sergeant of the guard finally came to the head of the Fifty-fifth Detachment. Then he walked down the line, counting each man for himself. Pickens sat on the ground at the head of the mess until the guard approached. Two members of the mess helped Pickens to his feet, then he and the sergeant of the guard worked their way down the line to Stanley at the end, where the fragile, wheezing Pickens leaned on Stanley's arm for support.

Twenty-seven men were counted. The three mice had remained in their burrow, too sick to stand for roll call, so Pickens hobbled away with the guard to their shebang to see for himself if those men still lived. The count complete, Pickens returned to the head of the mess and sat down heavily, and the sergeant of the guard went off to count other detachments.

The whole thing took over two hours, and yet not once did Stanley hear Pickens complain. But it was inevitable that one day soon, Pickens wouldn't be able to stand for roll call at all.

CHAPTER 12

ERE, MITCH, DRINK THIS." THE CAN AUSTIN HELD TOWARD Stanley was steaming hot. "I enjoy your visits, but you've been sitting there without a word for the last hour."

The can was nearly full with red root tea which Austin had brewed after reducing the root to a small pile of shavings. The tea would certainly help his arid, dusty throat, maybe quiet his throbbing head as well. And Austin had said it went down easy. "No thanks, Austin. Frank gave you that root for your scurvy."

"So, your canteen's full?" Austin's question carried hints of irony and sarcasm.

"You know it's dry."

Austin snapped his fingers as if he had just had a sudden revelation. "Right you are. I used the last of the water Stew gave you to make this tea. I can see it in your face, Mitch. Sitting, staring at nothing, feeling and looking hopeless. I told you, look for the good. Stew is sharing his place with you, and now a friend is offering a friend something to drink. These are good things. Now drink some tea, Mitch. Drink half. I'll drink the rest."

The tea was hot, strong, and a little bitter, but it was wet. Stanley's throat was soothed and his thirst appeased, but the slight easing of his distress would last for only a moment under the beating sun. And when Stanley handed the now half-full can to Austin, he longed to snatch it back and drink it dry.

"Now, get out of here," Austin said, firm, but not harsh.

"What?"

"Word of advice, Mitch. Got to be busy if you want to live. Get out and do something good."

"Like what? Stew's barbering."

The little man's dark eyes burned brighter than Stanley had ever seen them. "You say you're a Christian, Mitch. Your eyes should be open to what needs doing. Those three *mice*, as you call them, can you do anything for them?"

"I don't even know their names."

"God's put them in your path, and you in theirs. Now, get out and don't come back until you can tell me one good thing you did for someone this fine afternoon."

• • •

It was a walk of only fifty yards, maybe less, along the knotted pathways from Austin's shebang to the burrow of the three mice. Last night, it had been his burrow too, if he was honest with himself. Austin had told him to do something good—for them or for someone else? The three just didn't tug at his heart the way Denny Miles, one of Sherman's men, had. Denny's wounding at Vicksburg had caused him great agony, but he always fought to be cheerful, trusting God's goodness to the end. *I put my life on the line for that boy. I felt compassion for Denny and God helped me know what to do.*

The three shriveled fellows were still huddled together, sitting up now, awake. Almost as one, they eyed Stanley warily as he limped toward them.

"Hello. I shared your dugout last night."

The three men nodded.

"My name is Stanley Mitchell, Quartermaster Sergeant, Fifteenth Corps. You can call me Mitch. What are your names?"

Three sunken-eyed grimy faces stared in his general direction.

"It would be nice to know who I spent the night with, that's all."

"Taft," the one on the right said, so softly that Stanley almost asked him to repeat it.

"Harley," the second man said. Harley nudged the man on the left.

"Churchill."

"Did you fellows know each other before coming here?" Stanley asked.

The three men nodded again.

"Same unit?"

The three men nodded again.

"Where are you from?"

Taft glanced at the other two men before answering. "Illinois."

Stanley smiled when Taft pronounced the *s*.

There was nothing at all inside the shebang except the three men. One end of the blanket they had shared during the night was now supported by two thin poles, a roof to shield them from the sun. *Who did that?*

"Do you need anything?"

Not even a flicker of a response.

Perhaps an even more basic question was in order. Stanley pointed to a canteen hanging from the pole that supported the right side of the blanket. "Do you need water?"

Taft shook his head. He was apparently the spokesman for the trio.

"Look here," Stanley said, trying to keep his growing frustration from tinging his words, "Sergeant Stewart put me here last night. If you would like me to go away and leave you alone, just say so."

The three men looked at each other and shrugged.

Perhaps a softer tone. "Who looks after you?"

"Stew," Taft said.

"He gets you water. What about your rations?"

"Stew gets 'em."

Progress. A complete sentence. "When was the last time any of you had a wash?"

The three men seemed not to have heard the question at all.

"You really need to do something about the lice. They must bother you terribly. I can't walk very well, but I'll go with you down to the swamp to wash, together or one at a time, whichever you prefer."

The three men exchanged looks, then shook their heads.

"All right, what about your blanket? May I take it down to the stream to wash it?" A clean blanket on them during the night might keep the lice from spreading to others. It was long odds, but worth the effort.

Once again, Taft shook his head.

"Why not?" Stanley asked.

"Don't trust you," Taft said.

"I'm no Raider. I'm not going to steal it."

Taft looked at his two friends, evidently seeking their thoughts on the matter.

Churchill mumbled something to Taft, inaudible to Stanley except for the last three words, "...don't know him."

"Please, gentlemen," Stanley said. "I know it's hot and it's your only shade. I can see the bugs jumping on the blanket in the heat. Please let me wash it."

Finally, the three men began nodding.

"All right then," Stanley said, as he started to remove the blanket. "I'll be back in fifteen or twenty minutes. That's all it'll take, and I'll rig it up again just like it was."

CHAPTER 13

ONE OF THE BEST THINGS ABOUT WORKING IN THE Quartermaster Department was that Stanley rarely had to worry about food. It was the department's primary task, after all, to see that the army was supplied with everything it needed—meat, hard bread, vegetables, fruit, coffee, sugar, clothing, ammunition, weapons, mail, packages from home, fodder for the animals. It all rolled down the tracks from Nashville to Chattanooga, then south to the depot at the front.

It had become so routine that, even when the Rebels destroyed a portion of the railroad, there was a sufficient supply laid up to see the army through until new track was laid and the trains were able to run again, which was usually accomplished in less than a day.

But the daily distribution of rations at Andersonville, although routine, was something Stanley detested from the start. It was a cruel joke to call any of what was issued to the men food, because it simply did not do what food by its very definition is supposed to do, support the health and vitality of the person consuming it.

The mule-drawn ration wagon entered through the North Gate and rumbled slowly down Broadway. It was the same wagon Stanley had seen outside the stockade, the dead cart, as it was known within the walls.

The wagon halted. The driver called out a detachment number. A black laborer standing in the back of the wagon dropped heavy sacks of food to the ground. "Detachment Fifty-five" was called. Six sacks were dropped, over which Sergeant Beckwith stood guard until his sergeants of nineties, Stewart, Cleary, and a third man Stanley didn't know, carried the sacks back to their quarters.

Mess Sergeant Pickens, disabled as he was, designated Stanley to report to Sergeant Stewart to claim the rations for the mess. The allotment was the same as it was the day before, a sack of black-eyed peas weighing about fifteen pounds, on top of which were ten loaves of corncob bread.

When Stanley returned to the mess, a blanket had been spread on the ground. Whose blanket it was, or how dirty or infested it was, he didn't know, but he knew what was expected of him. Distribution of rations hadn't changed since Shiloh.

He lowered himself to the ground beside the blanket and opened the sack. He removed each of the ten loaves and stacked them neatly at one corner of the blanket. Then he went to the opposite corner and poured the beans from the sack into a neat pile.

Thirty equal portions. The eyes of all his new mess-mates would examine his every move to ensure equity.

"Does anyone have a knife?" Stanley asked.

A tap on Stanley's shoulder caused him to turn. He looked up the hilt of the long knife that was being offered and recognized its owner, the man who had asked him about prisoner exchanges the day before. "Ah, Poole. Thank you."

Stanley cut each of the ten loaves into three pieces, as equal as he could, lest anyone say he had gotten less than his *fair share*. When he was done, there was some murmuring, but no one voiced a challenge.

"A cup or a tin can?" Stanley asked.

"Use mine," Pickens said.

The peas were harder to ration out. A full can per man seemed too much and half a can too little, so Stanley added a small pile of about two-thirds of a can of peas next to each bread ration. There were still some peas left over on the corner of the blanket. Stanley scooped them up in his hand and added one to each pile until none remained.

Again, there was no protest regarding the perceived inequity of this ration over here or that one over there.

"All right," Pickens said. "Sergeant Mitchell will do the honors." Then he turned his back on the proceedings.

Stanley pointed at one of the rations. "Who shall have this, Sergeant Pickens?"

"Poole, for the use of his knife," Pickens said.

Poole stepped forward. He deposited his peas in a fire-blackened tin cup, picked up his bread, and walked away.

Stanley pointed at another ration. "Who shall have this, Sergeant Pickens?"

"Johnson, for the use of his blanket," Pickens said.

A man Stanley didn't know took his ration and headed back to his shebang.

On it went until there were five rations left.

"Who shall have this, Sergeant Pickens?"

"That will be yours, Mitch."

Stanley set the bread aside. He picked up his peas—a little more than a handful—and dumped them in the pocket of his trousers. "And this one, Sergeant Pickens?"

Pickens turned awkwardly around to face Stanley again. "That will be mine, Mitch. The last three are for Harley, Taft, and Churchill. Put them back in the sack and deliver them to Sergeant Stewart. He'll boil the peas for them. You did well, Mitch, not a complaint from the boys. Thank you."

Without a cane or a helping hand, it was a struggle for Stanley to get to his feet. But upright once more, he picked up his bread and the sack of rations for the three mice, and started along the path toward Stew's shebang.

Some of the men had tossed some of their peas down raw and hard—they would probably pass them out undigested. Hard peas had to be cooked, and the bread should be. Stew had firewood, but he would be busy cooking for Taft, Harley, and Churchill. Besides, Stanley didn't feel he was truly part of Stew's household yet, and Austin wanted a report. So, after he visited Stew, Stanley headed for the shebang with the strip of red cloth.

• • •

As usual, Austin was hovering over his cookfire. "May I add my ration to your pot?" Stanley asked.

"Tell me what good you did today. I said I would ask."

"I learned the names of the three mice. Then I went down to the swamp and washed their blanket."

"Was that for your benefit or for theirs?"

Stanley stared at Austin, then lowered his eyes. "For mine at first. I thought it would be a better for me whenever I visited them, that the blanket would have to be infested again before their bugs found me. But at the swamp, I thought about how miserable it must be for them to be so thoroughly inhabited, and I determined to do as thorough a job as I could, for their good as well as mine."

"Good. Anything else?"

"I divided and called the rations for the mess and took those of the three mice to Stew for cooking. That was at Pickens' request."

"How do you feel about what you did today?"

"Like I've accomplished something, Austin, a small but useful thing." *But there is so much more I can do.*

Austin smiled. "Look to do the same tomorrow and every day thereafter, just small and simple acts of kindness. Go ahead and throw your food in my pot. Haven't seen Dell for hours. Probably show up when he sees everybody firing their rations."

Stanley retrieved the peas from his pocket and began to examine them.

64

"What are you doing?" Austin asked.

"I'm checking for what else might have been in my pocket."

"Oh, like dirt or lice?"

Stanley shrugged.

"Extra seasoning, that's what I call it. Throw them in."

CHAPTER 14

Saturday, June 25, 1864

W HEN STANLEY RETURNED FROM HIS MORNING WASH AT the stream, he thought he should tidy up around Stew's tent—their tent, now. There was little to do because Stew seemed a tidy person by nature, so Stanley neatened their small pile of firewood and checked that each tent pole was securely planted in the ground. Then he opened his Bible and sat beside their tent on a small wooden crate that Stew had dubbed his "barbering stool."

It had been another restless, almost sleepless night for Stanley. Stew hadn't assigned him guard duty again, and the smells and sounds of the camp hadn't been as bothersome as the previous night, and there was no threat of an assault of bugs from Stew's direction. Instead, it had been Austin's bloody smile and the grotesque and twisted way Pickens had moved about at roll call that gave him no rest and drove sleep away.

Stanley skimmed the gospel of Matthew until he found the words that he had only half remembered during the night. *Lay not up for yourselves treasures upon earth, where moth and rust doth corrupt, and where thieves break through and steal, but lay up for yourselves treasures in heaven, where neither moth nor rust doth corrupt, and where thieves do not break through nor steal.*

It would mean a step of faith, but perhaps that was exactly what those words called for. *Austin, Pickens, and*

Frank are sick, but not at death's door, not yet, anyway. I think I can do something about it, something good.

Finally, Stew returned from his walk around the camp with Austin and Frank.

"Stew, may I speak with you?"

"Of course, Mitch. Should we be seen or unseen?"

"Unseen."

"Then I'll go in first and we'll sit facing each other. Keep an eye out if anyone stops to listen or look inside. I'll do the same."

Stew was the first to speak. "The three mice, Taft really, told me what you did for them."

"It needed to be done. Their blanket had so many gray-backs, I'm surprised it didn't walk away on its own."

Stew laughed. "I've had the same thought."

"Maybe we shouldn't call them mice anymore, Stew."

"It does suit them."

"I know," Stanley said, "and they seem to act more like mice than men, but they're still men. They deserve that much respect at least."

"How about the *triplets?*" Stew asked. "They closely resemble one another—short and wasted with gray, thin skin like old folks. They only differ in the color of their hair and eyes."

"Triplets it is," Stanley said, nodding. "But that's not what I wanted to talk to you about."

"I thought not."

Anything more than a whisper would carry beyond the enclosure of the blanket tent. A whisper would have to suffice. "Stew, I'm about to trust you with something no one else knows, not even Austin. It's something that could cost me my life, if word ever got out. You must give me your word as a fellow Christian that you will never mention any of this without my permission."

The arching of Stew's eyebrows was evident even in the dim, filtered light of the tent. "You have my word," Stew said.

"May I borrow your barber's razor?"

Stew reached into the pocket of his trousers.

The keen, slightly curved blade was exactly what Stanley needed. He slipped the suspender from his right shoulder and bent over it, making it impossible for anyone outside the tent to see what he was doing. He slid the razor slowly along the seam, gently cutting through each of six stitches.

Stanley closed the razor and returned it to Stew. Then he used the fingers of both hands to work the canvas backing of the suspender this way and that until a small folded piece of paper appeared in the slit he had opened.

Stanley gave the folded paper to Stew. "Open it very carefully." The words were mouthed more than spoken. "Hold it to the light just long enough to see what it is."

Stew did as he was instructed and held the unfolded paper so he alone could see it. Then he quickly creased the paper small again and gave it back to Stanley, his eyes big with wonder. "Ten dollars Federal?" Stew's soft whisper shouted.

Stanley nodded.

Stew pointed a finger at Stanley's right suspender. "More?"

Stanley nodded.

Stew pointed at Stanley's left suspender. "More?"

Stanley nodded again.

Stew drew a question mark in the air.

Stanley held up all ten fingers, then four more.

"Fourteen?" Stew mouthed.

Stanley nodded yet again.

Stew sat grinning and shaking his head for a while. Then he whispered. "Put it away. Then let's go for a walk.

It's almost time for roll call. People will think that's where we're headed."

Stew had but one simple question as they walked side by side away from their tent. "How?"

Their conversation would still have to be quiet, but at least they could dispense with the hand signals. "When I returned to the army last August and started receiving my sergeant's pay, I wanted to send it off to Anna for safekeeping until we could marry."

"There's always a girl involved when it comes to money," Stew said with a laugh. "I want to hear more of this girl, but please go on."

"I might have gotten a bill of deposit at Adam's Express, but then what? What bank in Tennessee could I send it to? Many of those bankers are probably still Rebels and shysters."

Stanley looked behind them. No one was following, trying to eavesdrop. "I thought about how to keep my money safe, not because I ever imagined I would be taken prisoner, but because of thieves. I know, it's hard to think of it, thieves in our own ranks, but I learned there were such soon after joining the Quartermaster Department."

Stew chuckled again. "A girl? Tennessee? Thieves? This is turning into an epic tale."

Stanley shook his head. "No epic, Stew, just a few morsels to explain why we're having this conversation in the first place." Stanley glanced over his shoulder again. "I began to think about what might happen if I was waylaid and robbed some dark night. I couldn't run away, of course, so I had to conceal my money on my person where no one would think to look."

"And your suspenders came immediately to mind," Stew said.

Stanley laughed a little. "Not immediately, but one advantage to being rather large, is that somewhat thicker suspenders don't look out of place. The standard issue canvas suspenders are all right, but they dig into my shoulders. So last winter, I went to a tailor in Huntsville—he was a good Union man, by the way—and I asked him to make me a wider pair. I also asked him to add another strip of canvas on the underside. I told him it was for added comfort. Then I bought a spool of thread, and a housewife kit to make repairs in the field."

Stanley checked again for followers. "When I returned to my quarters, I cut the thread along the entire inside seam of one of the suspenders. One by one, I folded the bills and tucked them inside. Then I took out my housewife kit, and stitched up the seam again, not as nice as the tailor did, but with practice, it was neat enough to pass any inspection."

"And when the Raider's searched you—"

"They found only what I was willing to give up to protect the rest."

Stew whistled low and long. "That's brilliant. Your bride will be very pleased."

"But like you, Stew, I've had a change of heart. I'm carrying a small fortune, and I can't hold onto it while others suffer and die."

"That *is* a fortune in this place," Stew said. "If any hint of it gets out, you'll be a marked man. If the Raiders don't kill you, someone else will. That you entrusted this secret to me is a great privilege, Mitch, but you can't help everyone."

"I *know* I can't help everyone," Stanley said, "but money is life here. I already feel the weight of it."

"What do you mean?"

"I must help Austin and Pickens, Frank too—they are friends, after all—but I haven't thought about any others."

"Because that means making decisions," Stew said. "You'll have to decide who is worthy of your help, and who isn't. Choosing life for some means death for others. It's a

70

fearful spot for any man to be in, Mitch. It will be a terrible burden."

"Yes, it will," Stanley said, "and I'm just beginning to understand that. But I've decided those bills are no longer mine, Stew, they're God's. He's going to help me bear that responsibility. And you too, Stew. You may be only five years older than me, but you seem an age wiser. I'm counting on your help."

"You have it, Mitch." Stew said. "But there's one other person we should bring into our confidence."

"Who?"

"Ogre," Stew said. "He knows the ins and outs of this camp far better than I. He's also a Regulator."

"A Regulator?"

"Yes, some of us are trying to organize a police force to oppose the Raiders. We call ourselves Regulators. I probably shouldn't be telling you any of this, but you trusted me with your life."

"Austin never told me."

"Nor should he, but his trustworthiness is assured. He's also a very frugal man. He knows what is absolutely necessary, and what isn't, so he should be able to help us get the most out of every dollar."

CHAPTER 15

AFTER ROLL CALL, STANLEY WENT FOR A SHORT WALK ALONG Broadway and then returned to the shebang to take a nap. Frank Griffin was speaking with Stew, so Stanley held back until their conversation ended.

Stew beckoned Stanley to approach. "Frank and I need to call on a couple of friends over on Sixth Street and we want you to come with us."

Stanley opened his mouth to ask why, but Stew and Frank started off immediately. They led Stanley through a maze of narrow paths between rows of shebangs until they stopped before a nondescript tent one block north of Broadway.

Frank and Stew peered into the tent and had a hushed conversation with someone inside. After a few minutes a large, strapping man emerged.

Stew laid his hand on Stanley's shoulder. "Sergeant Key, this is Sergeant Stanley Mitchell."

"Yes," Key said, "the new man you spoke of."

Key's smile was bright, his handshake firm and warm. He was every bit as tall as Stanley, when Stanley stood on his right leg rather than his left, and Key's broad shoulders revealed a strength of physique akin to Stanley's own during his wood chopping days at Matthews Hill Farm. Key's hair was light brown as was his full beard. Both were trimmed short, no doubt a defense against the gray-backs.

72

In fact, Key appeared to be a prime specimen of physical strength and young manhood, all that Stanley might have been, were it not for his infirmity.

Stanley watched Stew and Frank as they walked away. There had been no explanation. They had just escorted him a hundred yards across the prison and left him with a stranger who, despite his smile, looked like he could tear Stanley limb from limb.

Sergeant Key held open the flap of his shebang, a faded, tattered army blanket. "We should go inside and talk in private."

Private. A word that had very little meaning in what Stew had called a human anthill, where every personal, private act was of necessity carried out amid over 25,000 men, all of whom had been thrown together to survive or die.

Sergeant Leroy Key's shebang was a simple rectangular excavation in the earth, about six feet long by four wide and a foot deep. It was shielded from the sun by half a shelter tent and the floor was covered with a rubber blanket, upon which was a neatly folded woolen blanket. Key's accommodations were clean and tidy in comparison to others Stanley had seen.

Stanley eased himself down into the shebang and came face to face with a man who, until this moment, had remained hidden within the gloomy interior.

"This is Jim," Key said. No rank or surname was offered and Stanley didn't ask. "He'll be sitting in on our talk."

"What's this all about?" Stanley asked. "Stew and Frank didn't say a word to me. They just brought me here."

"Just following orders," the man named Jim said, and the way he said it put Stanley immediately on guard. *Orders? What orders?*

"And not a word of what is said here is to leave this tent," Key said. "That's an order too."

73

The three men sat close to one another on the edge of the dugout and kept their voices low, and all the while, Jim's dark eyes never left Stanley's.

Key leaned toward Stanley and looked him in the eye. "There are nine men wandering about this camp with the letter *T* tattooed on their foreheads. Do you know what that *T* stands for, Sergeant Mitchell?"

"No, Sergeant."

"Traitor." The word seemed to explode from Jim in the small space.

"Sergeant Stewart told me about you," Key said. "Says he thinks you're true Union blue, but Jim and I aren't so sure. I'm not judging you a liar, not yet anyway, but I must be cautious. Wirz is always trying to send spies in to see if anybody is planning an escape. They're usually loners like you that nobody knows. And it seems you were a guest of the Rebel president's brother."

Austin. News travels fast. I only told him about Hurricane Plantation last evening before we went to meeting.

"I was more a guest of Mr. Davis's slave," Stanley said. "He did me a great kindness."

Key held up his hand for silence. "Let's start at the beginning. Fifty-third Ohio, almost killed at Shiloh, and a Rebel woman saved your life. Then you took up with her daughter and you want to go back and marry this girl. Is that about the size of it?"

"There's a lot more to it than that."

"Always is," Key said, but he seemed calm, not accusatory. "You could have gotten a medical discharge. Why didn't you?"

"By the time I had recovered enough to travel, the army was less than twenty miles away at Corinth. The woman's slave was going to take me there to apply for a discharge, but the woman's son betrayed me to a local slave trader. He put me in chains and took me to Vicksburg."

"Did you stay there until Grant arrived?"

"No. The slaver sold me to the captain of a Confederate river steamer. I worked as his second clerk."

"What were your duties?"

"It was a hospital ship mostly, Sergeant Key. I kept the ship's log of the wounded being transported home."

"Sounds like giving aid and comfort to the enemy," Jim said.

Stanley met Jim's hard, cold eyes. "I was imprisoned aboard that vessel for being a Union soldier. And besides that, my helping those poor boys get home was basic human decency."

"And, Jim," Key said, "some of our boys work in Wirz's office, and nobody calls them traitors. Sergeant Mitchell, did you ever aid in the transport of Confederate war materiel or personnel?"

"The ship usually carried troops and arms on its upriver trips, but the head clerk did those manifests and logs personally. I kept the log of passengers and non-military cargo. I also stood my regular watches."

"Like watching for other boats?" Jim asked.

"Yes."

"Union boats?"

"Yes."

Jim looked at Sergeant Key. "What more do we need, Leroy?"

"Being impressed into the service of one's enemy is no crime. Tell me, Sergeant Mitchell, did you aid the war effort of the Rebels willingly?"

"Sergeant Key, I was in chains in Vicksburg when the captain of that boat rescued me and put me aboard the *Evangelina*. Anything I did that might be construed as aiding the enemy I did for the sole purpose of preserving the lives of the crew and passengers aboard that ship."

"You speak with skill and passion for one so young," Key said.

"Bah," Jim spat. He leaned back into the shadows again.

Key's brow creased. When he spoke, his words were soft and tender, not at all what Stanley expected from such a tough-looking man. "Tell us about the girl."

"I would much rather be with her than here with you gentlemen."

Key chuckled. "Humor. I like that. Go on."

"Her brother died beside me while we were being carried back to their farm. At first, she hated me for living instead of him. But by the grace of God, she softened and we pledged ourselves to each other. I saw her last October in Corinth when the Fifteenth Corps was passing through. I asked her to marry me. If I survive this place, I have no home back in Ohio, so we'll make our home in Tennessee."

Jim emerged from the shadows. "Sergeant Key is twenty-three and only Quartermaster Sergeant for his regiment. Stew said you're with the Fifteenth Corps Quartermaster Department. How did you get such a posting being so young?"

"Because of my bad leg. I was a civilian in Vicksburg during the siege. The family I stayed with knew I had been a Union soldier, but they were loyal Union people and they kept it to themselves. I worked in the Union ward of a Confederate hospital caring for some of our boys who were brought in from the lines. As a result, I became acquainted with General Logan. He ordered me to return to the army."

"McPherson should have let Logan loose at Resaca," Jim said.

"That's where Jim and I were captured," Key said.

"I know that place well," Stanley said. "It was our forward depot until we moved up to Cartersville. That's where I was taken prisoner on June 12th."

"How did you meet General Logan?" Key asked.

There was quality and depth in the sergeant's eyes— another man Stanley thought he could trust. Stanley

76

shifted uneasily. "It's not something I like to talk about. Sometimes, it seems crazy even to me. At the hospital, what little ether and opium we had was reserved for the Rebel patients, so during a ceasefire, I crossed over to the Union line and asked for some relief for the boys I was caring for. My request found its way to General Logan and he met with me in person. He said he wanted to see what kind of fool would make such a request."

"That was you?" Jim drew close and stared at Stanley as if he was examining him.

Stanley didn't look away. "That was me."

Jim turned to Key. "I heard of him when I was at Vicksburg—went all through the lines about this mad turncoat crossing over to get help. I still think he's a spy."

"He's no turncoat," Key said. "You see how lame he is. He's been wounded. He could have gone to the Invalid Corps, but Black Jack Logan himself wanted this man back in the army on active duty. Sergeant Mitchell is exactly who he says he is, Jim, and you know the kind of men we need for Regulators."

"Four things you say over and over, Leroy—smart, loyal, selfless, and brave."

"Right," Key said. "That stunt at Vicksburg sounds like the stuff heroes are made of, so that makes Sergeant Mitchell here a bona fide hero in my book."

Stanley felt the color rise in his face. "I'm no hero, Sergeant Key. I just did what needed doing."

"And you put your life on the line to get it done, Sergeant Mitchell."

"Please call me Mitch, Sergeant Key."

"Others may, but I won't. You earned your rank and I respect that."

"Thank you, Sergeant Key."

Key lowered his voice. "We're trying to build a police force to bring law and order to this prison because the Rebels won't. And we need all the smart, honest, and decent men we can get to do it, men of courage who won't shy away from a fight."

Key seemed to be the very embodiment of his own words. "Will there be a fight?" Stanley asked.

"There must be, Sergeant Mitchell, if we're to bring the Raiders to justice. Our hope is to arrest the leaders and bring them to trial, but we need numbers and weapons. We need hundreds of strong men, but only those who have been here less than a month have strength enough to fight the Raiders. Nearly every day we gain a few new men, but also nearly every day, we lose some to failing health. Frank Griffin just informed me that he is one such casualty."

"Frank?" Stanley closed his eyes and began to slowly shake his head. "I know he's been sick, but.... How many Regulators are there now?"

"About two hundred. Four companies of fifty."

"So, Sergeant Key, all you need is hundreds more men and hundreds of weapons."

"That's about the size of it. Shall we admit Sergeant Mitchell to the Regulators, Jim?"

Jim remained in the shadows. "No sane person would believe such a story."

Silence.

Then more silence.

"I guess that's why I believe it," Jim said. "And sitting here listening to you two—he seems the real article. I agree."

Sergeant Key shook Stanley's hand. "You are now a Regulator, Sergeant Mitchell. I'm assigning you to take Frank's place in Sergeant Stewart's company. He'll be your company captain. Stew said we can trust you and now I do to. Never betray that trust. You were brought here in secret because we are a secret society, and you are bound to keep that secret. You may never know who all the other members of your company are. Sergeant Stewart knows, but don't ever ask anyone if he's a Regulator. Also, do not ask anyone if he wants to become a Regulator. We admit new members only by recommendation of current members and through personal examination by Jim and me. We alone decide who will be Regulators and who will not."

"I understand, Sergeant Key," Stanley said. "I want to help, but what can I do with my bad leg? The Raiders took my walking stick."

Sergeant Key leaned close to Jim and whispered in his ear. Jim sprang up and left the shebang.

"Limber Jim, they call him," Key said, "and you can see why. He'll be back in a moment. What can you do for the Regulators? For now, just watch, listen, and wait. Watch the Raiders. Observe their tactics. You'll see they're formidable in large groups, but skittish and easily scared off if there are only two or three of them. Word will be passed down when we go against the Raiders. Just be ready to pitch in and do what you can."

Jim tumbled back into the shebang. "Here it is," he said, handing a long, thin staff to Sergeant Key.

"I've been keeping this in a secret place for use against the Raiders, "Key said, "but perhaps it has a nobler purpose." He handed the staff to Stanley.

It was old, maybe ancient, a simple walking staff about five feet long and an inch and a half thick, similar perhaps to the one Moses had held over the Red Sea. And it was heavier than it looked, probably cut from a maple sapling, then shaved and worn smooth. It would help him walk farther and more comfortably, but it could also serve as a weapon should anyone try to relieve him of any more of his possessions.

"Thank you, Sergeant Key," Stanley said. "I promise you, I'll put it to good use."

CHAPTER 16

AUSTIN WAS STANDING BESIDE STEW'S TENT WHEN STANLEY returned from his meeting with Key and Jim. "I found Rodgers dead this morning."

There was nothing Stanley could say to console Austin, only a promise to keep. He laid a hand on Austin's shoulder. "Let's go and do what needs to be done."

It was the most pitiful and disgusting thing Stanley had ever done. Rodgers had lain in his burrow until after roll call, covered in his own filth for at least a week; he had been too feeble to rise to go to the latrine. Unable to defend himself, he was nearly black with flies. Lice covered him from head to toe and attacked the hands and arms of Austin and Stanley as soon they began their work.

"Usually," Austin said, "the clothes are removed and salvaged for the living, but his are too far gone, and maggots are already at work underneath."

Stanley removed the blanket from atop the shebang and laid it on the ground. Then Austin and he lifted Rodgers from the burrow and placed him on the blanket. Stanley had already put down the urge to wretch several times, but now his defenses were shattered. All that came up was bile.

Austin began to turn over the earthen floor of Rodgers shebang with a spade he had borrowed. "No one will live here until the stink is gone. This will help, but rain will have to do most of the work."

Austin tied the corners of one end of the blanket together and Stanley did the same at the other end. Then they took hold of the knotted ends and picked up the blanket.

"Let's go," Austin said.

Stanley and Austin carried Rodgers' blanket-enshrouded remains out to Broadway, which was then teeming with prisoners engaged in buying or selling. If anyone gave them a passing glance, he more often than not quickly turned away.

A few minutes later Austin and Stanley stepped onto the bridge. The stream that provided some measure of cleansing now seemed like the River Styx of Greek mythology. Rodgers was making his final crossing, but there were no coins to pay the boatman, no boat at all in fact, just bare feet upon wooden planks.

Stanley's right arm began to throb as they started the final climb from the bridge to the South Gate. Austin had switched hands several times, but Stanley needed the staff in his left hand, so there was no relief. He counted down from a hundred the steps he thought it would take to reach the gate, but when he reached zero, they were still about thirty yards away. His right arm and shoulder were now taut with agony.

Finally, they reached their gory goal, the place beside the gate, next to the deadline, where the bodies of the dead were laid for removal outside the stockade to the deadhouse. There were already twelve bodies laid in a row on the near side of the gate, fifteen on the far side, and it was just past noon.

Stanley and Austin undid the knots and rolled Rodgers off the blanket next to another nearly naked corpse.

Austin took up the blanket and stood looking down at Rodgers. "You never said if you were a believer or not. I pray you were, my friend. May God have mercy on your soul." Then, turning to Stanley, he said, "I wish we could do more."

"We can," Stanley said.

Austin wiped his eyes with the sleeve of his undershirt and looked up at Stanley. "What can we do?"

"First, you must promise me you won't look at all surprised about what I tell you, and that you will keep looking like the little ogre you are, my friend."

Austin's left cheek bulged when he tried to smile. "I promise."

Stanley leaned down close to Austin's left ear, where the swelling from the scurvy was worst. "I'm now a Regulator," he whispered, "and I have one hundred and forty Federal greenbacks secreted about my person."

Stanley stood straight. Austin didn't move at all, his face frozen in the same half smile he had worn before Stanley revealed his secret.

"Let's go, Ogre," Stanley said, loud enough for anyone to hear if they chose to.

They started down the path beside the deadline toward the bridge. "First time you called me Ogre," Austin said.

"It's growing on me."

"Actually, I prefer it, Mitch. It's got a lot more character than Austin."

Stanley laughed. "Yes. That's it. Character. Then Ogre it is."

"You're a dead man if it gets out. Tell anyone else?"

"Only Stew. He says you know how to make it do the most good."

"Got some ideas," Ogre said.

"Frank should know too. The four of us are more than friends now; it's like we're brothers."

"That we are," Ogre said, as they stepped onto the bridge. "This is good, Mitch, very good. The four of us should talk after Sabbath meeting tomorrow."

CHAPTER 17

STANLEY WAITED AT THE NORTH END OF THE BRIDGE WHILE Austin washed Rodgers' blanket in the stream. He plunged the foul thing into the water, wrung it out, then did it several more times, just as Stanley had done for the triplets the day before—perhaps washing their blanket every day would get rid of many of their bugs. Finally, with the dripping blanket folded over his arm, Austin rejoined Stanley and they started up the hill toward the North Gate.

A rush of pounding feet came from behind, then the thudding of shoes and boots upon the planking of the bridge. Stanley knew who they were without turning around.

"Raiders," Austin cried out. "Get off the path."

Dozens of wild-eyed men rushed past. Nearly every one of them carried a club or knife at the ready as they charged up the hill. All were fully clothed, unlike the better part of the prison population, and from the variety of clothing they wore—regulation Federal blues, long riding coats, shirts and trousers in varied and sometimes garish colors, caps and hats of every style—it seemed each man wore what suited him. Now that he knew what to look for, Stanley was able to spot them easily, even amid throngs of other prisoners.

The gate opened. A long stream of new prisoners came in.

"They usually put new men in at the South Gate," Austin said. "Why the change and how did the Raiders know about it?"

Two large bands of Raiders converged on the new prisoners. The group that had rushed past Stanley and Austin drove headlong into the column of fresh fish from the side. The second group rushed down Broadway and struck the head of the column. The bewildered new prisoners were severed into small squads and clubbed to the ground. They were bloodied, defeated, and stripped of whatever possessions they had brought inside the stockade.

The battle ended as quickly as it had started. A signal must have been given, but Stanley didn't hear or see it. Leaving most of the fresh fish writhing in pain on the ground before the closed North Gate, the Raiders ran down the hill past Austin and Stanley, pounded across the bridge to the south side, and whooped and hollered all the way back to the Citadel.

Some of the new prisoners started down the hill after the Raiders.

"We have to stop them," Austin said, stepping into the path and pulling at Stanley's arm.

Ten men, all large and strong and furious, rushed toward Austin and Stanley.

"But what can we do, Ogre?"

Austin raised his hands toward a big, burly man in the lead whose mouth was completely hidden by his full mustache and beard. "Please," Austin cried out, "please, wait a moment."

The man raised his arm to swat Austin aside, but hesitated, his eyes wide with amazement. "A midget and a cripple? Out of our way."

"Won't do no good," Austin said. He stared up at the big brute while the man's followers gathered around. "Some bloody noses, knots and bruises, but if you go over there, you'll be beaten bad. Might kill you outright. Maybe you'll die later, but you won't get your things back."

"If we had weapons," the man said, "we could whip 'em, now that we know 'em. Maybe we'll just go over and take their weapons for ourselves."

"There are ten of you and hundreds of them," Stanley said, trying to match Austin's calm. "And they're organized. Their attack on you was well planned and executed."

"How many are you all told?" Austin asked.

"About three fifty," the man said. "Three hundred six are West Virginia boys."

"Oh," Stanley said. "Are you all from a single unit?"

"No. Five infantry, one cavalry, all taken at Kennesaw," the man said, "with a few artillerymen thrown in for color."

A few chuckles ran through the group.

"Are any among you leaders?" Austin asked.

"We got sergeants like any other," the man said.

"Not what I mean," Austin said. "Of your three hundred, are there six men you would gladly follow into battle?"

The man looked around at his fellow West Virginians. One by one, all started nodding.

"Good," Austin said, holding out his hand toward the man. "I'm Sergeant Austin Oglethorpe, Eighth Michigan Infantry."

The man shook Austin's hand. "Sergeant Jubal Case, Twelfth West Virginia."

"And my friend with the staff is Sergeant Stanley Mitchell, Fifteenth Corps Quartermaster Department."

Stanley raised his staff in salute.

Austin lowered his voice so no one beyond the small group could hear. "Most everyone wants to see the Raiders thrashed, but it won't be easy. Turn around. Walk back up to the gate. Help your friends and get settled, if you can. It won't be easy squeezing in three hundred and fifty more men."

"That German captain said there would be lots of room soon," Case said, "maybe in a few days. Said we'll have fine new land to set up camp."

"Blacks been working on that new section for a month," Austin said, "but had no word of it opening until now. Wirz always says everything is fine in here, but you can see for yourselves, it isn't. And he's not German, he's Swiss."

The West Virginians started back up the hill toward the North Gate.

Austin turned to Stanley. "We have to go see Sergeant Key. First day a Regulator, and you may have helped solve our personnel problem."

CHAPTER 18

Sunday, June 26, 1864

SABBATH MEETING WAS NO DIFFERENT THAN THE EVENING meetings Stanley had attended except that it was held at noon shortly after roll call. After the meeting adjourned and the gathering of two hundred or so dispersed, Frank, Stew, Austin, and Stanley remained in the open circular space of the wagon turn around.

"First, we should pray," Frank said. "What we are about to do will require much compassion and much wisdom."

The four sergeants bowed their heads while Frank prayed. The "Amen" was spoken in unison.

"Let's talk about security," Stew said. "None of us suspected Mitch was a walking and talking bank, so the bills should remain where they are. And when we must speak of it, I suggest we use a pseudonym, like Abraham, or Abe, since the President's picture is on each bill. Does anyone disagree?"

No one did.

"We are a small fraternity," Stew said, looking at each of the three men in turn. "Yes, a brotherhood founded upon our common Christian faith and mutual desire to keep God's commandments, to love him above all else and to love our neighbor as ourselves. I believe we should base every decision on these basic principles."

"Absolutely," Frank said.

"Yes," Austin said.

Stanley nodded and smiled. "Agreed."

"Good," Stew said. "Ogre, you look like you're itching to speak. Let's hear your ideas."

"All right. First thing to know," Austin said, "Federal money is worth more outside than inside."

The listening men exchanged quizzical glances.

"Basic economy, gentlemen," Austin said. "Say I want to make cabbage soup. The sutler wants one dollar Federal or ten Rebel for a head of cabbage. But I know this man who trades with one of the guards. Says the Rebels love our greenbacks because their Rebel scrip is worth less every day, and someday soon, it won't be worth anything at all. An honest fellow from what I've heard. For a small fee, he says he can get twenty-five to one from the Rebels, and it's going up all the time."

"Why would you want any Confederate money?" Stanley asked.

"Say I give this man an Abraham. He gives it to the guard and the guard gives him two hundred and fifty Confederate. Then he gives me two hundred and keeps fifty for his trouble. I give that same Abraham to the sutler and how many cabbage do I get?"

Stanley smiled. "Now I see it. Only ten, and if you gave him the two hundred Confederate you could buy twenty. You double the buying power with that exchange."

Austin grinned, swelling his left cheek. "And now, my friends, you understand the economy of Andersonville."

Stanley did the arithmetic in an instant. "Are you suggesting we invest in the soup business? The Rebel scrip will buy fewer than three hundred cabbages. That won't go far at all."

"But cabbage is the cheapest," Austin said, "and it's the best for nutriments. The sutler also has onions and leeks too. Very good for Mr. Pickens, Mitch."

"You and Frank too," Stew said. "I like the idea, Ogre, but how do we sustain it?"

88

"By making it a business rather than a charity," Stanley said.

"Exactly," Austin said. "Been thinking of making soup for a couple of weeks, not the little pot I make, but a big pot. Set up a soup shop and sell it. A small investment could go a long way, but I never had the small investment."

"So what would you need?" Frank asked.

"A large pot to start. Sutler's got a big kettle for five Federal. Then firewood and water, more than we get now."

"My friend's well is still strong," Stew said. "I'll have a talk with him, but I think we'll have to go outside for firewood."

"I'm feeling better," Frank said, "I think I can go out on wood detail."

"And I can swing an ax too," Stanley said.

"All right," Stew said, "so you have a big pot of soup. What then, Ogre?"

Austin grinned again. "We sell it to anybody who has five cents and a tin can. Got to keep turning the money over. Not saying we ought to make a profit, but we got to meet expenses, or the suspender bank will soon be empty."

"Brothers," Stew said, "I'm very much in favor of this venture, but what's to be done for someone who doesn't have five cents?"

"Got to sell twenty cans from every pot to break even," Austin said. "What's left can go to the needy."

"And that brings us back to the basic question," Frank said. "We can't help everyone, so how do we decide whose life might be saved by this vegetable soup and whose won't?"

"Does anyone think the four of us have been thrown together by chance?" Stew asked. "I used the word *fraternity* when we started. Are we not brothers in the Lord?"

The others nodded in agreement.

89

"Indeed, we are," Stew said. "Then we must trust each other in the Lord to make those decisions. Ogre, Frank, and Pickens must have portions, and Mitch too, for his generosity."

"You must, as well, Stew," Stanley said. "I insist that the health of all the brothers come first. This brotherhood must remain strong if we are to do lasting good."

For a few moments, the four members of the fraternity just looked at each other.

Ogre voiced their common question first. "What of the rest?"

"That's where the wisdom and compassion Frank prayed for come in," Stew said. "And we'll trust God to guide us."

The four Andersonville sergeants, now brothers in more than arms, clasped each other's hands, altogether, four as one, a mute pledge to carry out all that had been agreed upon. Then Frank prayed again for wisdom, protection, and provision from on high.

"Before we go," Frank added, "Josiah Talbot is not expected to survive another day. There will be a small gathering at his shelter this evening at the first sentry call. Please don't feel obliged, Mitch—you don't know the man— but Stew knows the way should you wish to attend."

Stanley walked with Austin back to his shebang. In the rear of the tent, back in the shadows where Dell slept, Stanley removed the first folded ten dollar bill from his suspender and handed it to Austin.

Austin palmed the bill and slid it into his pocket. "Were you saving it for something?"

"Not something. Someone."

Austin stared at Stanley for a moment. Then he nodded. "Anna." His eyes narrowed and he seemed about to reach into his pocket to return the money to Stanley.

"I must do this, Ogre. I'll never marry her if I don't survive this place, and I could never keep it for myself and watch others suffer and die. Besides, a can of vegetable soup once in a while along with my daily ration might quiet my gnawing belly and keep me going a little longer. Will the one Abraham be sufficient to get started?"

"Indeed, it will," Austin said. "That will pay for the kettle and keep us in cabbage for a week, maybe two."

CHAPTER 19

A S THE FIRST NIGHT-HOUR CALLS OF THE SENTRIES DIED away, Stanley, Austin, and Stew stood shoulder to shoulder with eight other weary and somber men around a small fire next to the tattered tent of Josiah Talbot. Within the tent, barely visible in the waning twilight, a companion, probably the man who had carried Talbot to meeting, held him upright so he could view the proceedings.

"'Precious in the sight of the Lord is the death of his saints,'" Frank said. "I say those words every time we gather to wish a brother Godspeed as he passes on to glory, but we can't hear those words often enough. God's saints are dying next to us every day. Every one of them is precious to him in life, but even more so in death. We are going to sing now, as we always do." He bent down and peered into the tent. "Brother Talbot, what hymn would you like your brothers to sing to God's praise this evening?"

Talbot's voice was thin and raspy, barely audible, but his words were clear. "Soldier of the Cross."

"I only know the first two verses, Brother Talbot."

Talbot heaved with a small chuckle. "That'll do."

"All right, but if any don't know it," Frank said, glancing around the group, "we'll sing each verse twice."

Am I a soldier of the cross,
A follower of the Lamb,
And shall I fear to own his cause,
Or blush to speak his name?

The tune was simple enough, and the pitch at which Frank sang was comfortable for Stanley, so he joined in when the verse was repeated. The second verse was likewise sung.

Must I be carried to the skies
On flowery beds of ease;
While others fought to win the prize,
And sailed through bloody seas?

"Frank." It was Talbot's friend within the tent. "Josiah has another verse for you."

Frank bent down once again. "Tell me, Brother Talbot, one line at a time."

The two spoke quietly for a few moments. "I think I have it," he said, standing and facing the group again. But let me speak while you listen, for this is what Brother Talbot would have us consider this evening. 'Thy saints in all this glorious war shall conquer, though they die. They see the triumph from afar, by faith they bring it nigh.'"

For a time, no one spoke.

"Frank." It was Talbot's helper again. "Josiah asks for one more hymn. 'Jesus, Lover of My Soul.'"

"I know that one well, four verses to the tune Martyn."

Frank began to sing and others familiar with the hymn did too. The tune sounded vaguely familiar to Stanley, but he remained silent, listening to the words, trying to grasp the depth of their meaning.

Hide me, O my Savior, hide,

Till the storm of life is past.

Other refuge have I none,
Hangs my helpless soul on thee.

Thou, O Christ, art all I want,
More than all in thee I find.

Raise the fallen, cheer the faint,
Heal the sick, and lead the blind.

Thou of life the fountain art;
Freely let me take of thee.

The men grew quiet again. Frank peered into the tent. "Brother Talbot, I'm about to dismiss this small gathering, but first, I would like to pray. I will pray for your wife, Nellie, and your children, of course. But how shall I pray for you, Josiah?"

Everyone heard Talbot's wry chuckle. Then he started to cough. When he spoke, he strained to make himself heard. "I know where I'm going, Mr. Griffin, and I'm ready to go. Pray the Lord not to drag it out. And pray for yourselves, Mr. Griffin, because in a moment, I shall see him like I see you, and he'll be far better looking."

The gathered men hooted and cackled and coughed their laughter.

Stanley bowed his head and closed his eyes to fight back the tears while Frank prayed. Such certainty—such unwavering faith—such joy that filled even the last words Talbot spoke—such utter peace.

As Frank neared the end of his prayer, he thanked God that Josiah Talbot had shown all who knew him that "to live is Christ, and to die is gain." Stanley had read those words himself, and even heard a sermon on them in Chattanooga. But those words had always troubled him,

94

that to die was better than life, even better than life with Anna.

I could die tonight, or next week, or many years from now. Will men gather around my deathbed? Will I remember Talbot and how he died amid all this squalor?

The funeral service ended. Each of Talbot's friends, some little more than ragged skeletons themselves, shuffled forward and leaned down into the tent to wish Josiah Talbot farewell.

Stanley, the last in line, stooped and looked into the tent. Talbot was nothing but the hollow shell of what once had been a strong, healthy man. He looked worse than some of the corpses Stanley had seen.

A smile spread across Talbot's sunken, withered face when he saw Stanley. His eyes sparkled, almost seemed to dance, and he held up his pallid, bony hand. "Josiah Talbot, son of God," he said. "You're Frank's friend."

Stanley shook Talbot's hand lightly. "Stanley Mitchell, also a son of God, I think."

"Don't think, Mr. Mitchell. Know."

Stanley looked at Talbot's helper, a dark-bearded, sallow man. "Are you in need of any pallbearers, sir?"

"No, Josiah has made his wishes known, but thank you anyway."

"Then, Mr. Talbot," Stanley said, "I'll pray you are granted your wish. May you go to God in peace, and—thank you. It's been an honor to meet you."

As Stanley and Stew walked quietly back to their shebang, it seemed to Stanley that a funeral for a still living man was as unusual as it was good. It had been much as Stanley had expected—a word of instruction, singing, and prayer. But he had not expected the laughter, laughter in the face of death, even laughter at death itself, or so it seemed. And Stanley couldn't forget Talbot's smile and his sparkling eyes.

Stanley had seen that look before. He had seen it on the faces of Grant's men when they marched into Vicksburg. He had seen on the faces of the veterans of Missionary Ridge. He had seen it on the faces of some of the most terribly wounded boys at Resaca when they were put aboard a northbound train.

And then Stanley knew why Frank had prayed as he had. Talbot had fought the good fight; he had finished the course; he had kept the faith.

And Talbot's face had glowed with that victory.

CHAPTER 20

Tuesday, June 28, 1864

MORNING ROLL CALL WAS NEARING ITS END WHEN A TRAIN whistle sounded. The fifteen-foot-high stockade wall of the prison followed the natural contour of the land. From the high ground north of the swamp, standing ranks of prisoners gazed toward the depot, which lay about half a mile distant and could be seen over the stockade where it dipped into the valley of the swamp.

More prisoners or more food? An obvious question for Stanley and every other man as well. And almost instantly answered. Squads of guards assembled and marched toward the depot. More prisoners would soon enter the already packed stockade. Had it been a supply train, slaves would have been put to work unloading the cargo.

Austin found Stanley immediately after roll call was dismissed. "We should go and see if we can help any of the new prisoners."

"You mean the fresh fish?" Stanley said.

"Not going to say that anymore," Austin said. "Don't like it. With the new section opening, I expect they'll be put in at the North Gate like the West Virginians were, but let's wait and see which road they take."

Stanley and Austin watched the procession of prisoners, with Captain Wirz in the lead, as they marched slowly up the lane from the depot. The column crossed the bridge over the stream, ascended the hill, and passed by Wirz's headquarters and the large star-shaped fort. But instead of turning toward the South Gate, as Stanley's squad had done the week before,

Wirz led the new prisoners down the hill toward a second bridge to cross back to the north side of the stream.

"The North Gate, just as I thought," Austin said. "At least we don't have to hurry. Stay behind me, Mitch, and don't interfere with the Raiders. Hang back in the crowd, just like I did when you were put in."

The gate opened and the first ninety entered. The guards marched the new squad part way up Broadway and then turned back toward the gate, leaving the shaken and bewildered new prisoners to the merciless Raiders.

Stanley looked down and closed his eyes. Thuds of clubs on flesh, cries of the wounded, and the boisterous whoops and jeers of the Raiders evidenced depths of cruelty Stanley had not seen before, except in one vile devil of a man—LaVache. *Ogre was right; I did get off easy.*

A voice penetrated the din—sharp, clear, and unwavering. "Go ahead, sinners, take my coat. Take my blanket and my wedding ring, too."

Stanley looked up. A solitary man stood erect, unbowed, his fists raised to heaven, every part of him a picture of defiance. Several clubs were raised to strike him down.

"Take my life, if you will," he said. "It will be glory for me, for I have already died to this world. Yes, my life is already hidden with Christ in God, and I shall be raised to glory."

Mouths were shut. Clubs were lowered. Loud, awkward silence followed.

"Let's go," one of the Raiders said. Taking their plunder, all of the attackers ran down the hill toward the bridge across the swamp.

Austin and Stanley pushed their way through the crowd of onlookers toward the man who had fallen to his knees in prayer.

When he finished, Stanley took him by the arm and helped him stand. He was a few inches shorter than Stanley, with dark hair and short beard, lightly streaked with gray, not neat and tidy, but acceptable by Andersonville standards.

Austin introduced himself and Stanley.

"First Sergeant Thomas J. Sheppard," he said, shaking their hands, "Company E, 97th Ohio Volunteer Infantry, taken at Kennesaw Mountain."

"Which detachment did they assign you to?" Austin asked.

"The hundredth. That Dutchman said we should camp on the new ground near the north wall."

"Twenty-seven thousand, now," Stanley said under his breath.

Sheppard brushed past Stanley and Austin and raised his arms high, quieting the crowd. "'This is the day which the LORD hath made; we will rejoice and be glad in it.' The LORD is my light and my salvation; whom shall I fear? The LORD is the strength of my life; of whom shall I be afraid?'

"Vultures gather wherever there's a body, but the problem for those vultures was—I'm not dead. Do you know the first words those robbers said to me? 'Welcome to hell,' they said. This may well be the nastiest place on earth, but it isn't hell. God is here. His word is here. And I am here. And as surely as you see me standing here, I am a child of God. Even now I feel his tender embrace; I feel the power of his love. Did you see? He shut the mouths of the roaring lions. He helped me in my hour of need, and there is none of that in hell."

He looked around at the crowd of half-naked, half-starved men, the miserable hovels that passed for shelter, the filthy ground on which he stood. "No," he added, lowering his voice as he turned back toward Stanley and Austin, "this place isn't hell, but it may be the place of the dead—Sheol, the Hebrews called it."

"You obviously know Scripture," Austin said. "Are you a pastor?"

"Nearly so. I was near the end of my second year of seminary at Granville when the war started. I remained to complete my final year. Then I was examined and approved for licensure. But when Father Abraham called for 300,000 more, I heard that call. I enlisted in August of sixty-two."

"If I may ask, Sergeant," Stanley said, "how old are you?"

"Twenty-eight, married for ten years, five children."

Austin laid his hand on Sheppard's shoulder. "That makes you the oldest man I know in here."

CHAPTER 21

A FEW MINUTES AFTER THE SENTRIES ATOP THE NORTH wall left their posts, a rope was thrown over one of the stockade timbers near the middle of the wall. Wooden ties that held one timber tight against the next were cut, also from the outside. The rope was pulled this way and that to loosen the freed timber from the ground, until the timber finally gave way, tearing up the earth around its base as it fell. A wild cheer went up. Then a second timber was likewise cut loose and pulled down.

Guards appeared in the narrow gap and threatened to shoot anyone who tried to force their way through. More timbers came down, ten in all, creating a passage into the new section of the stockade about fifteen feet wide. The guards filed through and marched off toward the North gate. A mad rush ensued as the mass of men picked up their pitiful shebangs and meager possessions and pressed through the narrow opening into the undefiled ground beyond.

The men of the Fifty-fifth Detachment had their orders from Sergeant Beckwith—northwest corner near the deadline, as far from the swamp as possible. Beckwith and his three sergeants of nineties would lay claim to their new acreage—a parcel about thirty paces square—while the rest of the detachment dismantled their dwellings, packed up all their furnishings and personal belongings, and moved onto the new, unspoiled ground.

Austin and Stanley worked together to move three households. The first was that of Stew and Stanley and the second was that of Austin and Dell. The third was the mansion belonging to the triplets. Stew had told them to be ready to move, but when Stanley and Austin arrived, it was obvious they had done nothing at all to prepare for departure and they were most unhappy about being forcibly evicted from their happy home.

"Orders from Wirz himself," Stanley said. He took the blanket from their feeble hands and shook it to get as many bugs out as he could, while Austin collected their tentpoles. Then he and Austin started for the gap in the wall and the triplets had no choice except to get up and follow their shebang.

Austin chose to establish his residence adjacent to that of Stanley and Stew. The new abode of the triplets was set up a dozen or so yards away. All the men of the detachment were required to pitch their tents upon the plot of ground Sergeant Beckwith and the sergeants of nineties had chosen, but beyond that restriction, Beckwith didn't care with whom or where the men lived. A man in the first mess of the second ninety could room with two friends in the third mess of the first ninety, and if each man stood with his own mess for roll call and rations, there would not be any problem.

Stanley and Austin finished with the triplets and all but tucked them in for the night. Then they walked up the narrow path toward their own dwellings. Stew had selected a small plot of ground that was, like all the other ground across the breadth of the new portion of the prison, heavily carpeted with pine straw. But the most important feature of their new homestead was a large stump, all that remained of a tall pine tree which had been felled for the new stockade wall. And anyone who possessed such a stump was considered very well off indeed.

Stew sat upon the stump, grinning. "I dare say we are ready for visitors, Mitch."

"We should invite Frank," Stanley said. "It's too bad he couldn't move up here."

"It would have been good for the four of us to live close together, but we don't make the rules. Lieutenant Davis said just the detachments from fifty-one and up. And Frank has always lived by himself down near the swamp."

"I know," Stanley said, "but he seems so far away now."

"Not so far," Stew said. "They only added six hundred feet. We can walk that in a few minutes."

"You would think this was the Promised Land," Austin said, looking around the new encampment of the Fifty-fifth Detachment, "but in a few weeks, this ground will be as corrupt as what we left."

• • •

Night fell over the prison. A waning crescent moon peeked in and out of low, billowing clouds. Hundreds of prisoners, including Stew, Austin, and Stanley converged on the still standing stockade wall that separated the new section from the old. No orders from on high were given. No one marched around the walls of the city of dugouts and shebangs. No trumpets blared, and no praises to the Almighty were shouted. But that night, the old northern wall of the stockade came tumbling down nearly as fast as the walls of Jericho. Only a few timbers remained of the hundreds, those at either end within the deadline that no one dared touch.

"This will last a month," Austin said, as he and Stanley toted a six-foot log toward Austin's shebang. "And did you see Key's squad? And Stew barking orders like he was in the field? Brilliant organization—like they had drilled for it. A strategic assault, the way they attacked those timbers.

You know what they're doing with all that wood, don't you?"

"Firewood, like everybody else," Stanley said.

"Eventually, maybe. But not now. Key's boys are going to do a lot of whittling."

"Whittling?"

"Clubs. They're going to make clubs, lots of clubs."

Stanley hadn't thought about the Regulators and the Raiders since Talbot's death. "Ah, we'll have the men if the West Virginians join us, and now we'll have weapons."

Austin was always on the lookout for anything he might borrow or work a trade for. He borrowed a wood rasp from one man, and promised one can of soup for each of the next five days to another man for the loan of a real knife with a wooden handle.

Stanley worked at cutting away the pine bark with the knife, while Austin scraped one end of the rasp back and forth, over and over again, across the same flat rock upon which he had sharpened his spoon, and which was never seen outside the pocket of his trousers unless it was being similarly employed. Saturday night passed on to Sunday morning, according to the regular calls of the sentries, before he pronounced his work good. "We now have a chisel."

Then they worked together; Austin held the chisel as Stanley pounded it with a large rock. The pine split easily, but only a little at a time, so the pair kept at it for hours, despite many pleas from Dell and other neighbors for peace and quiet. By morning, their hands were blistered, bruised, and bloodied, but the log had been reduced to a large pile of splintered kindling. And between the kindling and Stew's pine stump, there would be sufficient firewood to keep Austin's soup kettle warm for several weeks.

The sentries began to call half past four o'clock.

"I wonder where Stew is?" Stanley asked.

104

"Probably still with Key," Austin said. "Lot of work making clubs. Let's go wash. Then I'm sleeping on that fresh, sweet ground until roll call."

"Me too," Stanley said.

The path to the swamp took Stanley and Austin past the new quarters of the triplets. Stanley knelt to check on them. On the left, Taft was snoring softly. On the right, Churchill's breathing was shallow, but steady. But in between, Harley didn't move at all.

Stanley leaned over Harley and touched his forehead. It was cool to the touch. Stanley looked at Austin and shook his head.

Austin's nod was silent assurance. *Of course, I'll help you, just as you helped me with Rodgers.*

Frank and Stew were already waiting at the bridge when Stanley and Austin arrived.

"Harley died last night," Stanley said quietly to Stew. "I guess the move was too much for him. Ogre and I will take him to the gate."

After the four men washed, Frank was eager to see the new, much larger northern portion of the prison, so they set off up the hill toward the North Gate. They walked in silence for a while, being careful, as they always were, to step around anyone who had chosen to sleep on the path near the deadline.

They paused where the former northwest corner had been, conscious of the fact that they were about to step across the old deadline, which only the day before would have gotten them shot. The new section of the stockade lay open before them. Every part of it was already occupied. The old northern wall was no more. Only mounds of upturned earth marked where the pine timbers had been sunk in the ground. All that remained of the old deadline was a post here and there, obviously overlooked in the night.

105

A small squad of slaves was already hard at work removing the last few standing timbers of the old wall inside the deadline.

"You Yanks der, halt!"

The four friends stopped in their tracks.

Captain Wirz, gesturing wildly, stood in the first sentry box atop the wall inside the new portion of the stockade. "Vas ist das?" He pointed at the ragged trench line that marked where the old wall timbers had been. "Ver ist mein vood?"

Frank was the first to recover his wits. "Your vood, sir? What vood?"

"Da vall. It vas der last night." Then Wirz pounded his fist on the railing of the sentry box with each word. "Ver— ist—mein—vood?"

"Well, sir," Frank said, turning out his hands and looking up at Wirz, "it's plain to see none of us have it. In fact, the only wood among us is Mitch's walking staff, and the captain wouldn't wish to dishonor himself by depriving this wounded, needy man of his staff, would he?"

Wirz's eyes burned at the four young men. "Bah. Begone. I vill find mein vood. Soon. You see."

It was all the men could do to contain their laughter until they were out of earshot of the captain, who remained in that sentry box, ranting at anyone who passed about his missing stockade timbers.

But to Stanley, his own laughter felt hollow and forced. *Harley's dead. No joy of triumph there. He wasn't at all like Talbot. He was a lost and hopeless man, and someday soon, this place might reduce me to such. I can't allow it. I was almost dead at Shiloh and God delivered me. I was chained in that livery and nearly blown to bits in Vicksburg and God delivered me. Lord God, deliver me from this place too, and from that raving lunatic, Wirz.*

106

CHAPTER 22

Wednesday, June 29, 1864

STEW SEEMED A MOST CONTENTED MAN, PERFECTLY AT peace amid the constant clamor of the prison, as he whetted his razor on a small, smooth stone. Sunlight played through his light hair and added a lively glint to his bright blue eyes as he examined the blade this way and that before he pronounced it "good enough for Mitch's tough hide."

Austin and Frank sat side by side in the patch of shade afforded by Stew's two army blankets.

Stanley sat on their pine stump and waited for Stew to finish his preparations. The rains that had soaked the camp during June had ended. Now, as the summer sun blazed down upon prisoners and guards alike, Harley's kepi-style infantry cap covered Stanley's head and shaded his eyes. "Taft and Churchill said you should have it," Stew had said when he offered the cap to Stanley. "I debugged it mostly."

Stew took a dingy gray cloth from a steaming water pot and wrung the excess from it back into the pot. "I'm ready," he said.

Stanley removed his cap and tilted his head back.

Stew applied the hot cloth. "Sorry I don't have any soap, but this should soften the beard. You want it clean off?"

Stanley smiled and spoke through the cloth. "Yes, Stew. Got to keep the bugs down, and it's not likely I'll come across any ladies in this place."

"That may be more likely than you think, Mitch."

"What Southern woman would ever set foot in here?"

"None," Stew said, "but that's not what I mean."

"Then what *do* you mean?"

Stew removed the cloth and started shaving Stanley. "The same as it is outside, people tell their barber things they won't tell anyone else. I have it on good authority there are a few female prisoners inside the stockade."

"What?"

"Sit still, Mitch, if you want to keep that ear. I know for a fact, a number of women dressed as men and enlisted."

There had been rumors of such even before Shiloh, but Stanley had dismissed them as fireside talk.

"Only makes sense a few might end up here," Stew went on. "Seen two myself, smallish, no beards, soft-spoken, too. One joined up to be with her husband; the other was a patriot and just wanted to kill Rebels."

Stew paused to clean his blade in the pot of water.

"So," Austin said, his voice full of skepticism, "what's the good authority?"

"About the women? Ah, I've roused your curiosity." Stew chuckled and started shaving Stanley again. "Several days ago—I think it was just before Mitch was turned in—a fully-clothed dead body was left over at the South Gate. You can imagine that caused quite a stir. There was a fight over the clothing, and then *silence*," the word was whispered for full effect, "when the men discovered the body to be that of a young woman."

Stew rinsed the razor again.

"I don't believe it," Frank said. "Did you see her?"

"No," Stew said, "but a number of men have sat for my barbering and told me exactly the same story. It must be true."

Loud cheering erupted across the swamp—at least it sounded like loud cheering from over a thousand feet away. The four men stood and gazed across the camp toward the ruckus.

At first, Stanley saw nothing out of the ordinary, but then Stew pointed out where the cheering was coming from. A man was running between the rows of shebangs, turning this way and that along the narrow streets. He was being pursued by three or four others, who took different paths to turn his flank and trap him. Crowds of prisoners yelled after them, now just noise to Stanley's ears.

The man stumbled. He tried to right himself and continue fleeing, but his pursuers were upon him. Raiders. Even from across the swamp, Stanley could tell them by sight. They wore good clothes.

The man was thrown to the ground. The flash of a knife raised high, then down. Short seconds passed as the Raiders turned out their victim's pockets and rifled through his clothing. Then they ran away up the hill to their citadel.

The man's shirt was now bright red. He had been murdered in broad daylight, in full view of twenty-seven thousand men. And yet, even as a hush swept over the prison, no man went to his aid or to claim his body for burial.

Stanley donned his cap and grabbed the staff Sergeant Key had given him.

"Where are you going?" Stew's words were sharp, almost harsh.

"That man needs help," Stanley said.

"That man's dead already," Stew said. "And his killers are long gone. Only those close by could have saved him, but no one dared to confront the Raiders. There was nothing we could have done, and there is nothing we can do now except prepare to strike them when we have the advantage."

"And we should remember that man and his family," Frank said.

The four men stood side by side for a few moments, heads bowed.

"Amen," Frank said. Then he and Austin returned to their seats.

Stanley gazed across the way again. A few men had stirred themselves to look at the corpse. One had a blanket. The dead man would be gone within minutes and the incident nearly as soon forgotten.

Stanley laid the staff on the ground and removed his cap. Then he resumed his seat on the stump.

Stew began to whet his razor again. "I'm finished with your beard, Mitch. What about your hair? How much do you want me to leave for the ladies?"

Stanley eyed Stew's razor. "Take it all off, Stew, and make a nice, clean job of it. Just as bugs multiply if you don't keep your hair short, evil grows when good people do nothing. We've got to go over there and give those brutes a beating."

"Soon, Mitch," Stew said. "Very soon, I think." Then he began to cut Stanley's hair close to the scalp with the razor.

"Mitch," Austin said, "we still don't know much about you. Let's hear it."

"My tale of woe?" Stanley asked.

"Yes," Austin said, "the whole thing."

And Stanley did, an abridged version though, because how long would it take until Stanley's head was shaved clean like the rest of his face? He told of his early years which were filled with heartache—the death of his mother before he was three years old, taken by his father to Ohio, who then disappeared, leaving his unwanted child to be raised in the house of the boy's pitiless and loveless Aunt Bess and Uncle Charles.

110

At the age of sixteen the army had provided Stanley a way of escape, but his first action at Shiloh had ended abruptly with his wounding, not once, but four times. "Death seemed inevitable," he told his friends, "and I cursed God for my short, miserable life."

Stew lifted the razor away from Stanley's scalp. "You didn't get away with that, did you, Mitch?"

"No. I had never believed in God. Why had I cursed him? I lay there wondering if maybe God does exist. There was no help for me, so I called out again and again, 'Lord, help me.'"

"Attention!" Frank called out. He jumped from his seat and stood at attention with Austin beside the narrow path next to Stew's shebang. Stew helped Stanley to his feet and they filed into line shoulder to shoulder with the others.

Four prisoners pressed past, each holding the corner of a blanket upon which lay the motionless form of a comrade.

"It's the least we can do," Stew explained. "We're all enlisted here, so there's no saluting, but we try to honor the passing of each one who crosses our path."

"And we offer silent prayers for the poor man's soul," Frank added.

"Then I will do the same," Stanley said, "and I hope never to honor any of you in such a way."

The four men took their places again and Stanley continued with his story. He told of the desperate bargain he had struck with a local woman, who having lost both her husband and eldest son to the war, was forced to take a Yankee into her house and nurse him back to health.

Stanley's throat tightened and his voice grew husky when he spoke about Anna and their return to the battlefield at Shiloh. They had wept together where her brother had fallen, and in a few wonderful weeks, love had overcome hatred.

Stanley squinted his eyes to fend off the wetness. "Give me a minute, Stew."

Stew rinsed the razor with a little water from his canteen. Then he wiped it with the gray cloth.

Stanley pulled down the neckline of his undershirt, exposing the scar from Luke's hunting knife. "Her brother did that, and then he betrayed me into the hands of a slave trader who took me away in chains and sold me to the captain of a Mississippi River steamboat."

"You could easily have died from that wound," Stew said, returning to his work. "So, you were shot three times, an ornery mule broke your leg, and you were stabbed in the chest by a fourteen-year-old boy."

"And in Vicksburg," Stanley said, "my right arm was broken and I was knocked on the head by a brick during shelling by our own troops."

"I saw that scar just now," Stew said,

"When were you taken away from Anna?" Austin asked.

Stanley thought for a moment. "Oh. Two years and two days ago, June 27th."

"Have you seen her since?"

"Once. At church in Corinth, Mississippi last October." Stanley couldn't help grinning. "I kissed her right there in the street outside the church."

Stew clapped Stanley on the shoulder. "All right, Mitch. How about her brother, the boy who stabbed you?"

"Luke. He was quiet, but not mean like he was before. Anna and I forgave him, and judging from Anna's letters, he's looking forward to walking her up the aisle when we get married."

"Keep that hope alive," Frank said. "Don't ever let yourself think you won't return to her. That's an incredible story. God's been watching over you."

"But this is such a dreadful place." Stanley gazed past Frank and Austin and Stew at the unending grim scenes of deprivation, malevolence, and despair beyond. "In the short time we've been here, death has visited twice. I haven't been here a week yet, but I already know a man alone will quickly die. Why would God bring me here?"

"Why did he bring any of us here?" Stew asked. "I've known Austin and Frank for only a few weeks, but they're my brothers. You are too, Mitch."

Stew wiped his razor and wrapped Stanley's head with the hot, moist cloth. "There's more to your story, isn't there?"

"Yes, a lot more. The *Evangelina* was a good boat," Stanley said. "I worked almost seven months on her until she met with disaster in February of sixty-three. Then I spent two months at Hurricane Plantation."

"Where's that?" Austin asked.

The three men listened in fascination when Stanley spoke of his time at the war-ravaged plantation of Joseph Davis, brother of the Confederate President, and about Ben Montgomery, the well-educated black postmaster of the plantation, who had helped Stanley send letters to his beloved Anna.

"All I wanted was to return to her," Stanley said. "I went to Vicksburg, hoping to find a way north to Tennessee, but General Grant had his own plans. I was trapped in Vicksburg during the siege. I lived with a judge's beautiful family in a cave and I worked in a Confederate hospital tending some of our boys when they were brought in. Last May, I crossed the lines and begged for medical supplies. That's when I met General Logan."

Stew removed the warm cloth. "You did what?"

"I met General—"

"No, before that." Stew slid the razor up the back of Stanley's head. "That bit about crossing the lines."

"Yes, that," Stanley said. "It was just something I had to try. The hospital couldn't spare any ether or opium for the Federal patients, so I crossed over during a truce. Ended up speaking to General Logan himself."

113

"Well, I'll be...." Austin said, shaking his head.

"Did Key and Jim ask you about that?" Stew asked.

"Yes," Stanley said. "Jim said he had heard about that incident and I think it finally convinced him I was no turncoat. After the surrender, General Logan lived in the judge's house for a few weeks. The general and I sat at the same table every evening, and it was the general who ordered me back into the army with the Quartermaster Department."

Austin had stopped shaking his head, but his eyes were still wide with amazement. "How did you get taken prisoner?"

Stanley sighed. "We were abandoned by our cavalry screen." He kept his voice flat, without rancor. "We were the last unit in Cartersville, and we were about to mount up when Rebel bushwhackers appeared. Our cavalry screen chased them away, but then a second band of Rebels swooped down on us. All the other men jumped aboard their horses and sped away up the railroad toward Allatoona. But as you can imagine, it took me a bit longer to climb into the saddle, and the bushwhackers were on me before I could get away. The Rebels got one decent horse and one lame supply clerk in the deal, a small prize indeed, if you ask me."

A lean, well-muscled man, who looked somewhat familiar to Stanley, strode up the street through the camp of the Fifty-Fifth and greeted each of the four friends with a quick nod. "Frank. Stew. Ogre. Mitch."

"Key wants a meeting of the captains, Stew. Late. After dark. You know the place."

It was the voice from the shadows, Sergeant Key's man, Limber Jim.

"Just finishing up with Mitch," Stew said. "I can fit you in, if you like."

"No thanks," Jim said. "Looks like you made Mitch bleed a bit, but at least he's still identifiable, not like some of the butcher jobs you turn out."

Laughter filled the shebang and carried far beyond. And Stanley had thought Jim was devoid of humor.

"He didn't complain," Stew said. "Didn't even wince when I nicked him."

Stanley winked at Limber Jim so Stew couldn't see it. "That's because," Stanley said, straight-faced and somber, "once you've been kicked by a mule, nothing else draws so much as an *ouch*."

CHAPTER 23

CLOUDS MOVED IN AT SUNSET, JUST AT THE CLOSE OF THE evening prayer meeting. Austin placed his new soup kettle under the rear corner of the blanket roof to catch the dripping water in case it rained. Then he and Stanley ducked into the shebang and huddled close in the almost total darkness.

"Went to the sutler this afternoon to buy that kettle," Austin said. "Only took the fifty Confederate it cost, just to be safe. A few boys from the south side were there. Said the dead man had money, twenty-five or so he won playing euchre. Raiders watch those games, but usually go for the winner late at night. Getting more shameless every day."

Stanley swallowed. "Then you must be very cautious when you exchange another Abraham."

"But that's not all," Austin said. "For some reason, they trusted me. Said who the killer was, and I passed it on to Stew."

Approaching footsteps silenced Austin. A dark head-shaped form appeared under the blanket.

"Ogre, it's Stew. Is that Mitch in there with you?"

"Yes," Austin said. "Didn't get a chance to tell you, but nice, smooth job on his head. Don't care what Limber Jim says. Dell's here too, but he won't wake up until morning."

116

Stew, a black silhouette against the slightly less dark space outside, crowded into the shebang, four men now in a space barely large enough for two.

"Listen," Stew said, "things are happening fast." Eagerness and excitement filled Stew's hushed words. "That man's murder may turn out to be a good thing. When Key and Limber Jim learned about it, they immediately went to the gate and asked the guard for a meeting with Wirz. They returned an hour ago for the meeting of the company captains. Wirz has agreed to help us."

"Just like that?" Austin said.

The black shape of Stew's cap bobbed up and down. "Yep, just like that. The guards reported the murder to Wirz. Now he says the Raiders have to be stopped. Of course, Key never mentioned the hundreds of clubs he had made from the wall timbers. Key also said Wirz favors us having a permanent police force."

"Who else knows this, Stew?" Stanley asked.

"No one outside the Regulators or Wirz's staff," Stew said, "but there are spies and word may leak out. If the Raiders get wind of our plans, they may attack us before we attack them. Our orders are to always be on guard and never gather in numbers large enough to attract their attention."

"Sounds like they're having a grand old time now," Austin said. "Can hear them singing their stupid songs way over here."

Stanley nodded. "I've tried to ignore it, but—"

"But they keep on singing the same two songs over and over," Stew said. "Mark my words, Mitch, they won't settle down until well after the sentries call midnight."

"And how do you know that, Stew?"

"Because we have spies of our own," Stew said. "They have a new batch of that rotgut whiskey they make out of sweet sorghum. They'll hoot and holler tonight, but tomorrow or the day after, when we charge into them, let's hope they aren't feeling too lively."

"Then the fight is on," Stanley said.

"Without a doubt. No sense delaying. They probably know we're coming, so we should oblige them in the next day or two. I want to get after them and be done with it, and the sooner the better."

"And the West Virginians?" Austin asked.

"Key told me to pass along his compliments to both of you for the good work you did in bringing those boys into our camp," Stew said. "A couple dozen are too beat up to do anything, but the rest have fallen in line. They elected that man Case and five other sergeants to be their leaders. We now have ten full companies of fifty, and Key says that's more than enough."

Stew stopped and looked over his shoulder, more from habit, it seemed, than from any perceived threat. "Here's another surprise for you," he said in a whisper. "One of those West Virginia boys brought a pistol in."

Stanley opened his mouth to speak, but Austin beat him to it. "What? Weren't they searched?"

"They were, several times," Stew said, "but he had it in the bottom of his knapsack under a badly soiled pair of drawers. Obviously, the guards and Raiders didn't wish to look any deeper. Key has the gun now."

CHAPTER 24

Friday, July 1, 1864

AS THE SUN ROSE OVER THE PINE-TOPS BEYOND THE eastern wall, ripples of anxious fidgeting spread quickly through the Regulators. Their leader, Sergeant Key, had been assaulted during the night, his life threatened in the darkness.

Word of the attack went around as the men stood for roll call. There had been three attackers. They had walked right up to Key's quarters and called him out. Then they had the nerve to ask Key if there was going to be a fight. Key assured them there would be. The three Raiders closed in on Key. One of them drew a knife. Key drew the pistol. The Raiders ran off into the darkness.

"It's true," Stew said, when Stanley questioned him about the incident immediately after roll call. "But Wirz has the gun now. Key handed the pistol to the sergeant of the guard this morning and asked to speak with Wirz. It was a sign of good faith—that's what Limber Jim said—just to show Wirz he's got nothing to fear from us when we get after them Raiders this afternoon."

"It's today?"

"Sure is, Mitch. Last night's attack on our leader means it must be today. This is their last meeting before the fight. Wirz is a jumpy chap, and Key says Wirz needs to know our plan of attack, just to make sure he doesn't think we're

119

starting a revolt. Can't have Wirz ordering his artillery to fire on us."

• • •

At precisely half past three o'clock, according to Sergeant Stewart's silver pocket watch, a single whistle, loud and shrill, set the Regulators in motion.

"That's Limber Jim," Stew said. "Nobody can whistle like him."

From all around the prison north of the swamp, five hundred men jumped to the ready and ran to their assigned assembly points.

"Don't wait for me," Stanley called to Stew, who had raised his cap high atop his club to rally his fifty men. "I'll bring up the rear, but I will be there."

One hundred and fifty men in three companies, led by Sergeant Key and two West Virginians, ran down toward the bridge at the west end of the swamp, the same bridge the four sergeants and brothers gathered at each morning. Three more companies, led by Limber Jim, a big brawler named Ned, and Case the West Virginian, ran for the eastern bridge near the latrines.

A cry went up across the swamp; lookouts and cronies of the Raiders raised the alarm.

Stew started his company forward. It was the first time Stanley had ever seen most of the men. Some had clubs, others carried wooden poles or stakes, a few carried no weapons at all.

Austin held one of the stakes that had supported the roof of his shebang, and stayed close beside Stanley as he limped down the hill.

The twin one-hundred-and-fifty-man columns rushed up the hillside south of the swamp. As if their movements had been practiced many times on a parade ground, the two columns converged as they ran forward, coming together just before they drove headlong into the waiting throng of Raiders.

Stanley and Austin started across the bridge.

The result of the sudden attack was instantaneous. The body of Raiders was split in two; both sides attacked the Regulators who were suddenly in their midst. The Regulators faltered, withdrew a little, and seemed about to retreat when four more companies of Regulators rushed into the fray, two on either side of the combined center column. Both bodies of Raiders were now surrounded by club-wielding, revenge-minded Regulators.

Stanley and Austin reached Main Street near the North Gate and turned toward the battle. Here and there, a Raider managed to escape the press of Regulators and skedaddled. A few came in their direction, but they ran fast, too fast for Stanley, or even Austin, to give chase.

"They're like lice," Austin said. "They know the end is near."

The Regulators continued to press forward. Sergeant Key, Limber Jim, and many others fought side-by-side, or back-to-back swinging this way and that, smiting any Raider that dared stand against them with blow upon blow, until the Raider was beaten, bloodied, and usually knocked senseless. The ground behind Key and Jim was littered with their victims.

A thin man with a thin mustache, wearing a black slouch hat that looked several sizes too big for him, fought his way through the tightening line of Regulators, striking those on either side with what appeared to be a thick, dark shillelagh. He soon freed himself, and weaved toward Stanley and Austin.

Stanley recognized the man instantly. "I'll take this one," he said.

"I've got your back," Austin replied.

Stanley hobbled a few steps to his right, directly into the path of the fleeing man. Had the man taken any real notice, he would have seen nothing but a tottering cripple leaning on his walking staff, knuckles white as he gripped it tightly with both hands to keep from losing his balance. Instead, the man kept looking over his shoulder to see if any of the Regulators were giving chase.

The fleeing Raider was less than ten feet away. Stanley brought the staff up with both hands and, just as the man turned and raised his club to brush Stanley aside, the staff smashed into the man's temple. His knees buckled and he crumpled to the ground at Stanley's feet.

Stanley bent over the dazed man and picked up his weapon, the hickory walking stick that Levi Jackson had made. "Hello, Jack. You broke the beautiful carved horse's head off my cane. Today? During this fight?"

Blood streamed down the side of Jack's face. He raised a hand to cover the wound and nodded.

Austin recovered the black hat which had been sent flying several feet away. He offered it to Stanley. "Is this yours too?"

"Yes, it is, Ogre." Stanley looked inside the crown of the slouch hat. When he spoke, his words were flat, without emotion. "Where are the letters, Jack?"

Jack shrugged.

Stanley pressed the jagged, broken head of his walking stick into Jack's chest.

Jack groaned and writhed.

"What did you do with my letters, Jack?"

Jack shook his head slowly. "They're gone."

"What do you mean, they're gone?"

"Just gone. You don't want to know how."

Stanley leaned more of his weight on his broken walking stick.

Jack screamed, but hardly anyone heard because of the fight that still raged.

"Tell me, Jack. Now."

"All right, all right."

Stanley eased up on the walking stick.

Jack rubbed his sore chest. Blood seeped through his shirt. "Collins took them and read them. Then he gave them out, one by one, whenever one of his pals went to the latrine, to read and then use for—well, you know. Nobody ever brought one back."

A single blow would put an end to it—to Jack. Page upon page of intimate thoughts and desires poured out to Stanley, and only to him. Private, cherished words that he could have read back to her many years later when they were old and gray. Beautiful, loving, innocent, hope-filled pages, not only gone forever, but defiled, destroyed by the filthy hands of loveless, faithless fiends.

No. I will not become like them. Vengeance is mine, saith the Lord. Those words had come to him countless times during the last two years, ever since the days of his captivity at the hands of that demon LaVache. And in due time, that man had received justice in full.

Stanley raised his cane from Jack's chest. He searched the entangled mass of Raiders and Regulators. Wally, Jack's partner in crime was nowhere in sight. The Raiders had been driven back to the Castle, the huge black tent of their leader, Collins. One final push and the day would be won.

From the north side of the swamp a cheer arose. Thousands and thousands of men stood shoulder to shoulder on the slope to view the battle, and now that the issue was nearly settled, they raised their voices to salute those who had gone into the camp of the enemy and thrashed him soundly. Another thunderous cheer went up when the Castle came down.

Stanley looked down at Jack. "Get up."

Jack struggled to his feet, still holding the side of his head. "Now you have your hat, give me that cap you're wearing."

Stanley bristled at Jack's nerve. "What happened to my coat and boots?"

123

"Mosby got them, I think."

"Collins again. And my green checked shirt?"

"Wally's wearing it."

"Where's Wally, Jack?"

Jack shrugged again. "Sun's real hot. Give me that cap and I'll tell you."

"That's not going to happen. This cap belongs to the mess. Those letters were from the girl I *will* marry. Enjoy the hot sun, Jack."

The fighting had ended and the Regulators were rounding up all the Raiders they could lay hands on.

Austin pointed toward the Citadel of the Raiders. The fighting had ended and the Regulators were placing dozens of beaten criminals under arrest. "There's Stew," he said. "He'll know what we should do with Jack."

Stanley prodded Jack forward with his staff.

Blood trickled from an ugly gash near Stew's right ear and dripped onto his undershirt. He was breathing heavily from the exertion, but his blue eyes blazed with victory, just as Talbot's had.

"It seems you were in the thick of it," Stanley said.

"Just a glancing blow," Stew said, "and he got far worse."

"Still, you should wash it and cover it before the flies get at it."

"Thanks, Mitch. I will," Stew said. "And you boys got into the action too."

"It was all Stanley's doing," Austin said. "He got his hat and cane back."

"I see that," Stew said. "We've taken more than a hundred prisoners. Some escaped, but then again, they can't escape. We'll round them up tomorrow or the next day, or next week. Wirz said we are to use the North Gate as a jail for now. Take your man over there and turn him over to the Rebel guards."

Stanley and Austin joined the long, slow procession of jubilant, triumphant Regulators and dejected, defeated Raiders that filed down Main Street toward the South Gate and then down the hill to the bridge across the swamp. At the North Gate, they turned Jack over to the guard who ordered him to enter the gate through the wicket to await trial along with the rest of the prisoners.

Victory was sweet. The hickory walking stick, the only tangible remnant of his time at Matthews Hill Farm, was back in Stanley's hands. It was damaged, but he would smooth its broken head with a stone to fit his palm, just like some others he had seen. The black slouch hat he had purchased in Chattanooga now bore the sweat stains of another, but he would wash them away, and it would be his once more. The hat's broad brim would shade him from the sun, and when it rained, it would catch water to drink.

Tomorrow, Stanley would return Sergeant Key's staff. Then he would go across the camp in search of his coat and boots. The shirt? Stanley was plenty warm without it, even at night. However, if he did happen to stumble across Wally, Stanley would claim it from him by right.

But Anna's letters were gone forever. She had bared her soul. She had made him laugh out loud. She had brought tears to his eyes. She had made him love her more deeply than he ever imagined he could love anyone. How many long, cold nights had her words warmed him, even as they remained hidden in the crown of his hat?

Every evening since Stanley had entered the prison, pine smoke from thousands of cookfires had hung heavy over the stockade. But this evening, the air was clear and every cooking pot was empty.

The usual time for the ration wagon to enter had passed and the doors of the North Gate remained firmly bolted. Unrest within the prison was the excuse passed around the stockade by the guards. Captain Wirz would not risk opening the gates; unruly prisoners might rush through and try to escape. So on this day, when, thanks to the valiant efforts of the Regulators, every weary and sorry soul in Andersonville could finally sleep that night in relative peace and safety, most would do so under the constant torture of incessant, gnawing starvation.

Stanley and Austin returned to Austin's shebang. Stanley had first noticed Austin's limp when they had crossed over to the fight. His gait was even slower and more awkward now. His right foot dragged across the ground much as Stanley's left did. Dell was already asleep, so Austin sat in silence, hunched over his empty soup kettle. The scurvy was taking its toll.

"Tomorrow, go to the sutler and fill that kettle," Stanley said. "Do you need another Abraham?"

Austin shook his head. "No."

"Then I'm going next door to my place to lie down. Are you going to meeting?"

Austin nodded slowly, but he didn't look up at Stanley.

"Wake me, if I'm asleep. I want to go too."

One fight was done. Another fight would continue, the fight to survive—no, more than survive—the fight to live would continue, the fight for compassion, for mercy, for justice. Indeed, he would have to fight tooth and nail to feed the image of Almighty God within him, to keep it from slipping entirely away.

CHAPTER 25

Sunday, July 3, 1864

THE ROAD TO CORINTH WAS FAMILIAR NOW, THROUGH fields of cow peas that spread across a low hill known locally as Pea Ridge, then past Dismal Swamp, lower, boggy, dead ground, that was good for nothing except to be gotten through as quickly as possible. And after more than a year and a half of attending service in Corinth once or twice a month, Anna now knew many of the farmsteads they passed along the way by name, and some of the people by sight. But there was one place, just outside the town of Corinth, that Anna maintained a particular interest in.

"Luke, please take us by the camp. I promised Levi we would." It would take them out of their way, but only by half a mile, and they would still make it to church on time.

"All right, if I must," Luke said.

The words sounded curt and surly, but Anna knew it was an act. Luke loved to drive the family to church. His sour tone was just his way of reminding her, and perhaps himself, how mean and vengeful he had become after both his father and older brother died at the hands of the Yankees. And after he had been forced to live under the same roof with the wounded Yankee soldier, Stanley Mitchell.

The carriage began to pass a vacant parcel of land that lay to the left of the road. "Slow down, Luke," Anna said. "We haven't seen it since spring."

The land was dotted here and there with empty log huts. Just last year the huts had teemed with families of freed slaves—contrabands, the Yankees called them. The ground had been green and lush. Crops had been growing tall under the skillful care of the Negro residents. A bountiful harvest was certain.

"Such a shame," Anna said. "The fields are all overgrown. By next year, or the year after, the huts will be too. It'll be like it never was."

"I don't understand your fascination with this Contraband Camp," Luke called over his shoulder. "It's nothing but a ghost town now."

"It was important to Levi and Aunt Min," Anna said. "That little chapel on the left side of the road—Levi and some of the other slaves built it and his family went there with the other black folk. That's so sad, Mama, whites and blacks worshiping the same God in separate churches. And when the Yankees were here, they came to church to worship, and lots of our people stayed away."

"That's true," Mama said, "but most of our people never hugged a Yankee either."

Anna giggled softly, but something was wrong. Worry had plagued her the last three nights. It was best to think of other things. "Levi said just this week how sad they was—were—when the Yankees moved that camp to Memphis. They had to say goodbye to lots of close friends."

Luke half turned to look back at Anna. "But the contrabands are probably better off in Memphis."

"But they're people too," Anna said, "men and women and boys and girls. I hope it's better for them in Memphis, but maybe it ain't. I been thinking since the Yankees went away six months ago if I liked it better when they were here or when they ain't, like now." Only a few Confederate

128

soldiers had visited First Presbyterian Church since January, when the Yankees had burned the depot, destroyed the railroad for miles around, and abandoned the town.

"But now, my dear," Mama said, "I see you're actually paying attention to Rev. Peters' preaching instead of looking around at every Yankee soldier just to see if it's your Yankee. Are you worried?"

"Of course, Mama. I always worry, and with no letter this week, it's a little more. I've been telling myself all along not to worry if a letter doesn't come. It could be anything. He may be too busy to write, or he sent it a day or two late and it missed the weekly mail from Purdy, or the train carrying his letter went off the tracks and burned, or he just ran out of paper or ink."

"The mail is more regular," Luke said, "and the roads are much better, because of the Yankees. It takes us less time to make this trip than before."

"Do you think they'll come back?" Mama asked

"The Yankees?" Luke asked. "Patrols for sure, a column of cavalry maybe, but three weeks ago, General Forrest whipped the Yankees down at Brice's Crossroads. And this week I heard the Yankees are moving up toward Tupelo."

"Luke's right, Mama," Anna said. "There's nothing for the Yankees here—no depot, no railroad, no little mountains of supplies. We may see a few now and again, but not whole armies like we seen last year."

Mama looked sideways at her daughter. "So?"

Anna looked down at her hands which were folded in her lap. "So, I'll pray that someday soon these hands will touch his handsome face, Mama. And I'll keep praying for that boy, just like I always done. I'll hope he's safe, and I'll try not to worry so much, but even as I say it, I know I will until he's home again."

"Home, dear?" Mama smiled as she said it. "Our home?"

"Of course, Mama. But I don't think I'll be seeing my Stanley again until this war's done for good. Even then, it might be another month or two. Back in February he wrote that he'll have to return to Ohio to be discharged and enrolled for his army pension. Then he's coming back to Matthews Hill for good."

CHAPTER 26

Monday, July 4, 1864

I T HAD BEEN ALL STANLEY COULD DO TO RISE AT DAWN WITH Stew and Austin and head off to the stream to wash with Frank. A walk around the entire interior of the prison, a journey of almost a mile, was out of the question. Friday's fight and two days of searching for his coat and boots had wearied him. His feet were tender from the effort; more abuse might blister them and make them bleed.

The only bright spot was that, for the last two days, Austin had made a kettle of cabbage and onion soup. Pickens, the most severely afflicted, had received the first two portions. Then Austin, Frank, Stanley, and Stew received one each. The rest was sold, and there seemed to be no shortage of emaciated prisoners with five cents in their pockets and the will to walk all the way up to Austin's shebang near the northwest corner of the prison. Within two hours, the kettle was empty. Expenses for vegetables and water were recovered, and a profit of fifteen cents was realized.

But something strange was going on this morning. Throughout the entire prison, word passed on a whirlwind that a right and proper exchange of prisoners was set to begin on Thursday, the 7th.

The entire camp turned out for morning roll call, but there would be no regular counting of the prisoners. A host of guards entered the stockade accompanied by at least fifty clerks, some dressed in Rebel butternut, some in Union blue.

Lieutenant Davis, second in command of the prison, was held in slightly higher regard than Captain Wirz by most of the prisoners. Davis announced, through his cadre of clerks, that the roll for each detachment would be written anew in preparation for the exchange. The new rolls would be an accurate record of the names and regiments of every prisoner, and those rolls would be handed over to Federal authorities at the time of exchange.

It took Stanley a minute or two to understand the significance of the Rebel lieutenant's words. Then he went directly to Sergeant Stewart.

"Stew," Stanley said, "this recounting—it means they're throwing out the old roll call lists, and starting over. Would you have any objection to letting Austin and Dell join our ninety? Austin would jump at a chance to be out from under Cleary."

"Wouldn't we need to get permission from—?"

"Not that I can see, Stew. Look around. Lots of men are looking for friends to join up with."

"I might not be able to put Austin and Dell in Pickens' mess," Stew said, "and if the Rebs give me any grief over it, they'll have to go back to Cleary."

Stanley smiled. "Understood, Stew. Thanks. Any chance Lieutenant Davis is right about exchange?"

Stew pursed his lips and slowly shook his head. "I hope he is right, but I don't think so. I think it's another Wirz lie. He's a killer, Mitch. He kills hope, and that kills men. He does it to crush us."

"That's what I thought," Stanley said. "I'll go see Austin."

"By the way, Mitch, after this thing is done, Key wants to see you."

"Why me?"

"That's for him to say. He'll be over by the North Gate."

• • •

By two o'clock that afternoon, Austin and Dell had been added to the roll of the first ninety of Detachment Fifty-five. Stew had also gotten two men from Pickens third mess to transfer into the second mess, which needed two more men to fill out its compliment of thirty. The renumbering was completed and the guards and clerks went out the way they had come in.

Stanley's tired legs ached as he walked slowly along the deadline beside the western wall of the stockade all the way to Broadway. The jagged top of the cane where Duke's head had snapped off caused it to look more shillelagh than fine walking stick. It bit into his palm with each stride, but he didn't mind the little stab of pain, for it reminded him that Matthews Hill Farm was real. Levi Jackson was real. And above all, Anna Matthews was real.

Perhaps Stew is wrong. Perhaps exchanges will begin in a few days.

Sergeant Key stood with Limber Jim and several other men around a small desk placed in the empty space in front of the gate that was normally kept clear to allow the gate doors to swing open. A man Stanley didn't recognize sat at the desk hunched over a ledger book.

Key beckoned Stanley to approach. "Gentlemen, this is Sergeant Mitchell. Sergeant Stewart vouches for him, and I do too."

The other men standing with Key nodded at Stanley.

"Good morning," Stanley said.

"Sergeant Mitchell," Key said, "Captain Wirz says we may do what we wish with the Raiders that have been arrested. We believe that for law and order to take hold in this prison, we must conduct trials of the Raiders for the crimes they have committed." Key gestured at the man sitting at the desk. "Sergeant McCullough is an attorney in civilian life. He is the president of this court. Please answer Sergeant McCullough's questions truthfully. These other men and I will serve as witnesses."

"Yes, Sergeant Key," Stanley said. *What's this about? Do they want me to testify against Jack?*

"State your name, rank, and unit for the record," Sergeant McCullough said.

"Stanley Mitchell, Sergeant, Fifteenth Corps Quartermaster Department."

"What is your date of birth?"

"Twenty-second of September, eighteen forty-five."

"How long have you been in this prison?"

"This is my eleventh day here."

"Six men now under arrest have been charged with murder," Sergeant McCullough said. "I will now read each of the six names. You will answer in the affirmative if you are acquainted with any of them. Do you understand, Sergeant Mitchell?"

"Yes, Sergeant McCullough."

"Do you know a prisoner by the name of John Sarsfield, 144th New York Infantry?"

"No, Sergeant."

Sergeant McCullough made a mark in his ledger. "Do you know a prisoner by the name of Charles Curtiss, Fifth Rhode Island Artillery?"

"No."

Sergeant McCullough made another mark in his ledger. "Do you know a prisoner by the name of Patrick Delaney, Company E, Eighty-Third Pennsylvania Infantry?"

"No."

Sergeant McCullough made yet another mark, as if he was checking off a list. "Do you know a prisoner by the name of William Collins, also known as Mosby, Company D, Eighty-Eighth Pennsylvania?"

"I know him by name and by sight, but in no other way."

Key grunted. "As does everyone else in this pen."

"Has William Collins ever assaulted you, deprived you of your possessions, or otherwise aggrieved you?"

Otherwise aggrieved? As in giving Anna's beautiful letters to cronies on their way to the latrine? "Not that I know of for sure."

"Please explain."

"Some of the things the Raiders took from me are still missing. I don't know where they are."

"Did Collins take any of those missing items from you?"

"No."

Sergeant McCullough paused for a moment, then wrote a note in the ledger. "Do you know a prisoner by the name of Alfred Munn, United States Navy?"

"No."

Another name was checked off by Sergeant McCullough. "Do you know a prisoner by the name of Terence Sullivan, also known as W. R. Rickson, United States Navy?"

"No."

McCullough looked up from the ledger. "The purpose of this inquiry is to select thirteen men to serve as jurors during the trials of these six accused murderers, as well many others accused of less serious offenses. Each juror must be a sergeant deemed by his peers to possess sound judgment. Each juror must also be new to the prison, not acquainted with any of the accused, not long exposed to the depredations of these men, and a man whose mind and body have not been forced to endure the rigors of long imprisonment. Sergeant Stewart put your name forward as a man possessing these qualifications, and Sergeant Key has added his second."

Stanley swallowed hard. To sit in judgment on men like Jack and Wally—he hadn't thought it possible that he might receive some satisfaction for the wrongs they had done to him.

But it can't be about revenge. And it can't be about me, or Anna's letters. It must be about justice.

Stanley looked at Sergeant Key. "Thank you for your confidence, but aren't we to be exchanged in a few days?"

All the men, including Sergeant McCullough, howled with laughter.

Stanley waited for the laughter to subside. "I thought as much."

"Sergeant Mitchell," McCullough said, resuming his business-like tone, "do you hold any vengeful thoughts or feelings toward any of the six accused?"

"No, Sergeant McCullough."

"You are quite young and the evidence against these men may be quite gruesome. Do you believe you can listen to all the evidence, consider it diligently, and reach a fair and impartial verdict?"

Stanley looked at each of the witnesses in turn as he answered the question. "Yes, I can. I was nearly killed at Shiloh. I lived for a year in the hands of the Confederacy, and endured forty-seven days in Vicksburg under fire from our own guns. I witnessed unspeakable things at a Rebel hospital there, and I've seen a slave trader's brains blown out by a slave. I may be only eighteen, but I've known both justice and mercy. And in my eleven days here, I've already learned that Andersonville is no place for old men."

McCullough waited for the other men to stop laughing. "Are you, Sergeant Stanley Mitchell, willing to serve as a juror on behalf of your fellow prisoners?"

Stanley stood with both hands clasped over the broken knob of his walking stick. No one had asked him to swear an oath, and they were all enlisted men, so there was no saluting or adding "sir" to everything. "Yes, I will, Sergeant McCullough."

"The proceedings will be held at the South Gate," McCullough said, "in the chamber between the inner and outer gates. You will report to the wicket guard immediately after roll call tomorrow morning."

CHAPTER 27

Tuesday, July 5, 1863

SERGEANT MCCULLOUGH, THE PRESIDENT OF THE COURT, stood behind the same desk he had been seated at the day before in front of the North Gate. "Gentlemen of the jury, please be seated and come to order."

Two long benches had been positioned along the south wall of the chamber between the two pairs of timber doors of the South Gate for the jurors, where the walls would afford a narrow strip of shade from the beating Georgia sun. Stanley took his seat with the twelve other men, none of whom he had ever met before. Wooden desks were also provided for the prosecutor, a frail, sickly sergeant named Higgins, and another sergeant who was to serve as counsel for the defense, and who seemed to be there more for show than for any real purpose.

"We have much to do and little time to do it," McCullough said. "Captain Wirz has ordered us to clear the North Gate of prisoners before day's end."

Sergeant McCullough sat at the desk and referred to a sheaf of papers in front of him. "In all, the police, under the leadership of Sergeant Leroy Key, apprehended one hundred and twenty-nine men who stand accused of various crimes against the prison population. This court will first deal with ninety-six men who have been accused of lesser crimes, thefts of money, personal belongings, rations. Each case will be dealt with in a judicious and expeditious manner.

"Next, this court will hear the cases of twenty-seven others who have been accused of acts of violence against fellow prisoners, beatings, stabbings, and the like that did not lead to the victim's death.

"Finally, six men have been accused of murder and of inciting others to commit criminal acts. These six are being held separately in the guardhouse and will appear before this court when summoned.

"For each of the accused, your responsibility as jurors will be not only to determine guilt or innocence, but also what sentence this court should impose. This court has been given free rein to try, sentence, and punish these men by Captain Wirz. Therefore, you may impose whatever sentence you think just, including death."

The first accused Raider was called in and his trial began. The man stated his name, rank, and unit for the record. He was then asked to confess his crimes to the court.

Of the ninety-six cases, each of the accused eventually admitted his guilt. Some professed great shame at how they had treated their fellow man, others claimed they had been forced to commit such base deeds because of the privations of prison life. Still others showed no remorse at all, and instead shrugged their shoulders in apathy or laughed at the court as a sham.

Upon entering the "courtroom," first Jack, and later Wally, immediately spotted Stanley and pleaded guilty. Wally's nose had obviously been broken in Saturday's brawl, and the green checked shirt he had stolen from Stanley was now stained dark with Wally's blood.

The trials of the petty criminals at an end, McCullough addressed the jurors again. "You must now decide upon punishment. The only caveat placed on this court by the commandant is that the North Gate is to be cleared of prisoners by four o'clock so the ration wagon can pass through."

Stanley raised his hand, not sure if he was permitted to speak.

"Yes, Sergeant Mitchell?"

Stanley rose to his feet. "Mr. President, given the time allowed, we cannot impose sentence case by case, but must do so as a whole. Must we not agree upon a suitable penalty for all, or return them all without punishment?"

"I believe you are correct," McCullough said. "That is the question before you. Have these ninety-six suffered sufficiently for their crimes—through their thrashing at the hands of the Regulators followed by their being cooped up in the North Gate—or should some further sentence be imposed? A second issue is the disposition of the twenty-seven violent offenders. Their trials will be held tomorrow, but Captain Wirz wants the gate cleared."

McCullough stood. "It's now half past one. This court will reconvene in one hour to hear your decision." Then, McCullough and the two attorneys left the gated enclosure through the wicket

It was still and boiling hot between the inner and outer gates. The guards provided a bucket of water. Some of the jurors drank from it and pronounced it good, but Stanley was wary of its source. If the jury accomplished its task, and Sergeant McCullough approved the sentence, in an hour and a half, maybe less, Stanley could drink from his own canteen.

• • •

At precisely half past two o'clock the wicket opened. The three court officials entered and the thirteen jurors returned to their seats.

"Gentlemen of the jury," McCullough said, "have you reached a decision?"

A Sergeant Field of Wisconsin stood. He had been chosen to speak for the jury. "We have, Mr. President."

"What sentence shall be imposed upon our band of thieves?"

"We sentence them to run the gauntlet, Mr. President."

McCullough's eyebrows arched. "And how is this sentence to be carried out, Sergeant Field?"

"As soon as it can be arranged," Field said, "we ask the Regulators to form a double line along Broadway. One prisoner at a time will be released from the wicket in the North Gate. Sergeant Mitchell has calculated that, if one prisoner is released every fifteen seconds, the whole thing can be done with in less than half an hour."

"What of injuries, Sergeant Field?"

"That is rather the point, isn't it, Mr. President? However, we ask that you instruct Sergeant Key to impress upon the Regulators to punish the offenders and not to beat them to death."

"And what of the other twenty-seven?" McCullough asked.

"Mr. President," Field said, "the jury is unanimous in thinking they should be made to witness the punishment of the gauntlet. They should be put into the stockade in chains and held beside the gate until both the gauntlet and rations are done."

McCullough grinned, the first sign of emotion Stanley had seen from him since the trial began. "Two birds with one stone, carry out sentence and empty the gate at the same time. Wirz will be pleased. I hope he has enough chains."

• • •

An hour later, the wicket in the North Gate opened. One by one, the twenty-seven accused criminals doomed to watch the proceedings stepped through the doorway. The wrists of each man were manacled. Leg irons and heavy chains bound their ankles, each man to the man behind in three groups of seven and one of six. Sergeant Key

140

ordered two groups of criminals to stand to the left of the gate and two to the right.

The Regulators, armed with the same clubs they had used to vanquish the Raiders, stood in two long lines along Broadway, from the North Gate to a white flag about a hundred yards away that marked the end of the gauntlet. Stanley and a few of the other jurors stood near the white flag to ensure no punishment was meted out beyond the flag.

The first thief, at the point of a Rebel bayonet, was prodded through the wicket toward the waiting Regulators. He started to run toward the white flag of deliverance, arms folded over his head for protection. But one by one the blows hit home on his arms, back, sides, and legs. Onlookers flung taunts and insults at the man as well.

The man remained on his feet, fighting yard by yard through the gauntlet of clubs and curses. After passing the flag he collapsed in a heap. No one came to his aid. Another man came through and likewise fell, then a third, who, stumbling along blindly, tripped over the first man and lay unconscious for some time. Stanley recognized the green checked shirt and the bloodied face; it was Wally. After a few more minutes, the first man recovered enough to stand. He looked sadly back through the scene of his torment and humiliation, then staggered away through the crowd.

Stanley bent at the waist and leaned heavily on his cane. Nausea swept over him, but he forced himself to watch every man who came through. He had sat in judgment on each of these men. He had endorsed their punishment. These men would thieve no more. Law and justice would rule inside the prison. Some good had to come from all the violence.

Within half an hour, just as Stanley had estimated, it was done. Each of the convicts was left bruised and bleeding. A dozen or so had fractured arms or ribs or serious head wounds. Friends laid them on blankets and tended to them.

The Regulators dispersed, leaving two men prostrate in the street. The two were certainly dead. Prisoners gathered around each corpse, but no one bent down to help.

Stanley shouldered his way through the crowd around the first body. "Does anyone know this man?" he asked.

There was a general shaking of heads and several murmured nos.

"Is he to be buried unknown? Please, think of his family. He may have been a Raider, but he suffered for his crimes. Someone must know him."

But no one knew the man's name.

Stanley moved on to the crowd surrounding the second body. The man was face down; the back of his head had been smashed to pulp. Stanley knelt beside the man and turned him over. There was also a knot on the man's left temple, an older wound, still swollen and purple.

"Ah, Jack," Stanley said under his breath. *Just bumps and bruises. That's all it was supposed to be. A lesson taught and learned—not this.*

Stanley stood slowly. "I'm Sergeant Mitchell of the Fifteenth Corps Quartermaster Department." He pointed to a healthy-looking man at the front of the crowd. "Help me throw this man over my shoulder."

The man stepped forward. "Sure, Sergeant, but you need help taking him, seeing how as you're lame."

"No, I must do it." Stanley looked down at Jack. He looked about a hundred and twenty pounds. A month ago, Stanley wouldn't have thought twice about it. Even with the cane, he could have hefted Jack's weight. But the man was right. It was too much for him now.

"All right," Stanley said. "Thank you kindly. Now, let's get him up and take him over to the South Gate. I know his name and regiment for the clerk."

• • •

Shortly after Stanley returned to his shebang, the North Gate opened and the ration wagon rolled into the stockade between the two groups of chained prisoners who were now sitting dejected in the dust. It was then that Stanley learned he would receive a double ration, a reward for his service as a juror.

"Add this to your pot," Stanley said, as he turned his double portion of rice, beans, and a nice-looking chunk of beef, over to Austin. "Should make a nice stew with the cabbage and onions. I'll be back later."

Today he had witnessed justice, hard and swift. Had there been room for mercy? Tomorrow, his duty as a juror would continue. Harsher penalties would be asked for. And what of the six accused of murder?

Stanley took up his cane and headed for the only place inside the stockade where he might find anything approaching solitude to think over the events of the day, the bridge over the swamp where he and his friends bathed and talked and laughed every day. He had carried two dead men across that bridge, and to him, that swamp was becoming the valley of death.

CHAPTER 28

Wednesday, July 6, 1864

STANLEY HAD PASSED ANOTHER RESTLESS NIGHT, BUT HE had risen with Stew and Austin and headed for the stream as usual. After washing his clothes and body, Stanley once again excused himself from the morning walk around the prison.

Detachment One Hundred was located near the center of the new portion of the stockade. Sergeant Sheppard was sitting on the rim of his dugout with his Bible open on his lap when Stanley approached. Rather than interrupt, Stanley waited until the man looked up from his reading and acknowledged Stanley's presence.

"Good morning, Mr. Sheppard. May I have a word with you, please?"

"Yes, of course. Please sit down."

"I think I'll stand, Mr. Sheppard. My clothes are still damp from washing."

"Then I'll stand with you." Sheppard closed his Bible, stepped out onto the path beside Stanley, and stretched. "It's not good for a body to sit in the damp for long. You were one of the first kind faces I saw when I entered this place a week ago, but I can't seem to recall your name."

"It's Mitchell, Stanley Mitchell."

In the week since he had appeared in camp, Sergeant Sheppard had assumed the lead role in the evening prayer meetings. Frank was more than happy to cede his place to the well-educated Sheppard, who was also blessed with the gift of preaching. Some began calling Sheppard 'Reverend,' but he wouldn't allow it. He was not yet ordained, he told everyone, so 'Mr. Sheppard' was just fine. And he addressed every other prisoner as 'Mister,' rather than by the man's rank or camp name.

"What seems to be the problem, Mr. Mitchell?"

"Well, Mr. Sheppard, you're the closest thing to a pastor there is in here, and I'm troubled about something I must do."

"Speak freely, Mr. Mitchell."

Stanley sighed. "I'm a juror for the trials of the Raiders. Yesterday, I sentenced ninety-six men to run the gauntlet. Two of the men died and others were seriously injured. I knew one of the dead men. He and another robbed me when I was turned in. A stranger helped me carry him across to the gate."

"I heard about the gauntlet," Sheppard said. "Were all ninety-six convicted of criminal behavior, Mr. Mitchell?"

"Yes, Mr. Sheppard."

"How many jurors are there?"

"Thirteen."

"A moment ago, you said, 'I sentenced ninety-six men.' But it was you and twelve others who sentenced these men. Did you administer any of the blows?"

"No, but I witnessed the beatings."

"How were you chosen to sit on this jury?"

"Sergeant Stewart put my name forward," Stanley said. "Then I was questioned by the president of the court. Sergeant Key and six other men approved my nomination."

Sheppard looked deep in thought for a moment. "Did the commandant of this prison give these men the authority to conduct these trials?"

Stanley nodded. "Yes. According to Sergeant Key, Captain Wirz insisted that the trials, convictions, and sentences be handled entirely by the Regulators."

"It's a difficult thing to sit in judgment on another man, but from what you said, you're a civil magistrate."

"What do you mean?"

Sheppard looked down at the Bible in his hand. "The apostle Paul tells us in Romans that all earthly power comes from God, that the rulers and authorities are ordained by God. Like it or not, Mr. Mitchell, you are one of the powers in this prison."

"No," Stanley said, shaking his head, "how can that be?"

"Captain Wirz holds power over this prison. He granted power to the Regulators to judge the Raiders, and the Regulators granted that power to you and the other jurors. It is God who has ordained you to this, Mr. Mitchell."

Stanley shrugged. "So, God wanted me to be a juror?"

Sheppard pressed the spine of his Bible against Stanley's chest. "God knows you perfectly, Mr. Mitchell. He brought you to me this morning so we could speak of this matter, and he chose you to serve as his minister on that jury."

"His minister?"

"Yes, the magistrate is a minister of God for good to the upright and a terror to those who do evil. It's the duty of the magistrate to bear the sword 'to execute wrath upon him that doeth evil.' Those are God's words, not mine."

"But I'm a sinner," Stanley said. "How can I judge another and even sentence him to death?"

"It's good that you should tremble so, Mr. Mitchell." Sheppard spoke softly, but there was no mistaking the firmness of his words. "It's a heavy burden. You feel its weight. A man's life must never be taken easily; even the worst criminal bears something of God's image. But your power to judge doesn't rest in yourself; it rests in God. Let him bear you up, and remember that you are God's minister to this entire prison, for good to the good, and for terror to the wicked."

146

Stanley bowed his head. "Those two men who died yesterday—I feel responsible. That wasn't our intent."

"Were the Regulators told how to conduct themselves?"

"Yes, it was our stipulation to the court that they were to punish, not kill."

"Then the jury did its work fairly, the Regulators did not." Sheppard stepped a little closer and raised his hand to Stanley's shoulder. "Your sorrow for those killed is commendable, Mr. Mitchell. It shows your desire to be merciful. And the service you rendered the man who wronged you? Only God could have softened your heart in such a way. No, you are not to blame for the overzealous blows of the Regulators. Sergeant Key should address that matter with his men. Please, set your mind at ease."

Sheppard was an ordinary looking man with soft gray eyes, an engaging smile, and a gentle manner of speaking. It was hard to imagine this was the same man who had burned defiance at the Raiders. "Thank you, Mr. Sheppard."

"Please come by anytime and let's speak this evening at meeting. Now, we must take a moment for prayer. Then return to the South Gate, Mr. Mitchell, and finish your work as God's minister for justice."

CHAPTER 29

Saturday, July 9, 1864

A TRAIN WHISTLE SOUNDED OVER NEAR THE DEPOT. EVERY head turned toward the sound. A gang of slaves was already waiting along the siding, ready to empty the cars of cargo and cart it away to the storehouses. But only a very few of the thousands of turned heads remained fixed upon the depot. Those few who still looked, did so wistfully, longingly, seeking some small sign of deliverance, perhaps thinking the empty cars would soon be loaded with prisoners and sent north.

But no train cars had arrived at the depot on Thursday, the promised day of exchange, and no long lines of hopeful prisoners had marched out of the stockade to fill those cars. The prisoner exchange had been canceled—by the Federal authorities, according to the Rebel authorities. Instead, Stanley had spent the day within the confines of the South Gate again, the third day of trials, the day the six accused murderers were tried.

Stanley's walking stick felt comfortable in his hand now. Hours of rubbing it against the same stone Austin had used to hone the chisel edge on the wood rasp had shaped the jagged stub of the horse-head carving into a smooth round knob. Several times wisps of smoke had curled up toward his face, forcing him to stop lest it catch fire. But the blackening of the knob had, in his mind, only improved the walking stick, for he had burned away every trace of Jack's defilement.

It was dreadfully hot. His pace was slow as he labored up the slope toward the South Gate, but he would not—could not—remove his frock coat, except when he washed, and then only in the presence of one or more of his Christian brothers.

• • •

Collins had stood haughty and defiant, wearing Stanley's coat, as he faced the thirteen men of the jury. His trial had been the last of the six, and the evidence against him had been most damning. Limber Jim had testified that Collins had killed Jim's own brother. And beneath the bed in which Collins slept each night, a skeleton had been unearthed. Collins had refused to name the dead man, even after the prosecutor pleaded with him to do so, for the comfort of the man's family.

As a pair of guards prodded the chief Raider toward the outer wicket door, Stanley had demanded the return of his coat.

Collins had turned and sneered. "You cripple, I look far better in it than you ever could." Then he had shrugged and shucked off the coat. "Here, take it, but when I'm turned back in, I'll be looking to get my stripes back."

Stanley had recused himself when the jury began to deliberate the case against Collins. The members of the jury saw the return of Stanley's coat as an obvious ploy to soften their judgment of Collins, but it served only to harden their opinions of him. The vote to convict was unanimous.

• • •

His business at the South Gate had concluded the previous afternoon with the sentencing of Collins, so Stanley continued along the path that paralleled the deadline south of the gate. On Tuesday, he had observed the swift and brutal punishment of the ninety-six thieves

149

as they ran the gauntlet. Now, he felt compelled to witness the slow, agonizing torments being meted out on the men of violence who had grievously injured fellow prisoners.

The portion of the prison south of the valley of the swamp rose in a gradual incline, making the southwest corner of the stockade visible from anywhere in the prison, except for the low ground around the swamp. It was in that corner, between the deadline and the stockade wall, that the twenty-seven convicts were exposed day and night, both to the elements and to view, as they suffered various agonies for their crimes.

Twelve men in two lines of six sat or lay upon the ground close beside each other. Each man's ankles had been shackled and then chained to the man next to him. The last man in line was chained to a large iron ball. Each of the twelve had stabbed his victim, inflicting serious injury. Stanley tried to recall the names of the chained men, but only Lehmann, the German, came to mind.

Only a day of their sentence had passed, but already the ankles of each man were swollen, chafed, and bloody. Some of the jurors had argued for a sentence of thirty days, but Stanley had pleaded for mercy.

"Gentlemen," he had said, "I myself have been chained much as these men shall be. The bite of the iron on my flesh will always be a painful memory, the price of loving a girl an evil man thought I shouldn't. I know the pain these men will endure, and there is no doubt each has earned his punishment, but thirty days will be a death sentence to many of them."

The jurors had finally agreed to temper justice with mercy and a sentence of seven long, baking days under the Georgian summer sun was imposed. The convicts would receive water and diluted vinegar to drink, and rations of whatever the Rebel authorities wished to give them. And if any man had to get up and go to the latrine, the rest had to get up and shuffle along with him, dragging the ball all the way across the prison, and stand by while the man allowed nature to run its course.

A little farther up the path was what appeared to be two small gallows, thick beams supported at both ends by stout timbers. Eight men had used iron knuckles, or clubs with spikes in them to beat their victims senseless. The eight were sentenced to hang by the thumbs, four per gallows, also for seven days. The thumbs of each man were tied together. A rope was passed under his conjoined thumbs and thrown over the beam. Then the man was drawn up until his toes were lifted clear of the ground. Once per day, each man was given a short respite for water and rations, and an escorted visit to the latrine.

Whereas the men of the chain gang had been mostly silent when Stanley passed by, these kept up a constant discourse filled with curses hurled at each other, the Rebels, the Regulators, Sergeant Key, Abe Lincoln, General Grant, the Federal government, and God most of all. Stanley pulled the brim of his hat down low and moved on, lest he be recognized, and provide them a new target for their curses.

Seven convicts remained, all judged guilty of using clubs or their bare fists to pummel other prisoners into submission. These were sentenced to be bucked and gagged for ten days. At first glance, it appeared the men were sitting on the ground in a circle, as if they had gathered close around a campfire for warmth and a friendly chat. But each man's wrists were manacled to a stout stick that had been placed under his bent knees. He was also gagged with a small stick that was tied behind his head, in appearance much like a horse's bit. In this position, it was impossible for the man to speak or move, except to wriggle from side to side a little at a time.

Stanley turned around and walked back past the men hanging by their thumbs and the chain gangs. None of them had expressed any regard for their victims. The punishments they now endured were indeed brutal, but they were also fair. Some Raiders were still at large within the prison, but these, at least, would not trouble anyone for a long time.

As Stanley approached the South Gate, the heavy doors swung open. Stanley retreated a few steps. The guards tended to get a little jumpy whenever the gate was open.

A squad of a dozen guards marched in through the gate. Then the familiar ration wagon rolled inside. Several black laborers followed the wagon until it stopped a short distance up Main Street. The wagon contained a load of lumber, posts and beams and planks.

The guards unshouldered their rifles and moved through the mass of slovenly dwellings down the incline to a point about half way between Main Street and the swamp. "Make way, clear out," the guards yelled, as they drove dozens of hapless prisoners out of their shebangs, enforcing the order with the points of their bayonets.

The slaves emptied the wagon and stacked the lumber neatly in the cleared space.

"Leave that wood be," the sergeant of the guard shouted loud enough for all around to hear. "Don't none of you mess with it."

Then the guards, the wagon, and the slaves left the prison.

"What's Wirz up to now?" someone asked.

"I bet it's another sutler shack," another said.

"Maybe he's finally building them barracks he keeps promising." This brought hoots of laughter from the prisoners.

Stanley knew exactly what the lumber was for. Gallows would be built, not like the little ones up in the corner where eight men were hanging by their thumbs. This one would be much stronger and larger, a real gallows with space enough to hang six men by the neck until dead—all at once—in two days' time.

CHAPTER 30

Monday, July 11, 1864

ROLL CALL CAME EARLY, SHORTLY AFTER EIGHT O'CLOCK, and it was done in less than two hours. Under blistering hot sun the ten companies of Regulators assembled along Broadway. Two companies under the command of Sergeants McElroy and Case marched across the bridge over the swamp and took up positions near the South Gate.

Within a few minutes the gate opened. The ration wagon entered carrying a second load of lumber for the gallows. The first load had vanished sometime Saturday night. Captain Wirz had breathed fiery threats and his guards had spent much of Sunday searching throughout the length and breadth of the camp, but no trace of that lumber was ever found.

The wagon rolled down Main Street, just as Stanley had seen the wagon do two days before, although now it was surrounded by Regulators. It stopped at the same place. A large space was cleared of prisoners and shebangs. Slaves unloaded and stacked the lumber in a neat pile.

"Key says we're on alert until this business is done," Stew told his company. He pointed across the swamp. "McElroy's in charge of security. If there's any trouble, Key wants everybody over there to set a perimeter. Be ready to go anytime."

Austin nudged Stanley. "This will be my last day as a Regulator."

"Really, Ogre?"

"I told Stew before roll call."

"But there's still much to do," Stanley said. "The punishments we handed out cured many of them, but some didn't seem to mind it so much. And dozens of Raiders were never arrested."

"I'm more of a spy than a brawler," Austin said. "Keep my eyes and ears open for sure, but don't want to be a policeman."

Sergeant Key had been busy organizing the Regulators into a permanent police force, even as the trials of the Raiders were being conducted. Five hundred men now patrolled the camp constantly, looking and acting like ordinary prisoners, but ready at any moment to spring into action whenever a cry of alarm was raised.

"My duty as a juror ends today," Stanley said. "Tomorrow, I'll be sworn in as a policeman. I was looking forward to walking a beat with you."

Across the swamp a squad of carpenters began to lay out the framing for the gallows. A crowd began to gather—everyone knew of the impending executions—and soon the hundred Regulators were all but surrounded.

A high piercing whistle sounded—Limber Jim again. The assembled companies of Regulators rushed to the aid of their brothers. And as he had done the day of the fight, Stanley hobbled along behind as fast as he dared, with Austin at his side.

Key drove his column of Regulators straight through the crowd for the gallows. The Regulators pushed the crowd back, creating an open space, a three-sided square, with the place of execution forming the fourth side.

"Regulation execution formation," Austin said, as they fell into line with Stew's company facing the mob of prisoners.

"You'll never hang them," some shouted.

"Oh, they'll hang," others shouted back, "and good riddance."

Back and forth the yelling went, but no one tested the lines of shoulder-to-shoulder Regulators.

As each nail was hammered home, the crowd swelled. The platform was completed and soon the heavy cross member was lifted into place atop stout timbers at each end of the platform. Thick rope was cut, six nooses were tied and slung over the cross member. A short ladder was made for climbing up to the raised platform.

Shortly after midday a drum roll sounded outside the stockade. Hundreds of people, perhaps a thousand or more, had gathered on the hillside near the large fort—guards, officers, and private citizens, with a number of women in gay dresses holding handkerchiefs to their noses, no doubt perfumed against the stench—where they could look over the stockade to view the hangings. Off to the side, barely visible near the tree line, stood a few Negroes.

The gate opened. Captain Wirz entered first, riding his light gray horse.

"'And I looked, and behold a pale horse,'" Austin said, "'and his name that sat on him was Death, and Hell followed with him.'"

"What's that?" Stanley asked.

"Revelation, my friend, chapter six. Death on a pale horse. I'm surprised you haven't heard Wirz called that before now. Everyone does."

A pair of drummers followed Wirz into the stockade. Then the six condemned men, hands tied behind their backs and surrounded by a squad of guards, came single file through the gate—Collins first, followed by Delaney, Sarsfield, Munn, Rickson, and Curtiss. Finally, a priest entered several yards behind Curtiss, walking head down, reading from what appeared to be a prayer book.

The six men had been tried separately. In spite of the testimony of numerous witnesses against them, none had admitted any guilt; none had professed any regret or sorrow. Instead, each man had proclaimed his innocence and had remained defiant, even as they were sentenced to death. Collins had looked down the line of jurors until his fierce eyes settled on Stanley. "The Johnny Rebs will never let you hang your own men," he had shouted.

When the procession reached the gallows, Wirz drew his horse to a halt and raised his arm, silencing the drummers. Then he addressed the crowd. "Prisoners, I return dose men as good as I got dem. You have tried dem and found dem guilty. I had nothing to do wid it and I wash my hands."

"Just like Pontius Pilate," Austin muttered.

"Do what you like wid dem. May God have mercy on you and dem."

"Odd, that devil mentioning God," Austin said.

About thirty of Key's strongest men stepped forward and took charge of the six Raiders. Then the drummers struck up their cadence again until Wirz and his guards left the stockade.

The line of Regulators parted and the six were prodded through into the interior of the square. Each of the condemned now looked drawn and pale. Every trace of the arrogant defiance Stanley had seen only three days before had been wiped away, replaced with wide, tortured eyes that told Stanley each of the six murderers now knew this was no game.

"Key, do you really mean to hang us?" It was Collins, still trying to play the leader, but his voice broke with terror.

Sergeant Key's reply was firm and steady. "That's about the size of it."

Murmurs rippled through the crowd until Key raised his hand for silence. "Father Whelan wishes to speak."

156

Father Whelan stood between the six Raiders and the gallows. With impassioned pleas, he spoke on behalf of the condemned. He implored the crowd to show compassion and mercy, and to forgive rather than seek vengeance. For a time, out of polite respect for the priest, the crowd listened in silence, but as the minutes passed, the crowd grew restless.

"No! Hang them! Hang them all!" one man cried out.

A dozen more took up the chant, "Hang them. Hang them. Hang them all." Hundreds more joined in. Then the chant swept across the swamp through the many thousands gathered on the slope north of the swamp to view the spectacle. "Hang them! Hang them! Hang them all!"

Charles Curtis was shorter than most men, but built like a blockhouse. While most of the Regulators' attention was either on Father Whelan or the chanting mob, Curtiss rushed headlong into the line of Regulators directly across the square from Stanley. Clubs were raised to stop Curtiss, but to no avail. He simply lowered his head between his shoulders and butted his way through.

Once free of the Regulators, Curtiss ran through the crowd straight downhill toward the swamp and plunged in. Within seconds he was halfway across, but then his progress slowed.

Stanley started to shake with silent, nervous laughter.

Austin elbowed him. "Soon be six dead men at the end of those ropes."

"I know," Stanley whispered, "but this is a farce. What kind of escape plan is that—jump in the swamp with your hands tied behind your back? What if he sinks out of sight in that muck? Should he be left to die? Or should he be brought back and hanged anyway? It's like half Aristophanes and half Euripides. You know, a comedic tragedy."

157

Austin nodded slowly. "So you studied the Greek masters back in Ohio. No wonder General Logan took a shine to you." He pointed across at the line of Regulators that Curtiss had breached. "There's your answer. That's McElroy's company, and he looks hot as blazes. Just sent two of his best to fetch that man back. Now *that* is hazardous duty."

Austin was right. Stanley fought within himself to maintain an air of dignified solemnity, but it was indeed an odd scene. Old Father Whelan continued to stand between the condemned men and the gallows, head down, reading again. The five remaining Raiders also stood with lowered heads, unmoving, surrounded by Limber Jim and a dozen other Regulators ready to club them down if they tried anything. And there was absolutely nothing for Stanley, or Austin, or anyone else to do except watch and wait upon what developed down in the swamp.

Sergeant Key had evidently foreseen the possibility of an escape attempt for he had stationed Regulators at the north end of both bridges across the swamp. As soon as Curtiss plunged into the swamp, these men raced to keep him from making good his escape. But they need not have hurried.

Stanley knew the place well; men frequently had to be rescued from the deadly clutches of its pestilence-ridden, maggot-infested, knee-deep mire. Curtiss strained foot by foot toward the north side of the swamp. Then he stopped altogether and twisted this way and that, trying to free himself from the swamp's iron grip.

Four of the Regulators started into the swamp from the north side. They drew close to Curtiss. It was obvious the man was exhausted. He had no fight in him, but the Regulators clubbed him several times anyway. The four Regulators dragged Curtiss out of the swamp. Then they picked him up, carried him across the west bridge, up the hill, and through the waiting crowd, where they threw the panting, bleeding Curtiss to the ground next to the other condemned men.

"Let us proceed," Key said. "Climb up on the scaffold, or be carried up, makes no difference to me."

The six men obeyed while Father Whelan kept reading. It was quiet now. The priest's words were faint. It had been more than two years since Stanley had conversed in Latin, but he tried to make sense of the words.

"What's the priest reading?" Austin asked in a whisper.

"I think he's reading a prayer, a prayer for those about to die."

The six Raiders now stood side by side on the platform in the same order they had marched into the stockade, with Collins to the right and Curtiss to the left.

Key took out his pocket watch. "If you wish to say anything, say it now. You have two minutes."

Some of the condemned called out farewells to friends in the crowd. Others singled out one or two men as designated heirs of their stolen wealth. Only one man spoke a word of apology, and another claimed he would rather be hanged than suffer death by starvation. But not one of them cried out like the penitent thief upon the cross beside the Lord Jesus. Not one of them bowed his head in prayer, "Lord, be merciful to me, a sinner."

Key pocketed his watch. "Enough," he shouted. "Get on with it."

Six hangmen prodded the six Raiders onto a wide plank supported from below with two thick posts. Each hangman pulled a cloth corn meal sack over his man's head. A noose was placed around the man's neck and drawn tight. The six hangmen then jumped down to the ground behind the gallows.

Key raised his hand high. Father Whelan raised his voice in prayer. Key gave the signal. Two strong men stationed at opposite ends of the long, wide plank heaved at ropes attached to the support posts. The plank dropped.

The six Raiders dropped. Five stopped with a jerk, and remained swinging and kicking in the air. The rope of the sixth man broke. Collins fell to the ground in a heap.

Collins was dazed, but not dead. The noose and the meal sack were removed. "Where am I?" His voice was hoarse from the sudden throttling.

Limber Jim stepped forward and started working on the gallows. He replaced the posts under where Collins had been hung and topped them with a short piece of planking. Then he cut a length of new rope and tied the noose himself.

"Surely, you don't mean to hang me again," Collins cried out. "It was God that spared me. Mercy, that's what it is, God's mercy."

Limber Jim didn't say a word. Instead, he pulled Collins to his feet, threw the big, blubbering man over his shoulder, and carried him back to the gallows, where Jim and one of the hangmen hoisted Collins up onto the plank.

The meal sack was replaced; the new noose was tightened. Then Limber Jim jumped off the scaffold and kicked the supports out. This time the rope did not break and the infamous "Mosby" joined his fellow murderers in death.

Sergeant Key ordered the crowd to remain. Then he ordered the Regulators to form two parallel lines. The dead men were cut down, the meal sacks removed, and their bodies were laid out between the lines of Regulators. Then the crowd of prisoners passed through in silence to view the bodies. It was likely that only a few of them had ever witnessed a military execution, but every man knew the significance of this ritual and the graphic message it declared. *The same shall be done to you, if you do as these have done.*

CHAPTER 31

Saturday, July 16, 1864

STANLEY STABBED AT THE GROUND WITH HIS KNIFE. AT FIVE dollars Federal, it had been an expensive, though necessary purchase. Austin's sharpened spoon handle was still serviceable for small jobs, like chopping an onion for soup, but for more demanding work, like digging for roots, or splitting fire kindling, a long, thick blade was much more desirable. But best of all, the knife had belonged to one of the Raiders, who, when forced to cease his thievery, had discovered that selling off his few earthly possessions might be his only hope of survival.

Stanley removed his hat and wiped a hand across his brow. Nothing. Not a trace of sweat. His mouth had grown dustier each day since the fight two weeks ago. The head ache had started Wednesday or Thursday.

Water. Since the hangings, it was almost all he thought about. Water and exponents, something he remembered of the mathematics he had learned at the Portsmouth School for Boys beside the broad cold waters of the Ohio River. The well behind the Matthews house after a long day of work—how thirsty had he been as he drew that bucket of clear water up from the darkness? And how many times greater was his thirst now? How much greater his misery? Ten times? A hundred? More? Surely some exponent must apply.

"How many yesterday?" Stanley asked.

"Sixty-nine." It was part of Austin's daily routine to inquire at the South Gate the count of the dead.

"And the day before?"

"I told you, sixty-six," Austin said, shaking his head.

"Could be eighteen hundred for the month. Hard to believe it's been ten days since I helped carry Jack over there. Now, three minutes with the knife trying to dig up that last root and I'm done in. We have to find more water, Austin."

"When it rains, we'll fill the soup kettle," Austin said.

"And I'll be sure to turn up my hat," Stanley said, "but we haven't had a shower in a week. Mr. Sheppard's been praying for rain all along. We have too, and a lot of other people, but all it's been is stinking hot and dry. The stream is half what it was two weeks ago."

Austin stopped his whittling and looked at Stanley. "Did you see Pickens at roll call this morning?"

"I did. Looks a little stronger every day."

"And taller," Austin said. "Another two weeks and he should be walking as straight as any of us. I feel better too. My knees don't ache and my teeth are healing."

"And your left cheek almost matches your right," Stanley added. "I see what you did there, Ogre. You made me think about something good."

"Hmmm. That's your doing, Mitch. And that second blanket over our heads, and the extra canteen hanging from that pole. Stew said Taft and Churchill wanted you to have them."

The additional blanket had allowed Stew and Stanley to bridge the gap between their roof and Austin's, so that during the day the two shebangs were made into a single dwelling.

"But they died, Austin, and within a day of each other."

"True," Austin said. Then, with a nod toward Dell who lay sleeping in the rear, he added in a low whisper, "And soon, he will too."

162

"So?"

"So what, Mitch?"

"So, where are we going to get water to cook soup and today's rations?"

The first two weeks of the month they had received cooked corn mush for rations, with bits of meat and a few beans thrown in. "Chowder," Austin had called it, as he stirred his steaming pot. Stanley hadn't laughed. But on Friday, it was back to raw rations, a pint of meal per man, with exactly twenty hard beans and three ounces of rancid bacon—doubled, of course, with Stanley's extra police ration—and there was no water to cook with.

"Not like it was a month ago," Austin said. "Wirz sent in a load of picks and shovels for digging wells and that helped a lot. Then some of the prisoners started escape tunnels and Wirz found out about it. He took back all his tools and now, most of the wells have been filled in."

"Traitors," Stanley said. "I've seen several fellows with a freshly tattooed *T* on their foreheads."

"They're just the ones the tunnel diggers found out about."

"What about Stew's friend with the well?" Stanley asked.

Austin shook his head. "Mason's is only thirty feet deep. It's nearly dried up."

"Then it's the swamp or nothing?"

"There is a new well up near the northeast corner," Austin said, "over twice as deep as Mason's. Owned by a man named Weatherly and a couple of others. Water's good, they say, enough for a thousand men or more."

"Why were they allowed to dig a well?"

"Seems they made some sort of deal with Wirz, like they're the official prison water authority."

"Wirz again. What will it cost?" Stanley asked.

"Fifty cents to fill a canteen. We need three or four a day for the soup kettle."

Stanley plunged his knife into the ground. "Those fellows will get rich while others go insane from thirst. That's fourteen dollars a week for us. If we buy nothing else, we can make it two more months, maybe three."

"Longer than that, Mitch, if we keep selling most of the soup." Austin finished with the onion and started cutting into the large head of cabbage. "I know what you said about giving more away, but—"

"What I said, Ogre, was that I didn't care if I left here penniless, as long as my Abrahams allowed more men the chance to survive."

"Come on, Mitch. I know you can do the arithmetic. It's three dollars per kettle now. How many more days until there is no more soup?"

"Forty, give or take."

"All I'm saying is that we have to recover at least some of our expenses, or by the end of August your Abrahams will be gone and we'll be out of business."

Austin was right. It was easier to give away the soup, easier on his own conscience anyway. No one could ever accuse him of profiting from his fellow prisoners in their time of distress. "Maybe the police can do something," Stanley said.

"Like what? Seize the well?"

"I don't know, Ogre, but Sergeant Hill is now the judge. Maybe he can rule that the well is public property, and have Chief Mahaney enforce it."

Austin didn't look up from his cutting. "You'll start another war. Keep praying, Mitch, and trust God to provide our needs."

Stanley picked at the hard earth for a few minutes. Only a week's kindling remained from what they had split from the old stockade timber, and only one tree root remained within what Austin now called their estate. It was Stanley's job to dig it up for the cooking fire, but the root refused to budge.

"Do you think Key is all right?" Stanley asked. The day after the hangings, Wirz's guards had escorted Sergeant Key and several other top Regulators from the prison because of threats to their lives.

"Safe enough for now, I suppose," Austin said. "Got himself put in the cookhouse. Work isn't pleasant, but better than a knife between the ribs."

"He could have taken care of himself," Stanley said, "and he would know what to do about that well."

"It's property rights, Mitch, and I don't think Key or anybody else can do anything about it."

Stanley looked up at Austin. "Then we have to buy water again. Do you need another Abraham?"

Austin nodded.

Stanley looked warily around, then bent over his suspender. He removed another ten-dollar greenback and gave it to Austin. "That's number three."

Stanley attacked the stubborn root with renewed vigor—for a few minutes. "So," he said, laboring to catch his breath, "between us we have four canteens. How many do we really need?"

Austin stood and reached into his pocket. He counted out some coins, proceeds from his soup sales, and handed the coins to Stanley. "Two dollars for a trip to the well with all four canteens. Enough water for cooking, making soup, and maybe a little for red root tea until I can get your Abraham exchanged."

"Something I have to attend to," Austin said as he started to leave the shebang.

"Where are you going, Ogre?"

Austin looked past Stanley toward Dell who still lay in the rear of the shebang. "Something I should have done days ago." He touched Stanley's arm. "Mitch, I know you're out of sorts from that headache, but you got a good heart, looking out for Pickens, taking some of your extra rations to Mr. Sheppard. But look after yourself too. When I come back, I'll build a fire and boil that water you're fetching. Then you, my friend, are going to drink tea, or soup, or just plain hot water. And not just half a can like I've seen— two or three, maybe more."

"Thanks, Ogre, but if this headache doesn't let up—"

"It will," Austin interrupted. "Don't give up." He pointed at Dell. "Stay active, or you'll end up like him."

Austin was right again. Dell was indeed in a bad way, and it shamed Stanley that he had hardly noticed how quickly Dell was sinking away. The rains of June had given way to July's scorching heat, and for the last three days, Stanley had given into the desire to lie under the shade of the shebang and nap the day away, much as Rodgers and the triplets had done near the end.

I am becoming like them. It is so easy to surrender, to give up. But I cannot. I must not, for I would be giving up on Anna too.

CHAPTER 32

ABOUT MID-AFTERNOON, CLOUDS BEGAN TO ROIL UP FROM the south. The break from the beating sun and the prospect of a shower brought many of the prisoners out from the shelter of their shebangs in hopes of washing off a layer or two of accumulated filth.

Stanley paid Weatherly, the owner of the well, the money Austin had given him. Then he hefted the four filled canteens to his shoulder, walked across nearly the entire width of the prison back to their shebangs, and laid the canteens in the shade.

Stanley eyed the full canteens. *Just a quick drink, a sip or two to sooth my throat. That's all. Maybe it will lessen this headache.* He reached for the nearest canteen, but stopped himself. Austin's words had been etched upon Stanley's consciousness, indelible as a traitor's tattoo. *Never drink anything that hasn't been boiled.*

A few minutes later, Austin ducked his head under the blanket roof. "I brought Mr. Sheppard to see Dell."

Mr. Sheppard stooped and squeezed his way into the shebang.

"Dell," Austin said, "someone's here to see you. He's the leader of our evening meetings, Mr. Sheppard. Sit up for a few minutes and speak with him, or just listen." Austin helped Dell rise from the shadows. Then he sat next to Dell on his rubber blanket to help keep him upright.

Mr. Sheppard knelt before Dell. "Good afternoon, Mr. Dell."

Dell raised his eyes toward Sheppard. "Just Dell. Name's Robert...James."

"I'm sorry, Mr. James, I didn't know. Your friend, Mr. Oglethorpe, asked me to stop by."

Dell snorted with frustration. "Just Dell then, Parson."

"All right, Dell. How did you get that name?

"From Wisconsin, a town nobody knows...Kilbourn City...near the dells on the river."

"Oh, I see now. Dell it is. May I read from the Psalms for you?"

"You may, Parson...won't do no good." Dell's voice was raspy and frail. He had also lost a few teeth, and when he spoke, air whistled faintly through the gaps along with wisps of bloody spittle.

"Why is that?" Mr. Sheppard asked.

Dell pursed his cracked lips and eyed Mr. Sheppard. "You say it's the word of God—I'm supposed to fall down trembling. Men wrote them things. Men printed it. It's man's words like any other book."

Mr. Sheppard chuckled. "Seeing the state you're in, I don't think you'll be falling very far, but I won't stop you from trembling. Tell me, given your obvious hatred for the Bible, why would you allow me to read from it?"

"Pass the time, I suppose," Dell said, "and let you think you done your duty. I don't see any call for it."

"I see," Mr. Sheppard said. "Have you ever prayed, Dell?"

"Sure, as a child, then I got smart. Couldn't see what good it did me, so I quit. Ain't prayed since."

Mr. Sheppard nodded. A faint smile creased his face. "Who did you pray to when you were a child?"

"My father said God, but I never got no reply. I knew then there's no God. Nothing's changed my mind since. See what's going on here?" He tried to raise his arm as if to sweep it in a broad arc, but it fell limp at his side.

"Misery. That's all I see. I've had a terrible go of it. You think God is good. Tell me, what good is here? Death is better. I won't see or feel any of this. No, that book you think is holy—it's a damned lie, making people think they'll be all happy in the end."

"May I tell you about the Christian gospel?" Sheppard asked.

"Heard it before. It's all a lie too. Seen lots of dead men, dying by the hundreds in here, but none got alive again. No, sir. I don't see it."

"And does your wife think the same?"

"Oh no." Dell's bleary eyes burned at Sheppard. "She's got religion through and through...always reading that Bible and singing and going to meeting, or visiting somebody's Aunt Myrtle. She even prayed for me getting religion too."

Stanley saw much of himself in Dell—the way he used to be before he was changed. *There but for the grace of God go I—and the help of brothers like Austin, Stew, and Frank.* "If I may, Dell."

Dell turned his gaze upon Stanley, as if seeing him for the first time, even though Stanley had lived in the next shebang for almost two weeks.

Stanley lowered himself to one knee beside Dell and Mr. Sheppard. "You sound very angry. Might I ask, with what or with whom?"

"Of course, I'm angry, with the Rebels, with the army. Abe Lincoln too. And I suppose with me for getting caught by them Johnny Rebs."

"And God too, perhaps?"

Dell's expression soured further. He offered no reply.

"I was terribly wounded at Shiloh, Dell. I was shot and started for the rear. But then a mule kicked me and broke my leg above the knee. I was left on the battlefield helpless, bleeding, in terrible pain."

169

Dell had closed his eyes, but still appeared awake, listening, still supported by Austin.

"I was angry just as you are now," Stanley said, his voice wavering a little. "I cursed God for my miserable life and the miserable death I was soon to face. It started to grow dark. I knew I could not last the night. As a final, desperate act, I cried out again and again, 'Lord, save me.' I'm only here now because he heard and he saved me."

Dell opened his eyes. "For what? All this misery? I know what you're doing. You think I'll do what you did, but I can't—I won't."

"Why not, Dell?" Stanley asked.

"Because it's been a lie all my life." Dell coughed deep and wracking several times. "I know what truth is," he said, still coughing as he tried to speak, "and that ain't it. It would be a farce. I would be a hypocrite, and I ain't one. Nobody can ever say that about me."

"How can you hate the only God who can save you?" Sheppard asked. "Have you no fear of the one who holds your life by a thread? What if God is truly who he reveals himself to be and the Bible truly is his word? Have you no dread of the terror that awaits you, Dell?"

Dell closed his eyes again and lay back. "I'll know soon enough, and if I'm wrong, then I guess my misery will continue. Could it be worse than this? Your talk wearies me. Skip the reading, Parson."

• • •

After Mr. Sheppard left, Austin kindled a fire and set the kettle over it to heat the water.

Dell struggled to his feet. He picked up his walking staff, and without a word to Austin or Stanley, teetered off in the general direction of the North Gate.

Austin shook his head. "Where's he going now? Latrine's the opposite direction."

"It's another hour until rations," Stanley said. "He'll be back then for sure."

170

"Yes, probably." But something in Austin's tone wasn't convincing.

"Is there anything else we can do for him?" Stanley asked.

"I've tried, Mitch, you know I have. Comes a point when no more can be done, since the man won't lift a hand for himself. Food—I've offered it every morning and evening. Tea he takes from time to time to keep the scurvy down. But you heard him, Mitch. Dell has no God, no light in his soul, no hope in the hereafter, only his own despair here and now. It must be utter torture, so he's starving himself to death—that's the way I see it—to bring an end to his misery."

"I've never seen anything like it, Ogre."

"This prison, Mitch, it's a gauntlet—we're being pounded from every side. The constant beating changes every one of us. I'm powerless to stop it; so are you."

Austin looked down at the water in the kettle. A thin wisp of steam rose and was quickly carried away. "Making soup and tea is simple. Anybody can do it, but it's like God's called me to do it. I'm doing something useful. For me, there's purpose in all this unpleasantness, but for Dell, it's all just bad luck. Only he can change his luck for the better, and right now, he knows he's done in and empty."

Stanley sat quiet, watching the steam rise from the kettle. *Ogre's right. Dell is done in. Am I?* But Stanley felt better than he had for hours; his headache had diminished by half, at least. And he didn't feel quite as thirsty or as hungry as he had before. Stanley mused upon the possible cause of this welcome relief until he realized that, while Mr. Sheppard had been speaking with Dell, Stanley's attention had been entirely fixed upon Dell and not on his own discomforts.

About ten minutes later, the soup began to boil. "It's just about ready," Austin said.

Stew walked up the path, knelt beside the shebang, and peered in at Austin and Stanley. "Did you boys hear that shot a few minutes ago?"

Both men shook their heads no.

"Sergeant Beckwith said it's one of ours. Some fellow came running over from the South Gate where it happened. From his description, it sounds like Dell."

Austin set off at a run.

"Soup is done, Stew," Stanley said. "It can come off the fire." Then he hurried along after Austin as best he could. It was a long, long walk along the deadline from the northwest corner where the camp of the Fifty-fifth Detachment was, to the South Gate.

Stanley found Austin standing about fifty feet below the gate on the path that led up from the swamp. Dell lay face down about a dozen feet away, just inside the deadline, with an ugly, bloody hole in the middle of his back.

Tears streamed down Austin's face. "They said he was calm as you please. Told everyone around he was from the Fifty-fifth. Just stepped under the deadline and stood looking up at the guard. One shot in the chest. He killed himself, Mitch, and it's my fault."

Stanley put his arm around Austin's narrow shoulders. "No, Ogre. This was his doing."

"I pushed him to it. I never should have asked Mr. Sheppard to talk to him. He said Dell hated God."

"Ogre," Stanley said, "you did the last good thing you could ever have done for Dell. You gave him one last opportunity for salvation. You did right and Sheppard did right and Dell threw it all away."

Stanley took a step toward the deadline and looked up at the guard in the sentry box. "Sir, would you permit us to claim the body of our friend and place him with the others?" Stanley gestured toward the ever-present row of corpses near the gate.

The guard stared down at Stanley and leveled his rifle.

"Please, sir. If you wish, call other guards to aim their weapons at us. We only ask your permission to retrieve our friend's body and identify him for burial."

The guard shrugged. Then he nodded at Stanley and held up one finger.

"Just one of us? Me?"

The guard nodded.

Stanley handed his walking stick to Austin. *Lord, please keep me safe. Don't let this guard shoot me.*

Stanley bent low and stepped under the wooden railing of the deadline. Then he crept toward Dell, slow and stooped, never lifting his eyes from the dead man, uttering his silent prayer with every step.

Stanley knelt beside Dell and started to turn him over. He couldn't lift Dell. He would have to drag Dell back toward Austin, but Stanley simply couldn't leave Dell face down. Dell's eyes were half shut, unseeing, empty. Stanley stared at Dell, at death, at hopeless death, followed only by terrible, God-promised judgment.

"Get a move on."

The guard can speak. Lord, give me strength.

Stanley grabbed Dell's right ankle and tugged him inch by inch back toward the deadline. Then Austin and Stanley carried their friend up to the gate and laid him among the rest of the day's dead.

Robert James, Austin wrote on the card for the death roll, *Company B, 7th Wisconsin.*

"He did it real close to the gate," Austin said, as they turned away, "so we wouldn't have to carry him far. Known him since the train down here in May, but never knew his real name until today."

173

CHAPTER 33

STANLEY WALKED TO THE MIDDLE OF THE BRIDGE, TOOK HIS Bible from the pocket of his trousers, and turned to the page in Ezekiel Mr. Sheppard had marked. At each evening meeting, Mr. Sheppard asked several men to volunteer to read a passage of Scripture, to pray for an ailing prisoner, or to plead God's comfort for families and friends of the dead. And he asked everyone to pray for rain.

But Mr. Sheppard had something different in mind for Stanley. "Read it to the swamp every day," Mr. Sheppard had said when he assigned the text. "Proclaim these beautiful words of salvation to that dreadful place."

Stanley cleared his throat and began to read. His throat was parched and scratchy, and to his own ears, his voice sounded hoarse and lifeless.

> The hand of the LORD was upon me, and carried me out in the spirit of the LORD, and set me down in the midst of the valley which was full of bones, and caused me to pass by them round about: and, behold, there were very many in the open valley; and, lo, they were very dry. And he said unto me, Son of man, can these bones live? And I answered, O Lord GOD, thou knowest.

The stream had ceased to be a stream. The sun had baked it nearly dry. Only a slow, reeking trickle remained.

The putrid offal on either side had been baked half-hard, a temptation for some of the weakest to avoid the crowd near the bridge and attempt to crawl cross the stinking mire toward that narrow strip of life-draining water. The body of a man lay face down about fifty yards away, half-sunken into the maggot infested crust, a witness to others to stay with the many and await their turn.

> Again he said unto me, Prophesy upon these bones, and say unto them, O ye dry bones, hear the word of the LORD. Thus saith the Lord GOD unto these bones; Behold, I will cause breath to enter into you, and ye shall live: and I will lay sinews upon you, and will bring up flesh upon you, and cover you with skin, and put breath in you, and ye shall live; and ye shall know that I am the LORD. So I prophesied as I was commanded: and as I prophesied, there was a noise, and behold a shaking, and the bones came together, bone to his bone. And when I beheld, lo, the sinews and the flesh came up upon them, and the skin covered them above: but there was no breath in them.

And ye shall live; and ye shall know that I am the LORD. There were bones in the morass. He had seen them, cast up occasionally from the depths, stripped clean by the sea of maggots, bleached by the sun. It was indeed a valley of dry bones, but none of the bones came together, *bone to his bone.*

> Then said he unto me, Prophesy unto the wind, prophesy, son of man, and say to the wind, Thus saith the Lord GOD; Come from the four winds, O breath, and breathe upon these slain, that they may live. So I prophesied as he commanded me, and the breath came into them, and they lived, and stood up upon their feet, an exceeding great army. Then he said unto me, Son of man, these bones are the whole house of Israel: behold, they say, Our bones are

175

dried, and our hope is lost: we are cut off for our parts.

Stanley looked up from his reading. A small crowd had gathered in the stream and on both of its muddy, slimy banks. Washing had stopped, and the men were standing still, listening, nodding; a few even smiling.

"Yes, Lord, breathe on us," one man pleaded.

"...a great army...of skeletons," another said.

"We *are* all dried up," a weak, trembling voice added. "Are we all lost?"

Therefore prophesy and say unto them, Thus saith the Lord GOD; Behold, O my people, I will open your graves, and cause you to come up out of your graves, and bring you into the land of Israel. And ye shall know that I am the LORD, when I have opened your graves, O my people, and brought you up out of your graves, and shall put my spirit in you, and ye shall live, and I shall place you in your own land: then shall ye know that I the LORD have spoken it, and performed it, saith the LORD.

"Sheppard's right." Frank stood beside Stanley on the bridge. "It's not about bones and death, Mitch. It's about salvation."

"So, at dawn tomorrow, and the next day, and the day after, he wants me to stand here and read Ezekiel out over the swamp."

Frank nodded. "That's what he said."

"But I feel drained and my voice is pitiful. I'm becoming so weak that reading makes me short of breath."

"It sounded fine to me, Mitch, and to everyone else who was listening." Frank gestured at the small crowd. Some had resumed their washing, but many hadn't, and stood looking up at Stanley expectantly. "Remember, the power doesn't come from you, it comes from the word. It's the power of God for salvation."

"Not for Dell," Stanley said.

"No," Frank said, "but that doesn't lessen the power of God's word. Your special duty in reading it is to call every man to think about the state of his eternal soul and to seek salvation from God alone."

"Dell never figured he needed saving from anything."

"And like Dell," Frank said, "many folks deny death right up to the end." He nodded sideways at the men standing in the swamp. "But these men listened. You did well today, Mitch. Tomorrow you might follow up the reading with Psalm 23. There are no green pastures here, but the water certainly is still, and this is certainly the valley of the shadow of death. Besides, many men will know it by heart."

They turned to go. Frank caught Stanley by the arm. Frank's eyes were earnest and bright now, a testament to the benefits of Austin's soup. "Death is with us all the time here, Mitch, but I think there is much to be learned from it."

"What can I learn watching friends die?" Stanley asked. Not yet four weeks in the prison and death had become almost routine—Rodgers, Harley, Talbot, and the man murdered for his money, then Jack and the other thief, the six hanged Raiders, Taft and Churchill, and yesterday, Dell. But Stanley had learned nothing from death except that he should try his best to avoid it.

"Let me come at this from a different angle," Frank said. "What did you learn about life from Ezekiel?"

It was a good question. Stanley looked at the hundreds of men clamoring for a place to wash in the cleaner water near the bridge, and he thought about the half-sunken skeleton now screened from his sight. "God gives us life."

"Yes," Frank said.

"The wind gave the bodies breath, but they weren't truly living until God sent his spirit into them."

Frank smiled. "Exactly. So, what about Dell?"

177

"Dell believed his life was his own to do with as he wished. His life wasn't a precious gift from God, and when it got too hard for him, he threw it away."

"Mitch, the story of your life moved me greatly," Frank said, "and I've thought a lot about you since. I certainly hope, my friend—my brother—that you understand how precious you are in God's sight, in life now, and in death, whenever it comes upon you."

Stanley looked down at his bare feet. They were dark now by constant exposure to both earth and sun, and tough and leathery, just as Stew had said they would be. "I get it, Frank. A precious life and a precious death. That's why Talbot's face seemed so—so alive, even as he lay dying."

Frank grinned his broad Frank Griffin grin. "You really do get it, Mitch. So, did you learn anything else from Josiah Talbot?"

Stanley paused. His wandering gaze settled on Frank's hazel eyes. "Josiah Talbot taught me how to die."

CHAPTER 34

Thursday, July 21, 1864

HE ENVELOPE SLID FROM ANNA'S FINGERS AND FELL TO THE wooden planking of the veranda. "I can't open it, Mama."

Mama gathered her daughter in her arms and began to rock her, just as she had countless times when Anna was a child. "You know you must, my dear."

Anna sniffled. "But it's not his hand. It's to 'Miss Anna Matthews, near Shiloh, Tennessee,' and Stanley always writes "Matthews Hill Farm, McNairy County.' It's bad news. I know it is, or why wouldn't he have written for himself?"

Mama stopped her rocking. "Shall I read it for you?"

"Yes, Mama, so I can cry and cry my heart out."

Mama released Anna from her embrace. "Pick it up, dear."

Mama looked at the envelope. "Hmm. No sender's address, but there are four postal stamps—Chattanooga, July 9th, Nashville, July 12th, Paducah, July 17th, and Pittsburg Landing, yesterday. Not the usual route through Memphis and Purdy."

"*Please*, Mama, get on with it."

Mama opened the envelope and looked for the signature on the last page. "It's from that general Stanley wrote about in his last letter."

179

Anna raised her feet to the bench and hugged her knees. "Read it, Mama. Maybe I'll learn where he's buried."

Monday, July 4th, 1864
Camp of the XV Corps
Army of the Tennessee
Powder Springs, Georgia

My Dear Miss Anna Matthews,

It is my sincerest hope that this letter finds its way to the young woman for whom it is intended. A certain young man, who, I believe, is of mutual interest to us both, has gone missing.

Sergeant Stanley Mitchell was last seen on duty Sunday, June 12th, at the depot at Cartersville, just prior to dusk. This bit of unfortunate news came to me by way of my aide-de-camp, Colonel Kilpatrick. I first met young Mitchell about a year ago at Vicksburg during the siege, and became well acquainted with him when peace finally came to that city. It is I who convinced him to return to active duty, and recommended his promotion to sergeant. I, therefore, bear some responsibility for his current circumstances, whatever they may be, and feel obliged to inform you of those circumstances, to the best of my knowledge.

From our time in Vicksburg onward, I developed an abiding interest in Sergeant Mitchell's welfare, perhaps even friendship, if that is permitted of a senior commanding officer. It may be that I saw in Mitchell qualities I would have wished to see in my own son, had he lived beyond infancy.

While in Vicksburg, Mitchell told me about you and your family. When I was informed he was missing, I remembered his saying your family lived near the battlefield at Shiloh, but I could not recall your name. I inquired further of Captain Newell, Sergeant Mitchell's commanding officer, who also spoke very well of young Mitchell. In turn, Captain

180

Newell inquired of Mitchell's comrades, and a certain Private McCauley provided your name.

I also learned from Captain Newell the circumstances of Sergeant Mitchell's disappearance. On Saturday, June 11th, the construction of a crucial railroad bridge was completed. I ordered the Quartermaster Department to send all supplies and railroad equipment forward immediately to Allatoona, and to transfer the forward depot to Allatoona by the following evening.

Mitchell's detachment was the last to leave Cartersville. They were to ride their mounts the few miles to Allatoona under the protection of a company of cavalry. However, that evening, as they were about to depart, a band of Rebel irregulars came out of the woods. Most of the troopers set off in pursuit, leaving only a dozen or so men to escort Mitchell's detachment.

A second band of Rebels appeared, too many for the few cavalry troopers to fend off. Mitchell's detachment mounted quickly and dashed up the railroad toward the bridge, which was only a mile away. That was the last time any of them saw Sergeant Mitchell.

That is all I know with any certainty. I suspect Mitchell, being slow to mount because of his previous injury, was left behind and fell into the hands of the enemy. Several trains and many bodies of our troops pass through Cartersville every day, and no one has reported the discovery of the remains of a Quartermaster Sergeant. Therefore, I believe Sergeant Mitchell is now a prisoner of war.

Miss Matthews, I beg you, do not despair. From what young Mitchell told me, you and your family are people of prayer, which I am not, but perhaps ought to be. Pray to the Almighty then, if you will, for a short end to this war and deliverance for our mutual friend.

I remain your respectful and obedient servant,

John A. Logan, Major General

Anna wept quietly while Mama sat in silence.

A few minutes later Luke appeared in the doorway of the barn and made his way across the yard to the house. "Anna, what's the matter? Is it Stanley?"

Anna looked up at Luke, blinking several times to clear her vision. "He's gone, Luke. Missing, taken prisoner, maybe, or dead."

"But how?"

Mama handed Luke the letter. "Read it for yourself."

Luke's eyes brimmed with tears as he read. When he finished, he lowered the letter, knelt before his sister, and took her hands in his. "I'm sorry, Anna, I truly am. It's all my fault, all of this."

"Oh, Luke," she said. "I know you're sorry, but he's forgiven you everything. And if Stanley's still alive, he isn't blaming you for anything. He might be blaming the cavalry that ran off and left him, but not you, Luke, never you. I know that because I know his heart." She ran her hand gently through her brothers mop of dark hair. "And I think you know it too. And do you know what else I know?"

Shame and dejection pained Luke's gaze. He lowered his eyes and shook his head.

"You feel so bad because now you love him like he was your own brother."

CHAPTER 35

Saturday, July 23, 1863

THE DAY AFTER DELL WAS KILLED, STEW, AUSTIN, AND Stanley consolidated their holdings and began life as one family. Austin had inherited Dell's only possession, his rubber blanket, which Dell had never allowed to be used for any other purpose than for their bed, and Austin was particularly eager to see how much rainwater he could collect with it. If it ever rained.

"What shall we call ourselves?" Austin asked.

"We already have camp names," Stanley said. "What do you mean?"

"Heard many fellows have given their shebangs names," Austin said, "like Columbia House or the Herrington Rifles Mess."

Stew grinned. "How about Ogre's Mess?"

Austin didn't look pleased. "Really? Can't we come up with something a little more inspiring?"

"What do you think of the House of Stewart?" Stanley asked. He waited for a reaction, but none was forthcoming. "Stew's our most senior member, and it's a play on the Scottish House of Stuart."

Austin readily seconded Stanley's suggestion, but Stew withheld his approval.

"I may be a Scot," Stew said, "but I'm no royal. I wouldn't want our little homestead named for me, Mitch, but your

183

idea made me think of something just a little different. What do you think of calling ourselves Stalwart House?"

No one spoke.

Stanley mulled the name over, and the more he thought about it, the more he liked it. "Stalwart. It's what we ought to be—standing tall, unwavering, unbroken, persevering to the end."

"I agree," Austin said. "Stalwart House it is."

"Then I shall make a sign for all to see," Stew said.

Only a few weeks had passed since the opening of the new section, but the ground was now as barren as that of the old stockade. The hundreds of tree stumps that had populated the new stockade when it first opened had all been dug up, chopped up, and burned up. The network of roots had also been excavated, set in the sun to dry, and added to thousands of cook-fires. Stew's barbering stump had fallen victim to the ravenous cooking fire that Austin kindled every day to make soup. A rickety, wooden crate, which Stew had conjured from one of his wealthier clients, now stood in its place.

The only source of wood stood outside the camp. Daily details of prisoners were sent out of the stockade to chop firewood. Until now, Austin, through strict, economical husbanding of this precious resource, had sufficient firewood to cook their rations as well as the large kettle of soup for sale. But now, their supply would be entirely exhausted in a day or two.

Immediately after roll call, Stanley went to the North Gate and volunteered for wood detail. The guard looked at Stanley's walking stick, but made no remark, and jotted Stanley's name and detachment on the list. "You get an extra ration today. Wait over there," the guard said, pointing to a growing line of prisoners along Broadway. "We'll call you by squad. You're squad three."

• • •

184

With the arrest of the Raiders, and the hanging of the six leaders, peace and order had become the norm within the Stockade. Violence beyond fisticuffs was almost unheard of. Behind Stanley, a couple of "blocks" north of Broadway at the corner Tenth Street, stood a new shack built from rough-sawn lumber supplied by Captain Wirz—the police station.

Stanley had been inside the shack only once, three days before, when he had placed a man under arrest for stealing a haversack. The man was being pursued by two others who cried, "Thief! Thief!" as they ran. Stanley had stepped into the man's path. A quick, sharp rap with the head of his cane to the man's kneecap had sent him tumbling.

Stanley and the two witnesses had escorted the thief to the police station. Inside were two small desks, one for Chief Mahaney, which was vacant, and one for the officer of the day, an ordinary policeman named Stark who was chosen for the duty.

"You the arresting officer?" Stark had asked.

"Yes. Sergeant Stanley Mitchell of Sergeant Stewart's Company. These two men witnessed the theft."

Stark had recorded the particulars of the crime in a ledger, then locked the arrested thief in one of the three tiny cells with wooden bars that had been built along the rear wall of the shack. Each cell was devoid of any furnishings.

Stark had pointed at the floor of the cell. "Sit and be quiet. Judge Hill will be along later to try you."

A satisfying result, but even more so was how the hundreds of new prisoners were turned into the prison nearly every day. The chant of "Fresh fish, fresh fish" had continued, but it was more welcome than threat. The malevolent tone was gone, as were the sudden, violent assaults. The new men had retained whatever they were able to bring in, and then soon sold or traded away their goods for food. Little by little, these things had found their way into the general population, which had grown to over 30,000.

But what the crowd coveted most from all new prisoners was news from the outside. Within a few minutes, every new tidbit had rippled throughout the prison: "Sherman's well up on Atlanta," or "Grant's got Lee penned up at Petersburg." Every word was precious food for hope.

• • •

The North Gate opened—the massive twin doors, not the wicket. A band of sixteen black laborers entered under guard. Each of the slaves carried a pick or shovel on his shoulder and several carried pike poles. The work crew turned right immediately inside the gate and crossed under the deadline.

The twin doors slammed shut.

"First squad," the guard at the gate called.

Ten men walked toward the wicket. The guard checked each man against his list, then passed the man through.

The line along Broadway shuffled forward.

The second squad was called and then the third.

Like all the rest, Stanley gave his name to the guard. The wicket opened. Stanley stepped through, went toward the second wicket, and within a few seconds was standing outside the stockade with the rest of his squad.

He breathed deep and slow. The air was still foul, but less by half. To the left, slaves were digging up the earth and heaping it along the base of the stockade wall. *Austin said they had lots of rain before I arrived a month ago. Maybe it washed away some of the soil around the base of the timbers. The inside crew is probably doing the same.*

"Forward, march," a plain, colorless sergeant called out.

The detail moved forward at a slow pace—ten prisoners, ten guards, the sergeant, a wagon, empty except for a dozen or so axes and a large cask filled with water, two mules, and a driver. The small procession started north

186

along a narrow lane which led through one of the several encampments of the Rebel guards.

"Cemetery Road," one of the prisoners said. "Seen the dead-carts on it all the time."

Around the outside perimeter of the timber stockade, and about thirty feet from it, hundreds more slaves were digging a deep trench. Here and there were stacks of long timbers, pine trunks with their branches cut clean away and two sides sawed flat. A second stout timber stockade was being built around the first. Any attempt to escape would be twice as difficult when it was finished.

The detail turned off the road to the cemetery and passed beyond the northwest corner of the prison, not fifty paces from the shebang which Stanley, with much sorrow, had resigned himself to call *home*. The sergeant ordered a halt at the edge of the woods.

"Grab an ax and get to it. Four-foot lengths. Stack 'em neat and tight." Then, eying Stanley's walking stick, he added. "Each of you is cutting for a detachment, so do your bit."

One wagon load for ten detachments—twenty-seven hundred men. Stanley stepped up to the wagon and hefted one of the axes. He ran his thumb along the blade. It had been recently sharpened. There had to be hundreds of axes at Andersonville. Perhaps some slave worked every night over a grindstone to sharpen each of them.

Many trees had already been felled. Stanley chose one and measured off his first cut four feet from the end. He set his walking stick aside, then raised the ax high over his head. It seemed heavier than he remembered. He swung it down with all his might, driving the blade into the pinewood. He wrestled the ax handle back and forth to work the blade loose.

A second blow, then a third, and he had cut a sizable wedge from the log, but then he needed to rest. At Matthews Hill Farm, he had chopped wood for an hour at a time, stopping only for a drink from the well. But there was no well here outside the stockade. He took a small sip from his canteen. *I'll need to make it last the day.*

He hoisted the ax and began to chop again, groaning with every stroke. Anna. Her letters. She had written to him. She had seen him chopping wood that day in the rain when his left leg was still almost useless and he was in so much pain. She wrote that she had felt his pain. She had admired his strength and witnessed his determination to continue working despite the pain. That day her heart was softened. He was no longer just a Yankee. In her eyes and in her heart, she had confessed, he was a remarkable young man, strong of will and body.

Where was that strength now?

Stanley leaned panting on the ax handle. Just last Sunday Mr. Sheppard had preached on a verse from Isaiah. Stanley spoke the words aloud, to his own ears, and to anyone else who cared to listen. "The Lord Jehovah is my strength and my song; he also is become my salvation."

At the close of the meeting Mr. Sheppard had prayed for water, imploring the Lord to send showers of blessing upon the entire camp, prisoners and Rebels alike. And afterward he asked everyone to pray for relief without ceasing. "Never let a moment pass in idleness without looking to the Lord to supply our need for water."

Stanley looked at the water cask in the back of the wagon. The sergeant had pronounced the water good. Several of the prisoners had gone over to get a drink and seconded the opinion of the sergeant. Stanley ran his pasty tongue over his cracked lips.

Never drink anything that hasn't been boiled.

And that hymn they sang at Talbot's funeral. Thou of life the fountain art, let me freely take of thee.

188

Stanley took another small sip from his canteen and swallowed back the dryness in his throat. Then he picked up the ax again.

Later, he would be granted three rations, his daily ration, his police ration, and a wood detail ration. No matter how he looked at it, it was a small thing, but it was something to look forward to nonetheless. He smiled to himself. Perhaps roast pork and sweet potato pie was on the menu.

A breeze stirred the tops of the pines, abruptly freshening and cleansing the air around him.

Stanley breathed deeply of its sweetness. Then he went back to work.

The afternoon was well spent when the sergeant of the guard ordered the woodcutting to cease. The wagon was full and the prisoners assembled for the march back to the North Gate. Stanley gathered up several pine branches that he had laid aside, branches that appeared freshly cut and still oozed sap.

"Look for orange fatwood," Stew had said. "The brighter the orange, the more the pitch."

Stanley hoisted the bundle of branches over his right shoulder, took his walking stick in his left hand, and approached the wagon.

"What them sticks for?" the sergeant asked.

"We need pine needles, sergeant," Stanley said.

"What fer?"

"Medicinal purposes, sergeant." Stanley smiled at the colorless man. "Did you know, sergeant, these pine needles can be boiled for tea? It helps against the scurvy." It was Stew who had provided that crumb of backwoods New Hampshire wisdom. But Stanley withheld the primary purpose of the sap-rich branches from the sergeant; only more questions would have come of it.

The sergeant shrugged. "Keep up, or you'll have to drop 'em."

The walk back to the North Gate wasn't as bad as Stanley expected. It was mostly downhill and, had Stanley been fit, well-fed, and unencumbered, it would have been easy for him. He trailed along behind the slow-moving, heavily-laden wagon, and managed to keep pace with it. The driver had to proceed with great care, and he made frequent use of the handbrake, especially when he turned the rig onto Cemetery Road again.

No one challenged Stanley as he passed through the gate into the stockade. Apparently, none of the guards cared about a lame prisoner bringing in a few small branches for tent poles or firewood. But the value of his burden immediately attracted the attention of some of his fellow prisoners.

Stanley stood just inside the gate at the head of Broadway. No crowds could gather there, but several mean-looking fellows crept closer. They exchanged looks, as if plotting silent strategy. There was little Stanley could do if they assaulted him. They would knock him to the ground and take his pine branches and his long, hard hours of work outside the wall would have reaped nothing but a few scraps of a firewood ration.

Stanley raised two fingers to his mouth and whistled, loud and long. The creeping fellows froze. Within moments four men stood alongside him, all policemen, only one of whom Stanley recognized.

"Thank you, gentlemen," Stanley said. "Those men were looking rather keenly at my pine branches. Would you mind escorting me to my shebang?" He pointed toward the northwest corner of the stockade. "It's up the street near the deadline."

"You're one of Stew's men, aren't you," the familiar looking man said.

"Actually, these branches *are* for Stew. He's showing us how to make pine pitch glue." The glue was for Austin who had become convinced that rain, a lot of rain, would soon come, and that he would soon need a bucket for all that water.

The man reached for Stanley's bundle. "Let me take that. You look all done in. Left face. Forward, march."

CHAPTER 36

Friday, July 29, 1864

PRAYERS FOR WATER HAD GONE UP TO HEAVEN FROM hundreds, if not thousands, within the timber stockade at Andersonville. Monday evening, Mr. Sheppard had asked Stanley to plead with the Lord for water. It was the first time Stanley had prayed in public, so he had kept it short. "Lord God, we are your people. We aren't supposed to worry about what we are to eat and drink. But how can we not worry? We're dying every day. Please, Father, be merciful. Send us rain."

Hoping those prayers would be answered, Austin Oglethorpe made his bucket.

Work had begun six days before, as soon as Stanley returned from his first wood detail. It was a simple process, but much firewood and water was required, for which Stanley's sixth Abraham provided the funding. And Stanley went out on wood detail two more times to bring in more pine branches.

Stew, who usually spent many hours at the police station, stayed close to home and tutored Austin and Stanley in the fine, laborious magic of making pine pitch glue while he burned the letters of their new house name on a small signboard. Austin had cut the pine branches into short lengths and then Stanley had split the short pieces to expose as much of the orange heartwood as possible. The split wood had been boiled in the soup kettle to extract the sap, and after the wood was removed, the sap and water solution had been boiled until it thickened into syrupy pine pitch glue.

"Not too thick," Stew had advised. "You need to be able to pour it when it's hot." He nodded his satisfaction. Then Stanley carefully lifted the hot kettle and poured the glue into the smaller pot Austin usually cooked their rations in.

The glue making ritual had been performed for six days until this morning, when Stew finally pronounced the amount of glue in Austin's cooking pot to be sufficient. The fire was allowed to die to glowing coals. The pot of glue was set on the coals to make the glue liquid again and the larger soup kettle was placed upside down on the ground near the glue pot.

Stew scraped some charcoal from the end of a charred stick into the pot and stirred it. "That will make it set better."

The blanket which had formerly belonged to the triplets was deemed the poorest of the four Stalwart House possessed and was sacrificed to the cause. Austin used Stanley's knife to cut the blanket into strips about two inches wide.

Stew guided Austin through each step of the process.

"Put a strip of the blanket in the pot and stir it around."

"Make sure it's covered with the glue."

"The bottom of the kettle is your mold."

"Careful now, don't get burned."

"Use the stick to lift the strip and lay it over the kettle."

"Yes, that's good. Do another strip and lay it across the first."

One by one Austin laid the glue-covered blanket strips over the bottom of the soup kettle until it was completely covered. Then he added a few more, "to strengthen it," he said.

After roll call, Austin peeled the cooled bucket from the outside of the soup kettle. Then he and Stanley went to the swamp to test the new bucket. It wasn't much to look at. There was no handle and it seemed rather flimsy, compared to wooden buckets, of which there were several in camp.

Stanley sat on the bridge with his back to the deadline and his legs dangling over the edge. Behind him, the slave gang was still working on improving the stockade wall, singing and chattering among themselves. Below, Austin stood in the middle of the stream, holding his finished bucket. He looked at the ugly kettle-shaped fabric and pine glue bucket, then at the murky calf-deep water, then at the bucket again.

"We haven't got all day, Ogre," Stanley said.

"Actually, we do," Austin said, "but here goes."

Austin cradled the bucket in his arms and dipped it into the stream. He let it fill gradually and nearly to the top. Then he lifted the bucket clear. Water spurted from several holes, and the bucket emptied itself in less than a minute.

Austin was downcast. "It's no good. You said it wouldn't carry water, and you were right."

"Wait a minute, Ogre. I also thought it would break, but it didn't. There is still some glue left. It's probably because the blanket was in such bad shape. Let's go back home, patch the holes, and try again."

The holes were easy to spot when the bucket was held skyward, and almost as easily patched. The end of a pine stick was pounded until it split into thin fibers, which were then cut and added to the glue. Then Austin dabbed some of the glue onto each hole with a stick.

"Looks like a storm coming up." Austin said, as he and Stanley headed back to the swamp. "Stew knows how to rig our roof for catching rainwater, but we should make this quick nonetheless."

Austin didn't hesitate. He waded into the stream as soon as they reached it and submerged the bucket. This time the bucket didn't leak. "The sides are weak," he said.

"There's nothing to grab onto and I don't think the fabric is strong enough to take a handle. It's a lousy bucket for carrying water, but it will hold water. I now pronounce it our *cistern*."

A cool, fresh breeze swept over the camp. Thunder rumbled, not the close, sharp, crackling kind that accompanied a severe storm. Austin looked up at the lowering clouds. "I'm going back to camp," he said. "I think we just doubled our collection capacity. You coming?"

"No. I think I'll sit here awhile and enjoy the rain, if it comes."

Austin hurried off up the hill with his new cistern.

Rain began to fall. Stanley removed his hat and laid it beside him on the planking of the bridge. Then he lowered his suspenders and shucked off his worn and tattered undershirt. It slipped off so easily now; he was so thin. Many others tore off all their clothing and pranced around naked in the cleansing rain.

Stanley picked up his hat and moved to the other side of the bridge to watch the slaves, who continued to work in spite of the rain. Every day since Stanley first went out on wood detail, the slave gang had worked on the stockade wall between the swamp and the North Gate, where some of the timbers had become loose. They swayed side to side whenever a stiff breeze came up.

The slaves had used pike poles to maneuver each timber back into its proper position and earth was pounded tightly around its base. Then they had dug a trench several feet deep all the way from the North Gate down to the swamp and the excavated soil had been thrown up against the stockade wall to further strengthen it. Then the surface of the trench and the slope leading up to the wall had been tamped smooth.

Stanley hated to admit it, but it was an intelligent solution. The stockade wall was strengthened. Its pine timbers now stood tall and straight. The trench created yet

195

another obstacle to escape, and provided drainage to prevent rainwater from undermining the wall again. Now that the section of the wall between the North Gate and the swamp had been improved, the crew had moved on and had begun work south of the swamp.

Stanley lay back on the wooden deck of the bridge. The rain fell heavily on his face and into his open mouth. He rubbed his hands all over his face, neck, and chest, wishing above all else that he had just a little soap to do a proper job of it.

The rain stopped as quickly as it had begun. Stanley sat up and looked down at the stream. The flow had increased a little, but so had the amount effluvia it carried with it. It was muddy now due to a rivulet which flowed down the middle of the new trench into the stream.

The clouds parted and the sun reappeared. Within minutes, the heat and humidity had returned with a vengeance. A collective groan went up across the camp and the suffering returned to normal.

Thank you, Lord. That shower was a blessing, but we need much more.

As Mr. Sheppard had requested, prayers for rain had been unceasing. Stanley prayed the moment he awoke each morning. He prayed at odd moments throughout the day, and his last duty each night was to pray for Anna, for himself, for Austin and Stew and Frank, and for rain. The rain had come and the rain had gone, too quickly, not amounting to more than a drop in the bucket of what was needed.

Stanley wrung the rainwater from his undershirt. Too late, he thought to drink it, but was glad he didn't, for the shirt was as filthy as he had been. He pulled up his suspenders and donned his hat. It was wet on top, dry underneath—a good hat.

CHAPTER 37

Friday, August 5, 1864

THE MORNING DAWNED LIKE MANY A MIDSUMMER GEORGIA day, still, warm, and humid. Stanley read the Ezekiel passage over the swamp for the eighteenth time. The three members of Stalwart House and their brother Frank Griffin washed yet again in the sluggish, rancid stream, and then walked around the perimeter of the prison. The last week had been a constant war against bone-deep fatigue— Stanley felt anything but stalwart—but Austin wouldn't hear any excuse, and each day had pressed Stanley to walk with them.

Only six weeks inside the prison—an eternity with no end in sight.

Except death.

I feel more of its power every day.

Will my death be precious to God?

Stanley had lost at least a third of his body weight. Of that much he was certain. He couldn't weigh an ounce over one-forty. His joints had begun to ache the week before. At first, Stanley had attributed it to sleeping for so long on the ground, but a day later, his teeth also ached. Despite Austin's soup, the red root tea and the pine needle tea, and his extra morsel of rations, the accursed scurvy was setting in.

Stanley survived the morning walk. He stood for roll call and forced a smile when Pickens greeted him. It seemed

197

that as the mess sergeant's health had improved, Stanley's had worsened, the penalty for being large and lame rather than lithe and little.

A cloud appeared, low and cottony in the southwestern sky. It would probably pass by, as almost all of them did, without bringing any relief. At best, there might be a brief shower later, like the day Austin tested his bucket.

By the end of roll call, the cloud had grown higher and wider, lower and darker. A storm was building quickly, and it seemed headed straight for the prison. Stanley and Austin returned to the shebang while Stew went off toward the police station.

Austin took Dell's old rubber blanket from the floor and laid it over the woolen blanket roof. Then he tied the corners to keep the wind from blowing it off, and he retied the middle to form a channel down which rainwater would flow. On the ground, just below the bottom edge of the rubber blanket, Austin placed his kettle-shaped bucket.

Austin looked up at the building clouds. Thunder rumbled in the distance. "Could be a big one. Should give our new cistern a real test."

A stiff breeze blew across the prison for a minute or two, freshening the air. Then it grew still. Thunder rolled in waves over the valley of death. It was about midday, but the sun had been blotted out by dark, ominous clouds. A hush settled over the stockade.

Then the rain poured down.

It was a sudden cloudburst, as if a heavenly reservoir had been throw open, releasing the deluge. Stanley had known heavy rain before, and he had known the roar of a strong storm, but that roar had always been due to wind and thunder. Never had he witnessed rain so hard that it roared as it fell.

Stanley removed his hat and turned his face upward, as he always did when it rained. Water plummeted from above. It filled his mouth. He choked it down, then gasped for more.

"Looks like your prayer has been answered," Austin yelled into Stanley's ear.

"Our prayers," Stanley yelled back. He wrung the sweat and grime from his slouch hat and put it back on his head.

Austin's flimsy cistern was already about to overflow. He dipped the household's four canteens into the bucket to fill them, then hung them from the tent poles. Within a few minutes the cistern was brimming again.

Stanley and Austin carefully slid the cistern out from under the cascade from the roof and replaced it with the empty soup kettle.

"Nothing more to do here until it stops," Austin said. "Let's go check on Frank. His place is down near the swamp."

"Lead the way." The drink of rainwater had revived Stanley. He felt cleansed and strengthened by the pelting rain, which no longer roared as it fell, no longer stung his arms.

The streets had become small rivers. Nearly every shebang built over a dugout had been flooded. Their occupants stood by and tried to wash away the mud and filth that had suddenly swept in upon them. Indeed, it seemed the entire surface of the ground of the northern portion of the prison had become liquid and was sliding down the gentle incline toward Broadway.

Austin and Stanley pressed on across Broadway to the crest above the swamp, where the miry flow gathered speed as it went down the steeper slope toward the swamp. The sluggish stream was now a raging river, carrying away in mere moments months of accumulated pollution and pestilence.

"There's Frank," Austin said, pointing to the left.

Stanley couldn't distinguish their friend amid the rain-grayed host of milling prisoners, most of whom had hidden themselves under blankets, or jackets, or shirts.

Once again, Austin led the way, stepping carefully through the maze of flooded dugouts. He approached a man huddled under one half of a canvas shelter tent. "Frank," he called out.

The man turned and smiled. "Ogre," Frank said, "how did you ever spot me?"

"Knew the street where your shebang was," Austin said, "and there aren't many of those shelter halves in here. Good to see you're safe."

"Yes, and for now, the water hasn't flooded my little place."

Piercing cries came from a few streets away. Several men rushed toward the sound. Two men had been trapped in their dugout and were quickly being buried alive by the mudslide. Helping hands grabbed hold of the two and pulled them to safety, but a few seconds delay would have meant two more names added to the death roll.

"Look at the wall," Stanley said. The rain had abated a little more, but he still had to raise his voice.

Austin and Frank looked left toward the east wall of the stockade, which was less than a hundred yards away.

"Not that wall," Stanley said, "the west wall, where the stream enters. The water is above the bottom of the wall. See? It's trying to force its way between the timbers. They're swaying back and forth."

"Your eyes are better than mine," Austin said. "I see the wall shaking, Mitch, but I don't see the water coming through. Is it going to fall?"

Before Stanley could answer, the wall split in two. Pine logs fell in quick succession into the raging torrent, opening a gap about thirty feet wide in the stockade wall.

The sudden swell carried the fallen timbers swiftly across the prison. The bridge from which Stanley had read

200

Ezekiel each morning was smashed to pieces and swept away. Several men waded into the flooded stream and started grappling with one of the logs.

"Look at those fools," Frank yelled. "They'll die for firewood."

When the logs reached the eastern bridge by the latrines, it was likewise smashed. Timbers from the eastern wall swayed and fell, and a second large gap was opened in the stockade.

A clap of thunder came from the southwest. A shrieking whistle passed overhead. "That's Wirz," Austin cried. "He's opened fire on us."

"Look there," Stanley said, pointing toward the gap in the western wall. "Look at all the guards outside beside the stream. That was a warning shot in case anyone tries to escape through the gaps in the walls."

"We should go and see what's left of the bridge," Austin said.

"You boys go on," Frank said. "I'm going home to start putting it back together again."

The storm was moving on. The rain diminished to a light shower, then ceased altogether. The clouds appeared lighter gray. Soon they would part, and the sun would bake the earth dry again.

The bridge was indeed gone. The water still rushed. Another pine timber was undermined. It crashed into the stream and was carried past Stanley and Austin by the swift, powerful current.

"Water!" A fellow on the other side jumped up and down and pointed across the stream toward Stanley.

"Of course, there's water," Austin called over to the man. "Everyone can see it."

But Stanley followed the man's wild gesturing. The trench inside the deadline was flowing with water, just as it had the week before.

"It's just runoff," Stanley said. "When the sun comes out it'll stop."

But it didn't.

The sun reappeared and the heat returned. The rivulet of water in the trench slackened, but it didn't stop. The sentry boxes atop the wall were vacant; the guards had probably fled when the timbers began to fall. Stanley approached the deadline for a closer look. Up near the North Gate the bottom of the trench was muddy, but it was drying in the sun. The flow of water appeared in the trench about halfway between the North Gate and the stream, as if it was coming up from the earth itself.

The sentry returned to his box and Stanley backed away from the deadline. "Ogre," he called out, beckoning his friend to his side. "Remember what Mr. Sheppard preached on last Sunday?"

"Sure," Austin said. "About Moses striking the rock and water coming out, enough for all the people and their animals."

"And do you remember what he prayed for at the end?"

"He asked God to do it again."

"Well, Ogre, I think we have a spring of fresh water."

Others had noticed the spring. A crowd of prisoners gathered. One man, tin can in hand stepped under the deadline and walked toward the spring. Voices called out to the man, "Don't go in there. You'll be killed. Come back."

No word of warning was given. The sentry simply pointed his rifle down at the man and, just as the man lifted the can of fresh water to his lips, shot the man through the head, as calmly as he might have shot any jackrabbit or squirrel.

"Looks like God did his part," Austin said, "but now what? What good is fresh water if you get shot for trying to get some."

CHAPTER 38

Saturday, August 6, 1864

A T FIRST LIGHT, STANLEY STOOD UNCLOTHED IN THE stream. The current was still swift, the water chest high, and cool, wonderfully cool; he shivered a little. He wrung the water from his drawers and doused them in the water again. It was the first time he had taken them off and really washed them in almost two months. *If only there was soap.*

A few feet away, Stanley's three brothers were likewise employed, and with each passing minute more infested, filthy men waded into the stream. Stanley slipped his drawers on. Then he washed his undershirt and his trousers and made his way back to where he had left his frock coat on the bank of the stream beside the lone timber post, all that remained of the destroyed bridge.

As Stanley dressed, a Rebel quartermaster entered through the North Gate along with a squad of guards. A work crew of slaves equipped with saws, hammers, and nails followed the soldiers. A mule-drawn wagon loaded with lumber brought up the rear. *No hangings today. What are they up to?*

The quartermaster went to the place in the trench inside the deadline where the spring first issued forth from the ground. He made two marks with a stick and a slave pounded two wooden stakes into the earth, one on either side of the spring. The quartermaster then marked another

203

spot near the swamp beside the timber post from the destroyed bridge. Two more stakes were pounded into the earth.

There was much more shouting and pounding as two parallel rows of stakes were placed and driven into the ground from the source of the spring diagonally across the downward slope to the stakes near the swamp, a distance of about fifty yards. Pine planks were nailed to the stakes and a sluiceway began to take shape. Finally, a large oak cask was rolled off the wagon and trundled down to the end of the sluice. Black letters on the bottom of the rolling barrel proclaimed its origin—Old Oscar Pepper Kentucky Bourbon. The cask was half buried in the mud at the end of the sluiceway to catch the water.

The workers then moved to the middle of the swamp and began to build a new, wider bridge between the north and south sides, rather than replace the two at either end that had been washed away.

• • •

About mid-afternoon a loud cry went up from police headquarters and was relayed throughout the entire prison by every member of the police force. "All hands turn out. Swamp. West end."

As Stanley limped down the path from the North Gate toward the swamp, the reason the police had been called out became obvious. Pandemonium ruled as thousands of men fought to dip their canteens and tin cups into the cask for a drink of cool, clean spring water.

"Mitch," Stew called out from the crowd. He waved his arms to attract Stanley's attention. The police were trying to form a double line around the entire sluiceway from the cask to the deadline.

"This is fantastic." Stew's voice brimmed with joy; his face was streaked with tears. "We prayed for this and it happened. Someone called it Providence Spring and now everyone does. If the flow continues as it is, every prisoner will have enough to drink."

Stanley let out a low whistle. "Ogre said there are well over thirty thousand now."

"That's a huge number, I know, but look at that water. That's a stream of living water if I ever saw one. Chief Mahaney has declared it the property of all under the protection of the police."

"So what does that mean?"

Stew shrugged. "We don't know exactly, but the police will stand guard over this spring around the clock. By the way, he wants to see you."

"Who?"

"Mahaney. I think he has a special assignment for you."

Stanley found Chief Mahaney near the end of the sluiceway overseeing the water distribution. The men stepped forward two or three at a time, plunged their canteens or tin cans into the cask, and walked away drinking happily.

Stanley tapped Mahaney on the shoulder. "Sergeant Stewart said you wished to see me, Chief Mahaney."

Mahaney turned and looked Stanley up and down. "You must be Mitch. 'Tall fellow with a cane,' that's how Stew described you."

The two men shook hands. Mahaney was shorter than Stanley—almost all the prisoners were, for that matter—lean and about Stew's size. He was clean-shaven except for a reddish bushy mustache that hid his upper lip. He guided Stanley a few steps away from the throng surrounding the spring.

"Stew said you were a juror for last month's trials."

"Yes, Chief."

"And he said you were a corps level quartermaster sergeant."

"Yes, Chief, with General Logan's Fifteenth."

"Stew also said you're quite bright and that you got a gift for numbers."

Had Stanley's complexion been clean and fair, as it had been before he was captured, Mahaney would certainly have seen it redden. But weeks of pine smoke and hot sun had done their work, and now Stanley knew he looked as dark and ruddy as Mahaney did. "I guess that's true, Chief. I've always found numbers and figuring easy."

"Then you seem the right man for a job that I don't have the time or talent to take on." Mahaney waved his arm to encompass the still growing crowd. "There are one hundred and twenty-five detachments now. That's almost thirty-four thousand men inside this pen. Look at this mob. The only thing keeping them from tearing each other apart is that they respect the police since the hangings. But I can't keep the entire force on duty twenty-four hours a day."

"And, Chief, every man must have equal access to the spring."

"Yes, indeed, but I haven't even started to put a plan together."

Stanley smiled. "I think I can help with that, Chief. Would you be willing to reorganize the police?"

"How do you mean?"

"Well, Chief Mahaney, you have about five hundred men divided into ten companies. What if you reorganized the force into twelve companies of about forty each. Each company would guard the spring two hours each day."

Mahaney frowned. "How would only forty men control such a mob?"

"We would need to keep the mob from ever assembling, Chief."

"And how would you do that?"

"We're already grouped in detachments," Stanley said. "Maybe we call out each detachment in turn to get water."

206

Mahaney eyes widened with understanding. "Like we do with rations."

"Yes, Chief, and forty men can certainly keep order if the men approach one company of ninety at a time."

"How long would it take?"

"The whole camp, Chief?"

"Yes, how long would it take for everyone to get water?"

"Just a minute, Chief." Stanley knelt and drew some numbers in the sandy soil with a small, pointed stone. "One twenty-five...twenty-four hours......fourteen hundred forty...hmmm...."

Stanley looked up at Mahaney. "Chief, have you ever counted how many men got water in a single minute?"

"Not personally, but Stew did. He's got that watch, and he said sometimes as few as twenty, sometimes almost forty."

"That's good, Chief." Stanley returned to his calculations. Then he stood and faced Chief Mahaney. "Do you think we can maintain three orderly mess lines and a distribution rate of twenty-four men per minute?"

Mahaney squinted as he pondered the question. "I think so."

"So do I, Chief. According to my figuring, one detachment can go through the line in twelve minutes, and the entire population, in theory, can get water in twenty-five hours."

Mahaney laughed. "The days are long enough without you adding an extra hour."

"That's why I said, *in theory*, Chief. It's only an estimate." Stanley paused, reconsidered his calculations for a brief moment, then shrugged. "It may take more time, maybe less, and there is time for roll call and rations to consider. But by starting with a twenty-five-hour system, the detachments that have to line up in the middle of the night will continue to rotate. But we won't really know how long it takes for the whole camp to go through until it's done."

"Did you think all this up in the last few minutes?"

Stanley nodded once, short and crisp. "Yes, Chief."

"You mentioned roll call."

"If Wirz insists on carrying on as usual," Stanley said, "we'll have no choice but to shut down for those two hours. But it would be a shame to allow two hours of good water to run down into the swamp."

"How would we prevent line jumpers?"

Stanley chuckled. "Like I said, Chief Mahaney, numbers come easy to me. That's a law enforcement question."

"You're right, Mitch." Chief Mahaney eyed the crowd and appeared deep in thought. "I shall make the mess sergeants responsible for policing their own line just as they do at roll call. It'll be a three-hour penalty if they allow anyone outside their mess into their line."

"And have the mess stand aside and watch others pass, Chief?"

Mahaney smiled. "It would be a powerful message to everyone to maintain order in their own line."

"Indeed, it would," Stanley said.

"Then I think we have a plan." Mahaney clapped Stanley on the shoulder. "If I'm going to reorganize the police force, I'll need two more company sergeants. Are you interested, Mitch?"

Stanley looked down at his cane. "I'm not much of a fighter since I was wounded, and I'm always the last to arrive when the call goes out. Besides, Chief, you pay me for my brains, don't you?"

Mahaney guffawed. Then he grew serious. "I heard some very good news this morning from one of the new men in from Sherman's army. You know how we're penned up tight here? That's how Sherman's got Hood at Atlanta. Three big battles, the man said, and Sherman whipped Hood each time."

KARL A. BACON

Stanley was puzzled. "Hood? Johnston was their commanding general when I was taken."

"No more," Mahaney said. "Now it's Hood, and Hood's led the Rebels into disaster three times. It won't be long now. Sherman's cutting the railroads one by one, then he's coming down here to get us. Now, let's go over to the spring and I'll buy you a drink of that cool, sweet water."

CHAPTER 39

Sunday, September 4, 1864

STANLEY LOOKED DOWN INTO THE WATER CASK. HE WASN'T thirsty—he hadn't been since Providence Spring had opened four weeks before—it was just something he liked to do when he was on guard duty. It reminded him of the well behind the Matthews House.

Evening was his favorite part of the day. The sun had set and the heat of the day had passed. The nights were a little cooler now, and better for sleeping, a benefit of the shorter daylight hours. Most of the prisoners were settling down for the night. At the swamp, there were busy times for washing and slack times, and at the spring, evening was usually a slack time. To be sure, there was always someone dipping water from the cask, but the line was short and orderly. Now, only ten members of the police force guarded Providence Spring, to ensure no one jumped the line and no one took more than he should.

Stanley's plan for the distribution of water had lasted all of six days. Then it had been abandoned, because there was no longer any need to restrict access to the spring. It had been a rare thing indeed, before the great storm, for the dying to be offered a drink of water. "Why waste the precious resource?" was the common reasoning. But the spirit of the men throughout the camp changed entirely as they came to understand that there was plenty of water for all, and that the spring would still flow tomorrow.

All of Stanley's acquaintances knew the opening of Providence Spring was an extraordinary event, and many, including Stanley, believed it nothing short of divine intervention. Just as every man's empty cup was now full to running over, so the despairing tens of thousands had been filled with a new spirit of hope for eventual deliverance and goodwill toward their fellow prisoners.

Stanley stood guard duty every fifth or sixth day for three hours, sometimes in the heat of the day, sometimes at night, according to a schedule posted at police headquarters. It was easy, pleasant duty, except when it rained, and the extra rations he and Stew got for being members of the police force were added to Austin's single ration. Frank always dined with his mess down near the swamp, so the five rations were divided equally between the three members of Stalwart House. But the small amount of additional food each day only meant that Austin, Stew, and Stanley were starving at a pace slightly slower than those who were forced to subsist on a single ration.

At least that's how it seemed to Stanley before Captain Wirz went away.

● ● ●

About the middle of August, the rations had improved markedly. Of course, everyone was curious to know why. Captain Wirz had gone to Macon on medical leave, the guards reported. Lieutenant Davis was now in charge of the prison.

The food Davis allowed to enter the camp was actually edible—fresh, unspoiled beef with no worms, vegetables from local farms, even an occasional loaf of bread made from wheat flour. And thick, sweet sorghum molasses that instantly had Stanley craving Min Jackson's possum stew.

Stew removed the wool cover from his empty canteen and placed the canteen over the coals. The solder melted and he split the canteen into two halves. "We only need three canteens," he said, "and we now have two frying pans to cook our good meat properly."

Stanley's weight loss stopped. Perhaps he even gained a few pounds. His teeth and gums no longer ached from the scurvy, and he felt stronger than he had in weeks. And as the health of the men throughout the prison began to improve, talk of parents, wives, children, sweethearts, and homes became common. No doubt about it, Sherman was coming to free them

Stanley was no different. He thought of Anna. *I must be a horrible sight.* Every bone in his body seemed about to poke through his parchment-thin skin. How much did he weigh now? He and Austin were now equally emaciated— it was plain to see. Austin stood five feet three inches tall and estimated his own weight at one hundred and five. Stanley stood six feet two on his left leg, an inch taller if he stood on his right. It was only an estimate, but Stanley thought his own weight to be about one hundred and twenty-three pounds, maybe one twenty-five with the better food. But had he viewed himself in a looking glass, no doubt he would have had great difficulty recognizing the tall, gaunt, and spindly fellow looking back at him.

What would Anna think?

There was little Stanley could do to look well-fed and healthy again, but there was one thing he could do to improve his appearance. He asked Stew for another shave.

Their banter was as pleasant as ever as Stew readied his steaming cloth. "Since my last shave," Stanley said, "I've paid close attention to every prisoner that has crossed my path, but not one even remotely resembled a female."

Stew heaved with laughter.

"Please do a good job, Stew. Maybe we'll be out of here soon and on our way home."

"Maybe. Only God knows."

After Stew finished shaving Stanley, he washed his razor in a pot of boiling water. Then he showed Stanley a boil on the outside of his arm, a couple of inches below his elbow.

"It started to hurt two days ago," Stew said. "Now it's all swelled up and red, and it's got a nice round head on it." He grabbed his razor from the hot water.

"No," Stanley yelled. But he was too late.

Stew had shaved the head off the boil.

"Bandage it, Stew," Stanley said. "Don't leave it open for the flies."

Stew wrapped the wound tightly with a strip of cloth, but instead of healing, it began to fester.

"It's that swamp," Frank said when he saw it. "The miasma drifts up and fills the air, spreading sickness to everyone. I think it's gangrene."

Several similar boils appeared during the following week, and one particularly nasty looking open sore on the outside of Stew's right knee oozed clear liquid and a little blood. Austin, Frank, and Stanley took turns placing steaming hot cloths over Stew's wounds. Stanley removed two more Abrahams from his suspenders, and Austin purchased the best food he could get from the sutler, but to no avail. The flesh around Stew's sores became swollen and painful to the slightest touch.

There was no medicine. And even if they carried Stew outside to the small disease-ridden stockade known as the hospital, there was no guarantee he would get any treatment at all.

Six days ago Captain Wirz returned from Macon. The rations returned to their previous lousy state, corncob bread or meal, a few beans, and spoiled, rancid bacon or bits of moldy beef that always sent Stanley off to the latrine within a few minutes. The two or three pounds he had gained while Wirz was gone disappeared in two or three days. To Stanley, this was proof positive that Wirz would be satisfied only when all the prisoners at Andersonville were dead from starvation.

But none of that mattered to Stew. Fever set in and he shivered with chills. When he needed to go to the latrine, Stanley, or one of the other brothers, helped him get up and out of the shebang to a hole dug in the ground beside it. And when Stew was done, they shoveled dirt into the hole and dug a new one for the next time.

Then the headaches came on. Stew's eyes reddened with the constant pain and the tears which were wrung from him. And yet, nothing more could be done for him. Frank's prayers, Austin's vegetable soups, and another of Stanley's Abrahams spent on apples, eggs, sweet potatoes, and fresh wheat bread did nothing for their ailing brother.

Sergeant Albert Stewart was dying and he knew it.

Last evening, Stew's three brothers gathered around him, much as they had done for Josiah Talbot. Stew's words were taut with pain and sorrow. "Brothers, if any of you make it out of here, you must get word to my dear wife. My only grief is that I won't see her and my two girls again." His trembling fingers reached for Stanley's hand. "Promise me, boys."

"I promise, Stew," Stanley said. Austin and Frank said likewise.

"How shall we address the letter?" Stanley asked.

"Amanda Stewart, Portsmouth Road, Exeter, New Hampshire."

• • •

Stew was the one prisoner Stanley had thought certain to survive the rigors and horrors of the prison at Andersonville. With his lean, muscular body, iron constitution, and a will to match, he had never succumbed to the usual maladies that beset most of the prisoners. And Stew was the only man Stanley had met within the stockade who seemed not to wither under the daily assaults of filthy living, rampant pestilence, and disgusting food.

But three thousand men had been carted off to the cemetery during August.

A hundred more were dying every day.

And very soon, perhaps tomorrow, Sergeant Stewart would be one of those hundred.

Can I be far behind? Can I last much longer? Can I ever hope to see the outside of these walls? To see Anna again?

It was simple arithmetic.

The thin line of prisoners continued to shuffle past the water cask. Stanley eyed the three round canteens on the ground behind the cask. Stalwart House. The most stalwart among them would soon be dead. And then there would be only two members of the house left. Three canteens and two frying pans.

The sentries atop the stockade wall began to sing out the hour of the night-watch. "Post number one, half past eight o'clock, and all is we-ell."

Another half hour and my stint will be done. All is well. All is well. Can I say that? Can I say in my soul, Lord, that all is well?

Then came a call that caused every man within the sound of the sentry's voice to stop, turn to his neighbor, and ask, "Did you hear that?"

"Post number fo-ah, half past eight o'clock, and Atlanta's gone to he-ell."

CHAPTER 40

Wednesday, September 7, 1864

THE FOUR MEN TOILED UP THE PATH WITH THEIR BURDEN, Austin and Stanley at the front, Frank and Mr. Sheppard at the rear. The way was crowded. Hundreds of men stood in line, by their messes, nineties, and detachments, waiting for the grand exodus from Andersonville Prison. The announcement had come the previous evening. Come morning, the first ten detachments were to assemble and be ready for immediate transport to Savannah, where they were to be put on Federal ships.

"Make way," Stanley called out. "Please, let us pass."

The call was passed up the line. The sea of skeletal prisoners slowly parted, but the way was narrow, and for most, the passage of yet another dead comrade was hardly noticed. Only a few removed their caps, stopped their giddy chatter, and stood respectfully aside. A few offered pitiful sympathies.

"Poor fellow died a day too soon."

"Won't ever breathe free air now."

"Ain't never going back north to God's country."

"No, my son," Mr. Sheppard said, panting as he did so, "Sergeant Albert Stewart now resides forever in God's country."

The four men struggled up to the South Gate and laid Stew's body beside the others, their final service for their beloved friend and brother.

Stanley tied the identification to Stew's wrist. "It's a shame that Stew didn't live to see this."

"The Rebels are only sending those who can walk," Frank said. "They never would have let Stew go."

"Gentlemen," Mr. Sheppard said. "Would you wish him back in this dreadful place? No. His joy is now complete. His pain is not even a memory. Let us grieve for ourselves— we shall miss our dear friend. Let us grieve for his family— their loved one shall not return to them. But do not grieve for Sergeant Stewart."

• • •

That afternoon, about an hour before ration call, over two thousand five hundred men in ten detachments, tramped slowly out of the stockade under heavy guard. They marched up the lane past the deadhouse and the earthen fort, then down along the stream to the railroad depot. The prisoners were herded aboard two long trains of cattle cars until every car was filled. But there weren't enough cars. Hundreds of men were turned around and marched back to the stockade. At dusk, the lead train steamed away to the north. The second followed a short time later.

"Looks like it's true this time," Austin said.

Stanley was skeptical. "They're sending us away, but do you think it's really for exchange?"

"What else could it be?" Austin asked. "Wirz probably thinks Sherman will come down here as soon as he's done in Atlanta. The Rebels can't feed us. We're all about half-dead. Throwing us back to the Federals would remove a big burden from the Rebels and put it on our troops."

"But there are still over thirty thousand men here," Stanley said. "It would take a huge fleet of ships to send all of us north. I won't let myself hope for exchange until

217

I'm standing on the deck of a ship flying our Stars and Stripes."

Austin eyed Stanley the way he often did when Stanley grew cynical. "So if they call for Detachment Fifty-five, would you prefer to go out with the rest of us or remain here?"

"That's a stupid question." Stanley heard the pique in his own voice. "Of course, I'll go. Anywhere else would be better. But is it really possible? When?"

"Seven went out today. If seven more go out every day, it will take a week, maybe more. Have to say goodbye to Frank, and Mr. Sheppard too."

"We will?" Stanley hadn't given that possibility any thought, but it did seem the prisoners would be sent out incrementally by detachment number. "You're right. Frank should go out a day or two before us."

"Mr. Sheppard will go out after, maybe a week later. Hard to say goodbye, but there are only two ways out of this place, exchange or death, and either way means goodbye."

Stanley laid his bony hand on Austin's shoulder. "I'm sorry, Austin. Sometimes, I can't help but think I'll never leave this place alive. I try not to get my hopes up."

"And yet those hopes keep us alive, don't they? They keep us up and moving and doing."

"The day I was turned in here you said every day would be a battle. I'm weary of the fight, Ogre, and I'm ready to go home."

"But Mitch, the two of us are Stalwart House to the end, no matter where we end up. Come on. Let's go to the spring for water and make some soup."

"And then we should deal with Stew's things," Stanley said. He hadn't so much as glanced toward the dead pile beside the South Gate after they had left Stew there. *Busy work will keep me occupied, keep me from thinking about what will happen to his....*

"We'll take inventory," Stanley said, "so when it's our turn, we'll know what we can carry with us and what we must leave behind."

Austin smiled. "There you are, Mitch, back to your old quartermaster self again."

CHAPTER 41

Saturday, September 17, 1864

THE CARS ROCKED AND CLACKED SLOWLY ALONG THE RAILS, peaceful and soothing to Stanley's senses. The large doors on either side of the car had remained open since they left Andersonville the previous evening. As soon as the train had finally started to chug and clank northward, fresh, cool air had carried away much of the blended stench of sixty filthy prisoners and years of embedded livestock excrement.

Sleep had come easily during the night journey to Macon. A pair of guards rode atop the car and, for all anyone knew, they had probably slept too. Escape would have been as easy as jumping off the slow-moving train and disappearing into the dense pine woods. But no one in the car did, and no one even talked about it. It was pointless, after all, since the Rebels were giving the whole lot of them a ride back to the friendly Federal lines. Soon, very soon, they would all be in God's country; they would finally awaken from the horrific nightmare of Andersonville.

The train started to cross a bridge. Even as he dozed, Stanley had come to recognize the open, hollow sound under the cattle car. They had crossed many bridges in the last two days, bridges over every river, creek, and swamp from Andersonville to Macon, then on toward Savannah. At least that's where the guards said they were headed.

This bridge seemed longer than any of the others. Stanley opened his eyes. The train was crossing low, swampy ground, lush, green, and brightly speckled with the glittering reflections of afternoon sun upon marsh waters. A pair of brightly colored ducks paddled quickly out from under the trestle, trying to escape the thundering train. A large blue-gray bird with a long, curved neck and spindly legs paid the leviathan no heed and stalked its prey slowly through the shallows. *Savannah's on the coast. We must be very near.*

Stanley's stomach rumbled. The double ration they had been issued at Andersonville was supposed to last two days, but to the half-starved prisoners, the meager offering of salted pork and hard biscuits was a feast compared to what they had been issued within the stockade. Much of the food had been consumed by the time the train finally got underway late that night, and not a morsel was left until morning when the train had lumbered through Macon.

Across the bridge, the train slowed to a crawl and passed through a rail yard with only three sidings, very small compared to those Stanley had seen in Huntsville and Chattanooga. A string of ten aging passenger cars sat on the farthest siding. Hundreds of people milled about the cars. Children chased one another around, under, and through the cars. Women hung the day's laundry from ropes that stretched the entire length of each car or tended fires for cooking. There were only a few men, old and gray, sitting and talking.

"They're all white." Austin hadn't said much all day. The scenery of southeast Georgia had apparently been unremarkable until that moment. "Who do you think they are, Mitch?"

"They look like families," Stanley said. "Maybe they fled Atlanta when Sherman got close."

"You think they're refugees?"

Stanley nodded. "And who knows? Some might have been Atlanta's leading citizens."

Beyond the rail yard the train entered the outskirts of the city. Once again the train slowed. The car jerked a little as someone engaged the handbrake. The train squealed to a halt. Guards jumped down from their perches atop the cars and ordered all the prisoners out.

"I'll need a hand getting down, Ogre." Stanley's left leg was tight and sore, and he didn't want to fall to the ground as he had when he had arrived at Andersonville.

The train had not stopped at a depot, nor had it pulled off on a siding. Instead, the train appeared to have stopped on the main track at the edge of a fashionable neighborhood. Stanley had been raised in such a neighborhood, in the large, opulent house of his Uncle Charles near the center of Ironton, a few streets away from the noise and bustle along the Ohio River.

"Welcome to Savannah," the sergeant of the guard called out. "Columns of fo-ah. You Yanks know the drill."

The prisoners lined up quickly. Many, like Stanley and Austin, had canteens and blanket rolls slung over their shoulders. Both of their canteens had a tin plate strapped to the side, the two plates that had been made when Stew had split the extra canteen in half. The two straps were made from the only part of Stew's shoes that Austin and Stanley saw any worth in, the leather shoe laces.

Austin's blanket roll consisted of two woolen blankets with Dell's rubber blanket wrapped inside. The small cooking pot was tied up near Austin's shoulder along with his blackened tin ration can. The soup kettle had been too large to take along, so it had been "willed" to Mr. Sheppard who promised to make good use of it until the Lord called him elsewhere.

Stanley had also given Stew's rubber blanket to Mr. Sheppard. It just didn't seem right that he and Austin had two, when they could easily share one rubber blanket and give the other to someone who had none.

So, Stanley's roll of Stew's two woolen blankets was somewhat thinner than Austin's. Wrapped tightly within were Austin's spoon-knife, Stanley's large hunting knife, two split wooden sticks that served as handles for their plates so they could be used as small skillets, and their latest inheritance, Stew's razor. In addition, Stanley's possessions included a small ball of twine and string, the compact housewife sewing kit he had purchased in Huntsville, and his leather-bound, mud-stained Bible.

The column marched a short distance along the railroad track, then turned toward one of the city streets.

"Why so many guards?" Stanley asked. There were perhaps several hundred of them.

"To keep us from escaping," Austin said.

"They didn't guard us at all on the train. Why would we want to escape if we're to be handed over to our own troops?"

Austin looked sideways at Stanley and smiled. "Probably just their way. Want to put on a good show when they hand us over to our boys in blue."

Stanley hoped Austin was right, but he wasn't convinced. The guards weren't the usual reserves or home guards. They were all regular gray-backs, and they looked like they knew their business.

Stately homes of wood, stone, and brick stood silent along both sides of the beautiful tree-lined street. The spires of several churches stood bright against the sky several streets away. Except for the chorus of jays, warblers, and cardinals from the trees above, the only sounds in the street were the tramp-tramp-tramp of the guards and the muted shuffling of the barefoot prisoners. Not a soul walked or rode in the street, and no one sat in the shade on any of the many fine verandas to watch the procession pass.

"Looks like nobody's home," Austin said. "Looks too nice to be a ghost town."

"That's because it isn't," Stanley said. "Don't turn your head. Look around with your eyes. They're in their parlors watching us from behind the curtains. We must be quite a sight."

"You're right, Mitch," Austin said as they turned onto another street. "Should just come out and have a good look at us. We can't be that scary looking."

"Have you seen yourself lately, Ogre? Your name appears more fitting every day."

Austin laughed, drawing a glare from the guard nearest him. "No, Mitch. Wirz didn't provide me with a looking glass."

Stanley grinned at Austin. "That's all right. We'll be on the mend soon. What do you think our first meal as free men will be?"

"Tonight, we'll dine on hardtack and beef," Austin said without hesitation. "And coffee."

"Coffee? Real coffee?" *One of the few pleasures I enjoyed when I rejoined the army.* "I haven't had any since June 12th."

"Whoa, Mitch. We aren't there yet. Take a deep breath of that wonderful clean air."

"It is clean, but it's thick and humid like it was all summer."

"But there's something else. Don't you smell it?"

Austin was right, the air did smell different, but Stanley didn't know why.

"We're only a few miles from the ocean, Mitch. That's sea air. "

"I've never seen the ocean, Ogre, only read about it in books."

"Early in the war I was at Port Royal and Beaufort with the Eighth Michigan so I saw a lot of the ocean."

224

"To think we'll be out on the ocean for days on a steamer. I can't wait to see it for real."

The head of the column reached an intersection and turned to the left. A low, steady groan started up among the first prisoners to round the corner and worked its way rearward through the entire column.

The prisoners shuffled to a halt in front of the timber gate of another tall stockade. Gangs of shirtless Negroes were digging a trench around the outside of the stockade, deeper than the one that was dug between the wall and the deadline at Andersonville.

Austin had always tried to find the good in every circumstance, but now, no cheer brightened his words. "My first answer was correct, Mitch. All those guards were to keep us from escaping when we saw this."

Stanley stood, mouth open, shaking his head. "They lied again. Another prison. They knew it all along. There aren't any ships and there isn't any coffee." He spat in the dirt at his feet. "Rebels. They're nothing but skunks and liars."

CHAPTER 42

Thursday, October 13, 1864

Anna held Luke's hand as they walked down the narrow path that led from the barn to the Jackson's cabin. Luke carried a lantern in his free hand, and Anna, as she had done nearly every evening since her Stanley was taken, held her Bible pressed to her heart. Snorting hogs rooted about unseen in the woods and she smiled inside, remembering how Stanley had confessed his fear of being charged by them.

"What's it say?" Luke asked.

"You'll know soon enough," Anna said.

"But you let Mama read it."

Anna felt a spring in her step that had been missing for a long time. "And you will too. You're going to read it for the Jacksons."

"Me? Why?"

"Because I won't be able to keep from bawling like a newborn, that's why."

"But you seem happy," Luke said, "more than you been since General Logan's letter."

"I *am* happy he's alive, Luke, but not about what he wrote."

It was a familiar, comfortable gathering at the Jackson's cabin each evening. At first, after Stanley was taken, Anna had gone by herself, honoring his memory by doing what he had done, the simple service of reading Scripture to the slave family. And then there were the soft-spoken prayers, from Levi at first, then Aunt Min, and then each of their children in turn, all of them praying together with Anna for the safe return of Stanley—her Stanley.

When Luke had started to go with her, Anna had ceded the Bible reading to him. And even before they had seen Stanley last year in Corinth, Luke had joined the rest with his own prayers for Stanley. Now, Anna and Luke were teaching Levi and the older children to read simple passages like the first of Genesis and Psalm Twenty-three, passages they had memorized, or nearly so, so they could recognize the words.

And there was always dessert after prayer. Tonight, it was peach pie that Aunt Min had baked from the last of the season's peaches.

"I got a letter from Stanley today," Anna said.

"Praise be," cried Aunt Min. "That sweet boy's alive."

The seven Jackson children, from Jeremiah the oldest to Zechariah the youngest clapped, or oohed, or made some other happy sound, while Levi just smiled. Anna saw a trace of moisture in his eyes.

She handed the letter to her brother. "Luke's going to read it. The postal stamp is from Savannah, Georgia."

Luke looked at the address on the envelope. "This ain't his writing. That's a lady's writing. And it says 'Flag of Truce' at the bottom in the same hand."

"And a U.S. postal inspection stamp on the back," Anna said. "Stanley explains all that in the letter."

Luke removed the letter and unfolded it. It was several pages long.

Savannah, Geo.
Wednesday, September 28, 1864

My Dearest Anna,

227

I'm writing this letter from the hospital of a Rebel prison in Savannah, not as a worker, as I was in Vicksburg, but as a patient. I have been quite ill with pneumonia, and today I rose from my blanket on the floor for the first time since I was brought here last Friday.

The day after I sent my last letter, I was taken prisoner by Rebel bushwhackers. I lay no blame on them—we are at war with them. As for the cavalry patrol that was supposed to protect us, I leave it to God to judge.

"Remember, Luke?" Anna said. "He wrote about that cavalry troop he had thrown out of the church."

"You think they left him behind on purpose so he got caught?" Luke asked.

"Sounds like he be like Joseph," Levi said. "His brothers meaned him harm, but God meaned it for good."

"Well, Levi," Anna said, "I'm still waiting on the good. Carry on, Luke."

Until the 15th of September, I was held in Georgia south of Macon. Of that place I will not write, except to say that God preserved me through the aid of three Christian brothers—Sergeants Albert Stewart, Frank Griffin, and Austin Oglethorpe. Stew died a few days before we were sent here. Frank went out two days before Austin and me. We haven't seen him since. Only Austin remains with me.

We arrived at this prison on the 17th. The water and rations are better here, but I was weakened from almost three months at the other place. Within a few days I became sick with a bad cough and fever. My friend Austin insisted I report for sick call. The hospital at the other camp was miserable, so I resisted the idea. The following day I knew it was off to the hospital or die where I lay.

Anna couldn't help herself. She dabbed at her eyes with her handkerchief. "At the beginning, when he was helpless upstairs in bed, I took such pleasure in his pain. Now, him suffering like that? It just tears me to pieces inside. His birthday was the twenty-second—he's nineteen now—and he almost died. Now you know why I couldn't read it. I'm sorry, Luke. Please go on."

The hospital occupies a portion of the Savannah City Jail. I have been dry and, in the main, well looked after. Some of the nurses are sincere Christian women and bear us Yankees no special animosity, just the common Southern kind. I awoke once and found one of them, Mrs. Charlton, praying over me. She said she found my muddied, tattered Bible in the pocket of my trousers and thought I must be a Christian because of how well-worn it was.

Yesterday morning, I asked Mrs. Charlton if it might be possible for me to write and post three letters, the first to you in Tennessee, the second to Stew's wife in New Hampshire, and the third to Mrs. Adair in Vicksburg. Mrs. Charlton said she thought it was impossible. I explained the purpose of each letter and then she seemed to soften a little.

Later in the day she returned with her husband, an official with the Savannah and Gulf Railroad. Mr. Charlton informed me that, while it wasn't usual practice to allow prisoners of war access to the mails, a mail packet was sent out nearly every day under a flag of truce to the Federal ships blockading the river entrance. He also hinted that it was exceedingly rare for a letter from one woman to another to be rejected by the Federal postal inspector. So I asked Mrs. Charlton to write the address on each letter.

Mr. Charlton then said with some sadness, that delivery of the mail to ports such as Vicksburg and Memphis is a routine matter. Federal ships ply regular routes around the Florida peninsula and across the Gulf of Mexico to New Orleans. I have seen death in all its horror. I have smelled it, felt it, heard it, even tasted it. But all of that was—

229

Luke paused for a moment. Then he swallowed and took a deep breath. When he continued his voice was strained.

But all of that was swept away the moment Mr. Charlton assured me that my letters would likely reach their destinations.

I'm on the mend now. I feel stronger than I have in many weeks and I'm gaining a little weight. I don't know how much longer I shall remain here, but I will offer my services as a parolee here at the hospital until I am exchanged or sent off to another camp.

Anna—my dearest Anna—these last months must have been as dark for you as they were for me. Do not try to write to me—I expect my days here will be few—and please do not despair if this is the only letter you receive from me until this war is ended. I see the hand of God in the blessing the Charltons have been to me. I can't expect such kindness again until I'm out from under the press of Rebel heels.

Austin, my friend and brother through all of this, said his trials have reawakened and sharpened his faith. This morning he visited me on a pass from the prison and read these verses from Second Corinthians: "We are troubled on every side, yet not distressed; we are perplexed, but not in despair; persecuted, but not forsaken; cast down, but not destroyed; always bearing about in the body the dying of the Lord Jesus, that the life also of Jesus might be made manifest in our body."

I'm trying very hard not to be destroyed by all of this, and to return to you a whole man. Please pray earnestly that our God might be gracious and keep me from falling into the pit of despair—it's very wide and very deep.

Please give my love to your mother and your sister, Ruthie, and to your brothers, Luke, Willie, and Little Davy. And to Levi and Aunt Min and the rest of the Jackson tribe too. Please share this letter with them and ask them to pray for me too, "without ceasing."

230

I remain your most true and affectionate,
                    Sgt. Stanley Mitchell

Luke folded the letter carefully and put it back in the envelope. "We must do as Stanley asks," he said. Then he folded his hands and bowed his head. "Let us pray."

CHAPTER 43

October, 1864

STANLEY SAT ON THE STUMP NEAR THE MIDDLE OF THE OPEN
ground near the bridge over the clear as crystal
stream. It was a fine autumn day with a cool breeze and a
few fair-weather clouds that scudded across the sky, but
when they hid the sun for a minute or two he shuddered
from the sudden chill and longed for the return of brilliant
sunlight.

Four prisoners tramped toward the bridge carrying a
dead comrade on a torn and faded blanket. Stanley stood
and drew himself up to attention. At the bridge, the men
stopped to ask permission from the guards. Then the men
carried their friend across the bridge and laid him beside
the gate, just as was done at Andersonville. Fifteen to
twenty per day, that's what Austin said, all victims of that
wretch, Captain Wirz, even though he was hundreds of
miles away.

Stanley sat again and opened his Bible. He turned to
Isaiah, the fifty-fifth chapter, the chapter he had read at
the Jackson's cabin so long ago, the same number as his
detachment at Andersonville. His hope was simple as he
began to read, to recall the former place and try to forget
the latter.

*Ho, every one that thirsteth, come ye to the waters, and
he that hath no money; come ye, buy, and eat; yea, come,
buy wine and milk without money and without price.*

But how could he forget when he was still a prisoner inside yet another timber stockade. Millen—Camp Lawton, as the Rebel guards called it—was in every way better than the prison pen at Andersonville. The food was better—fine, well-ground corn meal that Austin baked into tasty cakes on a pine slab beside the fire, and a little fresh meat every day—but it was never enough for Stanley to feel properly fed. Still, the few pounds he had gained in Savannah had remained with him.

The water was infinitely better. There was always plenty of clean, cold water to drink or bathe in. Springs beyond the northern wall merged into a deep, clear stream that flowed gently through the stockade. Near the northern deadline, where the stream entered the stockade, the water was used only for drinking or cooking. A framework of latrines had been constructed over the lower end of the stream near the southern deadline, and the rest of the stream was used for bathing.

Firewood lay about in abundance. More prisoners had been turned into the stockade every day since Austin and he had arrived four or five days ago, but Frank and Mr. Sheppard were not among them. There were several thousand now, perhaps as many as seven, but even with that many prisoners inside, it seemed empty compared to Andersonville or Savannah. Plenty of open space lay between the stream and the "settlement," as Stanley called it, of prisoners' shanties and shebangs—plenty of room to find a stump to sit on and spend some time in solitude with the Scriptures.

Ho, every one that thirsteth, come ye to the waters, and he that hath no money; come ye, buy, and eat; yea, come, buy wine and milk without money and without price.

There were still four Abrahams tucked away in his suspenders and a small wad of Confederate bills that he and Austin had split. The days were still pleasant enough, but the nights were getting chilly. They had already spent two sleepless rainy nights wrapped up tight in the rubber blanket, the only advantage Stanley could think of to being so thin.

So many stumps. He had seen some men chopping away at them with their pocket knives, only to leave with a few chips, hardly enough to boil a single tin of water. And the stump upon which he sat had been blackened from several attempts to set it ablaze.

Winter was coming. Exchange was not.

Fire. We must have fire.

A Rebel officer walked across the bridge followed by two guards marching in step and carrying their rifles at right shoulder arms. The officer looked neat and professional in his cadet gray uniform. Gold-colored braid adorned the sleeves of his jacket, brass gleamed in the sun and the top of his gray and black kepi bore the twin braids of a captain of infantry.

The officer came directly toward Stanley, and as far as he could tell, the officer wasn't armed with a pistol or the ceremonial officer's sword so many of them wore. Stanley closed his Bible, grabbed his cane, and stood as the officer approached.

"Good day, sergeant," the captain said. He seemed pleasant and polite, not at all what Stanley had expected—certainly not another Captain Wirz.

"Good day, sir."

"I am Captain Vowles, the commandant of this prison, and I have come to address the prisoners. I had hoped to send you off to spread the word." Then the captain smiled, a true smile that made his eyes twinkle. "But I see you aren't much for running. Corporal Tunney. Private Bennett. Go tell those men up in the camps that I should like to speak with them. Not long, ten minutes should do it."

The corporal eyed Stanley. "You'd be on your lonesome with this-un, sir."

"He won't trouble me," Captain Vowles said. "He's a soldier too, Corporal Tunney. Now run along and round up the men."

"Yes, sir," Tunney said. Both soldiers snapped sharp salutes and ran off up the hill toward the settlement.

"What's your name and division, sergeant?" the captain asked.

Upon entering the stockade, the prisoners had been grouped in divisions of one thousand each. "Mitchell, sir. Stanley Mitchell. Second Division, Second Hundred."

"I see you're a quartermaster sergeant—that is your coat, isn't it? One never knows inside the stockade."

Stanley smiled. "That's true, sir. Yes, this is my coat. I was with the Quartermaster Department of the Fifteenth Corps."

"Oh, one of General Sherman's minions." It seemed a matter-of-fact statement rather than an accusation.

"Yes, sir."

"What were your duties with the corps?" Captain Vowles asked.

Stanley looked at the captain, trying to perceive why he was questioning him. He appeared close to middle age and on the verge of corpulence, a man who had likely never endured a single day on short rations.

"I ask only from curiosity," Vowles said. "This is not an interrogation."

"My unit handled the routing of supplies to the corps at the front and the evacuation of our dead and wounded to the rear."

"Important work, all of it. Have you been schooled in mathematics, Sergeant?"

The conversation seemed light and cordial to Stanley, the sort of good-natured exchange that would normally pass between new acquaintances, except for the fact that the prison commandant and he were sworn enemies. "Yes, sir," Stanley said, keeping his tone amiable, "back in Ohio at the Portsmouth School for Boys."

"I could use a man like you."

"Sir?"

"At my commissary," Vowles said. "Only three of my enlisted men had any schooling before the army. And none of them possess the skills necessary for a good quartermaster, which, it seems to me, you do."

"You want me to go outside and organize the prison commissary, sir?"

"Yes, Sergeant Mitchell."

From the higher ground to the west, fellow prisoners were walking down the slope toward the Rebel officer and the Yankee sergeant.

"That would be giving aid to the enemy, sir," Stanley said, "and I couldn't do that."

"I can't argue that point," Vowles said, "but you would also be helping to improve the procurement and distribution of rations for all of your comrades. You will, of course, be granted a parole to pass through the gate to the commissary. And you will be granted an extra ration daily—no, you're a tall lad—let's make that two extra rations daily, as payment for your service."

The captain's offer had merit. Four rations per day for two men; it would make a big difference. "I must think this over, Captain Vowles. May I give you an answer tomorrow?"

"Yes. Speak to the guard at the bridge." Vowles looked down at Stanley's feet. "Seems you have a rather large pair, but I'm sure the quartermaster has something to fit you."

It had been four months since his boots were stolen and winter was coming on fast. Stanley smiled and nodded. "That would be nice, Captain Vowles."

"There is one more thing," the commandant said. "I will ask you to sign an oath of loyalty to the Confederacy. It's

236

a simple statement that you will not use your position to do harm to our cause."

"Then I can give you my answer now, sir. No."

"It was only a request, Sergeant Mitchell, not a demand, but signing that paper will mean freedom for you. I can promise you that."

There was no doubting the captain's earnest eyes and words, but several hundred prisoners were gathering around, and the conversation was no longer private.

"My answer is still no, sir," Stanley said.

"Suit yourself. Might I borrow your stump to speak to the men?" Captain Vowles asked.

"I believe it's your stump, sir," Stanley said, "and it is I who was borrowing it."

Captain Vowles smiled again, but this time the smile didn't reach his eyes. "Right you are, Sergeant Mitchell. Think about what I said."

Vowles climbed atop the stump and began to speak to the men. Most of his speech was the usual laying down the rules of the camp, but the captain spoke in a pleasant, casual manner, the opposite of the fire-breathing Wirz. No cursing colored this commandant's speech and more than once he called the prisoners *gentlemen*.

As he concluded, Captain Vowles stunned the gathered prisoners by telling them that, if they had any reasonable requests, they should submit them in writing to the guards. Then, after promising to return the following Sunday afternoon, he stepped off the stump and walked back across the bridge.

● ● ●

Austin was sitting within their crude dwelling, tending his cooking fire. It was a great improvement over their blanket tent shebang at Andersonville. When they had arrived several days before, the ground had been strewn with thousands of longleaf pine branches, debris from the construction of the stockade walls.

Following the examples of their neighbors, Stanley and Austin had dug a shallow rectangle in the sandy soil with their canteen halves. Then they had erected a small pine-bough hut, intertwining the tufts of long needles to form a roof about four feet above the earthen floor. Lastly, they laid more pine boughs on the floor of the dugout and spread out their rubber blanket atop the pine needles.

It was not a place of comfort, not by any means, but it was *better*. When it had rained the previous night, the pine bough roof had shed most of it, and wrapping themselves up in the rubber and wool blankets had kept them warm and dry. And in the morning, the two men agreed they had built for themselves a first-rate shanty and that their days of lowly shebang living were a thing of the past.

"Saw you coming from a mile away in those plaid trousers," Austin said as Stanley ducked into the shanty.

"And I will wear them until they fall to rags like the old ones," Stanley said. "The Charltons were very good to me and others in the ward. When I awoke, my old rags were gone. I had no choice." In fact, Mrs. Charlton had provided Stanley with most of his clothes. Mr. Charlton had donated the trousers. They were a few inches too short in the leg and much too large in the waist, but Stanley thanked her just the same. She also gave him a clean ivory-hued shirt, white undershirt and drawers, and a pair of white stockings that Stanley had not yet worn, because the one item the Charltons were unable to provide was a pair of shoes large enough for Stanley's feet.

"Thought I had lost you," Austin said. "Seems you did very well for yourself though. Good thing I kept your coat and suspenders when you were carried to the ambulance."

"And thanks for staying here and guarding our fortune," Stanley said.

"Still some thieves among us. No need for me to go down there to hear the commandant. Figured you were there."

"More than that, Ogre. Captain Vowles and I spoke just as we are now. He seems as decent as any Rebel I ever met. He offered me a parole to work in the prison commissary."

Stanley waited for the obvious question, but Austin didn't oblige.

"He also offered me triple rations and a new pair of shoes. Think of that, Ogre, shoes and stockings again."

"Rebel shoes?" Austin asked.

Stanley nodded.

Austin shrugged. "They won't last."

"That's what I thought," Stanley said. "I declined the offer."

CHAPTER 44

November, 1864

STANLEY HELD THE WIRE BAIL OF THE TIN CAN OVER HIS head as he forced himself step by step through the icy chest-deep water. In stark contrast, the heat from the embers in the can nearly seared his fingertips, but he held the wire fast between his thumb and forefinger and pressed on. He had swum up and down the stream only two days before. The water had been cold then, but he had warmed with the exercise of his first real swim since the Etowah back in June.

His legs ached from the cold. There was no turning back. Snow had fallen lightly since dusk—an uncommon thing for early November back in Ohio, a rare thing indeed so far south in Georgia—but he waited until it was fully dark for fear of being shot by one of the guards.

Those men must have fire, or they will be dead by morning.

• • •

As October ended and November began, the weather had turned sharply colder. Scores of prisoners who had been sick upon arrival had already died, but constant exposure to the cold and the pelting rains that swept through the camp every few days laid even the hardiest of men low. And among those whose constitutions had already been eroded through months of severe deprivation of food, clothing, and shelter, and by hopes for release

240

raised high and then dashed to pieces, sickness ran unchecked, and death followed close behind.

The Rebel authorities had established a hospital inside the prison. Rows of tents had been pitched on the forbidden side of the stream near the southeast corner of the stockade. Gravely ill prisoners in search of medical treatment reported for sick call every morning, but only those deemed "sick enough" were allowed to cross the bridge to report to the hospital.

To Stanley, it had seemed like an improvement over Andersonville, and indeed, it would have been, had it been May or September. But there were too few tents. Dozens of sick men lay on the ground exposed day and night to the elements. Most afternoons were still pleasant enough, but the nights were becoming downright cold. No one was permitted to cross the stream to try to ease their suffering, and no one had dared test the resolve of the Rebel guards.

Stanley had never seen the warm glow of a single campfire across the stream at the hospital. There were still plenty of pine branches close at hand, but no one had gathered any and no one had lit a flame to warm the cold, shivering, dying men at the hospital.

Yesterday afternoon, a light flurry of snow had blown through. This morning, the dead wagon had entered the prison and was driven across the forbidden land to the hospital. Eight more corpses were thrown into the cart and hauled off to the cemetery.

• • •

The water grew shallower, to his waist, to his knees. Stanley stumbled out onto the bank. He wanted to lie down, to recover his breath, but no warmth could be found there, only death from freezing. His cold, wet undershirt and drawers clung to his flesh. He had left his shirt, trousers, and frock coat with John so he would have something dry to put on later.

241

Stanley blew gently into the can until the embers glowed brightly again. Then he moved through the trees toward the line of white tents.

Men huddled together under blankets. Some lay on their sides on the ground, spooning front to back for warmth, in lines of eight or ten.

Stanley found an open space. It wasn't hidden from the guards in their roosts, but it would have to do. He knelt and scraped together a small pile of pine straw. The straw was a little damp, but it would have to do too. He dumped the glowing embers onto the ground and covered them with some of the pine straw. He bent low and blew deep, gentle, steady breaths until first a flicker and then a small flame curled up from within.

Some of the men began to stir.

"Shh," Stanley said to the nearest man. "I need more straw. Can you crawl over here and blow on this to keep it going?"

The man did so and Stanley returned to the stream where the trees grew thickest and where the pine straw was plentiful and drier. He also gathered up as many twigs and small branches as he could carry.

Within a few minutes, Stanley had a small, hot fire burning. He collected some pine branches and added them to the fire. Sick men closest to the fire had to move back because of the heat. Others of the sullen, sunken, hopeless faces were now smiling and nodding their thanks to Stanley.

"It's your fire now," Stanley told them. "If you can walk, you must get firewood. There are still a lot of cut branches on this side of the stream. If you let that fire die, you will die."

Stanley wanted to stay to warm himself and dry his clothes, but his work was done. He edged away from the blaze toward the shadows to conceal himself from the guards. Then he slipped back through the pines and into the frigid stream again.

Once across he picked up his walking stick where he had left it and started hobbling up toward the settlement. The cane trembled in his hand with every aching, shivering step. He had never been so cold, but his own home fire would soon warm him, and a tin can full of Austin's hot beef broth would make him whole once more.

CHAPTER 45

STANLEY COUNTED THE PASSAGE OF WEEKS BY THE SUNDAY afternoon appearances of Captain Vowles within the stockade—four more since the time they had spoken. The abysmal conditions at the prisoners' hospital had continued to distress Stanley and, during the commandant's third visit, Stanley had asked him what could be done to alleviate their suffering.

Vowles answer still rankled Stanley. "They are being well cared for. They are attended by the same doctors that attend my own men."

"But, sir," Stanley had said, boldly meeting the glaring eyes of the commandant, "many of our brothers have no shelter at all."

"Yes, well," Vowles said, "it's all we have."

Stanley didn't go to any more of the commandant's meetings, and as the days wore on, nothing of any substance changed for the good. Bathing in the frigid waters of the stream and walks about the camp became solitary activities. Whenever Stanley left the shanty, Austin had to remain to guard against thieves. The rubber blanket was their most prized possession—it's protection against cold and rain was coveted by all.

The rations remained edible, but totally insufficient, so Stanley slipped another Abraham out of his suspenders and handed it to Austin. "I only have three more."

"Make it last as long as I can," Austin said. He went off to the sutler's shack next to the bridge to purchase potatoes and vegetables for soup, and just as he had at Andersonville, he established a small soup shop outside their shanty. Austin's business thrived for about three weeks, and many of Austin's regular patrons began to look healthier, but the dead cart continued to make its daily runs back and forth to the cemetery outside the stockade wall.

About the middle of November, on a Wednesday, as near as Stanley could figure it, a squad of eight guards led by a lieutenant marched up the path from the bridge and through the settlement to the section occupied by the First Division.

"Silence," the lieutenant ordered the gathering crowd. "I have an order from Captain Vowles. First Division, you are to prepare to depart immediately for exchange. You will be sent out as soon as the cars arrive."

The squad moved a few blocks to the Second Division. The order was repeated, except that the Second Division would be sent out the following day. "One more thing," the lieutenant said, raising his voice above the stir of the prisoners, "Sergeant Mitchell, show yourself."

Austin elbowed Stanley. "What's this about, Mitch?"

"No idea," Stanley said. He stepped forward through the ranks of prisoners until he was face to face with the lieutenant. "I'm Sergeant Mitchell, sir."

"The commandant has ordered you to report to him immediately."

"May I ask what for, sir?"

"You may not," the lieutenant said.

● ● ●

Captain Vowles appeared very different from the pleasant, confident officer Stanley had talked with weeks earlier. He sat huddled over his desk in the dimly lit and sparsely furnished parlor of a simple log house. One hand cradled his brow. His face was creased with worry, and he seemed weighed down by life itself, just as every prisoner under his control had been for months.

Vowles waved Stanley to a chair next to the desk. "I've been ordered to close this prison. In one week's time, all the prisoners must be gone from here. And I find that, once again, I must ask for your help."

Why? Stanley bit his lower lip to keep from blurting out the question. He knew why. *Sherman. His army must coming here.*

"When we first spoke," Captain Vowles said, speaking slowly, his voice nearly monotone, "you mentioned your service to your dead and wounded comrades. You have also expressed your concern for the sick of this prison."

The commandant took a pipe from the top drawer of his desk. The bowl held no tobacco, but he held it to his mouth anyway. "I would like us to discuss how we might evacuate the sick from this prison. We shall probably never become friendly, but for their benefit, I would like our conversation to be as cordial as it can be between two men who find themselves on opposite sides of this conflict. May we agree to that much?"

"Yes, sir."

"Good," Vowles said, smiling the same weak smile Stanley had seen inside the stockade, "and I won't ask you to sign any oath."

"All right, sir. What can I do to help?"

"I'm not asking you to divulge any military secrets, but how did you transport the wounded of General Sherman's army?"

"We had special cars, sir, passenger cars fitted with two tiers of bunks. Each car carried two dozen patients. It had its own small privy and a stove for heat."

The captain wrinkled his nose and drew on his empty pipe. "Our provisions will have to be more modest."

"How modest, sir?"

"The usual freight or cattle cars, whatever they send me. I'm not an evil man, Sergeant. I want as many of these men as possible to survive the journey to the point of exchange."

"Are they really going to be exchanged, sir?"

The commandant gazed steadily at Stanley. "Yes. These men will never fight in this war, and they are—" He stopped suddenly, as if he was about to say too much.

"They're hindering your movements, sir, and your superiors wish to rid themselves of that burden."

Captain Vowles stared at Stanley for a moment, then nodded.

"Then, sir, it's a matter of how many sick men there are, how far they will be expected to travel, and how long you expect to hold them until they are exchanged."

"According to Surgeon White's last ration count, we have four hundred thirty-one this morning. They will be sent to Savannah, and I'm told exchange is to be immediate. Take a few minutes to think over the arrangement, Sergeant."

"I don't need to, sir," Stanley said, shaking his head. "Our sick men won't be able to sit for the journey as we did on the way here. Many will need to lie down all the time. Thirty men per car instead of sixty should allow for this. That's fourteen or fifteen cars."

The captain's eyes widened in amazement. "You wrote nothing down, Sergeant. Did you figure that in your head?"

"Yes, sir. I find numbers easy."

"Fifteen cars then," Vowles said. "Continue."

"Each should have his own blanket, sir. And straw too."

The commandant arched his eyebrows at Stanley.

"Yes, sir, straw," Stanley said. "The floors of the cars should be covered with it a foot or two deep, for warmth, sir, but also to absorb their excretions. Some of those boys won't be able to make it to the bucket."

"I see," Vowles said. "Straw we have. There are plenty of hay bales in the fields of this county. But four hundred blankets could be a problem. Is there anything else?"

"I believe it should take twelve hours or so to reach Savannah, sir, but it could take an entire day." Stanley waited a moment for Captain Vowles to respond, but he remained silent. "Please make sure they have plenty of water, and if it's at all possible, sir, please grant them double rations."

Captain Vowles held out a piece of paper and an old quill pen toward Stanley. "Write it all down, Sergeant, and I'll pass it on to my adjutant."

"Captain Vowles, is there someone on your staff I can review the details with, someone who can oversee this operation after I'm gone?"

"Gone, Sergeant?"

"Yes, sir. Your lieutenant said my division is to go tomorrow."

"And they will, but you will not. You will see to your sick men first. Then you will go out with the last division." Vowles handed Stanley another sheet of paper. "That's a parole granting you permission to leave the stockade. Show it to the guards whenever you pass the gate. You will report here each morning at eight o'clock to report on your progress."

CHAPTER 46

STANLEY SAT ON THE LOW RAILROAD EMBANKMENT FOR several minutes massaging the tight muscles of his left leg. Too much sitting in the cars. Too much of being forced to push the train up a slight grade. Stanley had tried to do his part, but his leg wouldn't take much strain, and he had to hobble along behind the last car as it had inched toward the low crest. Mr. Charlton would have been horrified, had he bothered to come out from his office in Savannah, for this was his railroad, the Savannah and Gulf.

Stanley uncorked his canteen and lifted it to his lips. He drained it dry. Less than a mouthful. The engine had stopped just before a short bridge. The half dozen slaves who rode on the fuel tender dashed back and forth to the stream with buckets, filling the boiler.

After a while, the slaves went into the woods under guard and began felling several trees. If the past three days were any indication, it would take the six slaves about two hours to chop enough firewood to fill the tender.

One carload of prisoners at a time was allowed to go down to the stream to fill their canteens. Stanley was in the third car. When his turn came, he eased himself down the slippery bank into the slow-moving stream. Most of the men plunged their canteens under the water within a few feet of the bank, but Stanley waded several yards into the stream and waited for the sediment he had stirred up to settle.

Stanley removed his hat and rinsed it in the stream. He splashed water on his face and on the back of his neck. Then he uncorked his canteen and lowered it slowly into the water, tilted at an angle, so the water flowed into the canteen at a slow trickle.

Stanley returned to the water's edge and made his way back to his place along the roadbed. The locomotive had broken down for the third time in as many days out of Savannah, though not as completely as it had late last night near a place called Doctortown. Then, the locomotive had failed completely; the train had lurched to a halt. The prisoners had tumbled out of the cars for fresh air and slept beside the rails until morning, when a mechanic had come out from town. The train had finally gotten under way again about noon.

They must be moving us again to keep us from Sherman, but where are we now? And where are the Rebels sending us? Am I any closer to Anna than I was at Millen?

All Stanley knew from the angle of the sun was that they were crawling their way southwest deeper into Georgia. And even with his aching leg and his walking stick, he thought he could have made better time on foot.

Three prisoners, gaunt, dirty, and rough-looking, walked up the shoulder of the roadbed toward the front of the train.

"Whoa there." One of the guards stepped into their path. "Where you-uns think yer going?"

"We can help get this rattletrap moving again," the middle man of the three said.

The guard spat a dark stream of something nasty at their feet. "Us-uns'll fix it."

"Like the last time, and the time before that," the man said. "We're sick of sitting by and starving. We're mechanics. We can fix anything. Don't you want to get where you're going and get something to eat?"

The guard pondered the question for what seemed a long time, but his gnawing belly must have convinced his mind of the wisdom of the Yankee's offer. Finally, he turned and escorted the three mechanics forward to the stricken locomotive.

• • •

Stalwart House was no more. Stew was dead and Austin was gone. Frank was gone too. Stanley had heard talk in the quartermaster's office of a new large camp in South Carolina. Maybe they had been sent there. When Stanley said he would be staying behind when the rest of the Second Division was sent out of Millen, Austin had been crushed. The following morning had been somber indeed as they divided their possessions equally.

Stanley's inventory didn't amount to much, but it was more than many others had—two wool blankets, one canteen, a half canteen for use as a plate, frying pan, or shovel, one fire-blackened tin can with a wire handle, his Bible, his hunting knife, Stew's razor, a small ball of twine and string, his housewife sewing kit, thirty dollars Federal, and twenty-seven Confederate. The three Abrahams were still tucked away safe inside his suspenders, and the Confederate scrip was stuffed in the pocket of his trousers. All of the other items were rolled up inside his two blankets.

Austin and Stanley had wished each other safe travels. Each had promised the other that he would keep an eye out for him wherever he was sent. They had embraced, as brothers often do, and then they had bidden each other farewell.

Stanley had shouldered his blanket roll and walked down the slope from the settlement to the bridge over the stream. The guards had let him pass with hardly a glance at his parole. That evening, when Stanley had returned to the Stockade from his work at the prison quartermaster's office, the shanty was bare and empty.

• • •

Stanley sat with his face buried in his hands. There were many prisoners nearby talking or sleeping. One group had built a fire and took turns holding their trousers over the flames to smoke the lice out. *Good idea. I'll try that next time rather than skirmishing.* Stanley recognized several men from the car, but not one he could call a friend. *No doubt about it. Were it not for Austin, I would have died at Andersonville.*

"You can't do it alone," Austin had said that first day. "Got to have friends, good friends."

And countless times, Austin had proved himself a true friend. Perhaps he was sent along this same route, just a few days earlier. Perhaps his train broke down too. Perhaps he sat along this very same stretch of track.

But Stanley really didn't really think so. He had heard the Rebels talking when they thought no one was listening, or perhaps didn't care if anyone overheard. Some of the trains were returning to Savannah; others were headed for Charleston, and still others for a place Stanley had never heard of—Florence.

At least the weather had been good since Savannah. The sun was strong on his back, the air fresh and clear. And the nights spent locked inside the crowded car had been bearable. The guards had chained the doors open a little, not enough to let a man slip through, but enough to admit the cool night air.

A prisoner about thirty feet away stood and began walking toward the tree line, a common enough occurrence with so many men needing to relieve themselves from time to time. The guards stood straight and raised their weapons in case the prisoner made a sudden dash for freedom.

The prisoner was from Stanley's car and it seemed that he was alone too. His clothes weren't complete tatters. He didn't look thoroughly unkempt the way most of the other prisoners did, and he looked only quarter-starved rather than half. He always seemed to be off by himself, far away and sad, even when he was crowded in the car with dozens of other prisoners—very much like Stanley himself.

The prisoner stopped short of the tree line and fell to his knees amid the grasses and wildflowers of the roadside. He bent over and clawed at the ground with his hands, trying to unearth something, perhaps a plant. The man straightened a little and examined his find, a plant with a long, tapered root. Then he started digging again.

Stanley stood and walked toward the man. The guards had lowered their weapons and were talking among themselves again.

Stanley tapped the man's shoulder with the tip of his walking stick. "Will this help?"

The man looked up. "Yah, sure. Thanks." He reached for the cane.

"It's strong," Stanley said, "but try not to break it."

"I'll be careful. Name's Wendell Brooks. What's yours?"

"Stanley Mitchell. Mitch, if you like. What are you digging up?"

"Bull thistle. Them prickles ain't fun, but you can eat the rest." He stabbed the tip of Stanley's cane into the earth beneath another plant a couple of feet away. "Yah, sure, ain't nothing to recommend it. The root don't taste good, and the greens ain't exactly delec'able, but it's better than what I got in my belly, which is nothing."

"Where are you from, Wendell?"

"Minnesota. Near St. Cloud. Got this stuff up there too. There's lots of stuff just laying around to eat it in a pinch. Dandelion's better. Seen some back a ways, but I ain't seen none here."

"Do you have a partner?" Stanley asked.

"Nah. My brother died real terrible at Andersonville. I tried another chap on for size at Millen, but he died too."

Stanley slipped his blanket roll off his shoulder. "We left about eight hundred in the graveyard there," he said, as he untied the end of the blanket. "I was in the quartermaster's office figuring out transport for our sick. They didn't record the names of the dead, so all our boys were buried as unknowns."

Stanley removed his prized hunting knife from the blanket and slid it across the ground toward Brooks. "Here, this will work better. Don't let the guards see it."

Brooks smiled. "Thanks, Mitch. I'll give you some root. It ain't cooked so eat just a little and see if you abide it good."

Stanley stood between the guards and Wendell as he dug up several more bull thistles. "Say, Wendell," Stanley said after a few minutes, "I'm in need of a new partner too. You interested?"

Wendell finished digging up another thistle. He picked up his small harvest and the knife, which he kept hidden among the thistles, and stood facing Stanley. "Yah, sure, but my luck with partners ain't been good, just so you know."

The guards started to call the "All aboard." Along the roadbed, grunting, groaning, starving men rose wearily to their feet. There was no hopping into the cars, and only a little actual climbing aboard. Mostly, it was a mixture of heaving and hoisting and swearing and flopping that got the thin, sickly men back into the cars.

The six slaves had filled the fuel tender, but as it had been each of the past three days, they were hard at work again. Whenever the train stopped for any reason, their final task was to dig one or two or three graves just within the tree line, unmarked graves that would probably never be noticed, for men who would be forgotten as soon as the train rounded the next bend.

254

CHAPTER 47

ONCE AGAIN, THE TRAIN RATTLED AND SQUEALED TO A STOP. Curses and groans rose from the suddenly awakened prisoners.

Guards rapped the butts of their rifles on the metal sides of the cars. "All out. Column of fo-ah."

Stanley nudged Wendell. "I think we're finally at wherever it is we're supposed to go."

"Yah, sure, Mitch. At least the engine didn't break again."

Wendell helped Stanley down to the ground and the two lined up with the rest of the prisoners. A man had died in their car. His body was removed and laid beside the rails with several others.

It was late at night, perhaps very late. And it was raining, not pouring down torrents, but enough to soak every man to the skin. Pitch-pine torches were lit and handed to prisoners in every fifth rank down the length of the column. The guards carried only their rifles, primed and ready, in case any prisoner bolted for the trees.

"You were right, Wendell," Stanley said. "That thistle root didn't taste like much, and it gave me a stomach ache, but keep those leaves for tea."

"You think we're going to another camp, Mitch?"

"Yes." The affirmation forced Stanley once again to admit that his prospects for ever returning to Matthews Hill Farm were growing fainter with each passing day.

The column started forward. They shuffled along the tracks past a shack of a depot. Torchlight illuminated a peeling sign with faded letters on the side of the small building—B-L-A-C-K-S-H-E-A-R. The column entered a narrow, wooded lane that led away from the railroad. *Any minute now the gates will slam shut behind me. Again. Then it will be more endless days of being, just existing—not living—using all my meager energy to survive one more day. And when the end comes, who will care? Who will even notice? Will my name ever be recorded?"*

An hour later the guards ordered the column to halt. Far ahead, more flames flickered through the trees, not torches, but large, blazing fires. Tiny black silhouettes of soldier figures with rifles on their shoulders paced back and forth.

Shouted orders were passed down the column. The prisoners went forward again. There was no gate and no stockade of pine logs, only a well-defined perimeter, protected by hundreds of guards and several batteries of artillery. The prisoners were counted by hundreds, turned into the camp, and told to settle down for the night.

By morning the rain had stopped and it grew quite warm. Stanley and Wendell set out to find a place to set up their own camp.

It wasn't a large place, a fraction of the size of Andersonville, tiny compared to Millen. Hundreds of small huts and shanties had been built among the trees. Campfire smoke hung in the still morning air. The ground was entirely forested, except for the narrow strip of land around the perimeter where guards patrolled and artillery pieces threatened.

"It is rather clever," Stanley said.

"What?" Wendell asked.

"At Andersonville and Millen, the Rebel forts were outside the prison. Here, the prison is inside the fort. Each guard has his own narrow sector to watch and the cannon can rake the entire camp."

"It's a cattle pen," Wendell said.

As Stanley and Wendell walked around the camp, Stanley asked dozens of men if they had seen a small man, with short, dark hair and beard who went by the name Ogre. Nobody had been there more than four days. Six to eight hundred had come in every day, almost all from Millen, but nobody had seen Austin.

Wendell Brooks had other questions for the men. "What about rations?"

"Guards go out every morning and drive in some beeves. They slaughter them right outside. Freshest beef there is, but not much of it. There's rice too, and now and again a farmer stops by with a wagon of fruit or taters."

"And the guards, who are they?" Wendell asked.

"Georgia reserves, from what I heard, several hundred of them down from Savannah. Either of you know what day this is?"

There had been a calendar on the wall of the quartermaster's office at Millen. Stanley counted the days. He had left Millen at night on the seventeenth, boarded the train for Blackshear the next evening, then four more days. "I think it's Wednesday, the twenty-third of November."

"Ha," the man said, "then tomorrow's Thanksgiving Day, thanks to Mr. Lincoln. Can't you smell the turkey them Rebs is roasting for us?"

A small stream ran through the middle of the camp. Stanley and Wendell claimed a spot under the trees near where the stream entered the camp, where the water was cleanest. Wood was abundant, even more so than at Millen. Stanley built a small campfire and filled their canteens at the stream while Wendell went about gathering branches for building shelter.

Stanley chopped some of the bull thistle roots and leaves. "I wish I had a pot to make a proper soup," he told Wendell, "but my friend Austin took it when he went out from Millen." Stanley poured some water into his tin cam and threw in some of the thistle cuttings. Then he hung it over the fire to boil. Wendell did the same.

"What do you think, Mr. Brooks? Shall we throw up a simple shanty or improve the neighborhood with a log hut?"

"That's up to you, Mitch. I don't plan on being here long term."

"How's that?"

"I'm done with trekking about this Confed'racy. Yah, sure, they'll keep at it until I'm dead, so I ain't giving them the chance. I got to go home or Mama won't never know what become of Billy. Or me. You ain't a spy, are you? You said you done work for the Rebs."

"No, Wendell." Stanley's ire stirred a little. "I didn't work for them, I worked for our sick comrades. They did go to the coast for exchange, I can assure you, and those who survived are well on their way home by now."

Stanley paused, deciding if he should speak further. "I'm as Union loyal as you are, Wendell." He lowered his voice to a bare whisper. "I wish I could run off with you, but I would only slow you down. But when I'm finally free, I'm going back to Tennessee to marry a beautiful Southern gal, and that's where I'll make my home." Stanley shook his head slow and deliberate. "No, I'm no spy. Your secret is safe with me."

● ● ●

Six days later, after Stanley prayed over their evening meal of rice, boiled sweet potato, and fire-roasted beef, Wendell set his tin plate aside.

"I'm going out tonight."

Stanley didn't respond. He wasn't surprised. Wendell had slept every day since they had come to Blackshear,

258

and he had stayed awake every night, watching the guards, studying their habits, looking for an opportunity.

"Yah, sure, I'll dash right through them and into the woods. They ain't cleared but twenty yards of trees away for their pigeon walk. And them guards is supposed to turn the same to keep proper watch. But they don't, 'specially late at night. It ain't the same distance between the guns. They get lazy and sometimes one guard turns at one time, and another turns later. Sometimes there's a gap of a minute or more."

"And they don't have any dogs to chase you down," Stanley said.

"No dogs." Wendell picked up his plate and ate a few bites more. "I'm taking only my blanket and my knife. Clanky stuff will only give me away."

"What about your canteen?" Stanley asked.

"Yah, sure. I thought about that a lot." Wendell shrugged. "When it's full, it's heavy. When it's empty, it's clanky."

"But you must have water, Wendell."

"Yah sure, but it ain't no desert out there. Saw lots of streams on the train. Must be one every mile, maybe more."

"Then keep water in it, and you'll risk being spotted at a stream less often."

Wendell shrugged and nodded. "That's good advice. I'll take the canteen."

Stanley chewed his beef slowly, savoring its juicy, smoky, fatty goodness. "So, it's tonight?"

"Yep, been watching the moon, wasn't but a trace last night. Should be none tonight."

"We're in the middle of nowhere. Where will you go?"

"North a bit, then west a bit, then south to the railroad. Should shake anybody trying to follow. Then it's back through Blackshear and on to Savannah. A hundred miles or so. I'll follow that rickety railroad all the way back and travel only at night. I can hide easy if a train comes along. You said they sent us out of Millen because Sherman was going for Savannah. I'll be there to welcome him. Yah, for sure."

When darkness fell neither man slept. They sat side by side in their shanty, speaking little, listening to the guards call out the half hours.

"You see?" Wendell whispered, shortly after the call for two o'clock went around the camp. "They're stumbling along half asleep. Now, the one turns and they're both facing each other." He counted the seconds under his breath. "Now, the one on the right turns. Forty seconds. When that one on the left turns again, they'll be facing opposite and I'll be running between them." He grabbed Stanley's hand and shook it. "So long, Mitch. Hope you get back to that girl."

"Godspeed, Wendell."

And then he was off, running between the inattentive sentries for the trees beyond. An alarm was raised. The guards quickly realized what was happening and unslung their weapons. A couple of shots rang out; then it was silent. A detail of torch wielding guards was dispatched into the woods, but no cries of discovery were heard and no bloody corpse was returned to the camp.

And so it seemed that early on the morning of Wednesday, November 30th, as Stanley reckoned the passage of days, Wendell Brooks had indeed made good his escape from the Blackshear prison camp.

CHAPTER 48

December, 1864

THE VERY NEXT DAY, AT FIRST LIGHT, THE COMMANDANT OF the prison entered the camp. A call went up from one guard to the next all around the camp that the commandant wished to address the prisoners. He was a slender man with light hair and long bushy sideburns that almost joined at his chin, much like Dr. Lord back in Vicksburg. Stanley moved to the front rank of the gathering crowd to hear every word.

"My name is Colonel Forno. It has always been our intention, to return you to Federal authorities as soon as possible, but your own people have thwarted those efforts at every turn. Their lack of ships or the raids of their cavalry have prevented honorable Confederate officers from completing the necessary exchange of prisoners."

It sounded like more of the same—promises and excuses—but then Colonel Forno held up a paper.

"This is a certificate of parole. I had five thousand of them sent down here from Savannah. Any man that signs this parole will be put aboard a northbound train for immediate exchange."

"Read it!" a voice came from well behind Stanley.

The sergeant next to Colonel Forno took a step forward, as if to search out and silence the voice in the crowd, but Forno grabbed him by the arm.

"It's all right, Sergeant." Then Colonel Forno read the certificate.

"Let one of our boys read it," the voice said.

Waves of murmurs went back and forth through the crowd of prisoners. "Yes, yes. One of our boys."

Forno scanned the front ranks of prisoners. His eyes settled on Stanley. Perhaps he thought Stanley was one of the leaders because of the chevrons on the sleeve of his long frock coat. "Sergeant, take this parole down to that tall sergeant with the cane in the front. Go ahead and read it, son."

Stanley scanned the paper. It certainly looked official. He cleared his throat and raised his voice so all could hear, just as he had done whenever he read over the swamp at Andersonville.

I, the undersigned Prisoner of War, hereby give my parole of honor not to bear arms against the Confederate States, or to perform any military or garrison duty whatever, until regularly exchanged; and further, that I will not divulge anything relative to the position or condition of any of the forces of the Confederate States. Signed this First day of December, eighteen sixty-four.

December first. So, my counting of days was correct.

"Thank you, Sergeant," Forno said. "Are you willing to sign that parole? If you do, son, you will very soon be back within your own lines."

The war would end soon. Everyone knew it. Even the Rebels were realizing their cause was doomed. Stanley knew he wouldn't be fit for any military duty for months, if ever. And the part about not divulging anything? That was hog slop. Everybody knew that too.

Stanley looked up at Colonel Forno. "Have you pen and ink, sir?"

• • •

In the light of day, the ramshackle Blackshear depot fit in well with the small chapel and about two dozen other simple wooden structures of the tiny hamlet, and that included every cabin, coop, barn, shack, and shed. Someone said it was the county seat, but Stanley didn't see anything that resembled a courthouse.

It had been two days since Stanley signed the parole, and the train he boarded was the second to depart northbound from Blackshear. The train wheezed and clanked several hours along the rails back the way it had come just days before, and much to Stanley's surprise, the locomotive didn't break down at all. Late in the day, however, the train came to an abrupt halt at Doctortown again, just before a long bridge over a wide river.

The train backed onto a siding and the prisoners were ordered out of the cars. A few minutes later the locomotive chugged past in reverse and disappeared in the direction from which they had just come.

The guards were peppered with questions which they only answered with shrugs, if at all. "Where did the loco go?" "How long will we be here?" "What's happening?"

It was nearly dark when the locomotive returned. It had obviously paid a visit to a turntable, for it was now pointed in the opposite direction—back toward Blackshear.

"Sherman's cut the railroad," a prisoner near Stanley said. "Has to be, and now they can't send us to Savannah."

"Why don't they just send us to Sherman then?" a comrade asked.

"Because," Stanley said, "these little excursions are never about exchange."

"And you was the first to sign that parole," the first prisoner said.

"Yes," Stanley said, "and I would do it again just on the remote chance that there might be one honest Rebel left in the South."

"Bah," the man said, "we're all hoping that, and probably will until one day it's for real."

"The only ones I know who were actually exchanged," Stanley said, "were our sick from Millen. As soon as that engine's hitched, they'll put us back in the cars and send us back to Blackshear or some other camp."

● ● ●

It was back to Blackshear.

The six hundred men from Stanley's train shuffled back into camp between two long lines of prisoners, all eager to hear the order to march to the depot.

"Back so soon?" one man asked as Stanley passed.

"Another hoax," Stanley said. "I should have known."

Stanley's shanty had remained untouched during the day and a half he had been gone. It was nothing but a few pine boughs propped up with sticks. Who would want it? He gathered a few sticks, asked a neighbor for an ember, and built himself a small fire. It was almost time for rations.

Months of winter lay ahead. How long could he wait? How long could he waste away a little more each day, wander about shoeless, and huddle under a threadbare blanket by a small fire—if there was any wood? How long until the finish of it all? How long could he endure? *How long, O Lord?*

There was a psalm that started with those words. Stanley took out his Bible and, starting from Psalm One, quickly found the passage and read the words aloud.

"How long wilt thou forget me, O LORD? Forever? How long wilt thou hide thy face from me? How long shall I take counsel in my soul, having sorrow in my heart daily? How long shall mine enemy be exalted over me?"

Have you forgotten me? Are you hiding your face from me? Will my sorrows last until the day I die? Until my enemies exalt over my death?

"Consider and hear me, O LORD my God: lighten mine eyes, lest I sleep the sleep of death; lest mine enemy say, I have prevailed against him; and those that trouble me rejoice when I am moved."

Literally moved. Hither and yon at their whim. Up the tracks a ways, then right back here, and Forno and the rest are probably laughing long and hard about how easy it is to trick "them damn Yankees."

"But I have trusted in thy mercy; my heart shall rejoice in thy salvation. I will sing unto the LORD, because he hath dealt bountifully with me."

Have you, Lord? Have you dealt bountifully with me? Austin told me to look for the good. Where is the good? And what good can I do when I'm so in need? Death still surrounds me—six more men were buried beside the tracks this morning—and yet I'm supposed to trust you. My friends are all gone. Only I am left. Is this what you want? What am I to say, that there is no one else but you, Lord? That I love you more than all others? More than Anna? Did she ever get my letter from Savannah?

After cooking and eating his meager supper, Stanley folded one of his blankets in half and laid down on it. Sleep wouldn't come for hours, if at all, but there was no one he cared to talk to. He drew the second blanket over himself, not because he was cold, but because that thin, frayed blanket was the one comfort he could touch and feel and hold onto.

And beneath its covering, Stanley clutched his hunting knife and his Bible over his chest, the entire arsenal of a lame, emaciated prisoner alone in the night.

CHAPTER 49

*T*HERE HAD BEEN YET ANOTHER TRAIN RIDE FROM Blackshear, west rather than east, and away from Sherman to another camp in a village at the end of the railroad line called Thomasville.

After a week or so, Stanley noticed that Colonel Forno's guards, who paced the perimeter of the camp and who had been with them since Savannah, had been replaced by a new cohort. And this new bunch looked meaner and nastier than Forno's toughest men ever had.

One of the new guards looked somewhat familiar to Stanley—faded butternut uniform, sergeant's stripes on his sleeves, a long, bushy red beard. Although it was a warm and pleasant day, a cold shiver of dread raced through Stanley's body, for in that moment, he understood his fate.

The new guards had come from Andersonville, and Stanley could think of only one reason for their sudden appearance: to escort the prisoners back to that deadly place. And there was only one way to get there—walk.

A few days later, four or five thousand Federal prisoners, almost all of whom were shoeless like Stanley, started to march north from Thomasville to Albany, a distance of sixty-three miles, according to the signpost.

The marchers had no shelter. Only a scant ration of corn meal and a morsel of beef per man was provided each evening. And firewood was in short supply, only enough to cook their rations, never enough to warm more than their hands.

Cold rain pelted them the first night. Stanley didn't sleep at all. He wrapped himself in his blankets, turned up the collar of his frock coat, and forced himself toward prayer, but he could only groan his miserable burden heavenward, little believing that even God could provide any relief. Frosty wind finally drove away the rain. Stanley, chilled to the bone, shook uncontrollably. His jaw ached from clenching it to keep his teeth from chattering.

In the gray, cloudy half-light of the first dawn of the march, the wretched prisoners were ordered to rise and form a column in the road. But several men couldn't hear the order; they couldn't rise and obey; their earthly march was done.

A score of slaves that trailed along at the rear of the column collected the corpses, dug a shallow trench beside the road, and laid the dead to rest, unmarked and unknown, just as had been done along the railroad. And even while the slaves were shoveling dirt over the bodies, the order rang out to march on.

It became common for a man to fall out of line and drop dead beside the road. After the first few times, hardly anyone glanced down at the dead man as they shuffled past. Stanley took out his Bible and tried to read as he plodded along. The print was small and he had to keep his eyes steady to keep his place, but the reading helped pass the dragging hours and fix his attention on better things, spiritual and eternal things, rather than on the shadow of death and his own misery.

On the fourth day of the march, Stanley was deep into the troubles of the prophet Jeremiah when a man in front of him suddenly stumbled and fell in a heap. Of course, Stanley didn't seen the man fall, so he tripped over the man and tumbled to the muddy road.

"Damn you." How quickly the curse displaced the words of Scripture. Stanley looked at the dead man—about his own age, perhaps a year or two older, but it was so hard to tell when every man hardly looked like a man at all. No doubt his heart had given out.

It could have easily been me, a hundred times or more. Lord, please forgive my sin and have mercy on him.

"I'm sorry," Stanley said to the dead man. "I don't wish you damned forever. I only wish you God's grace and peace, and comfort for your loved ones."

"On yer feet, Yank, or you'll get buried next to him." The red-bearded sergeant stood over Stanley, trying to look fierce despite his own hunger and exhaustion.

"Ah, Sergeant Peck," Stanley said, "I'm at your feet just as I was when I arrived at Andersonville six months ago." And just as he had done then, Stanley used his hickory walking stick to struggle to his feet.

"Maybe yer oughta quit the reading," Peck said, with a sneer on his face and in his words, "and keep yer eyes to the front."

"If it's all the same to you, Sergeant," Stanley replied, "I find God's strength in the reading. I'm weak and wasted, and it's only his strength that will save me."

After six days of plodding along, the column arrived at the Flint River across from Albany, a town with a railroad, and that railroad went north toward Andersonville.

Stanley hobbled down the bank and plunged into the river. There was no reason to ease his way in, for the frigid water wouldn't be less of a shock to his wasted limbs, and if he got it over with, the sinking afternoon sun might dry him enough so that his clothes wouldn't freeze during the long night. And the aching cold assured him he still lived.

The next morning, before dawn, the prisoners were roused and marched to the Albany depot. Stanley's clothes were still damp from the previous afternoon, and everyone stood shivering and stamping their feet until long after sunrise.

The stationmaster arrived. Word passed through the ranks that a train would be coming in later that morning to take as many men as the cars would hold north to Andersonville.

"What day is this?" someone asked the stationmaster.

"Why, boys," he drawled, "don't ye know?" The gnarled old man smiled and his eyes gleamed. "Today is Saturday, the twenty-fourth of December. Tomorrow, it's very special, you know. It's both our Savior's birthday and his resurrection day."

More waiting. Rations were distributed, two hardtack crackers and a small square of cooked bacon, better than they had seen for a week.

Finally, the train whistled and wheezed into the depot. After the engine's boiler was filled with water, and its tender filled with firewood, the prisoners boarded the foul-smelling cattle cars. Stanley was one of about sixty wedged into the eighth car in the train of twenty.

The train chugged northward for several hours and stopped when the winter sun was low in the western sky. The doors of the cars slid open and the prisoners were ordered to form a column along the siding. The familiar, dreaded man on a pale gray horse pranced up and down the line of prisoners who were once again under the cruel whims of his iron fist.

"Merry Christmas, Yanks," he cried out again and again. "Velcome home. Vee must celebrate your return. Tomorrow, vee make special Christmas feast in your honor."

CHAPTER 50

Sunday , December 25, 1864

*F*OR AS LONG AS ANNA COULD REMEMBER, THE MATTHEWS family had gathered around the fireplace in the parlor each Christmas morning, Bibles in hand, to read the story of the nativity. Years before, Papa had written an order of passages for the occasion, and the reading always immediately followed breakfast, before any gifts were exchanged.

"You may begin, Willy," Mama said, when her four children were settled in their places.

Willy stood. "From the ninth chapter of Isaiah."

The people that walked in darkness have seen a great light: they that dwell in the land of the shadow of death, upon them hath the light shined. For unto us a child is born, unto us a son is given: and the government shall be upon his shoulder: and his name shall be called Wonderful, Counsellor, The Mighty God, The Everlasting Father, The Prince of Peace.

Anna's eyes stung a little. Willy always went first. He held no Bible, but his recitation was flawless. His eyes had begun to fail shortly after he had learned to read, and he had worked hard at remembering what he called the *important parts.*

Willy had taken to Stanley from the moment Stanley finally awoke days after he had been carried almost lifeless into the house. And helping Willy memorize some of those passages had helped Stanley heal from the wounds to both to his body and his soul.

But there has been no word from Stanley for months. Where is he now? Is he still alive, Lord? Does he have any joy this Christmas Day?

Anna, Ruthie, and Davy took turns reading Luke's account of the birth of Christ. Then Willy recited the account of the visit of the wise men from the second chapter of Matthew.

Finally, it fell to Anna to read the final passage.

And when they were departed, behold, the angel of the Lord appeareth to Joseph in a dream, saying, Arise, and take the young child and his mother, and flee into Egypt, and be thou there until I bring thee word: for Herod will seek the young child to destroy him. When he arose, he took the young child and his mother by night, and departed into Egypt, and was there until the death of Herod: that it might be fulfilled which was spoken of the Lord by the prophet, saying, Out of Egypt have I called my son.

Anna closed her Bible. "That must have been hundreds of miles, and they probably walked the whole way. Imagine that. It must have taken months, but Stanley's last letter came all the way from Savannah in two weeks."

"By the sea route," Luke said, "I think that's more than two thousand miles."

"But it's easy with a steamship. You just sit on the deck while it carries you along." Anna smiled brightly and looked at her mother. "Mama, I want to try to find Stanley."

Mama's mouth fell open. "You what?"

"I want to go to Georgia and try to find Stanley."

"Whatever for?"

Anna's smile disappeared in an instant. "Last winter, I did almost nothing except read books I already read and wait for Stanley's next letter. I can't just sit and wait all winter. I must do something. I must try to find out what's become of him."

"Alone? I won't allow it."

"I could go with her," Luke said. "Levi and Aunt Min can look after you and the children, Mama."

Mama looked back and forth from Luke to Anna. "The two of you have talked about this?"

Both Anna and Luke nodded.

"How do you think you're going to get there?" Mama asked.

"There's a stage coach out of Purdy every Wednesday," Luke said. "Gets to Memphis Thursday evening."

"And then what?"

"Stanley's letter came by steamer," Anna said. "I think we can take a riverboat down to New Orleans, then hop on an ocean steamer to Savannah."

"Hop? You'll need to buy a ticket first." Mama's cheeks were becoming rosy pink. "And there will be stage coach fare and lodging and meals to pay for. Do you have money for all that? And to get home again?"

"We were hoping you could give us some money, Mama," Luke said.

"*I will not.*" Mama took a deep breath and calmed herself. "What will you do *if* you get to Savannah?"

"Maybe we can find the people that helped him—the Charltons." That idea had come to Anna when she had reread Stanley's last letter.

"But Sherman's taken Savannah," Mama said. "His men will be all over the place."

Anna looked across the table at Luke for help, but it was plain to see he had given up the fight. "What about General Logan's letter?" Anna asked. "I'm sure it will open a lot of doors."

"Probably," Mama said, "but not the kind my daughter will ever enter. And will it open any Confederate doors?"

"No, but maybe the smile of a pretty Southern girl will."

"Listen to me." Mama was dead earnest, looking Anna in the eye. "Sherman's army is at Savannah, so Stanley won't be. Georgia's a huge state, and truth is, you don't know if Stanley's still in Georgia. They could have moved him anywhere. If Stanley's still a prisoner, nobody in the Federal camp will know anything about him, and if he isn't...."

"Then I would just be searching for an unmarked grave somewhere? Is that what you're saying?"

Mama nodded slowly.

"And I will just have to accept it?"

"Yes, my dear, just like I had to accept that I would never know where your father was buried."

Anna fought off a sob, and when she replied, her words were bitter. "Well, I won't accept it, Mama. I can't."

Mama reached for Anna's hand and held it with both of hers. "Believe me, my dear, I do know how much you love Stanley, and how bad it hurts not knowing what's become of him. Don't you know it hurts me to see how you ache for him? If I thought there was any hope of finding him, I would go myself, but I won't have you and Luke running off to try to find him, and I won't provide one penny for such a foolish venture."

"Foolish?" Anna snatched her hand from Mama's grasp. "If I had money of my own—"

"But you don't, so that's the end of it." Mama's words were hard and unbending. Then she softened and touched Anna's hand again. "Please tell me one thing, my dear."

"What, Mama?"

"You haven't seen Stanley in over a year. Do you love him less for being gone so long, or more?"

Anna wiped her eyes with her handkerchief. "More, Mama. So much more."

"Then be patient and let your love grow even more, my dear. The war can't last much longer. Please, keep waiting on the Lord and pray he'll bring our Stanley back to us."

CHAPTER 51

Tuesday, December 27, 1864

STANLEY AWOKE STIFF AND ACHY. A COLD NIGHT ON COLD, hard ground always did that to him in spite of his two blankets. The sun had risen, but he was not yet ready to rise. There was no reason to hurry down to the swamp to beat the crowd, for the crowd was only a quarter of what it had been during the summer. And Providence Spring still flowed. He could wash later, when the sun was high in the sky, when he might actually feel a little of its warmth.

Christmas Day had passed almost without notice, except that Mr. Sheppard had preached an excellent sermon on a single verse from Luke's account of Jesus' birth. *For unto you is born this day in the city of David a Saviour, which is Christ the Lord.* The day of the Savior's birth was supposed to be a special day of peace and comfort and joy. Stanley was supposed to feel reborn, *a new creature,* according to the promises of Scripture, except all he felt reborn to were the deadly promises of Andersonville.

Stanley lay quiet, waiting for the others in the shebang to rise. His feet were the worst of it. He could always put his hands into his pockets or tuck them under his armpits to warm them, but what could he do to warm his bare, near-frozen feet?

• • •

When Stanley was turned into the stockade through the South Gate for the second time, no one had attacked him and no one had tried to steal any of his possessions. Instead, there had been many tempting offers of accommodations, as anyone who saw his thick blanket roll coveted the warmth his two woolen blankets might provide, no matter what condition those blankets were in.

Stanley had stood at the ready, his hand on the twine that tied the end of his roll closed. A quick jerk of his hand and his large hunting knife would have been in his hand. Instead, he had asked, "Can anyone tell me if the Christians still meet at the turnaround on Broadway?"

Several heads had nodded. Some of the men had looked disappointed and walked away.

"Who leads the meetings?" Stanley had asked.

"Mr. Sheppard does the preaching," a voice had answered. "Should be gathering soon."

Stanley limped down the hill, crossed the swamp on the new middle bridge, and was half-way down Broadway when the singing started. The hymn was still the same, "Come Ye Disconsolate," but the voices were weaker and fewer than he remembered. Stanley joined his voice to the chorus of the gathering faithful.

Mr. Sheppard led the meeting and preached a short sermon. He looked and sounded much as he had when he had defied the Raiders. Six months within the stockade had done little to diminish the passion and conviction of his preaching.

After the meeting, Stanley approached Mr. Sheppard.

"Ah, Mr. Mitchell." Sheppard grabbed Stanley's hand and clapped him on the shoulder. "I'm so glad to see you safe, but not that you have returned."

"And it's good to see you are well, Mr. Sheppard."

"You're still wearing your blanket roll. Do you need a place to call home?"

Stanley smiled. "I do, Mr. Sheppard, if someone of this group has room to spare."

"Nonsense," Sheppard said. "It's me and four others under my roof, and half that roof is the rubber blanket you gave me. You are more than welcome. And do you still have your Bible?"

"I do."

"Good," Sheppard said. "Then if you agree, I have a different passage for you to read down at the swamp."

• • •

Stanley dipped cold water from the ice-lined cask at Providence Spring and washed as quickly as he could. The cleansing was a despised, but daily necessity for himself and the other members of Sheppard's Shire. Like the now-defunct Stalwart House, Sheppard and the other four men—Caldwell, Munson, Stiles, and Wheaton—had committed themselves to wash and skirmish regularly, and to keep their residence, and the grounds around it, as clean as possible.

The men had greeted Stanley warmly and at once tried to make him feel welcome in their midst. For his part, Stanley had untied his blanket and displayed its contents. "These now belong to the shire," he had told them. His new housemates had gazed in wonder at Stanley's large hunting knife, but what particularly captured their fancies was Stew's razor, for all of the men were in desperate need of barbering.

Stanley wrung as much water as he could from his clothing, then drew each article on slowly. He had never grown accustomed to the dreadful discomfort of donning cold, damp clothing. Only his frock coat was dry, because he never washed it. An occasional rainstorm was all that was needed to keep it from offending anyone.

Stanley took his Bible from the pocket of his coat and stepped onto the bridge over the swamp. The simple duty of reading to the men had sometimes chafed him last summer, but now it felt good and necessary, an important way to mark each day. Stanley read from the nineteenth chapter of Job, the passage that Mr. Sheppard had chosen.

> Oh, that my words were now written! Oh, that they were printed in a book! That they were graven with an iron pen and lead in the rock forever! For I know that my redeemer liveth, and that he shall stand at the latter day upon the earth: And though after my skin worms destroy this body, yet in my flesh shall I see God: Whom I shall see for myself, and mine eyes shall behold, and not another; though my reins be consumed within me.

Stanley had come upon those words during that long, wretched trail of misery from Thomasville to Albany. The words had stayed with him. He knew them by heart. The promises had buried themselves deep in his soul, and had brought him some relief. He prayed it would be the same for all who heard those words day after day.

When Stanley returned to Sheppard's Shire, Munson looked quite ill.

"We need to take him to sick call," Mr. Sheppard said.

"Sick call's a farce," Stanley said, "and nobody gets better at the hospital."

"That was true three months ago," Sheppard said, "but the doctors have made some improvements while you were away, Mr. Mitchell. Half our boys come back better than they went out."

Stanley wasn't convinced. It must have shown on his face.

"Mr. Munson can walk," Sheppard said, "but he needs help. Why don't you help him across the camp to sick call at the South Gate and see for yourself?"

Munson looked miserable. Fits of coughing racked his body. His teeth chattered and he quivered uncontrollably. Stanley helped Munson to his feet and wrapped his right arm tightly around him. The man felt warm, too warm. Probably pneumonia.

And Munson had shelter. Hundreds, perhaps a thousand or more, had none. Last night, Stanley had been shocked to see lines of fifty to a hundred men form here and there throughout the camp. They lay on the open ground, spooning front to back, trying to keep warm during a long, frigid night. And when cold rain mixed with sleet had fallen, the suffering of those men was as keen as anything Stanley had endured on his recent march.

The doctor at sick call took one look at Munson, paroled the sick man to the hospital, and gave Stanley a pass to help Munson get there. The hospital was inside a small stockade outside the southeast corner of the prison.

Stanley waited with Munson until a doctor arrived to examine him. Then Stanley wished his new tent-mate well and went out through the gate of the hospital stockade to return to the prison.

"Ho there, lad."

Stanley turned around, seeking the owner of the cheery, reedy voice. A white-haired Catholic priest—the same priest who had pleaded for the lives of the six executed Raiders—had just left the hospital stockade.

"You're Father Whelan," Stanley said, when the priest approached.

"Aye, that I am. I don't believe we've met. How do ye know me, lad?"

"I saw you many times inside, when I was here before."

"Ah, a prodigal." There was a twinkle in his eye that matched his lilting brogue. "And who might ye be, lad?"

"Sergeant Stanley Mitchell of the Fifteenth Corps Quartermaster Department." And as the two men walked down the lane toward the South Gate, Stanley told Father Whelan of his experiences at the Green Hospital in Vicksburg.

Apparently, the priest was favorably impressed. "It seems ye have a heart for the downcast. Do ye think ye might wish to work at the hospital, lad?" he asked, when they reached the gate.

Stanley answered without hesitation. "Yes, Father. I must keep busy, and the hospital seems much improved over what it was."

"It is, lad." He turned toward the gate in the second of the three stockade walls that now surrounded the prison. "I must be going, for I'm chaplain to all the men, inside and outside."

CHAPTER 52

Monday, January 1, 1865

W ITHIN A FEW DAYS, STANLEY RECEIVED A PAROLE detailing him to work as a steward among the one hundred and twenty patients in Ward 6. *Ward* was the preferred word when anyone referred to one of the long, low sheds that had been built inside the hospital stockade to house sick prisoners. The sheds had roofs to protect the patients from rain, but no walls, and the bedridden suffered through the long, cold winter nights every bit as much as the rest of the prison population inside the stockade.

Father Whelan was nothing less than a hero to the men of Stanley's ward. Every other day, each man received a third of a loaf of soft wheat bread—not the usual coarse corncob bread—a gift from the priest, the men told Stanley. He had spent sixteen thousand dollars of his own money, all he had, they said, to buy barrels of fine wheat flour for the prisoners.

The priest visited Stanley's ward every day at least once, sometimes five or six times, to ease the suffering of the men, to pray with them, to administer the final sacrament, or to close their eyes when death took them. And Father Whelan never failed to speak a few kind words to Stanley.

"It's good work you're doing, lad. Is there anything you need?"

"No, Father, not for me, but many of these men will soon die. All of them have asked me to get word to their families. Is there anything I can do?"

"Aye, lad. Don't ye know the new rules Captain Wirz distributed today?"

"My company sergeant posted them at his tent, but I didn't read them."

Father Whelan took Stanley by the arm. "Come with me, lad."

The priest walked Stanley to the guard house next to the gate of the hospital stockade. He pointed to a sheet of paper nailed to the wall. "Read Rule Eight."

"'The prisoners have the privilege to write twice a week. No letter may be over one page in length and must contain nothing but private matters.'"

Stanley stared at the words and then read them a second time, just to be sure. He had heard of a few letters being sent out during the previous summer, but never had he heard of anyone receiving a reply. "Father, I've just returned after a three-month holiday, so I find this hard to believe."

"Aye, Sergeant, by order of our Swiss host himself. Ye know his guards will read them, so ye can write only personal things for the men, but that may be a hard thing, lad. Do ye think ye can write such letters for them that can't?"

"I'm willing to try, Father Whelan."

"That's all I can ask, lad. I know ye to be an educated young man. Ye will do a fine job of it, and the men shall have that small comfort at least. I shall appeal to the commandant for paper and pens and ink."

"And might I be allowed to write a letter of my own, Father?"

"Aye, lad. Anyone can, and your kin will likely get it."

• • •

Sgt. S. Mitchell, Det. 29
Camp Sumter Hospital - Ward 6
Andersonville, Geo.
Monday, January 2, 1865

My Dearest Anna,
Another year has begun and once again I write from a hospital, but not as a patient, as in Savannah. I returned to this place Christmas Eve. It is the same camp I mentioned in my last letter. There have been improvements since I was sent out three months ago. There is clean, fresh water for all from Providence Spring and the hospital is helping the prisoners. But the best is that I may now write two short letters each week which the authorities will read and post. Many in the camp have already written letters to loved ones at home with high hopes of receiving a reply soon.

My work at the hospital has several advantages. My Bible has often been my only comfort, and I read for the patients whenever they wish it. Father Whelan, supplied me with paper, pen, ink, and a small wooden lap desk so I could write letters for those who are too feeble to write—last thoughts of wives or sweethearts or parents, remembrances of happier times, or pleas for forgiveness of some insignificant, near-forgotten sin. Their words often tear at my heart.

For me, I'm passing the time more profitably and quickly in this important work than within the stockade where there is little to do. Austin, my good friend during my previous stay, told me I could not survive alone. He was right, and I'm never alone when I'm at the hospital. Perhaps I depend more upon the sick and dying than they do upon me.

Beyond these things that warm my spirit, the hospital wards are now long sheds with roofs as shelter from the rain, but no walls to keep out the cold. Still, I'm dry most of the time, and my work earns me an extra daily ration of food.

I have filled up my sheet front and back and must close. My hope has nearly gone out several times, but flickers once again with the thought that I may soon have some word from you.

I remain Your Affectionate and Devoted,
Sgt. Stanley Mitchell

• • •

Thursday, January 19, 1865

Anna clutched the letter to her breast with both hands. *Thank you, Lord.* The envelope was smudged with many filthy fingerprints. The post office imprints were faint, almost unreadable, and the ten-cent postage stamp looked odd, even for the Confederate postal service. Anna tore the envelope open. The page inside was smudged as well.

Stanley's handwriting was legible, but shaky, like it had been written by a much older hand. She compared the new letter to his letter from Savannah. His hand had been shaky then—an effect of the pneumonia, she had thought—but it was worse now, and he said nothing of being ill again.

Of course, I'll write, my darling boy. And you will get it just as soon as it can be carried to you. She laid the two letters aside and reached for her quill pen.

Miss Anna Matthews
Matthews Hill Farm
Purdy P. O., McNairy Cty., Tenn.
Friday, January 20, 1865

Dear Stanley,
I got your letter yesterday, and didn't sleep all night thinking about what to write, and put it all on one piece of paper. It's snowing now, but as soon as it's light out, Luke and me we're riding out to Purdy to get this in the mail that

284

goes out at noon. By the way, Mr. Burns took the C patch off one side of his mail bag, so he's got C. S. Mail on one side and U. S. Mail on the other. I should ask him who pays his wages.

I showed Luke where your in prison in Georgia and he looked real dark. At first he wouldn't say anything about it, but he keeps up on war news when he can, and I thought he knew, so I pestered him about it. Luke says he heard rumors and none are good. I can only cry out my heart to God and maybe He'll be kind and send you back here—to me.

I always think about you and sometimes dream, too, about you coming home and us getting married, but that's as far on as I ever get. Even when I think hard about how we will get on after we're married, I can't see anything clear, like leaves on a tree shaking in the wind, nothing stays still. Perhaps when you get home—never think if, only when— things will get more clear.

I'm very sad indeed thinking of you spending the long, cold winter with no shelter and poor food—part of the rumors Luke heard. I do hope and pray the weather there is better than here. Please write as soon as you can. Perhaps warm words between us both will make winter less cold.

Be well, my Beloved. Come back to me.
Anna Matthews

• • •

Saturday, February 4, 1865

Father Whelan sat straight is his chair and looked across his tiny desk at Stanley. "How much?"

"Shh." Stanley leaned toward the priest. "Thirty. Federal. Many men continue to die from scurvy, too many. I want to help."

"Fruit is rare this time of year, much too dear for my short funds."

"I heard of your generosity, Father. Are there other like-minded men who might help?"

"A few, but our dollars are almost worthless now. A hundred-dollar barrel of flour now costs a thousand."

"What about onions, Father?"

"Aye, lad. Lots of onions about, and cheaper than fruit. But even thirty Federal—how far can it go, lad?"

"What's the going price?"

"Fifty a bushel."

"What can one Federal dollar get in Confederate money?"

"Sixty, maybe seventy-five—depends how needy folks are."

"Do you think any of these farmers would accept three Federal dollars for five bushels? That would mean fifty bushels for our men."

Father Whelan paused to consider Stanley's proposition. "Aye, lad, I think two or three might, so I best be getting on my way before noon."

"One more thing, Father." Stanley removed Stew's old razor from his pocket and opened it. Then, one by one, he sliced the nine brass war eagle buttons off the front of his frock coat. "I was hoping to take these home to a beautiful girl, but some of the guards will pay handsomely for these."

"Aye, that they will, lad. I pray your sacrifice will be honored in heaven."

An orderly approached. He took a sheaf of papers from a satchel that was slung over his shoulder. "Excuse me, Father. I have the mail for Sergeant Mitchell's ward." The mail came in twice per week. Every letter was opened and, everyone assumed, read by prison authorities. The orderly handed the small stack of envelopes to Stanley and left for his next delivery.

286

Stanley wished Father Whelan success in his scouting mission and returned to his ward. It was now an ordinary and rewarding duty, moving from bed to bed as he delivered letters from home to longing, hopeful men, many of whom were sick unto death. About halfway through the score of envelopes, Stanley came across one addressed to him in Mrs. Matthews flowing script. He stuffed it in his pocket and waited to read it until all the other letters were delivered.

• • •

Stanley wept as he read Anna's letter. The scurvy had returned since he had written her. Once again, his gums were sore. Sometimes they bled, and it was a chore to chew any morsel of food. His legs ached all the time and he leaned more heavily on his cane. *My Beloved*, she had called him. If she could see him, would she still think him so?

Of course, he would reply to her letter—next week, maybe—and it would be as cheerful and hopeful as he could possibly make it. He would take great care of the darkness that so often crept over him, to hold the doubts in check, to cleanse his words of every taint of despair. Only the good would he write, never the bad—death taking some every day, fewer than before only because there were fewer for death to visit.

No, Anna must never know how very far he had been taken from her, and how very deep was the chasm of horrors into which he had been thrown.

• • •

Sgt. S. Mitchell, Det. 29
Camp Sumter Hospital - Ward 6
Andersonville, Geo.
Thursday, February 16, 1865

My Dearest Anna,

Your letter of Jan. 20th arrived on the 4th and I can tell you I must have smiled for a day or more. A doctor said I looked as if I had just come into money, and a patient thought I had suddenly been granted my freedom. But knowing you are still praying for my safe return and that I am constantly in your thoughts—well, that is indeed precious beyond words.

I continue working as an aide to my fellow prisoners at the hospital. The weather here is changeable, warm and pleasant for a day or two, then cold and rainy, then windy and cool, then warm and pleasant again. There is much to do to ease the suffering of the sick under the hospital sheds, but we are making some progress. Nearly one hundred bushels of onions were delivered to the hospital, thanks to the good graces of our commandant. Many patients who were suffering with scurvy are now on the mend, but new patients are brought in every day.

I have developed a friendship with Father Whelan. Pastor Blackwell would no doubt call the priest a papist, but not one Protestant clergyman has set foot in this prison. Mr. Sheppard, a fine preacher and good friend I knew when I was here before and who remained here during my journeys, said that Father Whelan is a fine example of "loving thine enemy."

I believe both men are true servants of the Lord and that both would agree with something I learned while I lay abed in your mother's house: Man is powerless to heal himself. Only God can. What small services we render to our fellow man are but our duty to God. I speak this to myself every day.

Yours with much affection,

Sgt. Stanley Mitchell

• • •

Stanley kept a strict account of the patients in his ward—the rations issued to each man, who was improving and who was not, who had recovered enough to be sent back into the prison, who was failing and near death, who had died during the night, and who now occupied the dead man's bed. The task was every bit as important as the ship's manifest he had maintained while aboard the *Evangelina*, or the log he had kept of sick and wounded soldiers awaiting transport from Sherman's front to the rear.

"The best records of any ward, lad," Father Whelan said, as he reviewed Stanley's ledger, "but one name seems to be missing."

"Hmm. I thought I accounted for every man," Stanley said.

"You did, lad, all but one."

"Who, Father?"

"You, Sergeant Mitchell."

Stanley shook his head, not understanding. "Orderlies don't list themselves as patients, Father."

Father Whelan's eyes burned at Stanley. "Still, I suggest ye add your name to that ledger, for ye shall soon be a patient."

The priest was probably right, but Stanley didn't know how to respond.

Father Whelan stroked the stubble on the side of his face. "I learned long ago if I'm to do unto others, I must do unto me too. The men depend on me, and they will suffer more if I'm not here to help them. So, I must look after meself, and remain healthy so I can serve them. Is this not your wish too?"

Stanley nodded.

"Then, unless you want to go abed and martyr yourself, you must have onion soup every day along with the rest."

• • •

289

Anna laid Stanley's letter aside—only his second letter from that place called Andersonville, when he could have written twice each week. Had someone read the letter to her, his words might have warmed and uplifted her, but his handwriting was that of a stranger now. The script of his earlier letters, smooth, flowing, and easy to read like the letters from Hurricane Plantation, had been reduced to a barely recognizable scrawl.

Your words sound fine, but what aren't you telling me? And what's this "with much affection," like you're writing a sister or friend? And what makes your hand tremble so? Are you all right, my darling, or are you far worse than I can imagine?

CHAPTER 53

*T*HE WAR WAS COMING TO AN END AND EVERYONE KNEW IT. Apparently, Captain Wirz was ordered to empty Andersonville to free the South of the burden of caring for thousands of Yankee prisoners of war. Prisoners from eastern states were to be sent to Savannah for exchange, while prisoners from states west of Pennsylvania were to be exchanged and paroled at Vicksburg.

For Stanley and eight hundred other prisoners from Ohio, Michigan, Wisconsin, and every other western state, the heavy timber gates of Camp Sumter opened on the twenty-first day of March. They traveled by train from Andersonville to Columbus, then on to Montgomery, Alabama. A river steamer carried the hopeful, ragged men to Selma, and then another slow train took them to Meridian and Jackson, Mississippi.

Except for the spring rains that soaked them three times and chilled them to the bone, the journey was not difficult. Rations were limited to hard crackers and a little meat. The scurvy Stanley had fought all winter returned, and when the train had finally stopped at Jackson, it was all he could do to lower himself to the ground. His gums had started bleeding again; his knees were swollen, and as hard as he had tried, he could not straighten his legs. But the health of the Yankee prisoners, or lack thereof, was of no concern to the militia at Jackson.

"Take up thy bed, and walk," Jesus had told the cripple, and the words of the Rebel sergeant at the Jackson depot had been nearly identical. "Take up your rations, and walk. Only way you'll get there, thanks to you-uns."

There was the Union line on the western bank of the Big Black River, the gateway to Vicksburg and the Mississippi River, and the route north to God's country.

Stanley groaned. He knew how far it was from his time in Vicksburg during the siege. "That's almost fifty miles, Sergeant."

"And you-uns got plenty for two days. Best you don't dawdle. Just stay on the Vicksburg Road or the railroad, what's left of it anyway."

Many of the prisoners who were in better health went whooping up the road. For them it was a lark, a short hike to freedom, and they probably would make it to the Big Black in two tiring, but joyful days.

Others, like Stanley, straggled from the start. He chose to walk along the railroad, for there would be no steep inclines, and the route would likely be more direct than the Vicksburg Road which passed through several towns along the way. The road would also be dusty from wagon traffic when it was dry, and a quagmire if it rained.

About two hundred other prisoners made the same choice. At first, they tried to stay together, to help one another along, or to lend an arm if a comrade stumbled. But as the first day wore on, those in better health adopted a quicker pace, while others lagged far behind. Men limped along in pairs or threes, but soon these units also separated, and each succeeding mile became a more lonely and solitary struggle for all but the hardiest.

Late on the fourth day, Stanley hobbled into the tiny railroad station at Bolton. He had made his cornmeal last two days, but now his belly was sore and swollen from eating bull thistles and wild onions. The more he ate of the thistle root, the more he hated it, and the more his stomach ached. And his fingertips bled from pulling thorns from the thistle leaves. Worse still, his tattered clothing had chafed his thin, drawn skin, and several open, oozing sores had appeared on his arms and legs.

"Ain't allowed in here, Yank," the stationmaster growled.

Stanley knew very well how he looked and how he smelled. Had it been the other way around, he probably would have spoken just as the stationmaster had. "Yes, sir, I know, but I if I may, what day is it?"

The man glared at Stanley. "Third of April, Monday. Now get along, Yank. Bunch of your kind been passing through, so keep passing and let us alone."

"Yes, sir. How far is it to the Big Black?"

"Fifteen miles, give or take. Now, git."

Stanley backed toward the door. "One last thing, if I may, sir, I was wondering if an acquaintance of mine still lives up the road."

"An acquaintance, you say. Here? Who?"

"Mr. Joseph Davis, sir."

The man's eyes widened. "You say you know Mr. Davis?"

"Yes, sir. Before our army came through, I had dinner with him and stayed overnight in his house."

"Oh." The stationmaster squinted at Stanley. "You looking to board with him tonight?"

It was almost sunset, but Stanley banished any thought of a warm bath and a soft bed. "No, sir. Mr. Davis said he and Mrs. Davis were moving east."

"They did." The man's stern, wrinkled face softened. "They moved east to Lauderdale, almost to Alabama. Mrs. Davis died there in October after the Yanks got Vicksburg."

"I never met Mrs. Eliza. She was ill when I visited. Thank you, sir." Stanley turned toward the door. "I'll be on my way."

"Hold on, son, hold on."

Stanley turned and looked the stationmaster.

A faint smile now warmed the old man's face. "This war's done," he said, "all but the parades. And some way, we got to start putting it all back together. I lost my eldest at Stones River, and my youngest is a prisoner up in New York. Says he's in good health, though—he writes every second week—and he's looking forward to being released soon. But you look in a real bad way, son. What's your name?"

"Sergeant Stanley Mitchell, sir."

"Is there anything you need?"

"Food, sir. A cabbage maybe, or onions. Fruit, if you can spare any. The scurvy's been keeping me low and slow." Stanley held up his empty canteen and shook it. "Have you any good water, sir?"

Mr. Lavery nodded. "Me and Mrs. Lavery live up the road not fifty yards. You're welcome to use the well. Wash too, if you want. I'll walk you up there myself. I was just about to close anyway."

"Close, sir? But there aren't any trains. Why would you be open?"

"The telegraph, son." The stationmaster pointed out the window toward a pole beside the track. "News comes down that wire, and folks want to know right away. It's all bad now, so the Yankees keep stringing new wire whenever it's cut. Just so we'll know, I think."

The well behind Mr. Lavery's house was a simple wooden frame over a hole in the earth, but the water was sweet to the taste and cool on Stanley's skin. He filled his canteen, drank it dry, and filled it again. He removed his clothes and washed them in bucket after bucket, until the water no longer looked dirty. Then he carefully washed each of his sores with clean water and prayed they wouldn't fester like Stew's had.

Stanley walked back to the station. The water had revived him and cleansed him. He laid out his blanket among the tall grass behind the station, where the

294

stationmaster had told him to bed down. Fifteen miles to the Union lines. Something to eat and a good night's sleep, and then two more days of teetering along on legs that would not—could not—straighten themselves out. In a week or two, if his diet didn't improve, he would be all bent up like Pickens had been.

It was almost dark when the stationmaster returned with a plate of fresh green beans, a wedge of boiled cabbage, a half-dozen small strawberries, and a thick slice of bread.

"You gave Mary a fright when she saw you at the well, but when she saw how you was, all she could say was, 'Poor thing. Could just as easy be our Randall.' We got ham and pork, chickens too, and some rabbits, but don't know if you can handle it, being so starved."

"This is a feast, Mr. Lavery. Thank you."

"Mary says you should stay tomorrow, and I agree. You look all done in and more food and rest will do you good."

Stanley devoured the beans and cabbage and strawberries within a minute or two. Then he laid down on his blanket, gazed up at the stars, and nibbled at the soft, wonderful bread until it was gone. There would be more bread tomorrow, Mr. Lavery had said, and more besides bread.

Lavery's well, simple and wooden, was so unlike the well behind the Matthews house, which was built of stone and deep. And for the first time since his return to Andersonville, Stanley allowed himself the secret pleasure of thinking that he would live to see that well again.

• • •

Stanley's frock coat was the only item of clothing that marked him as Union, and it lay under his blanket behind the station. And so, wearing only the remains of the clothing Mrs. Charlton had given him in Savannah and his black, sweat-stained slouch hat, he spent much of Tuesday sitting on a wooden bench beside the doorway of the station. Had any local citizen happened by, Stanley's lack of shoes and the old hickory cane in his hand, and the fact that he appeared to be dozing, made him look like any other poor and worn out wounded veteran.

About mid-afternoon, Mr. Lavery's telegraph clacked to life. The responding taps of Mr. Lavery's key lasted only a few seconds. There was more clacking from the telegraph, and then the sound of the stationmaster's chair scudding across the floor.

Mr. Lavery came to the door. "Seems it's really over, Sergeant. The Yankees marched into Richmond yesterday. General Lee is trying to escape with his army. Won't be but days now, I think."

Stanley stood and faced the stationmaster. "We're all ready for it to be over, and for our lives to be normal again, if such a thing is possible. But you and Mrs. Lavery have shown me great kindness, sir. May I ask why?"

"I've seen a hundred of your men go by, but when I seen you, Sergeant, it hit me on the head that my people made you that way. And your thinking kindly of Mr. and Mrs. Davis shamed me, so I needed to set that right."

Stanley extended his right hand toward Mr. Lavery. An odd, wondering look crossed the old man's face. Then he smiled and shook Stanley's hand.

"Thank you for everything you did for me," Stanley said. "A good friend of mine—a brother, really—told me I couldn't survive alone, and you proved him right once again, Mr. Lavery. I'm stronger and rested, and my knees aren't as swollen. I'll be on my way at first light tomorrow."

• • •

Thursday afternoon, the sixth of April, as a bell atop some faraway church chimed five, Stanley Mitchell stumbled onto the planking of the long bridge over the Big Black River. A mast stood tall at the far end. Its flag hung limp; there was no breeze to unfurl her stars and stripes.

296

Old Glory. He had lived to see her again. Two hundred more steps and he would stand beneath her.

One shaky, bowlegged step after another, Stanley started to cross the bridge. His walking stick thudded hollow upon the uneven planking; he would need to take care with each step. His toe caught the edge of one of the planks; he almost fell. Cries went up from the far end. Boots thudded upon the bridge deck. A half-dozen men in blue ran toward him. Strong arms caught him; hard hands patted his back. Voices shouted. Fresh, cool water was poured down his throat.

Other men ran up with a stretcher and laid Stanley upon it. Then the men carried him to the end of the bridge beneath the now-stirring folds of Old Glory. They carried him about two hundred yards farther to a railroad siding and lifted him into a car, the same type of car Stanley had seen daily when he was with Sherman, a car furnished with bunks for the sick and wounded.

"Where are you taking me?" he asked.

"To the hospital at Camp Fisk just this side of Vicksburg. Only a ten-minute ride, Sergeant."

CHAPTER 54

Friday, April 21, 1865

STANLEY LIFTED THE LATCH ON THE HEAVY IRON GATE AND pushed it open. With a deep unburdening sigh, he started slowly up the cobbled walk to the stairway of fourteen steps that led up to the massive veranda that surrounded Stonehaven Manor on three sides. It would be good to be among friends again.

It had taken more than a week for Stanley to feel up to making the four-mile journey into town, and five more days to obtain the pass. The day he applied for the pass would be forever etched in his memory, for cries of horror and indignation had swept through the camp even as he was signing the form in his still feeble, scrawling script. President Lincoln was dead, shot down by an assassin. The elation of Lee's surrender at Appomattox, and of the prisoners' own anticipation of finally being truly freed and sent homeward, had vanished in an instant, and a somber, sorrowful, and, at times, vengeful mood had settled over Camp Fisk.

Stanley was but one of the thousands of haunting specters from Andersonville who found themselves in a military purgatory between prison and freedom. No unparoled prisoner could leave Camp Fisk, except with a written pass granted for a short time and for a specific purpose. The officer of the day signed each pass, and with right hand raised, the not-yet-free man swore to return by the agreed upon time or face arrest and court-martial.

Stanley raised his hand to the door knocker. The fact that his stated purpose was to visit one of Vicksburg's most

298

prominent citizens had certainly aided his cause. He felt for the new watch in the hip pocket of his new jacket. Almost one o'clock—the same hour he had approached that same door two years before. He would have to take his leave at three to return to the camp by five.

He rapped three times.

Shuffling footsteps approached. The door opened slowly to reveal Old Nate, now stooped a little with age, his woolly hair whiter than Stanley remembered it.

Nate's tired eyes looked Stanley up and down, then settled on his face. "Master Stanley? Is that you?"

"Yes, Nate."

"Mrs. Olivia told me to expect you, but you look a whole lot different."

"It seems I've escaped the grave, Nate, at least for now."

Nate opened the door wide. "Come in, sir, and leave your hat with me. Mrs. Olivia's in the parlor. I'm sure you know the way."

Livvy was standing at a small table against the far wall of the parlor, tending a bouquet of flowers. Her back was toward the door, so Stanley stood still and watched her, not wishing to disturb the moment, and only half believing he was there at all.

"Are you going to stand there all day," Livvy said, "or are you going to come over here and give your big sister a hug?" She turned toward Stanley. Astonishment, then fleeting hints of shock and horror, then astonishment again. She tried to hide it well, tried to recover the brilliant smile that usually graced her face.

I must look ghastly. He had examined himself in the looking glass at the barracks that morning. The camp barber had done good work, and his new uniform looked perfect, but it hung loose. He was but a hollow shell of the man she had known before.

Then Stanley realized that he was looking back at Livvy with nearly the same degree of amazement, for Livvy was heavy with child.

Livvy saw him staring at her. "Yes, Stanley, I got married last April. I'm expecting a baby brother or sister for Earl and Newton in about a month."

Stanley leaned his cane against the settee and crossed the room. He wrapped Livvy in his arms and held her. "I'm so happy for you. Is he a good man?"

"He better be. He's one of your officers, Colonel Matthias Wright. Matt was one of the officers of the occupation force that came in shortly after you left with General Sherman." Livvy gave Stanley a squeeze and released him. "I hosted a gala here one fine day in October. I invited about a hundred townspeople and an equal number of Union officers along with their wives, if they were in town. I had hoped the townspeople would get to know some of our Federal occupiers and come to view them more as protectors than captors. But I don't know that it made a bit of difference."

Livvy laughed, bright, airy, high, the kind of laughter that could fill a house and lift every spirit within its walls. "You might say the principal result of that party was that one of those officers captured me. It just happened the way these things sometimes do."

"And how is your father-in-law?" Stanley asked.

"It seems Dada's age is telling on him more each day, but he almost leaped from his chair when the messenger arrived with your request for a pass. He's outside with Matt, waiting for us in the gazebo."

Livvy took Stanley's right arm and the two walked toward the rear of the mansion. The garden looked very much as Stanley remembered it, and the gazebo appeared as if it had always remained at the rear of the garden, that it's timber framework and planks had never been used to support the cave below and cover its earthen floors.

Colonel Wright stood as Livvy and Stanley approached. Stanley paused at the base of the steps and raised his right hand, palm out, in a crisp salute.

"At ease, Sergeant Mitchell." Colonel Wright was an impressive looking man, tall, lean, and confident looking, with sandy colored hair cut short, and a closely trimmed beard and mustache.

Livvy and Stanley, arm in arm, climbed the three steps to the gazebo. Judge Adair hadn't risen with Colonel Wright, but Stanley clearly saw his red, swollen eyes, and the tears that coursed down his cheeks.

The colonel offered his right hand to Stanley. "Livvy's spoken often of you, Sergeant. It seems you've been a good friend to this family."

"More than a friend, Matthias," Judge Adair said, wiping his eyes with his handkerchief. "I think of Stanley as a long-lost nephew, and he's been like a brother to Livvy."

The judge reached out for Stanley, who bent down, allowing the judge to draw him into a tight embrace. "Hugs are for family," he said in Stanley's ear. "I can't begin to tell you how pleased I am to see you safe."

Judge Adair released Stanley and turned to Colonel Wright. "I know this boy's history. Trial and hardship have been Stanley's companions for all his young life, but he has endured all that the Lord has put before him. Do you still intend to return to Tennessee and marry that girl Anna?"

"If she'll have me now." Ten months of unspeakable degradation had obliterated all but the faintest shadow of Anna's face. Grisly scenes of torment, brutality, horror, and death seemed to occupy every thought, whether he was awake or asleep, and the wasting corruption of his flesh had left him most pitiable indeed. The scurvy had left him—of that he was thankful—but it had left its marks. His legs were now as straight as they had been, and his teeth and gums had healed, but the sores on his arms and legs still bothered him.

"What do you mean *if she'll have you now*?" Stanley had heard Livvy's strident tone more than once during the siege. "I know you, Stanley. Your strength and will saw this family through six weeks of living in a cave, and what you did for those Union boys at the hospital? That was nothing short of heroic. Have you written to her?"

"Yes, Livvy, a short note a week ago to let her know I was once again within Federal lines. I wanted to write more, but she knew me as I was before—before that place."

"Was it as bad as they say, Sergeant?" The colonel's eyes were kind. His concern seemed genuine.

"It was worse, Colonel Wright," Stanley said, "far worse than anyone who wasn't there could ever imagine. Many men in better health than me didn't survive. I don't know why I did."

The judge pulled at Stanley's sleeve. "That was God's doing. He saved you again—for Anna. Like that cane you hold, you have been damaged, but not broken. You have passed through the fire and you have been polished smooth. And just like that cane, you are dreadfully thin—I wept at the sight of you despite myself."

"And I nearly did too," Livvy said. "I know you saw how I first looked at you. I saw it in your eyes, but I couldn't help myself. It wasn't revulsion, Stanley. It was pity, my dear, and anguish that you suffered so. And sorrow, too, that you were forced to endure such treatment. But as Dada said, God spared you for Anna. I truly believe that. You're still young, Stanley, not yet twenty, I believe. You will regain your strength and vitality, and you can have a long and happy life with her."

But my youth is spent. That will not return. Will Anna look at me the way Livvy did? Will she break into tears at the very sight of me like the judge did? Can Anna still love me? Can I still love her?

"Please, sit and let's break bread together," Judge Adair said. "Matthias, please ask the blessing."

The colonel's prayer was the usual thanksgiving for the food and asking God's blessing upon it. But then Colonel Wright thanked God for answering "many prayers" for Stanley's preservation and he asked God to continue to preserve and bless Stanley all the days of his life. It was a simple earnest plea that touched Stanley's heart.

Stanley opened his eyes. *Livvy—she still loves me, and the judge's tears were proof positive. And Colonel Wright?* "Thank you for the prayer, sir."

Colonel Wright smiled at Stanley. "It's true, Sergeant Mitchell. I feel I met you before today through Livvy's many prayers, and those of the judge, especially since Livvy received your letter from Savannah. And Earl and Newt have prayed for you every evening. They'll be overjoyed to see you when they return from school shortly after four."

"But I must be on my way before then, sir."

"Nonsense, I'll send word that you will be staying with us until the army arranges transport for you. I'll have your things brought up here and you'll have a real bed to sleep in and dine on real food rather than army rations. Do you know when you expect to head north?"

"No, sir, but I'll probably be sent upriver with a bunch of other men from Ohio. The army is trying to keep units together. It makes sense for expediting delivery of the men to their home states."

"Ohio?" The concern in Livvy's voice was obvious. "You're not going to Tennessee?"

"Not at first, Livvy. I must return to the state in which I enlisted to be discharged and to sign the papers for my army pension. Then I'll take a steamer up the Tennessee River. I think it will delay me about a week, and maybe I'll gain two or three more pounds."

"Then it's settled," Colonel Wright said. "You'll remain here at Stonehaven until the army orders you to report for transport to Ohio."

"Thank you, Colonel."

"Now, Sergeant, Livvy told me that General Black Jack Logan is a friend of yours. I heard he was brilliant during the Atlanta Campaign. Please tell me first-hand how the two of you became acquainted."

CHAPTER 55

Monday, April 24, 1865

IMMEDIATELY UPON THEIR RETURN FROM SCHOOL, EARL AND Newt burst into the parlor, where Stanley sat chatting with Livvy and Judge Adair, and began to pepper Stanley with questions. From the moment they had seen Stanley Friday afternoon, the boys had been eager to ask Stanley about where he had gone with Sherman's army, and what he had done, but Livvy's insistence that they allow Stanley to rest had kept her boys at bay Friday evening and all of Saturday. And on Sunday she had told them to select a topic for discussion more appropriate to the Lord's Day.

For a while, Stanley satisfied the boys' curiosity with tales of the battles around Chattanooga and of Sherman's strategic campaign to take Atlanta—at least as much as he knew of it. He also told them of his own activities in the Quartermaster Department of the Fifteenth Corp. But soon, the boys' questions became more personal and difficult for Stanley to deflect. They wanted to hear the full story from their Yankee friend, so they could relate his exploits to their classmates.

"Why are you so skinny, Stanley?" Newton asked

"You didn't say much about Savannah," Earl said, "only that you went there. Were you with Sherman during his march through Georgia?"

"It's all right, Stanley," Livvy said. "They should hear about that side of the war too. It wasn't all grand strategies and glorious victories. Earl and Newt still talk about the terrible siege, but please remember they are but eight and six."

A short time later, after recovering from astonishment at hearing Stanley had been a prisoner of war, Earl and Newton rolled this way and that on the floor laughing, because Stanley had just told them about his good friend Ogre.

Old Nate shuffled into the parlor. "Messenger just came for Master Stanley. He says he delivers his messages in person, but I signed for it and assured him I was nothing if not reliable."

Nate handed the folded note to Stanley and left the parlor.

Stanley stood and walked toward Livvy. "It seems my time has come. Once again, the army orders me away when I would much rather stay a little longer. I'm to report by seven o'clock this evening to the river steamer *Sultana* for immediate transport north to Cairo, Illinois. It's signed by Col. Reuben B. Hatch, Chief Quartermaster, Department of Mississippi."

Livvy stood slowly, using her arms as much as her legs to rise from the soft-cushioned chair. "I'll have Matt ready the carriage." She hugged Stanley and kissed him on the cheek, then took his arm and walked with him to the base of the broad stairway in the hall. "Your time with us has been so short, but it has pleased me beyond words that you were able to return this way."

"I knew I had to see you again, Livvy." Stanley swallowed against the tightness in his throat. "And even if we never meet again, I'll always know the people of Stonehaven truly cared for me."

"And still do." Livvy squeezed his hand. "You said you wanted to write Anna when your plans were definite, so I shall write her a note saying you're on your way home. Now, go upstairs and collect your things."

● ● ●

At first glance from the seat of Judge Adair's open carriage, the *Sultana* was a fine-looking vessel. She gleamed white in the low evening sun, and except for the large black letters on her paddlewheel housing, Stanley thought Captain Gauthier's *Evangelina* had somehow been salvaged and brought back to life.

The *Sultana* was tied alongside a wharfboat. A long line of blue-clad soldiers snaked its way across the landing, across the wharfboat, over the stageplank, and onto the main deck. Every section of deck space looked packed with men. Perhaps a thousand were aboard already, with hundreds more in line.

"I've never seen so many people on one boat," Colonel Wright said. Livvy had insisted he drive Stanley to the riverfront rather one of the servants, and the colonel had been more than willing.

"Neither have I, sir," Stanley said. "The *Evangelina* was about her size and she could carry four hundred passengers."

"General Smith wants to get our prisoners of war home as soon as possible, but I should think you fellows have had enough of being packed in on top of each other."

Colonel Wright pulled the carriage to a halt near the end of the line of waiting men. "This war has meant great tragedy for some, Sergeant, and great blessing to others. Before I was posted to Vicksburg, I was thinking I might never marry. But then the war threw Livvy and me together, and now I consider myself a most fortunate man, truly blessed."

"She is a remarkable woman, Colonel." Stanley scanned the crowded railings of the *Sultana*, not expecting to see anyone he knew, but hoping just the same he might see Austin one last time. "Did she tell you about the night she saved my life?"

"No." Colonel Wright's eyes gleamed. His chuckle sounded low and wry. "So, my wife hasn't told me everything about you, Sergeant. I shall ask her as soon as I get home." Then he grew more serious. "I must thank you again for helping Livvy and the boys, and Judge Adair too. You were a blessing amid the terror, and you will be warmly welcomed at Stonehaven should you ever pass this way again."

• • •

An hour later Stanley finally reached the stageplank and handed his written order to the boarding clerk.

The clerk scanned the order. "Fifty-third Ohio. Lots of Ohio boys going upriver, but none from the Fifty-third. Squeeze in wherever you can."

Stanley limped across the stageplank onto the bow of the steamboat. His favorite place on the *Evangelina* had always been the stern of the hurricane deck, but that meant a long, tiresome walk up two flights of stairs, and shouldering his way the entire length of the ship through crowds of boisterous, singing, laughing, homeward-bound soldiers, most of whom had also narrowly escaped death in a prison stockade.

"Where you headed, Sergeant?"

Stanley turned toward the voice. A young private sat on the deck against the larboard gunwale, just one of a hundred or more who had claimed a spot in the bow of the ship. "Ohio," Stanley said, "Fifty-third."

"Fifty-ninth myself. Name's Andy. Could be we're both headed for Camp Chase. We was at Andersonville."

"I was too, twice." Stanley held up two fingers. "And four other prisons in between."

"Merle," Andy said, nudging the man beside him, "whyn't you scoot over a bit, and I'll scoot the same, so this injured sergeant can set down?"

Stanley lowered himself and slid into the small patch of deck between the two men, Andy slightly astern to Stanley's right, and Merle slightly forward to Stanley's left. Stanley introduced himself.

"Me and Merle," Andy said, "we're both Fifty-ninth, but most of these other fellas are Kentucky cavalry. Their horses and a pack of mules are in pens back of the boilers, a bunch of hogs too. Know why we picked sitting up front here?"

Stanley shook his head.

"Tell him, Merle."

Merle seemed to be the thinker of the two. His speech was slow and deliberate, as if he was trying to speak in a proper and dignified manner. "I thought of what to do when we have to go to the latrine. We cannot stumble our way through the throngs up to the privy in the main cabin, so I thought staying here and doing what we have to do over the side would be easiest."

"Yes," Stanley said, "but about two thousand others will do the same, and I haven't seen any fresh water aboard, so it's drink that same river water or nothing."

Merle screwed up his face. "Almost makes me long for Providence Spring. Still, it's better with no decks above and we're upwind of most of it, especially the hogs."

"They say we'll reach Cairo late Thursday, Friday at the latest," Andy said. "After what we been through, we can abide anything at all for three days."

CHAPTER 56

THE *Sultana* DEPARTED VICKSBURG AFTER MIDNIGHT AND churned steadily northward through the dark, mud-tainted waters of the Mississippi. The festive mood quieted, and Stanley, as did nearly every other soldier aboard, remained in the place he had claimed for the duration of the voyage, and slept as he was able.

Throughout the following day the *Sultana* steamed onward without stop, rounding bend after bend, sounding it's bright, joyful steam whistle as it passed every town. Once, and thankfully, only once, as a large down-bound riverboat appeared upriver, crowds of boisterous men on the upper decks rushed to the starboard rail to wave and holler at the passing ship.

Stanley felt the *Sultana* heel over. She seemed about to capsize, but the men above, seeing how near they had come to dooming both themselves and the ship, dashed back to larboard, and the ship righted itself.

"Keep your places, men," the captain out called from the pilothouse through a shiny brass speaking trumpet. "Please keep your places. We must keep the ship on even keel."

Stanley passed another quiet, restful night. He awakened to the clanging of the ship's bell, a sure signal they were approaching a landing. The *Sultana* slowed and nosed up to a wharfboat on the west side of the river—Helena, according to the sign on the wharfmaster's office. A few passengers disembarked and several sacks of mail were delivered to the wharfmaster's office. A small band of civilians approached the stageplank and appeared in deep discussion, pointing here and there, as if trying to find a place among the horde of Yankees who occupied nearly every square foot of deck space. Finally, they marched back to the wharfmaster's office, no doubt to exchange their tickets for passage on the next up-bound ship.

The fuel bins were filled with coal and the *Sultana* started up river again. Stanley leaned over the gunwale and lowered his canteen into the water which streamed past just a few feet below. Then he sat against the gunwale and held the canteen still for at least five minutes to allow the sediment to settle. He took but a single mouthful. It wasn't too bad, better than he had expected. He swallowed it. Then he shook the canteen vigorously and poured the rest over the side. He did this several more times until he thought he had drunk enough. Surely, there must be good water at their next stop, Memphis.

The lights of the city appeared a few miles ahead off the starboard bow shortly after sundown. A line of men formed in the bow near where Stanley, Andy, and Merle sat. These men wished to see the city, if only for a couple of hours, and the regular occupants of the bow were forced to move aside to allow the stageplank to be moved into place as soon the *Sultana* was made secure at the wharf.

Stanley stood and massaged the muscles of his left leg.

"You getting off?" Andy asked.

"I'm thinking about it," Stanley said. "It's only three days ride to that girl I told you about."

"But, Sergeant," Merle said, "you would be going out on French leave. From the way you talked, I thought you were a different sort."

"I am, Merle," Stanley said. "I doubt the army would care one way or the other. Nobody would miss me either here or up in Ohio."

"Then you're going?" Andy asked.

"Like I said, I'm thinking about it," Stanley said. "But no, I'm not taking French leave. I must go with you boys up to Camp Chase and get properly discharged. The army owes me back wages which I intend to collect. I will not return to Anna with nothing in my pockets, but I am going to get off to stretch my legs."

It felt good to move around, to work off the stiffness that seemed to have settled in every joint and muscle from two days of nearly total immobility. Stanley paced up and down the length of the wharfboat, careful to keep clear of the hundred or so hogs that were driven off the stern of the *Sultana* to a holding pen on the landing. Rations of hardtack and cooked beef were brought aboard and distributed, enough for a single day, for they were due to reach Cairo the following afternoon.

About midnight, the *Sultana* cast off and steamed directly across the river to the Arkansas shore, where she moored to a coal barge and refilled her bins. The night was cool. A steady breeze blew downriver from the north, so Stanley, as the *Sultana* started upriver again, wrapped his frock coat tightly about himself and leaned back against the gunwale.

Stanley slept. He must have slept, for his next awareness was of the boat suddenly trembling and lurching. *Oh no! A snag, just like the* Evangelina. A hot blast seared the right side of his face.

Andy screamed.

Stanley opened his eyes. His gaze, already upward because he was leaning back against the gunwale, fixed upon one of the *Sultana's* tall, majestic stacks which was toppling toward the stern. It fell with a loud crash an instant later.

Andy screamed again. "She's blowed up. We're done for." He put a hand to the left side of his face which Stanley couldn't see. "My face is blowed off too."

Andy turned wild-eyed toward Stanley. The right side of Andy's face, the side toward the boilers, had been severely scalded. The skin and some of the flesh beneath seemed to be in tatters, the way everyone's clothing had looked at Andersonville. But it was still a face. And Andy had shielded Stanley from the worst of the blast. His own injury was minor, probably just some pain and redness, nothing a few days and a little salve wouldn't heal.

"Andy," Stanley said, straining to make himself heard amid the chaos and building panic. "Your face is still there. The boilers blew, and the *Sultana* has lost power, but lots of boats have survived blown boilers. I've been on the river. I've heard the stories. You must calm down."

But they were wasted words. The man next to Andy was terribly injured and looked about to die. Perhaps a dozen others closer to the boilers lay dead from the sudden blast of steam.

"Fire!" The cry came from a single voice raised above the din. Then it was taken up by others. Shouts and screams rose from all parts of the stricken vessel.

The odor of smoke. A flicker of flame. The furnaces of the boilers must have broken apart, strewing their glowing embers upon the wooden deck.

Andy jumped to his feet. Tears streamed down his face. "We're doomed," he cried, "and I ain't burning." He vaulted over the gunwale and vanished beneath the black surface of the water. Others in the bow followed Andy's example and likewise disappeared into the river. And heavy splashes from aft meant that people from the upper decks had also jumped into the river.

To Stanley's right, Merle started to rise. "Maybe Andy's right."

Stanley pulled at Merle's arm. "I've been shipwrecked before, and panic will kill you. Andy's dead unless he's a good swimmer. So are the others. The wind is from the north. The flames will be driven aft—those poor souls back there—so many doing just as Andy did—pray for them."

Merle settled back against the gunwale.

"Take a few deep breaths to calm yourself," Stanley said. "We need three things if we're to survive, Merle—self-control, a clear head, and prayer. Father in heaven, please deliver us in our time of need. Amen. Now, let's keep ourselves calm so we can think clearly."

"We *are* going into the water, aren't we, Sergeant?"

"It's possible, Merle, but not yet. The engines have stopped. The wheels have stopped, and the ship will drift with the current back toward Memphis. Other boats will come to our aid. And there is plenty of water to douse the flames."

312

But no one rose to fight the fire while it was still in its infancy. Instead, the flames matured with each passing minute, and just as the appetite of a child becomes insatiable as he matures through his teens, so it was aboard the *Sultana*. From about midship, where the furnaces were, the flames swept upward and sternward, driven along by the northerly breeze and their own desire to consume increasing quantities of the ship's wooden structure.

Hundreds of men, all of them soldiers except for a few civilian men and one or two women, rushed from the forward portion of the deck above the boilers, which the flames had not yet claimed, down the shattered main stairway to the bow of the ship. Most jumped straightaway into the cold, dark water. What became of them, Stanley couldn't see, nor did he wish to, but if anyone hesitated at the brink of probable death, the press of others from behind quickly decided the issue for all eternity.

Some of this crowd broke ranks and went for the long heavy stageplank across which every one of them had walked to board the *Sultana*. They hoisted the stage onto their shoulders, pitched it over the prow of the ship, and then jumped in after it. How many of those who had gone in before, who were fighting against sinking into the river, were crushed to death under the weight of that stageplank?

A fight broke out—at least it sounded like a fight—for ownership of the stageplank. Weak, desperate pleas for rescue, too many to count. Shouts of derision, curses, and damnings told Stanley who had control of the stageplank.

More terrible screams came from aft. Stanley peered along the larboard side of the *Sultana*. The flames had reached the paddlewheel housing. Several figures had taken refuge atop the housing, but the flames wanted that part of the ship too, the part that proudly bore the doomed vessel's name. The flames must have eaten through the support structure of the paddlewheel, for the top of housing pulled away from the side of the ship. Something snapped, and within seconds, both the paddlewheel and its housing fell with a loud crash, killing many who were in the water below, and the men who had taken refuge atop the housing were thrown into the river.

But the wheel and housing were still attached to the ship. As the *Sultana* drifted slowly backward, the increased drag on her larboard side caused her bow to slowly come about. This was almost unnoticed by Stanley until he felt the change in the direction of the wind. Soon, the wind would come from the stern. The flames would be driven forward toward the unburned bow, and then the death throes of the *Sultana* would end.

Stanley removed his black slouch hat and started to unbutton his frock coat.

"What are you doing, Sergeant?" Merle asked.

"Getting ready. Fifteen minutes at most and we'll have to abandon ship. Go over near the stairs and try to find a plank or something else that will float."

Merle crept over to the base of the stairs and rooted around in the debris. He picked up a piece of wood about three feet long and started back toward Stanley. Then someone rushed down the stairs and snatched the board from Merle's hand. The thief was gone over the side before Merle had time to throw a curse at the man's back.

Merle returned to the pile of debris and found something even better, a split newel post, longer and twice as thick as his previous selection.

Stanley took off his Frock coat, folded it carefully, and laid it on the deck. He untied and removed his shoes—he had just gotten accustomed to wearing them again. He shrugged off his suspenders—no Abrahams were hidden within these new ones—and he unbuttoned the suspenders from his trousers. He reached into the pocket of his trousers, took out his Bible, and opened it. The short letters Anna had written to him at Andersonville were tucked within.

Stanley fingered each letter, remembering Anna's words and trying to recall her face. Then he closed the Bible, fixed the clasp, and returned the Bible to the pocket of his trousers. He took off the new green-checked shirt Livvy had bought for him the previous Saturday in Vicksburg, folded it, and laid it atop the coat. Lastly, Stanley removed his trousers and placed them, also folded neatly, atop the shirt.

"Do you want to share my post, Sergeant?" Merle asked.

Stanley took Levi Jackson's walking stick from where it had lain against the base of the gunwale. "No. I have my cane. I think it will be enough for me."

Fewer men remained in the bow of the ship now, a score maybe, not hundreds. Taut ropes and chains revealed others over the side, and dozens more, unseen but for their white-knuckled fingers, held on desperately to the gunwale.

Stanley stood and turned away from any who might be watching in the bow toward the blazing stern where the cries of anguish were now few and faint. All must have either perished or gone into the water. He slipped the hickory walking stick inside the waistband of his drawers and slid it down along his left leg. Then he tied his suspenders snugly around his left leg to hold the cane in place.

Minute by minute the flames crept forward. Wind-driven smoke billowed overhead.

Stanley nudged Merle. "We must wait for the last moment, after all the panic and madness has died away. It won't be long now, Merle."

"No, it won't. I can't say it's been a pleasure traveling with you, Sergeant."

"Remarkable," Stanley said, "a bit of humor at such a time shows self-control. Here's my plan, Merle. We were on the Arkansas side of the ship, but since she turned, we're on the Tennessee side. We must cross to the other side of the bow, because the ship is closer to the Arkansas side. I can just make out the shore. I'm going to try for it anyway."

"Then I will too." Merle held out his hand. "I'm glad to know you, Sergeant Mitchell."

"Likewise," Stanley said, as he shook Merle's hand. "May God protect you. You already lost one board to a thief, and men are still fighting among themselves in the water. Before you go, Merle, pray to God to save you. Look for an open place and jump in. It'll be cold, but it was colder at Millen and Andersonville. Then get away from the boat as fast as you can."

The flames were close now. The forward section of the deck above was now ablaze. Waves of heated air and smoke swept over him. Glowing cinders fell upon his skin and scant clothing.

A sudden splash and Merle was gone, stroking away furiously with his post under his armpits. *Lord, be merciful to him. He seemed a decent fellow.*

A few more minutes, that was all, until Stanley would burn as many others had. But he would not burn. The fingertips of those still clinging to the bow seemed to ripple as they inched closer to the pointed prow of the ship, trying to flee the approaching flames. How long could they hang on?

A gap formed between those clutching fingertips and the advancing flames. *It's now or never. I'm in your hands, Lord, to save my life or to take it.*

Even as the heat seared the already scalded skin on the side of his face, Stanley crawled over the starboard gunwale of the *Sultana* and lowered himself into the cold, swift water of the Mississippi. The nearest man was about six feet away, intent on clinging to the ship with the last of his strength. Stanley slid Levi Jackson's hickory walking stick out from inside his drawers and draped an arm over it.

Lord God in heaven, please save me again.

Then Stanley released his hold on the hull of the *Sultana* and pushed himself out into the darkness.

CHAPTER 57

*H*USHED VOICES—FEMALE VOICES. STANLEY LAY STILL, WARM and comfortable in the soft bed, trying to catch the words.

"...only the dead coming in now...."

"...seeing all them bodies on the wharf, I just cried...."

"...I heard over eight hundred yesterday...."

"...they say more perished than lived...."

"...after all they been through—it's pitiful, just pitiful...."

Once again, Lord Jesus, you brought me to the brink of death and then drew me back. Is this how my life is to be? Why can't you let me live in peace? Have I not yet learned whatever it is you're trying to teach me? Is my faith still so weak?

Stanley opened his eyes. Glowing oil lamps hung at regular intervals down the entire length of a large hall, a hospital ward with a row of beds along each wall and a third row in the center. Three nurses were huddled about a dozen feet away beside the door to the ward.

He started to rise.

A nurse hurried over. "Just a minute, soldier. Let me help you."

She sounded pleasant enough, but her face was hidden in shadows. "Where am I?" Stanley asked.

"Overton Army Hospital, Memphis. What's your name, soldier?"

"Sergeant Stanley Mitchell, ma'am. What day is this?"

"Why, it's Monday, first of May, almost three in the morning."

317

"How did I get here?"

"You was found on the Arkansas side and brought over on a steamer. Do you need the privy, Sergeant Mitchell?"

"I do, ma'am. Just hand me my cane and point the way. I believe I can do the rest."

The nurse giggled softly. "There was no cane, Sergeant Mitchell. When you was brought in, all you had was what you was wearing—a lady's nightgown."

Wonderful. No doubt with all the frills and lacy stuff Rebel women love.

"There are clean drawers and an undershirt at the foot of the bed. Do you need help dressing, Sergeant?"

Stanley shook his head. "No, ma'am, I can manage."

"Then I'll go fetch you some supper," the nurse said. "I'm Mrs. Percival. Just call for me if you need anything else."

Shortly after Stanley returned from the privy, Mrs. Percival appeared with a steaming plate of food. Sweet peas, soft bread with butter, and a nice piece of roasted pork—not the sumptuous fair of Stonehaven, but a feast nonetheless. Stanley forced himself to eat slowly. He had always been the last to finish during those few days at the judge's table. It would take time for his digestion to recover from the almost total shutdown it had known for ten long months.

• • •

Several hours later, Mrs. Percival shook Stanley awake. "Sergeant Mitchell, you have a visitor."

Stanley sat up. Mrs. Percival looked the way she sounded, middle-aged, plump, and pleasant.

"This is Corporal Hoadley from the quartermaster's office."

The corporal was a small man attired in a spotless uniform and wearing a dour expression. He stood beside the bed holding an open ledger and looking like he would rather have been anywhere else.

"Good morning, Corporal." Stanley didn't offer his hand in greeting.

"Hullo." The corporal spoke barely above a mumble. "I'm here to draft an order to reissue new clothing for you."

"A new uniform?"

318

"Yes. What's your name, regiment, and rank?"

"Stanley Mitchell, enlisted December, 1861 in the Fifty-third Ohio Volunteer Infantry, wounded severely at Shiloh, readmitted to active duty August, 1863, Quartermaster Department, Fifteenth Corps. Current rank, sergeant."

"We've seen cases of a person passing himself off as someone else to gain a better pension. Do you have any proof of your identity?"

"You mean other than the fact that I suffered for ten months in Rebel prison camps, or that I was plucked from the cold waters of the Mississippi River, or that I'm lying in *this* bed in *this* hospital?"

The corporal nodded.

"No. You have only my word on the matter. But you might check the regimental records. The surgeon recorded my physical description—six feet, three inches tall, brown hair, blue eyes, one hundred eighty pounds. And from this moment on, Corporal Hoadley, you will refer to me as Sergeant Mitchell."

"Yes, Sergeant Mitchell." The corporal's condescending tone was unmistakable.

And Stanley wasn't about to let it pass. "And one more thing, Corporal. If the army still needs more proof that I am who I say I am, they should wire Colonel Matthias Wright of the Vicksburg garrison, or Judge William Adair, also of Vicksburg, and should you still not deem their word sufficient, then wire Major General John Logan and ask him to describe his friend, Sergeant Stanley Mitchell. And please present my compliments to the general when you do."

Hoadley took a step backward. He blinked twice, slowly, and when he spoke his tone was markedly more respectful. "I think your word is enough, Sergeant Mitchell. Would you stand up, please? I need to take some measurements."

Stanley turned sideways toward the small table beside the bed, intending to use it for support. A cane had been leaned against the table—a gift from Mrs. Percival, no doubt.

Stanley eased himself out of bed. Every part of his body ached from his battle with the river, but each of his members still seemed to work. He stood to his full height, and looked down at Corporal Hoadley, who was already stretching out his tape measure. "Make sure those are quartermaster sergeant's stripes on my sleeves, Corporal."

"Yes, Sergeant."

"And please do a particularly fine job of measuring my feet, Corporal. After so many months without shoes, it was a shame to leave them behind on the *Sultana*."

"Yes, Sergeant."

"And I want the long nine-button frock coat, not a sack coat or shell jacket. Brand new, never worn before, and three sizes larger than I am now."

"Yes, Sergeant. Why all the particulars, if you're just going to wear it for a couple of weeks until you're mustered out?"

"Because Corporal Hoadley, I sold the buttons from my old coat to the Rebels for food. I was hoping to save those buttons for a certain young woman. Now, I'm hoping she will treasure these new ones instead."

• • •

Two days later, Stanley Mitchell, well-rested, well-fed, and feeling better than he had since he was taken prisoner, dressed in his new uniform. It was exactly what he had asked of Corporal Hoadley, with the exception that his stripes had not been sewn on. This task Mrs. Percival gladly did during the small hours of her night-watch.

Stanley tied his new, stiff brogans, and grabbed the plain wooden cane in his left hand. Then he hobbled down three flights of stairs to the ground floor, walked through an open-air portico, and emerged from the hospital onto Poplar Street.

Following Corporal Hoadley's directions, Stanley walked down Poplar to Front Street, the busiest street in Memphis, because it ran along the entire length of the city's bustling riverfront. He paused at the corner and gazed beyond the storehouses, saloons, and dancehalls that lined both sides of the street, down to the levee where the river steamers were tied nose to tail. He could only see a few riverboats from his vantage point, but there must have been dozens. Another day or two and he would have to board one of them and resume his journey back to Ohio, unless there was another way.

Stanley skirted the crowded wharf area and headed north. Three more blocks of walking brought him to his destination, the depot of the Memphis and Ohio Railroad where the quartermaster of the army had established his office. Upon entering the office, Stanley took a piece of paper from his coat pocket and handed it to a private seated at a desk. "I received this order to report today to arrange transport."

The private glanced at the paper. "Yes, Sergeant Mitchell. I'm Private David Thorpe." He set Stanley's written order aside and opened a thick journal. "We're sending as many survivors home as soon as we can, but first I need to check your name against my Ohio list. We try to keep it in alphabetical order, but there are additions when men are located and erasures, of course, when others die." The private scanned two or three more pages. "Ah. Here you are. Will you be fit to travel Friday?"

"I'm fit enough now, Private."

"Yes, but all our steamer allotments for today and tomorrow have been filled. We're being quite careful now."

"Now?" Stanley wished to make a more pointed remark, but stopped himself. The private had nothing to do with the disaster on the river. "I would like to travel by train, Private."

"But that's impossible, Sergeant Mitchell. This railroad doesn't go to Ohio; doesn't even go as far as Brownsville because the bridge over the Big Hatchie was burned to cinders."

"What about the other railroad, the one to Corinth?"

"Same thing, Sergeant. I'm sorry, but like all the other boys from Ohio, you must report to Camp Chase at Columbus to be mustered out. I know you don't want to board a steamer again, but it will only be for one day up to Cairo, and the rest will be in the cars."

The private bent over another paper that looked like a shipping schedule. "I can send one hundred up on the *William Burke*. Departs at ten in the morning. Be aboard by nine."

Burke. The name of Captain Gauthier's pilot on the *Evangelina*. An omen? Stanley shrugged it off. He had never

321

been superstitious. "That will have to do, Private. I've survived two shipwrecks; I pray there won't be a third."

The private scribbled something on the back of the paper Stanley had given him and handed it back. "Go to the paymaster's office at the rear of this building and show him that. All the survivors were granted twenty dollars to see them through until they get home."

The private stood and offered his hand to Stanley. "I'm sorry for your troubles, Sergeant. I wish you Godspeed. Is there anything else I can do for you?"

"Yes, there is," Stanley said. "Where might I post a letter?"

CHAPTER 58

Saturday, May 6, 1865

A NNA RAN INTO THE BARN WHERE LEVI JACKSON WAS CLEANING the stalls of the twin horses, Duke and Earl. She held the letter up. "Look, Levi. Stanley sent it only three days ago from Memphis."

"So, when that boy coming home, Miss Anna?"

"Don't know for sure," Anna said, "but it has to be soon. I already read it, but I want to hear you read it, Levi."

"But Miss Anna, I got work to get done, and Mastuh Stanley—"

"It's Stanley now, Levi, just Stanley."

"Yes, maybe, but Stanley, he uses them big words, you know."

"And I'll help you read every one. He'll be so pleased you know how to read."

"Won't be a moment, Miss Anna." Levi finished his cleaning and went off to get fresh water for the horses.

Anna leaned against the pillar between the two stalls, just as she had that thrilling evening almost three years ago when she first admitted to herself that she loved that wounded Yankee, Stanley Mitchell. That love was still alive and strong, and more so every day since his short letter from Vicksburg. And the terror that Luke had caused, and the long time apart that had followed? Those dark things were truly forgiven, but they would never be truly forgotten.

Levi returned with fresh water for the horses. Then he and Anna went to the wide doorway of the barn where the light for reading was best. Levi read slowly, sounding out each word, and as Anna had promised, she helped him whenever he stumbled.

Memphis, Tenn.
Wednesday, May 3, 1865

My Dearest Anna,

As I start this letter, I'm keenly aware that I'm but eighty miles or so from you. I hope and pray this is the last time pen and ink and paper are required for me to "speak" with you.

I left Vicksburg on the 24th of April but unforeseen circumstances have delayed me here in Memphis. As much as I wish it, I will not be traveling directly back to Matthews Hill, because the army requires that I return to the state of my enlistment for discharge.

On Friday, I'm scheduled to board a river steamer to proceed on to Cairo, Illinois. From there I will travel in the cars north to Mattoon, then east to Indianapolis and Camp Chase at Columbus, Ohio. Once there, I expect to receive twelve months wages. The last I received was a year ago for January through April, so this should amount to a tidy sum of about two hundred dollars.

The surgeons at Camp Fisk at Vicksburg told me I should qualify for an army medical pension because of my disability. This will take some days in Ohio as I must wait for an appointment, then fill out the required forms, and then be examined by yet another surgeon to prove that my left leg is indeed a casualty of the war.

My months as a guest of the Confederacy were hard times indeed. I lost fully one third of my weight. I write this not to elicit your pity, but to prepare you for the day when we shall finally see each other face to face. When you saw me last at Corinth, I was healthy and strong. Remember how I lifted you in my arms? Now, such a feat would be impossible, for I'm still very weak. And even though I have gained twelve pounds in the last month, I am still, as they say, "thin as a rail."

Anna, is it proper for me to presume the pledges we made to each other long ago still bind us? We were so young then. Now,

I feel so old. I have no home to return to but yours, and no family of my own—only yours and Levi's, and the judge's family as well, have prayed for my safe return.

In a few weeks, perhaps a month, I shall return to Matthews Hill—if the remainder of my journey is blessed with safety—and I shall return a different man from the one you met in Corinth, perhaps not for the better in your eyes. And it may be that the man who returns to you is so changed from what you knew that your affections for him have cooled. If that is the case, you must tell me outright. I would not wish to hold you to your pledge if it meant a lifetime of misery for you.

Yours with great affection,

Sergeant Stanley Mitchell

Anna sniffled into her handkerchief. "How could he doubt me?"

Levi put his arm around Anna and held her until her sobbing ended. "It ain't doubt, he's saying, Miss Anna. He left a boy and he's coming back a man. And you ain't no girl no more. You both been changing and growing while you been apart. War can make one man real good, another real bad. You know that, Miss Anna. He's seen lots of evil, Miss Anna, too much for most folks. All he's saying is you might not like what he become. He's saying see for yourself, and he ain't holding claim on you unless you want him to."

"After all we've been through, could I just cast him away? 'For better or worse,' that's what the vows say."

Levi held the letter up to Anna's tear-filled eyes. "Don't you hear our Stanley in this letter? He still wants you to love him, hoping for that too. But it might take time, maybe a lot of time, until he like he was. All he's saying, Miss Anna, is that you ain't said them vows yet."

CHAPTER 59

*T*HE REGULAR BEAT OF AX-FALLS ECHOED AMONG THE PINES beside the narrow lane to Matthews Hill Farm. Less than a hundred yards ahead, the woods ended at the pastureland below the homestead. *Levi. It must be Levi and his boys chopping firewood.*

"I'll get off here, Colley," Stanley said to the driver of the wagon.

Colley had been waiting at Pittsburg Landing for anyone or anything that needed transport to a nearby farm or community. Crooked letters—L-I-V-R-Y—had been painted in white on the side of his old buckboard wagon. The young black man had refused to accept payment from a former Union soldier, but Stanley had pressed a five-dollar bill into the man's hand and said, "Feed your family with it."

Colley turned the rig around in the lane and started back toward Parker's Store Road. It was quiet now—perhaps the woodcutters had seen or heard the wagon. A high whoop erupted from the woods, followed by the crash of feet running through underbrush. Almost simultaneously, Jeremiah and Micah Jackson appeared dodging this way and that among the trees. The brothers froze at the tree line.

Levi loped up behind them, wiping sweat from his brow with a red kerchief. "Don't just stand there gawking, boys. Go say hello to Sergeant Stanley."

Jeremiah stepped into the lane and took a few uncertain steps toward Stanley. He lowered his eyes and bowed slightly. "Hello, sir."

"There will be no more *sir* or *master*," Stanley said. "Friends call each other by name." He offered his hand to Jeremiah. "Please, Jer, just call me Stanley."

Jeremiah pumped Stanley's hand with great vigor. "Welcome home, Stanley."

"Now, Jer," Stanley said, once he had recovered his hand intact, "watch how I shake Micah's hand."

Micah stepped forward and then stood mute and grinning while Stanley shook his hand.

"Your grip," Stanley explained, "should be firm and warm, but it's not a contest of strength. And three or four gentle shakes are usually enough for a friendly greeting. Now, Jer, let's try it again."

"Time to get back to work, boys," Levi said. "I'll be along in a few minutes."

Levi stood beside Stanley and watched Jer and Micah disappear into the woods again. Within moments the drumbeat of axes had resumed.

"Do you have another project going, Levi, or is it just more firewood?"

"Can't say, Sergeant Stanley."

Levi's wiry hair was almost entirely gray now, but there was still a youthful presence about him. And he was smiling broadly.

"What do you mean, you can't say?"

"Can't say." Levi hesitated a moment, then added, "not my place."

Stanley shrugged. No use pressing Levi further. He would have to ask Mrs. Matthews. Stanley held up his cane. "Army issue. I kept that fine walking stick you made me until I lost it a month ago. But it saved my life more than once."

"I'll make you another, Sergeant Stanley."

"And thank you for your many prayers, Levi."

The smile remained on Levi's face, but the mirth was gone from his eyes. "We always pray for them we love."

Stanley swallowed hard.

Levi turned and looked Stanley in the face. "Anna and Luke are up the lane herding the cattle and sheep, but I got to say something before you see her." He paused, as if asking permission to continue.

"Speak freely, Levi."

"All right. She had me read your last letter."

"Really? You can read now?"

"Yes, but slow. Anna teached me."

Stanley grabbed Levi's hand and shook it. "That's wonderful."

"Yes, but I got to tell you something important."

"Go ahead, Levi, I'm listening."

Levi spoke soft and slow, as if he was measuring every word. "Now, I know this for sure, as sure as I know anything—that girl loves you. You said she might not and it near broke her heart."

Stanley had written those words at the hospital just after he had returned from the quartermaster's office. The words had come hard, but they were necessary. *Dry bones—that's how dead I feel sometimes, as if all the good and decent and lovable that Anna saw in me was buried beneath that putrid swamp at Andersonville. Somewhere deep inside I still love her, but I had to write that letter. I had to give her a way out.*

Levi touched Stanley's arm, a gentle, simple gesture that commanded Stanley's immediate attention. "I say this now, Sergeant Stanley, 'cause you and Anna is real dear to me. You know I like Isaiah. Since I read that letter I been thinking a lot on this one particular bit that Jesus said was about him, 'He hath sent me to bind up the brokenhearted, to proclaim liberty to the captives, and the opening of the prison to them that are bound.'"

Stanley had heard Levi's soft, earnest, and pleading tone years ago during some of their night walks along the dark wooded lane that led from the Jackson's cabin to the barn.

"You was in prison," Levi said, "but now you ain't. I thank God for that every day. And you ain't a captive no more, unless it's what's inside you that's holding you. You probably seen all kinda evil and death. Maybe you is broke inside, in your heart, like you said in that letter. Good old Isaiah said Jesus can fix that, Stanley. Anna can love you and do all kinda good for you, but she can't fix your heart. You can't either. Only God can do that. And he will, if you let him."

• • •

The last of the sheep were finally in the southwest pasture. Luke jumped down from his horse, Duke, and began replacing the rails in the fence while Anna turned Earl up the gentle slope toward the northern edge of the pasture, where leaf-laden oak boughs overspread, and the shade was deepest. She loved to cool down there after the herding was done.

Luke mounted his horse again and started slowly across the pasture to the gate at the lane. He had grown broad in his shoulders, and he was now several inches taller than she. Best of all, Luke had become a decent, hardworking young man, a fine son in whom Papa would have taken great pride, had he lived.

About thirty yards from the gate, Luke reined Duke to a halt. Then Luke looked to his right toward the lane where it emerged from the woods. Anna followed Luke's gaze and squinted across the distance. A dark figure appeared in the sunlight—a man walking slowly up the lane. Only his head and shoulders were visible above the rail fence and the tall grasses that grew along the fence line. He wore a black slouch hat and what appeared to be a Union soldier's dark blue jacket.

It was Stanley. There could be no doubt. She started to dig her heels into Earl's haunches, but stopped herself. Instead of racing across the broad pasture, she backed Earl farther under the shade and sat quiet, nearly hidden.

Stanley spotted Luke and gave him a wave. Luke jumped to the ground and led his horse toward the gate. He was tying Duke to a fence rail when Stanley approached the gate.

A few words were exchanged. What were they saying to each other? Were the words spoken at Corinth just words? Were they still heir and interloper? Or were they truly something much more?

Luke opened the gate, not all the way, just enough to allow Stanley to enter the pasture. Her brother took hold of Stanley's shoulders and drew Stanley into a bear hug. Anna almost cried for joy. The secret doubts that had for so long haunted her nights vanished. But Luke was so strong now, and Stanley seemed but a rag doll. *Luke! Don't crush him, now that he's home.*

Anna flicked the reins and started Earl across the pasture at a slow trot. *They look so much like brothers.* She had hoped and prayed for it; now there it was, so much better than she could have imagined it.

You know he's hurting, Lord. Give me the right words.

CHAPTER 60

STANLEY COULDN'T BELIEVE HIS EYES. *HOW IS IT POSSIBLE THAT she is even more beautiful than I remember?* Anna rode high and light in the saddle as she steered Earl straight for Stanley and Luke. Her honey-brown hair bounced lightly upon her shoulders to the rhythm of Earl's gate. And as she came nearer, her brilliant hazel eyes beamed at him, even from under the shadow of her broad-brimmed straw hat.

Stanley removed his hat and lowered his gaze. How many times had he bathed since he was freed? At every opportunity, he had washed with lye soap, but he still felt unclean. Even the two hours in the Mississippi hadn't been sufficient; the filth of Andersonville still clung to him. He could still taste it. He could still smell it. He could still feel it. And so would she.

Anna eased Earl close to Stanley. "You're late, soldier. Tater day was Thursday."

Stanley longed to look up at her, but he couldn't. Not now. She was too good, too pure. A sob rose in his throat; he heaved a deep sigh to suppress it.

"Luke," Anna snapped, "go on and tell Mama to set another place for supper. We'll be along in a while."

Anna waited until Luke had ridden away up the lane. "Soldier, put your hat on so the sun doesn't boil your brains."

Stanley flopped the broad-brimmed hat back on his head.

"Help me down, soldier."

Stanley looked up at her through wet, bleary eyes. "Really? You need my help? I've seen you jump on and off that horse a dozen times."

"No, I don't need your help. I want your help—and I want you to touch me."

"Touch you?" The words escaped before he thought them.

Anna stared down at Stanley. "That's right, soldier. I'm sweaty and dirty, and I probably smell of horse, so if you can bear touching me, please help me down."

Stanley shrugged. "If you insist."

"I do. A man should always help his lady off her horse."

Stanley tossed his cane aside and reached up for her with both arms.

Anna slid quickly out of the saddle and into his arms. It was all he could do to keep them both from tumbling to the ground.

"Next time," Anna said, "we'll try to do that without the shrug and with a little more grace. A nice smile would help too."

Stanley's eyes dropped earthward again.

Anna stood close to Stanley. Hardly an inch separated them. She put a finger under his chin and pressed gently upward until he had no choice but to look at her.

"Did you come all this way and forget to bring your beautiful smile?"

She sounded teasing and playful, just as she had before.

"And so few words? Remember how we used to talk for hours?"

"I remember," Stanley said, "but...."

"But what? We can't talk about the terrible things they did to you?"

"No." It was barely a whisper.

"Because I'm a woman and I shouldn't have to hear those things?"

"No, you shouldn't."

Anna pulled his face down to hers and kissed him tenderly. "I love you, soldier," she said, her lips still touching his. Then she drew back to look into his eyes again. "Do you still love me?"

Stanley started to turn his face away.

"No. Look at me. Do you still love me?"

Yes, he wanted to scream a thousand times, *but how can you still love me? I'm not who I was before.* But what of her words of love? Her letters filled with hope? Her worn and faded image that he had carried inside of him for so long? Did he not think of her only with warmth and affection? Didn't he desire her above all else on earth?

Stanley smiled, thin and forced, but it was all he could manage at that moment. "Yes, I still love you, but there were times when I thought you unreachable, like an unearthly illusion that I could only view from far away, but never approach or touch."

"But you have touched me, Stanley." Anna took a handkerchief from the pocket of her duck trousers and wiped his eyes. "And I'm touching you now. I *am* real. We kissed."

"I know. I dreamed of this day for a long time, but then I didn't anymore. I didn't think it could ever happen. Even now, I'm wondering if I'm really here with you, Anna. Tomorrow, I could wake up and find I'm gone from here and this was all a cruel dream."

Anna's slap stung Stanley's face.

"Did that hurt, soldier?"

Stanley rubbed the side of his face and nodded.

"That's real pain," Anna said, "not an illusion. You won't be gone, not tomorrow, or the next day, or ever, unless you want to go. I want a full life with *you*, a happy home with *you*, and happy children with *you*. We could live to be a hundred—who knows? But even then, I know there will be times you'll go into the darkness of what you just come through. I want to be there to help you through those times."

"But how?"

"We can start right now." Anna took Stanley by the hand and led him across the pasture to the deep shade at the northern edge.

"It's cooler here, and the sun won't beat on us." Anna sat in the grass, leaned back against a fencepost, and removed her straw hat, which she placed on the ground beside her. She tugged at Stanley's hand. "Take your hat off too, Stanley. Then lie down here and put your head in my lap."

Stanley did as Anna wished.

Anna cradled Stanley's head in her arms. "Now, soldier, tell me all of it, every detail of what happened after you were taken prisoner." She ran her fingers softly through Stanley's sweat-damp hair. "Tell me—what will take you far away from me, or give you fits all night long, or make you wake up screaming? I'm the one you'll cling to in those dark hours. I must know."

CHAPTER 61

FROM THE MOMENT STANLEY BEGAN, ANNA STARTED TO WEEP. He might never speak of those things again, so she entered those gates beside him and shuddered when they slammed shut behind her.

He tried to describe the filth and degradation within the stockade. "Imagine your barn with not only one team of horses, one team of mules, and some chickens running about, but also a hundred hogs, and imagine what it would be like if the manure was never cleaned out, not for a week or even a month, but for a whole year."

Anna's heart swelled with pride when Stanley spoke of the fight with the Raiders and his part in the trials, but his voice was flat and emotionless when he spoke of the hangings, and of how quickly death had become common and routine. "The tears came only for Stew," Stanley said, "and after that, not at all."

Anna had known her own griefs. He still had his. And when he told her of his constant struggle to hold onto the three fairest of all Christian virtues—faith, hope, and love—and to remain decent and human, Anna was again powerless to hold back the tears.

"You looked ashamed when you first saw me," Anna said. "I seen—I saw the same in Luke when he saw how bad he hurt me after you were taken away. But God took care of Luke. I saw that when he hugged you."

She paused and looked down at Stanley. His blue eyes had always been soft and warm, alive with hope and dreams for the future, even at Corinth when she had last seen him. But they were darker now, harder and cooler. *Lord, let those eyes blaze with life again and let me be the cause of it.*

"And me? I know you said this was done with, but I hated you for Father's death. I hated you for Aaron's death. I hated you for being a Yankee, and I even think I hated you just because I hated you, and I never ever hated anybody before. How often did I tell you it was God that changed me? You had a part, I know, but only God could beat that hate out of me."

Anna bent down and kissed Stanley lightly on the forehead. "I didn't hear from you from October to January."

Stanley told Anna about the other camps he had "visited"—Millen, Blackshear, and Thomasville—and she gasped when he said he had returned to Andersonville on Christmas Eve. And a shiver swept through her when Stanley spoke of counting the minutes during a cold, rainy night, and praying for sunlight with the dawn so that he might dry and warm himself.

When Stanley finally spoke about his journey home, his voice trembled as he spoke of the wreck of the *Sultana*, and of the deaths of hundreds of people he had witnessed within a scant half hour. But the effort drained Stanley. His voice trailed off as he spoke of his rescue, his eyelids drooped and soon he was asleep.

Your terrors are so many, my darling. Will you ever be free of them? I'll be right here when you awake, my love. I'll be right here, my love....

• • •

Anna woke with a start. *What time is it? Mama must be worried. Not yet dinnertime, but soon.*

Stanley shifted a little, jostled perhaps when she awoke. He opened his eyes and squinted up at her. Then he stretched, yawned, sat up, and reached for his hat.

"Not yet," Anna said. Something about him seemed different. "Look at me, please."

As Stanley turned his face toward her, Anna placed her hand on the side of his bearded face. He turned slightly as she did so and kissed her hand. Then he looked directly at her. His eyes were now brighter, bluer, more like they had been before, but not completely so.

"Ah, there you are," Anna said. "Welcome home, Stanley."

She helped him stand and the two held each other for some time beside the rail fence. "Stanley, my darling?"

"Yes, my dearest Anna?"

"I know you were tired, but you said you jumped off that ship and woke up in the hospital. Surely, there was more to it."

Stanley relaxed his embrace and looked down at Anna. "I suppose I must tell you that part too. I didn't jump off the *Sultana*. I lowered myself slowly into that cold water. I slipped Levi's walking stick out and held onto it while I swam away from the boat, first with one arm, then with the other. The walking stick kept me afloat, but I soon grew very tired. My little strength and stamina was all gone, and I thought in a few minutes I would sink below the surface."

"So? What happened?"

"I prayed. I prayed as I did at Shiloh, and as I have done many times since. 'Lord, save me.' Once again, I knew I could do nothing for myself. Only he could save me from a watery grave."

Anna clung tightly to Stanley, her face pressed to his chest, both hearing and feeling the trembling of his voice.

"I swam a few more strokes toward the Arkansas side of the river, because it was nearer the burning hulk. Then some large dark mass floated by a yard or two away. With the last of my strength I pushed myself toward it. I thought it might be a piece of wooden furniture, but it was an animal, a large, dead animal.

"I clung to this animal's hindquarters and hoisted myself partly out of the water. I inched my way farther forward to be in a more pleasant position, and then I thought it would be even better if I could hold onto the beast around its neck. That's when I saw its ears. It was a mule."

Anna tried to suppress her giggle.

"I'm at death's door again and you find that funny?"

"No," Anna said. She loosened her hold on him so she could look up at him again.

"Then what?"

"God has sense of humor," she said. "Think about it, Stanley. You prayed for him to save you, so he sent you a mule. A live mule broke your leg and started this whole business. Then a dead mule saved your life, and now you're back so we can finish that business."

"What business?"

"What are you doing a month from today?"

"The twenty-seventh of June?"

"It's a Tuesday."

Stanley shrugged.

"Another shrug. Is that what you'll do when you take your vows?"

Stanley took a step backward. "You still want to marry me, Anna?"

"Of course," she said. "You made me cry and you made me laugh. What more could a girl want? The question is, Stanley Mitchell, do you still want to marry me?"

Stanley's jaw went slack. His mouth hung open. His eyes narrowed, then shut altogether. A few moments passed. Then he began to weep. "I love you, Anna, more than I can ever say. I do still want to marry you, I do."

Anna drew close and used her handkerchief to wipe away Stanley's tears. Then she kissed him again and hugged him until he quieted.

"Tomorrow," she said, "we're going to church in Corinth, and me and you are going to ask Reverend Peters if he can come out here and marry us on the 27th of June. What do you think of that, Sergeant Stanley Mitchell?"

"Why the 27th?"

"Have you forgotten, Stanley? That's the day you were taken away by that evil man three years ago."

"And you think that's the best day for our wedding?"

"Yes, I do. What better way is there to turn that terrible day into a happy day than by me becoming Mrs. Stanley Mitchell."

"All right. It's soon, very soon—"

338

"And Mama's already making my dress and—"

"I can see you're way ahead of me on this, Anna, but where will we live?"

"Didn't you hear all that chopping and banging when you came up the lane?"

Stanley nodded.

"Levi and his boys and three other hired men are building us a house, not a cabin, a two-story house."

"That's why he couldn't say what he was doing."

"You'll wear your uniform, of course. You know how I like those pretty brass buttons, and I asked Mama if you could wear Papa's gold sash. It's the only thing of Papa's that General Forrest returned to Mama. She thinks it's a splendid idea."

Anna took a deep breath. There was more, but it could wait. She moved slowly toward Stanley, her eyes fixed on his. He drew her to himself and kissed her—long and soft—just as he had three years before beside the cool meandering waters of Owl Creek.

❧ The End ❧

If You Enjoyed This Book,
Please Share the Message with Others

❑ Mention *The Gates of Sheol* on Twitter or Pinterest, or in a Facebook post or blog post.

❑ Recommend this book to your friends, discussion group, book club, or classmates.

❑ Like my Facebook page: facebook.com/karl.bacon.7 and post a comment about what you enjoyed most about the book.

❑ Visit my website: kbacon.com

❑ Email me: kb@kbacon.com

❑ Give a copy of this book to someone who might enjoy and be encouraged by it.

❑ Write a review and post it on amazon.com, bn.com, goodreads.com, etc.

Books by Karl A. Bacon

Available from Amazon.com and other retail outlets

An Eye for Glory: The Civil War Chronicles of a Citizen Soldier
- *Publishers Weekly* Top Pick Spring/Summer 2011
- 2012 Christy Award Finalist (First Novel)

The Shiloh Trilogy
Until Shiloh Comes (Book 1)
- Winner: 2016 National Indie Excellence Award - Historical Fiction
- Bronze Medal Winner: 2016 Independent Publisher Award (IPPY) – Best Adult Fiction E-Book
- Finalist: 2016 Selah Award – Historical/Biblical Fiction

Prairie Dog Town (Book 2)
- Winner: 2017 Selah Award – Historical/Biblical Fiction
- Winner: 2017 Director's Choice Award for Fiction (Blue Ridge Mountains Christian Writers Conference)

ABOUT THE AUTHOR

From youth Karl A. Bacon has been a serious student of the
Civil War. Countless hours of detailed research supply the
foundation for each novel, including copious reading,
internet research and personal visits to battlefields and
historic sites. For *The Gates of Sheol,* he toured the
Andersonville National Historic Site and the Andersonville
National Cemetery. Research included reading dozens of
diaries and memoirs written by Andersonville prisoners and
two detailed accounts of the *Sultana* disaster. The research
provides depth and realism to the stories so that the novels
might be as historically accurate and believable as possible.
Karl lives with his wife, Jackie, in Connecticut.